the works of Katharine Marlowe

"Absorbing psychological drama. Marlowe's smooth, suspenseful narrative offers a satisfying read."

—*Publishers Weekly* on *Secrets*

"The author is adept at creating tension. [*Heart's Desires* is] a real page turner."

—*Library Journal*

"A psychological drama of the first magnitude, *Secrets* entertains from beginning to satisfying end."

—*Tulsa World*

"A pleasure to read."

—*Booklist* on *Heart's Desires*

"A psychological mystery [and] a page turner. Read this one for fun."

—*Florida Times-Union* on *Secrets*

Previous works by Katharine Marlowe

Heart's Desires
Secrets

Nightfall

Katharine Marlowe

A TOM DOHERTY ASSOCIATES BOOK
NEW YORK

NOTE: If you purchased this book without a cover you should be aware that this book is stolen property. It was reported as "unsold and destroyed" to the publisher, and neither the author nor the publisher has received any payment for this "stripped book."

This is a work of fiction. All the characters and events portrayed in this book are fictitious, and any resemblance to real people or events is purely coincidental.

NIGHTFALL

Copyright © 1993 by Katharine Marlowe

All rights reserved, including the right to reproduce this book, or portions thereof, in any form.

A Tor Book
Published by Tom Doherty Associates, Inc.
175 Fifth Avenue
New York, N.Y. 10010

Tor® is a registered trademark of Tom Doherty Associates, Inc.

ISBN: 0-812-52415-2
Library of Congress Catalog Card Number: 93-12453

First edition: May 1993
First mass market edition: August 1994

Printed in the United States of America

0 9 8 7 6 5 4 3 2 1

Nightfall

PREFACE

Rebecca drove mechanically through the downpour, signaling her turn onto the Post Road even though it was past midnight and there wasn't another car in sight. It was slightly over three miles from Agnes's house to her own, and she was better than halfway home. She hiked up the volume on the radio and glanced at the speedometer. The last thing she wanted was a speeding ticket.

The rain was sheeting across the windshield, and even with the wipers going at top speed, it was hard to see. She hated driving in the rain, and the trip back from the city would have been a nightmare if Agnes hadn't been along.

Up ahead about a quarter of a mile she could see a car pulled to the side of the road. The hood was raised, and two boys were peering in at the engine while a third stepped out into the road and waved his arms at her to stop.

"Are you kidding?" she murmured, mildly alarmed. She'd have to be crazy to stop at this time of night to offer help or a ride to three teenaged boys. She wouldn't have stopped for anyone, but especially not a trio of young men.

When she was about fifty feet away, the boy who'd been waving suddenly darted out in front of her. Fear leaping into her throat, she spun the wheel hard to the left, swerving to avoid hitting him. Thank God there was no oncoming traffic. Trembling, her heart racing, she swung back into the outside lane, then glanced into the rearview mirror. "Maniac!" she gasped, seeing the boy shaking his fist at her. As if she'd done something wrong, and not him. Whatever he was shouting was drowned out by the radio. Her right knee was quivering. She was doing over fifty in a thirty-mile-an-hour zone.

Sweating, she eased back on the accelerator. What the hell was wrong with that kid? Her hands were wet, slippery on the steering wheel. Scared the hell out of her. Staying in the outside lane, she kept her eyes on the road ahead. Another two minutes and she'd be home. *God!* Was he out of his mind, doing a thing like that? The pulse in her throat was hammering painfully. She felt as if she might throw up. What if she'd hit him? He might've been killed. She longed to be home and had to stop herself from putting her foot back down hard on the accelerator.

"*Bitch!*" Pete yelled, shaking his fist in the air as the car went past.

"Hey, forget it, man!" Cal said, wiping his grimy hands down the sides of his jeans. "No woman's going to stop for us. You probably scared the living shit out of her, jumping in front of the car like that." He shook his head disdainfully; he couldn't believe Pete had actually pulled such a dumb stunt.

"Serve her goddamned right," Pete snapped, watching the car's right taillight flashing for a turn. "It'd like kill her to help us out?"

"I think maybe I've got it," Tim called over. "I've cleaned the sparks. Cal, get in and try it."

Cal stared at Pete a moment longer, then got behind the wheel and turned the ignition key. The starter made a grinding noise; the engine wouldn't turn over.

"Shit!" said Tim. "I guess we'll have to walk."

"My dad'll have a fit," Cal said unhappily.

"It's not like you did anything. I mean, it just died," Tim said, looking over to see Pete still watching the taillights of the car he'd tried to stop. "Be serious!" he said. "You're lucky she didn't run you down."

Pete pushed the wet hair out of his eyes, saying, "Yeah, right. So what's the deal here?"

"The deal is, we walk."

"It wouldn't've killed her to give us a ride," Pete said hotly. "What a bitch!"

"Forget it. Okay? I can't believe you did that. You know?" Tim looked at his watch. "Man! I'm way past curfew. My mom's going to have my ass. Come on, Cal, lock 'er up and let's go. I figure if we jog it, we can make my place in half an hour. You coming, Pete?"

"You know who that was?" Pete said excitedly, still gazing down the road. "That was Leighton, from school. Shelley had her for junior English last year."

"So?" Tim said, exchanging a look with Cal, who shrugged and turned to lock the doors. After pocketing the keys and tying his handkerchief to the antenna to let the cops know the car had broken down, Cal looked at Pete. "You just going to stand here all night in the rain or what?"

"That was her," Pete repeated, convinced that his recognizing the teacher was significant somehow.

"You coming?" Tim asked again as he and Cal moved to go.

"Fuck it!" Pete said. "You guys go on." He'd make it

over to the service center on I-95, maybe score some uppers from one of the long-distance drivers. He had a twenty he'd scammed from his mother's purse that morning.

As Cal and Tim gave up, exchanging another look before taking off at a run, Pete started toward the turnpike. The rain dripping down his neck, his jeans saturated, he got more and more steamed with that bitch Leighton for leaving the three of them stranded. Jesus, it *really* pissed him off.

CHAPTER

One

Rebecca let herself in the back door, threw off her coat in the mudroom, and went into the kitchen to pour some Stoli into a glass. She dropped in an ice cube, stirred it into the vodka with her finger, and took a long swallow. She shuddered, closed her eyes for a moment, feeling the cool burn, then put the glass down on the counter, thinking how glad she was to be home. The telephone rang. She jumped, and put a shaking hand out to pick up the receiver.

"Just wanted to be sure you made it home safely," Agnes said.

"I'm okay now," Rebecca told her, relieved to hear Agnes's low, rich voice. "Some kid jumped right in front of my car as I was coming down the Post Road. Scared the hell out of me."

"Jumped in front of you?"

"Literally. There were three boys about eighteen, and it

looked as if their car had broken down. Anyway, I'm all right."

"You didn't stop, did you?"

"God, no!" Rebecca said, too readily able to imagine being attacked by a trio of sturdy young men.

"You're sure you're all right?"

"I'm fine. A little shaky, that's all."

"Good. Well, will I see you this weekend?"

"Maybe Sunday evening, if I can get through those junior essays. Let me call you."

"Of course." Agnes sighed, then said, "I am sorry about the play."

"It wasn't that bad."

"Wasn't good, either. So, my dear, I'm glad you're home safe and sound. Enjoy your evening tomorrow with Mister X, and we'll talk on Sunday."

Rebecca was tired, but still rattled by the incident on the Post Road, and by the unexpected late-night ringing of the telephone. Not that Agnes's call was out of the ordinary; Aggie usually checked to make sure she got home safely. Carrying her drink upstairs to the bedroom, she thought about how Agnes seemed to have changed in the past month or so. She'd noticed it again this evening, when Agnes had been deeply offended by an actress of almost sixty attempting to play a forty-year-old. Rebecca had agreed about the miscasting, but Agnes had appeared to take the matter as a personal affront.

"Imagine what a decent actress could do with a part like that!" she'd said. "Once upon a time, I might have played it."

"I bet you'd have been wonderful," Rebecca had said, wishing not for the first time that she could have seen Agnes perform. She must have been brilliant. It stood to reason that someone who'd made her London West End debut at the age of seventeen had to have been very special. "Didn't it kill you to give it all up?" she'd asked. Agnes rarely talked about her early life, and Rebecca had been curious.

"Apparently not any more than it did you," Agnes replied coolly.

"Aggie, all I ever did were a half-dozen television commercials and two plays miles off Broadway. But you did West End shows, and won awards. You were there."

" 'There,' my dear, is a relative term. I was an impudent child who didn't give a damn. Back then that sort of attitude was so rare it was considered rather attractive. Nowadays it's the norm. In any event, I'm far happier teaching than I ever was treading the boards. Did it kill *you*, Rebecca, giving up your theatrical career?"

"I moved to the city right after graduating from college, you know, convinced I'd be in a Broadway show by the time I was twenty-five," Rebecca answered, trying to stay well away from the other cars on the rain-slicked road. "For three and a half years I worked lunches waitressing, and got my Master's credits going nights to NYU. I did speaking parts in three industrial films, two voice-overs for commercials that went national and paid great residuals for two years, four on-camera commercials, and those two pretentious plays I mentioned before.

"I guess what I miss most is being constantly on the go—to dinner, plays, gallery openings, movies. And all the available men," she added meaningfully.

"I seem to recall men in London," Agnes said with a wry smile. "Go on."

"Well," Rebecca said, "on my twenty-fifth birthday, instead of celebrating, I stayed home to take stock of my life. I thought about the over-forty hopefuls who invested their savings in face-lifts that left them looking grotesque and who showed up at every audition wearing too much makeup and dressed to the nines. All in the hope of that break that might still happen.

"I thought about how various people in the business had suggested I dye my hair white-blonde, maybe get a small chin implant to strengthen my profile, and have my wisdom teeth pulled to emphasize the arch of my cheekbones . . . on and on." She'd smiled and glanced over to see Agnes listening soberly.

"I couldn't see the point. I mean, tinted contact lenses, bleached hair and spike heels weren't going to make much of a difference, because underneath it all I'd still be five-foot-three with black hair and blue eyes.

"And what does plastic surgery have to do with making a career, anyway? Talent counts, too, but nobody seemed to care much about that. So I decided to bail out before all I could talk about was parts I'd been *that close* to getting after three callbacks. I had the qualifications to teach, and the house Dad had left me. So I gave notice to the tenants, packed up the Manhattan studio, and moved back to Connecticut. That was just over eight years ago, and I don't regret it.

"Sometimes I miss the panicky excitement I'd get when my agent called to say she'd put me up for something. Maybe this would be my big break, I'd land the part that'd make me a star." She gave a self-deprecating shrug. "But I'm happy teaching, too. Of course every time one of the kids expresses any interest in an acting career, it's all I can do not to launch into an impassioned speech about the heartbreak and humiliation of it."

"Quite so," Agnes had agreed, once more recognizably herself. "It's their right to dream and to be disillusioned."

Now as she prepared for bed, Rebecca wished she could pinpoint what was wrong. The change in Agnes was so subtle she doubted that others would notice it. But she was closer to Agnes than anyone else, and there was definitely something going on.

Climbing into bed, she finished the vodka, then reached for her book on the bedside table, again saw the boy throwing himself into the path of her car, and shivered. What if she'd hit him? God! It'd been such a close call. A brief, nasty episode. But it was over. She was home, safe in bed. Nothing bad had happened. But, God! She could feel the car lurch as she spun the wheel, could see the pale blur of his features as she went past him. He had to be crazy to do a thing like that. He could've been killed.

For a second time she reached for the book. As she did, she thought of seeing Ray tomorrow and sank back against the pillows with a sigh. She'd pretty much lost interest in the man Agnes had, from the outset, referred to as Mister X. Mister X, she thought tiredly. It sounded far more exciting than it really was.

The disadvantages to life in a small town were the lack of unattached men and the lack of much to do if one were unmarried and had no children. Everything shut down by ten P.M. The streets were deserted, and initially, after life in Manhattan, the silence had been particularly difficult to adjust to. Now she was so acclimated to the nighttime quiet that the slightest unusual noise instantly caught her attention. She saved up "unusual noise" stories to tell her mother on Sunday afternoons when she drove down to Greenwich to visit.

She had to admit her existence in Nortown became a lot less boring after getting involved with Ray Hastings seven months earlier. They'd met at a local nursery one Saturday afternoon. Rebecca had been buying flats of pachysandra to plant along the western side of the house, and while waiting to pay, Ray had approached to ask if she knew anything about house plants. He was attractive and, thinking it was a pity he had on a wedding ring, she'd made several suggestions. Grateful for his help, he'd asked if he could buy her lunch. After deliberating for a moment or two, she agreed to meet him at a restaurant in the nearby shopping center. What harm could come from eating lunch with the man?

While they ate their sandwiches, he explained that he was in the process of getting a divorce after twenty-two years of marriage. He'd stayed with it longer than he probably should have because of his sense of obligation to his two children and because he hoped something might reawaken his one-time affection for his wife. The children hadn't appeared to benefit from his sacrifice, and his affection for his wife had not been rekindled.

Finally, he'd told a sympathetic Rebecca, he'd been sitting one night with the Stamford *Advocate,* scanning the real estate ads. The next evening he went to view several apartments, and without ever having planned it, he took a lease on one. Over dinner that night he announced he was leaving.

"The kids nodded and went on eating," he'd said, "and Marla said, 'If you think I'm giving up this house, you're crazy.' I said that wouldn't be necessary, and that was pretty well that." A week later he was installed in his furnished apartment. He'd been living there for close to nine months when Rebecca met him.

There were problems with the affair almost from the start. Not only did Ray commute into the city to his job as commercial claims director for an insurance company, which meant he left early and got home late, but he also traveled extensively for the company. So he was rarely able to see Rebecca more than once a week, and sometimes not even that. At first she hadn't minded, thinking it was better to see someone infrequently than not at all. And after more than a year of celibacy, it was good to be sexually active again.

Lately, though, despite Ray's passionate declarations of love, she was feeling increasingly like "the other woman" and hated the idea that she was in a clichéd situation. She also could no longer ignore the nagging suspicion that Ray was happy to keep things just as they were. If she had to explain this, she knew it would sound lame. After all, she was involved with an attractive man who claimed to love her. There were plenty of women who'd jump at the chance to have him around, regardless of what was going on his life. She wasn't one of them. She'd already compromised her primary rule never to date married or separated men by dating him in the first place.

Matters were further complicated by the fact that Ray's son was a student at the high school and in Aggie's senior English class. Ray assured her that neither of his kids nor his wife knew of his involvement with her. "For the time being, it's better if we both keep a low profile," he said. "I'd hate to get you messed up in the divorce, or put your job in jeopardy." That had made sense, and she'd resisted the fleeting impulse to ask Aggie to point the boy out to her. Knowing what he looked like wouldn't improve her relationship with Ray, or speed up the divorce. So what was the point?

At last she turned out the light, anxious to go to sleep. But her brain kept relentlessly ticking over. In the morning there was the grocery shopping to be done; in the afternoon the junior essays had to be marked; then there was dinner to prepare for Ray. And after dinner he'd want to make love. That was the usual pattern. She could summon up very little anticipation, the surest sign that the relationship was in trouble.

At the outset she'd been very optimistic, wanting to believe things would be different this time. Well, they were different all right, but not better. The time had come to end the affair. It was admittedly cowardly, but she kept stalling, hating the idea of a scene. And somehow you couldn't announce you wanted to break up without there being one.

She sighed again. These things happened. She'd enjoyed life well enough before Ray came along; she'd enjoy it again after he was gone. It was sad when things didn't work out, but she should never have broken her rule and become involved with someone in the midst of a divorce.

It was better by far to be a little lonely than locked into a go-nowhere romance. On the plus side, she had a good job. The hours were terrible, the pay scale barely adequate, but the kids were terrific, and she treasured her friendship with Agnes. She admired Agnes's striking good looks, enjoyed her eccentricities, her wicked sense of humor, her generosity, and her theatrical flair. They shared a compatibility Rebecca had never known with any other friend. Continuing the credit side of this mental balance sheet, she owned her own home; she was independent and entirely self-reliant. She had a wonderful mother, and friends among the other teachers. She had some savings, and a car she owned outright.

On the minus side, Agnes was acting a bit peculiar, forgetting some things and overreacting to others, and Rebecca found this worrisome. As well, she was going to have to break up with Ray, which was bound to be unpleasant. And to top everything off, she couldn't get to sleep. Perfect, she thought, shifting over to her left side. Instead of going to sleep, she was busy running down the pros and cons of her life.

She'd concentrate on relaxing her body, an old exercise from her acting classes. The rain drummed down on the skylight overhead. The wind whipped through the branches of the old copper beech outside. She breathed slowly, deeply, starting to descend, the blackness spreading. Then suddenly she was back in the Jetta, swerving to avoid the figure that leaped into her path. At once overheated and upset, she turned over again, trying physically to get away from that frightening incident.

It was hours before she finally fell into an exhausted sleep.

CHAPTER

Two

Rebecca had known a fair number of men, even one she'd briefly considered marrying. But she'd never dated anyone quite like Ray Hastings. His custom-tailored suits were a kind of camouflage, intended to reassure those he met in the course of his investigations.

If a claim reached his desk, it was almost certain some element of fraud was involved. Ray looked for holes. If he saw them, he returned the annotated file to the adjustor. If he didn't, he took charge, reviewing all the paperwork before going out into the field to interview the claimants and anyone else who might be involved.

"They say," he'd told Rebecca a number of times, with a show of pride that had made her slightly uncomfortable, "if Hastings can't find the needle, forget the haystack."

He loved his work, and he loved to talk about his twenty-four years of dealing with people who burned down their buildings, incinerating their goods, when business was bad. For some reason, they always believed they could get away with it. After paying the premiums, sometimes for decades, they felt the insurance company owed them something.

"They're so ridiculously easy to spot, for the most part," he'd told her. "I mean, it's not as if arson's an accredited college course. A torch gets his know-how on the street or in jail. I've run into a few guys with some education and technical training, usually picked up through military service. But mainly a torch is just a bum who'll burn down your place for a thousand or two. And they make mistakes. *Always*. They forget and leave their empty solvent cans outside on the loading bay, or they choose a spot where a fire simply couldn't occur, or they use chemicals they don't know how to handle and wind up in the emergency room with burned hands. And if there's nothing that obvious, nine out of ten times an examination of the company books will turn up some very interesting numbers. I love the tough ones. I love nailing those guys."

At the beginning Rebecca enjoyed hearing him talk about his work. He was one of the rare men who had a job he liked. He was also one of the few she knew who actually liked to read. He made it a point to ask what she'd been reading, and jotted down titles she recommended. On several occasions they'd disagreed strenuously. He was fond of South American novelists, whose books, she insisted, were about as exciting as watching paint dry.

"They're precious!" she'd argued when the previous week Ray had praised yet another South American effort. "Who cares what happens to a couple of boring academics sitting in some Bolivian café discussing philosophical fine points? I want to be entertained and enlightened. I want to read about people I can care for. Can you honestly tell me you'd like to meet two pontificating professors?"

"I might," Ray had said with a laugh.

He was attractive in a faintly battered, homey sort of way; tall, brown-haired and blue-eyed. He had a good smile, a nose that took a pronounced turn to the left as a result of a collision with a baseball bat in high school, and an offbeat sense of humor. He was attentive sexually and didn't rush off the moment their lovemaking was over. But he'd never spent an entire night with her because, he said with tiresome regularity, "This is a small town, and people notice things like a strange car sitting in your driveway all night."

At the outset, she'd accepted the logic and truth of this. But when it began to seem as if the divorce was taking an unusually long time to happen, her dissatisfaction took root. She wanted to dine out, to go see a movie or a play, to do the ordinary things couples did. She wanted to be able to be seen in public in the company of a man she cared for. And that man wasn't Ray. All their meetings had taken place in her home, and she couldn't help thinking that their relationship was terribly convenient for him. For her, it had evolved into a predictable sameness. Her sympathy and patience had just about run dry.

That Saturday evening when Rebecca routinely asked how the divorce was progressing, he set down his knife and fork and drained his glass before replying finally in what seemed carefully chosen words.

"I've got Marla and the kids to consider. We're working on a no-fault divorce. If she finds out about you, Rebecca, I could wind up on the street with nothing but my jockey shorts and an empty briefcase. As rotten as I know it sounds, I really can't afford to have us seen together.

"Then there's the matter of the kids. My girl's great. She'll be graduating from college next June and off on her own. But my younger boy's something else. His grades last year were down the toilet, and he's moody as hell lately. Be patient with me, will you?" he asked, reaching across the table to stroke her arm. "You've never been through a divorce, so it's probably a little hard for you to appreciate what a horror show it can be."

"Neither have you," she said quietly, irked by this patronizing remark.

"True. But I'm up to my eyeballs in it now."

"I know," she said, fed up with all the secrecy and endless rationalizations. It was possible that twenty-four years of delving into the nefarious activities of allegedly upright businessmen had taught him to be extremely careful in all his dealings, but her tolerance had also run dry.

He gazed at her with a helpless expression. "These things take time, Rebecca. I don't like it any more than you do. I know it's hard on you. I'd love to be able to take you out, show you off. Don't you think it bothers me too, all this sneaking around?"

"Does it?" she asked.

"Of course it does! Hell! I'm starting to feel like one of those white-collar guys who're forever trying to scam the company. I've never been involved with anyone but Marla, and I feel kind of guilty." He looked down at his half-eaten dinner. "Unfortunately," he said, "you seem to be getting the pointy end of the stick."

"I'll survive," she said, wondering if maybe she'd been misreading him. He appeared sincerely upset.

"I looked forward all week to being with you tonight," he said with the barest hint of recrimination.

"Did you really?" She had no idea how his mind worked. Seven months and the only thing she knew for certain was that she was tired of hearing him repeat himself. He made this same statement every time she saw him.

"You know I did." He looked up at her suggestively. "All week I've been thinking about nothing but you."

He blotted his lips on his napkin, then rose halfway out of his chair and leaned across the table to kiss her. She accepted the kiss without responding. He didn't seem to notice. Sinking back into his seat, he said, "After dinner I'll show you just how I've been thinking about you. Don't give up on me yet. I'm trying my best to work things out.''

Had he guessed she'd been thinking of calling it off? The heat of her uneasiness rushed into her face and she lowered her eyes, chagrined by the transparency of her reactions. She'd been told that as an actress, one of her major assets was the way her features mirrored her emotions. As a woman, and nowhere near a stage, she wished she were better able to mask her feelings. She had no difficulty doing it in the classroom. But now, when she was most anxious to maintain some control over the manner in which she dealt with this man, she couldn't seem to do it.

"I love the way you blush," he said fondly, misinterpreting her reaction. "You're like a teenager."

"I'm not sure that's a compliment," she said, forcing herself to go on eating. "At thirty-three, I'm hardly a child."

He paused to drink more of the Reisling he'd brought along, studying her over the top of his glass. "I know that," he said. "Is something wrong?"

Did he actually believe her comparative youth automatically made her somewhat gullible? She may have been young by his standards—he was forty-seven, after all—but she was old enough not to take at face value everything she was told. And there was plenty wrong. Among other things, she had questions about his extraordinary need for secrecy. The few times she'd tried to phone him at his apartment in Stamford, she got his answering machine and she'd hung up without leaving a message. When she'd mentioned it, he'd laughed and said, "I keep the ringer turned off, so I don't have to listen to Marla leaving threatening messages. To be honest, half the time I forget to check the thing."

He phoned her almost daily, from wherever he happened to be. If he was going to be away for a day or two, he'd warn her in advance. He was so faithful about calling that she'd never felt any need to phone him at his office. Besides, the thought of having his secretary ask, "May I say who's calling?" or "What company are you with?" was more than enough to put her off.

As usual, she'd made a special dinner: chicken breasts in an apricot-mustard glaze, with wild rice, an arugula salad with a light vinaigrette dressing, and a crusty baguette with sweet butter. She should've just served leftovers, thereby sending the message that she no longer considered *him* special. She was so preoccupied with her dissatisfaction that she could scarcely breathe, let alone eat. She knew she should tell him they couldn't go on seeing each other, but her horror of ugly scenes kept her procrastinating. And that made her angry with herself. She wanted to end it, but she just couldn't make the move. The result of this inner conflict was a weight loss that over the past month totaled close to ten pounds.

Aggie had noticed and remarked, "Mister X, my dear, may well turn you anorexic. I seem to recall several hundred years ago when I was in my prime and playing naughty games with the boys, lovemaking gave me an astonishing appetite. I remember, after one fairly pyrotechnical performance, eating most of a cold leg of roast lamb, several slices of bread, the better part of a pound of raw carrots, and half a custard pie."

"What's so amusing?" Ray asked now, smiling reflexively.

"I was just thinking about something Aggie said."

"She's the head of your department, right?"

"That's right."

"What did she say that was so funny?"

"Oh, nothing worth repeating."

"Does she know about us?"

"She knows I'm seeing someone. She refers to you as Mister X."

"You talk about us, Rebecca?" He lost his smile and looked on the verge of anger.

"I don't discuss my private affairs with anyone, Ray. But Agnes is my closest friend. Of course I've mentioned you."

"Not by name, I hope."

A sudden constriction in her chest, she kept her voice low as she asked, "Would that matter?"

"You're damned right it would. Are you forgetting my son goes to that school?"

"My conversations with Agnes are strictly between the two of us. She's entirely trustworthy, and even if she did know your name, it's unlikely she'd gossip about us. You don't think maybe you're overreacting just a little?"

"I'm sorry." His smile returned and he reached for her hand. "I'm living on a powder keg these days, but I shouldn't take it out on you. Am I forgiven for that brief paranoid display?"

"I'm not stupid, you know, Ray," she said, freeing her hand. "And I don't like your implying that I'm indiscreet. I'm not some addled teenager having her first affair, and I resent your treating me as if that's precisely what I am. Don't be fooled by the fact that I look younger than my age. I've lived in the real world for a good long time. You've made it abundantly clear that you're having a rough time with this divorce, and I sympathize. But when you start questioning my judgment, maybe we have a problem. As a matter of fact, it might be a good idea if we stop seeing each other."

"No, I'm sorry," he said quickly, stunned. "Please forgive me. The last thing I want is to upset you. Could we forget it, please?"

She got up from the table and carried the dishes to the sink, then switched on the coffeemaker, saying, "I'm really not sure we should keep on, Ray. I don't like having to censor everything I say for fear of triggering what you call 'paranoid displays.'"

When he failed to speak, she turned to see he'd dropped

his head into his hands. Returning to the table, she stood waiting for him to say or do something.

"I was a jerk," he said thickly, finally lifting his head to look at her, "and I'm sorry. Don't give up on me, Rebecca." Tears came to his eyes. "You're the best thing that's ever happened to me. Maybe I'm not too good at showing it, but I love you."

Embarrassed for him, she watched the tears slip down his cheeks as he pulled a handkerchief from his pocket. "You're not a jerk, Ray," she said softly. "It's just that there are too many problems. And when it gets to where I don't feel free to say what I think, I have to wonder what it's all about."

"I know," he agreed. "You're right." He wiped his face impatiently, then got up and stood facing her. "I don't want to give you up. And I don't want you to give up on me."

Her inner voice was saying, *Call it off right now! Do it and get it over with!* But he was so abject, and she felt such an unexpected surge of sympathy for him, that she simply didn't have the heart to do it. She gave him a hug and said, "Why don't you go sit down in the living room? I'll be in with the coffee in a couple of minutes."

"I love you, Beck," he said urgently, searching her eyes.

"I know you do." She smiled, feeling like a complete fraud. "Go on. I'll just get the coffee organized and be right in."

With the expression of a wounded little boy, he stood looking at her for another moment, then turned, retrieved his wine glass from the table and carried it with him to the living room.

She watched him go, disgusted with herself for not taking advantage of the chance she'd had to make the break. As she quickly cleared the table, she berated herself for being too softhearted, too much of a coward to tell the man the truth. God! He'd actually sat there and cried. The longer she waited, the worse it was going to be when she finally did call off the affair.

Rinsing the dishes before loading them into the dishwasher, she made up her mind not to make love with him again. That would be the first decisive step, and one he'd be unable to misinterpret. Never again! she thought, getting two cups. If she had to spend the rest of her life alone, fine. But this was the one and only messy divorce she intended to be involved in, no matter how peripherally. He'd actually cried! God! It was positively mortifying. What would he do when she told him it was over?

She wished she had Agnes's aplomb. Agnes would never get herself into a mess like this. She could just imagine the comments Agnes would make if she told her about this.

CHAPTER

Three

Y ou should sell the house to Mr. Givens," Rebecca was telling her mother, not for the first time. "For more than two years he's been saying how perfect it would be for his daughter and her family, how thrilled he'd be having his grandchildren right next door. You really should do it. You could buy one of those gorgeous new condominiums down on the Sound, and even when you've paid the capital gains tax on what's left in profit after you bought the new place, you'd still have enough money to do almost anything—go on one of those ninety-day around-the-world cruises, and take along a friend; hire a full-time daily housekeeper instead of having to make do with Coral coming in once a week to move the dust. Why are you so determined to hang on to this enormous old barn?"

"I've lived here for forty-five years. I'm used to it."

"But, Mother," Rebecca tried to reason with her, "it needs so much maintenance. Why not sell it now, while it's still in reasonably decent condition? What's the point of sinking more and more of your capital into something that's way too big for you, when you could have a lovely, far more manageable apartment? Think of it! Plus there'd be no broker's fee, just the closing costs. You could make a real killing."

Evelyn Leighton's head shook resolutely back and forth throughout her daughter's declaration. "I don't want to move. And besides, what would I do with all my things?"

"You don't *need* most of this stuff. Artie and Bill would probably be glad to take a lot of it off your hands."

"Don't talk to me about your brothers!" Evelyn said, her face creasing into stubborn folds. "I never see them from one year to the next. They have no interest in their mother or in the contents of this house."

"That's not true," Rebecca disagreed, promising herself she'd call her brothers as soon as she got home and give them hell. She adored her mother and was happy to make the visits and the phone calls. "I'm sure they're just busy and forgot to call."

"For three months?" Her mother gave her a you-must-be-joking look.

"Okay. What can I say?"

"You just said it," Evelyn gave one of her heart-melting smiles. "I gave birth to two typical men, and," she added, the smile heating up several degrees, "one pint-sized sweetheart." Her smile now took full charge of her face, making her at once younger looking and, for Rebecca, completely irresistible.

Evelyn had been far and away the most beautiful of all the mothers Rebecca had encountered while growing up. She had then, and still had, that rare combination of lovely features and a loving, generous nature that shone in her large, wide-set eyes and her marvelously mobile mouth. A petite but large-breasted woman, she carried herself with innate dignity and grace and, in reality, looked a good ten years younger than her age.

Rebecca had always thought it a pity that she scarcely resembled her mother. The only characteristic they had in common was the color of their eyes. Otherwise, they couldn't have looked more unalike. Evelyn's once auburn hair was now primarily gray with a few tenacious russet strands remaining. Her skin was a warmer hue than her daughter's, and the shape of her face was more square, her jaw wider, her chin less pointed. They had at one time been the same height but, as Rebecca had begun to notice in the past year or two, her mother was becoming gradually smaller. Evelyn still dressed with casual elegance, most often in narrow trousers that showed off her legs to advantage, and loose-fitting tops that concealed her heavy breasts. She wore her hair in a short, shaggy cut that nicely framed her still lovely features.

"I'm crazy about your face," Rebecca said, giving her mother's cheek a gentle pinch. "You are the best-looking senior citizen in the entire state."

"This face has more wrinkles than a Chinese laundry," Evelyn said with a laugh and a dismissing motion of her hand.

"You could get yourself a boyfriend in no time flat if you'd relent and go just once with Aunt Bertha to that club of hers."

"First of all," Evelyn said, lifting the lid to check on the peas, "I wouldn't be caught dead spending an evening with a bunch of old codgers. My sister has no self-respect and no taste in men. You'd think after surviving twenty-nine years with that old fool, she'd have had enough of men to last a lifetime. But no. There's Bertha every week, decked out in her best bib and tucker, looking for love at the Seniors' Singles Club. I'd rather stay home and read cookbooks. Second, I'm not interested in having a boyfriend. I had your father for thirty-eight wonderful years. It'll be eight years in February since he died, and I still half the time expect him to shout down the stairs asking where's his blue shirt. There'll never be another Arthur Leighton, and I have no desire to go through that whole dating song and dance again, thank you very much. Once was more than enough. And I was lucky. I only had to date a half dozen 'nice eligible young men'—as my mother liked to refer to them—before I met your father at Ethel Simpson's twenty-first birthday party."

"But aren't you bored?" Rebecca stood, her hands in padded mitts, ready at a signal from her mother to lift the roasting pan out of the oven.

"Okay," Evelyn said, "you can take it out now."

Once the roast was set on the platter and Rebecca had tipped the pan juices into the pot on the stove, Evelyn added her special mix of sherry, flour, salt and pepper, and began stirring what would be the best gravy Rebecca had ever tasted.

"I am never bored," her mother finally answered. "Don't cut the slices too thick, sweetheart. I have my books and my music and the VCR. I've got my Saturday night poker game with the girls and my two afternoons a week volunteering at the hospital. I'm an old woman. Doesn't that sound like a pretty full schedule to you?"

"Don't tell me you've finally figured out how to run the VCR. I can't believe it!"

"How quickly they forget!" Evelyn addressed the simmering contents of the gravy pot. "Do I have to remind you who had the mechanical skills in this family, who it was who fixed the toilets, the fuses, the stove? Who put up the bookshelves in your bedroom? Who knew how to jump start the car? We all know it wasn't your dear father, bless his heart. So who could it have been, I wonder?"

Rebecca put her arm across her mother's shoulders and gave her a squeeze. "I inherited all my skills from you," she said, profoundly aware of the delicacy of the frame she embraced. Every time she came into close contact with her mother's body, she felt a stab of advance sorrow at the knowledge that one day this dear woman would be gone from her life forever. She couldn't imagine what she'd do with the abundant residual love she'd be left with then. Unless Evelyn lived to be well over a hundred, Rebecca would never be able to use up all the affection she had for her mother. "God!" she exclaimed lightly. "You really are shrinking!"

"That is correct," Evelyn confirmed. "Old people shrink. Everybody knows that except young people, who think it's something that's never going to happen to them."

"I wish you'd stop talking about yourself that way. You are *not* that old!"

"Sixty-seven is old enough, thank you. I earned every minute of it. Put the peas in that bowl, please. We're almost ready."

Once they were settled at the table in the dining room, Evelyn said, "So, tell me all the news. How's your crazy redhead friend from school?"

"Agnes is . . . I don't know. We went into the city Friday night. Saw the *worst* performance." Rebecca told her mother about the play, quoting several of Aggie's more pithier comments. "It was strange," she said. "At first it was all right. But then I kept thinking she'd stop, and she didn't. Lately she hasn't been herself at all. She completely forgot about a staff meeting last week. That's just so unlike her."

Evelyn shook her head. "Maybe she's having an early menopause. It's been known to make women forgetful."

"Maybe," Rebecca said doubtfully. "But I don't think that's it."

"Talk to her. She might surprise you and tell you what's on her mind."

"I'll think about it."

"What's the latest on the married boyfriend?"

"Separated," Rebecca corrected her.

"Whatever."

"The lawyers are trying to thrash out an agreement."

"Sounds as if it's going to be one of the longest divorces on record," Evelyn observed mildly.

"It's beginning to feel that way to me. I'm fed up with the whole thing."

"So stop seeing him," Evelyn said simply.

"It's not that easy."

"What's so hard about it? He calls up and you say you've decided not to see him again."

"I can't just do that," Rebecca said.

"Why not? Other women do it every day."

"I don't want to hurt him."

"Oh, please, Rebecca! I've been hearing you say the same silly thing since you went out with your first boyfriend at fourteen."

"Well, I don't like hurting anyone," Rebecca defended herself.

"I'll never forget the year you were seventeen, when you broke up three times. Three times you wanted to see other boys, and three times you couldn't bring yourself to be the one to end it. So you let it drag on. The boys dropped you. And I had to nurse you through your broken heart. You'd think by now you'd have learned how to make a graceful exit."

"Evidently I haven't quite got the knack of it yet. This is delicious," she said, eating with gusto. "Next week Aggie and I start casting for *The Philadelphia Story.*"

"A wonderful movie," Evelyn said, going along with the change of subject.

"A wonderful play, only a tiny bit dated."

"The movie was better."

"You saw the play?"

"Sure. The movie was better. Hepburn and Cary Grant."

Evelyn gave an appreciative sigh, then said, "Have some more potatoes." Obediently, Rebecca served herself as her mother said, "Talk to me some more about what you think I should do with this place."

"You'll sell it?" Rebecca asked eagerly.

"I said talk to me. I might think about it. And you might think about giving this fellow the push before you end up getting hurt again."

With an abashed smile, Rebecca said, "Okay. We'll both do some thinking."

"And how was your divine little mother?" Agnes asked, curling up on the sofa and retrieving her cigarette from the ashtray.

"Are you being sarcastic?" Rebecca asked warily.

"Not at all." Agnes looked surprised. "I love your mother."

"She was as terrific and as stubborn as ever," Rebecca said, satisfied by the answer. She pushed off her shoes before settling in the overstuffed armchair. All of Aggie's furniture seemed to have been transported directly from the twenties into her living room. Despite its stark contrast to the fifties' ranch-style architecture of the house, it was exceedingly comfortable. "But she's actually promised to consider putting the house on the market."

"Oh, I will be sad at having to curtail my infrequent visits to the House of Usher. I do so enjoy the crypt-like atmosphere, the dankness, the sudden drafts."

"All right!" Rebecca laughed. "Message received. Where did *he* come from?" she asked, pointing to a brown teddy bear sitting in the companion armchair.

"What do you mean, where did he come from? Teddy's always been here. Haven't you, Teddy?" She got up from the sofa and retrieved the bear from the chair, holding it in the bend of her arm. She addressed her question to the bear as if fully expecting it to reply. Cradling it like an infant, she returned to the sofa and sat holding the toy securely to her breast. Rebecca was captivated by this performance. In the eight years of their friendship, she'd grown accustomed to Aggie's impromptu theatrics. She'd drop a quote from Shakespeare into the middle of a conversation, or, out of the blue, quote snippets of doggerel; limericks, poems, even snatches of dialogue she'd overheard in the supermarket.

"Have you always had him?" Rebecca asked.

"Not always," Agnes answered, taking a puff of her cigarette. "My first teddy was *taken away,*" she said in cool, accusing tones, her hold on the bear visibly tightening as if Rebecca had threatened to take it from her. "This teddy's been in residence eleven years now."

"No kidding," Rebecca said, thinking Agnes was playing this scene to the hilt. "Eleven years. He's in very good shape."

"Only children abuse their teddies, Rebecca," she said, stroking the bear's nose with the tip of one long finger.

For a moment Rebecca wondered if she could actually be serious. Agnes was staring meaningfully at her, her mouth tight, eyes narrowed. It was a bit frightening to think she really meant any of this. Rebecca felt all at once apprehensive, but then, to her relief, Agnes grinned and said, "And how was Mister X? Tell all! These days I'm living vicariously through your exploits."

Grateful to be back on normal territory, Rebecca said, "Mister X was the same as he always is, thank you."

"No breakthroughs on the divorce-wars front?"

"Not yet. Possibly not ever. I don't really care anymore, but I'm not in the mood to discuss it. Anyway, what's all this bull about living vicariously through me? You and my mother both talk as if you're so old all that's left is to sit around waiting to die. You're only forty-three, for God's sake, Aggie. And you're way more attractive than most of the women around town."

It was true. Agnes was five-ten, with long red hair, most often worn in a topknot pierced by half a dozen tortoiseshell pins. She had perfect, translucent skin with scarcely a line on it, slanted green eyes, and a beautifully delineated mouth she invariably accented with clear red lipstick. She had a model's lanky body and dressed with eccentric flair in simply-cut clothes of either black or brilliant primary colors.

"My personal interest in men, darling, terminated some time just after the Crusades," she said archly, putting out her cigarette before recrossing her enviably long, slim legs, all the while holding the teddy bear to her breast. "My interest in them now is purely academically prurient. I prefer to remember them fondly rather than grapple with them presently."

"What a load!" Rebecca scoffed. "What about that guy two years ago?"

"A mere bagatelle," Agnes insisted, lifting her chin. "A brief refresher course, wasn't he, Teddy?" She addressed the bear in the doting tones of an adoring mother.

Rebecca laughed, beginning to feel uneasy. "Until someone else comes along."

"I very much doubt that, darling. What with rather nasty diseases and all the contrivances one must resort to nowadays for personal protection, I'd as soon give it a miss. How were the essays, by the bye?"

"Fairly terrible, except for Lisa Owens. That kid's so talented it's scary. She writes like an angel."

"She *is* good," Agnes agreed judiciously, propping the teddy bear on the sofa beside her so that it sat squarely facing Rebecca. "She was in my sophomore class last year, turned in some truly inspired essays. Never fails to amaze me that a little bugger like that actually has a functioning brain. Trish was saying the other day in the staff room the girl's a whiz at computer sciences, too."

"Every college in the country will be fighting to get her," Rebecca said, glancing again at the teddy bear. It had, if such a thing were possible, a serious little face. Its shiny brown eyes reflected the light from the table lamp, making it seem as if the bear were real and not merely a toy. Just a trick of the light, she told herself.

Agnes shrugged and lit a fresh cigarette. "She's bright enough, but I suspect she's ingesting alien substances."

"You mean drugs?"

"Why the great show of surprise, my dear? She's certainly not the only little bugger popping out to the parking lot between classes to take a bit of this or that. If we ever raided the students' lockers, I expect we'd turn up enough pharmaceuticals to keep a fair-sized hospital stocked for a year. Not to mention the liquor these kids consume. I'll wager a good half the senior class gets pissed every weekend."

"It's depressing," Rebecca said quietly. "Why do they do it?"

"Don't be naive!" Agnes chided. "We've ruined the world for them. Haven't we, Teddy?" She gazed at the bear for a long moment before looking back at Rebecca. "We've put holes in the ozone layer, thrown our raw sewage and our laboratory waste into the water supply; we've polluted the air, the rainwater, the beaches, and our food; we're in the process of cutting down the rain forests just to be certain we destroy the ecology of the planet completely. Sex is potentially lethal. Property values are so inflated kids can't afford to leave home without parental subsidy. The only things left are angry music, drugs, and alcoholic beverages. You're forgetting that this is a generation that's been 'entertained' electronically, one way and another, since birth. Unlike Teddy," she ran a loving hand over the bear's head, "they've all got alarmingly foreshortened attention spans, little if any ability to entertain themselves, and the majority are functionally illiterate. Aside from that, things are simply super," she said with bitter gusto.

"I expect if I were growing up today, I'd take drugs of one sort or another just to be able to see things somewhat differently."

"You don't mean that," Rebecca said, shocked.

"Don't be too sure. I'm not overly fond of the world in its present state."

"Well, neither am I. But it's not completely rotten."

"Not completely," Agnes said. "Only about seventy-five percent."

"Come on, Aggie. You know you don't mean what you're saying."

Agnes shifted, looked penetratingly at Rebecca for a few seconds, then smiled and said, "Not really, no."

"What did you do this weekend?" Rebecca asked, hoping to lighten the mood. She was finding it hard to keep her eyes off the bear.

"Not a great deal. Went to a meeting of the Medieval Society Friday night, did the marketing yesterday, watched the Britcoms on Channel Thirteen, did some marking today, and the laundry. The usual thrilling stuff."

"What's the Medieval Society?"

"Oh, you know, Rebecca," she said somewhat impatiently. "It's this group that likes to get all rigged out in twelfth-century gear and drink mead and talk a load of old rubbish."

"When did you join?"

"I've belonged for ages, and you know it."

"I've never heard you mention it before," Rebecca said. "I'd certainly remember if you had."

"Well, I'm sure I have and you've simply forgotten."

"Maybe you have," Rebecca backed down, looking at her watch. "I should be going. I've got a few papers left to mark, and I want to wash my hair."

Agnes laughed. "Yes," she said. "Attending to all the joys

of a teacher's life. Teddy and I have an equally exciting evening planned."

"Right!" Rebecca laughed, wishing as she pushed her feet into her shoes that Agnes would stop this game with the bear. "On that happy note, I'll make my exit, stage left."

Agnes got up to see her out. "I'll see you in the morning," Rebecca said, looping the strap of her bag over her shoulder. "What do you medievalists eat at these meetings, anyway?"

"Oh, the usual things: venison haunch, wild greens, Uncle Ben's rice."

"You're out of your mind!" Rebecca said fondly, giving Agnes a kiss on the cheek before opening the front door.

"It's why you love me," Agnes said. "It's why most of the civilized world loves me." She leaned against the open door as she watched Rebecca climb into the Jetta. "Drive carefully!"

As Rebecca backed the car out of the driveway, she looked over at Aggie, who smiled and lazily raised a hand before stepping back inside and closing the door. Heading home, she made a mental note to phone her brothers. Then she thought about Agnes. For a few minutes back there, that business with the teddy bear had been kind of creepy.

CHAPTER

Four

Pete hardly thought about Leighton until he saw her walking down the corridor at school after lunch on Monday. When he saw her, all his anger fused and focused on her. Wasn't for her things would've been fine; he wouldn't've been out there at the service center on the thruway in the pouring rain at one o'clock in the morning, with not a thing happening, the drivers all crashed in their cabs, the McDonald's about empty with just the staff cleaning up, everything dead. He'd had to walk four and a half miles; took him *hours*.

He finally gets home and all he wants is to hit the sheets, but the minute he comes through the door his mother's all over him, like a goddamned storm. She's been sitting there waiting for him. Where's he been, why's he so wet, how come Tim and Cal didn't bring him home? She's bent all out of shape and has maybe a million questions, and all he wants is to sack out. But no way is she going to save it for the morning.

She goes, "You get out of those wet clothes, then come right back here and give me some kind of explanation."

And he goes, "Could it wait?"

And she goes, "No, it can't wait! Have you any idea how worried I've been? Why didn't you call? You know you're supposed to check in so I don't have to sit up half the night thinking you're probably lying somewhere dead."

He's thinking he blew it totally. Long as he remembers to pick up the phone, she'll go to bed, not sit in the dark in the living room, chain-smoking and waiting for him. But did he remember? No way. So then he has to get into the apology number, say all the sorry stuff she wants to hear so she'll get off his case and let him go to bed.

So he goes, "Cal's car died on the Post Road. I couldn't call you. We had to walk home."

And she goes, "You couldn't've used a pay phone?"

And he goes, "What pay phone? We were down on that stretch of road by the cemetery. You don't think I would've called if I could've?"

That stopped her for like five seconds while she scoped out his face like she could read if he's lying, which she used to be able to do, absolutely, until he learned how to make himself look completely blank. Now there's no way she can tell zip from his face. So he's standing there with his face hanging out, like this is the total truth I'm telling you.

"What time did this happen?" she wanted to know, eyes squinty, nose almost twitching like she could smell bullshit if he started dishing it up.

"Like one-thirty," he goes, looking her dead in the eye. "You know what it's like out there?" He points toward the windows and the rain. "Plus we tried to get it going. We didn't want to just leave it there. We tried to start it up."

"And where were you until one-thirty that you couldn't have called?"

"I forgot. I'm sorry. Okay? Can I go to bed now?"

"If you knew what went through my mind, Peter. Why do you have to keep putting me through this? When are you going to develop some sense of responsibility? I *worry* when I don't hear from you. Would you prefer to have parents who don't care?"

He'd have liked to say, Yeah, I'd love it. It'd be beautiful. I could have a *life*. But no way he could stand there and say anything like that. She had this temper lately, this unbelievable thing where she'd go completely off her head, like this one time when he'd been horsing around and she didn't like it and she'd just snapped and come at him with her knitting needle. Scared the crap out of him, she'd been so insane. You wanted to keep on living, you didn't screw around with this woman, because she could be normal one minute and the next she was coming at you with a knitting needle or a screwdriver; she'd stab you if she didn't buy what you were saying or doing.

"Course not," he answered, clued in to all her buzz words. "I said I'm sorry. Could I please go to bed now?"

"You're grounded for a week," she goes. "You'll spend the rest of the weekend doing yard work. I want those leaves raked and bagged and taken to the dump."

"It wasn't my fault!" he goes. It's so unfair, he's ready to cry. And he'll die before he cries in front of her.

"I don't care whose fault it was, you're supposed to check in. You didn't, so you're grounded. That's it! End of discussion. Now get the hell to bed. And don't leave those wet clothes on the floor or I swear to God I'll brain you. Put them in your bathtub. I come in tomorrow and find them on the new carpet, Peter, I'll ground you for the *year!*"

"Fine!" He heads off to his room, hating her. Which is okay, since he knows how much she hates him.

So the whole of Saturday he has to do stinking yard work, raking up goddamned wet leaves that weigh a ton. Bugs and shit every time he lifts the stuff. And he couldn't find the stinking work gloves, so he has to use his bare hands to push this soaking crud into the plastic bags. He's practically puking, trying not to think about the slimy gunge he's handling. Only decent thing is, she lets him haul the bags to the dump in the station wagon, so he gets some time in behind the wheel for a change without having to beg.

Then she makes him do his own laundry, which is okay, he doesn't mind doing the stuff. But she's hanging over him screaming not to mix the whites with the colors until he'd like to shove her into the machine with the jeans and the socks and watch her drown. "Can't you do *anything* right?" she's shrieking, pushing him out of the way to reset the water temperature, the load size. "Go do your homework!" she tells him, standing there programming the goddamned washing machine like a rocket scientist.

He goes, "I don't have any," and she gives him one of those knitting-needle looks, so he goes, "Okay," and heads for his room wishing she'd go away somewhere and leave him alone. If he turns on the stereo, she'll come screaming at him to turn it off and get his homework done. And he can't wear the headphones because she likes to trap him; she'll come knocking on his door and he won't hear, naturally, 'cause he's got the headphones on with the volume up full. Then she'll come exploding into the room with more screaming. So he's stuck, doesn't have even one single pill. Nothing. He should've taken a couple more from the prescription bottle in Cal's parents' bathroom. Stupid! Head up his ass.

He's stuck, so he cracks the books, gets the theme written for that lunatic English giant Tyrell, aces the trig assignments, copies Shelley's physics notes, actually finishes every last bit of work since the start of the semester. Amazing! He won't have to do dick for weeks. He throws on a Zeppelin tape, then thinks the room sucks; it's a shit-heap, and he hates when everything gets all out of torque. The only thing he hates more is when his mother decides she's had enough so she's going to clean up for him, and she throws stuff out, goes through all his pockets. She'd probably read his diary if he had one. That's the way she is. It's her *right* to go through every-thing. They fight every time she does it, and he'd like to kill her, just wrap his hands around her stinking throat and choke the shit out of her. He's cleaning up when he gets the idea that maybe the tapes would be better in the bookcase instead of all jammed into the drawer, so he starts sorting stuff out, separating the bootleg Dead tapes and homemade dubs from the store stuff.

He's really getting into it when she comes charging in, doesn't knock or anything like she'd do if it was Lee's room, no knocking, just shoots on in and starts accusing him of all kinds of stuff. She went and called Cal's mother, checking up on his story. And Cal was home by one-thirty, so where the hell was he and why was he forever lying to her? *"And didn't I tell you to do your homework?"* she screams so loud it's like knives in his eardrums, not giving him a chance to say word one.

"You're grounded for a *month!*" she goes, and before she slams his door so hard it's miraculous the sucker doesn't split in half, she goes, "And clean up this pigsty!" which is the killer blow, because what's he been doing for hours if not cleaning his room?

So Monday after lunch when he sees Leighton, he decides she's the one to blame for all of it, and she's gonna pay for messing him up. And for the rest of the afternoon he's figur-ing out stuff, his brain all centered and cooled from some Valium he scored in the parking lot at lunchtime. He's tuned in on that winking turn signal he can still see perfectly as the red VW Jetta zooms past them like they're garbage; he's got a close-up on the car making a turn onto the Shore Road.

That night he checks the phone book. She's not in there. Then he calls 411 and gets the "That's an unpublished num-ber" routine, which really ties it for him. Here he's all set to do the heavy-breathing gig over the phone to freak her out and she's got this unpublished number. So he's got to rethink the thing. And he's definitely into it now because it's a toughie. So he's scoping it out, kind of glad in a way he couldn't get hold of her number, because the heavy-breathing gig's bullshit. Any jerk-off can pull that kind of crap. What he wants is something more in the way of pay-back. He's considering various gigs to pull when Cal calls, wanting to know what happened.

"I'm *grounded,*" Pete goes, "for an entire *month!*"

"Holy shit!"

"Yeah. Tell your mother thanks a lot!"

"Hey! Don't go blaming my mother, man!" Cal tells him. "She just told the truth. Where the hell were you anyway, you didn't blow in there until like four-thirty?"

"I was checking out the service center on I-Ninety-five."

"Looking to score, right?" Cal's making it sound on a par with murder or something.

"Yeah. So?"

"You're a head case. You know that?" Cal goes.

"Oh, fuck you, man!" Pete puts the phone down. He doesn't need this grief. Everybody on his case. He's so bummed he turns off the phone; let whoever calls talk to his machine. The hell with it! He's fed up with the entire world.

He's sitting there, too peaked even to bother with some music, when there's a knock, and he knows it's his dad because Lee's at college and she's the only other one who knocks around here lately. So he goes "Yeah?" and his dad comes in, gives him this sad/disappointed smile, and sits on the end of the bed for a talk.

"Why didn't you check in?" he goes, and Pete can't get up the energy anymore, he just shrugs. "And why the hell did you lie to your mother?"

"I didn't lie, okay?"

"Come on, Pete," his dad goes. "You know you did, and

I know you did, and your mother knows you did. Why does everything have to be a battle with you? If you'd just told her the truth, you'd have been home free."

Pete gives another shrug, feeling his high starting to go. He's got a couple of pills left he'll take as soon as his dad's finished the good-father routine and leaves.

"Well," his dad goes, "you'll be happy to know I got her to knock it back to a week."

"No shit?" Pete can't help looking over at his dad now.

"No shit." His dad takes in the room, like he's thinking what to say. Then he goes, "When're you going to stop fighting all of us? What's it going to take?"

Pete has like fifty things he could say to this, but it's so totally useless he can't waste his breath. He just shrugs again and goes, "Thanks."

"For what?"

"For getting it down to a week."

His dad gives him one of his high-voltage conspirator smiles. "It was hard work," he goes, so Pete gets ready to hear what the pay-back's going to be. "Just do me a favor and try to get along with your mother. A matter of months and you'll be a free man, out of here, off to college. It isn't even all that long."

Not that long? Eight months until next June and it's not that long? Pete can't even begin to deal with any of this. He just nods and waits for his dad to go. But his dad keeps on sitting there; then he goes, "You know your message light's flashing?"

Pete turns to look. His head weighs about two hundred pounds and he's so tired he could sleep for a week. "Yeah, I know. I don't feel like talking."

His dad goes, "Anything you need?" and Pete thinks of a dozen things he could say, but he's tried saying them all before and it didn't change a thing. So what's the point of bothering? His dad's quieter maybe, but he's just as big a loon as his mom.

"You okay for money?" his dad asks when Pete doesn't answer.

It's what his dad always does, offers him money. Forty bucks allowance a week; ten here, twenty there. Pete wants to go, Keep your money, man! You can't buy me the way you do Lee. But he only goes, "I'm fine, thanks."

"Okay." Finally his dad gets up, but he stands there looking at Pete like he's got all this other stuff he wants to say.

So Pete goes, "Thanks again," and at last his dad leaves.

"Jesus!" Pete goes out loud to himself, and reaches into his pocket for the last of the Valium he's been saving. He goes into his bathroom, runs a cup of water, then stands looking at the two little light-blue tablets. They've got this line down the middle on the one side and "Valium 10" on the other. Nice color. He throws back the pills, then turns on the tube and stretches out on the bed to run the channels, see if there's anything halfway decent on. Nothing. He's seen all the movies, didn't like them enough the first time to watch them again. No biggie. His mind's clicked back to that bitch Leighton, and he's getting an idea.

The next day after school he tries to follow her on his bike—riding the bike's completely embarrassing but no way the downer it'd be to ride the school bus every day—but she doesn't go home. She's heading for the shopping center, so he gives it up, hangs a U-ey, and heads back to his place.

The day after, he tries again, but she drives too fast and loses him almost right away. At home that night, nicely dosing on some 'ludes he scored from Jenny Baker, whose father just happens to be a doctor, he rethinks things and decides on a better plan. Because it's getting to be this major challenge, and no way he's going to give up. It wasn't for that bitch, he'd be out over at Jen's place, or with the guys, instead of being stuck in his lousy room with his mother in the den in front of the Trinitron with her knitting. Christ, but it's pathetic the way she just sits there, all dressed up like any minute she's going out somewhere when she practically never goes anywhere anymore, with her lap full of the stuff, the needles clacking while she watches hokey shit like *Rescue 911* or *Unsolved Mysteries* or *America's Most Wanted*.

Thursday after school, he's stationed at the junction of the Post Road and the Shore Road, waiting. This was the way she was headed last Friday night. He figures she has to live somewhere along here. He's got the bike parked against a hedge—nobody looks at bikes around here—and he's hunkered down behind the hedge so he can get out in a hurry when Leighton drives by, or in case somebody from the house up the driveway spots him and wants to know what he's doing. He'd love to drop one of the reds he scored from the guy who hangs out lunchtimes by the school, but he knows the second he does, something'll happen, and he wants to stay completely tuned in, so he just squats in back of the hedge and waits for the red Jetta.

He starts to get into this whole other mental state after a while. His brain is way off somewhere else; he's spaced, not even thinking. So when the Jetta does go by, he almost misses it. But the color flashes to him and he has this major jolt realizing it's her. He's waiting to let her get up the road a ways so he can hop on the bike and follow far enough back that she won't notice him. Except that she's signaling to make a left and as he watches, she turns into the driveway of the first house up from the corner. He's so blown he nearly breaks out laughing. She lives not a hundred yards from where he's been waiting.

He gives it some time, then comes out from behind the

hedge, grabs the bike and casually starts to walk it along the road, going nice and slow so he can check everything out.

It's a small white two-storied house with a lot of windows; all the ground-floor ones have these boxes of flowers. A white picket fence protecting this maybe four-foot-deep strip of front garden from the road, stockade fencing around the perimeters. The property's five times the size of the house, at least half an acre, with a bunch of trees at the corner where the Post Road goes by, and one of those prefab metal storage sheds on the left of the driveway. He can't get a look at the near side of the house because what he assumes is the living room at the front is like the long side of an L lying on its back, so you can't see anything from the road. No matter. Now that he knows where she lives, he can come back to take a good long look during the day while she's in class.

He's on a major natural high as he cycles home. He can hardly wait until tomorrow so he can seriously scope out the place. Ideas are racing through his brain; all the things he can do to rattle her cage. It's gonna be beautiful! He just wishes he could tell Shell or Tim, or even Cal. But he knows they wouldn't get it, so why bother?

"You're in a good mood," his mother goes over dinner, all suspicious.

He goes, "Yeah. Is that okay with you?" and instantly knows it's the wrong move. "I didn't say that. Okay?" He gives her a two-hundred-and-fifty-watt display of the teeth. "Eighty-six it. Okay?"

"Pete," she goes, all serious, "do you have any idea how much I love you?"

He hates it when she does this. It's like she's begging for him to go, I love you, too. He won't do it. He's not a parrot he has to say it every time she wants to hear it. She does it to all of them. Lee just goes, I love you, too, Mom. Pete can't and won't play this game, not even when she puts on her injured look. The most he'll do is go, "Yeah, I know." But she's caused a major buzz kill. He hates her when she does this number, and wishes she'd give it up. He's no little kid anymore. He knows it's bullshit, all this love stuff.

She didn't used to be such a loon. She used to be on the run: tennis games with her buddies, lunches at the country club, into the city for shopping and a matinee. It all just kind of died. Every day she gets dressed up like it's showtime, but the only places she goes are the supermarket—spends hours taking a cart up and down the aisles like it's the most amazing place she's ever seen—and the handicraft place to buy a shit-load more wool so she can keep on knitting. She makes these unbelievably hideous sweaters. Lee makes a fuss and goes, "This is great, Mom," and takes them away to school. Probably gives them to her friends, or burns them or something.

If she'd just back off some, give him some breathing room, he thinks things could actually be decent, the way they used to be. But it's way too late, and he knows it. He can remember when they had serious good times, though. It's like it was a whole other bunch of people, or this movie he saw once. But he thinks he remembers how she was pretty decent. He loved to do stuff with her and his dad and Lee. What he can't remember is when it all turned so weird and depressing, and his mom and dad got into major warfare, using him like this weapon they kept shooting off at each other. He wishes they'd all just leave him alone, but it'll never happen.

To hell with that garbage! He's got to concentrate on the number he plans to pull on Leighton. Teach her a little lesson about how to treat people.

CHAPTER

Five

Rebecca loved her eccentric little house. Some hundred years ago it had been a one-room artist's studio for the wife of the merchant who owned the considerably larger house about three hundred yards away.

In the twenties a doorway was cut into the studio's far wall and a tiny kitchen, a bedroom, and bathroom were added, thereby creating a new wing that extended the front of the house and went deeper into the property at a right angle. In the thirties a second story was added over the first addition. In the sixties the rear wall of the kitchen was moved back to within six feet of the huge old copper beech that sheltered the house. The narrow bedroom above was also enlarged and a new spiral staircase led down to the corner of the kitchen below. The bathroom under the eaves was expanded, and a new furnace and water heater were installed in the eight-by-twelve-foot space beneath what had been the old kitchen. This basement area could be reached through a trapdoor in the floor between the kitchen and living room, or via a pair of metal storm doors at the side of the house.

During the years of her residence, she used some of her inheritance on new carpeting and appliances, and for the addition of a skylight in the roof of the master bedroom on the second floor. The only part of the house that remained much as it had always been was the living room—the original studio. It had a cathedral ceiling with a north-facing skylight, and each of the three outside walls contained a pair of windows.

Because the back door was closest to the driveway, Rebecca invariably entered and left the house through the mudroom. The only times she used the front door were in the mornings to grab *The New York Times* off the doormat, and in the afternoons to get her mail from the box.

When the weather permitted, she spent much of her free time on the flower beds and window boxes. The work took her mind off the stresses of a job whose worst feature was the hours. In order to be at school by eight in the morning, she had to be up by six-fifteen. She found it hard to get going at that hour, especially since she rarely went to bed before midnight.

By the time she got home on Friday afternoon, she was ready for a relaxing weekend. After changing clothes, she opened the front door and took the half-dozen steps to the mailbox. Magazines, junk mail, a couple of bills. She closed the box and turned to admire the window boxes.

For a moment it didn't really register. She blinked, as if to improve her vision. Her mouth dropping open, head turning stiffly, she gazed at each of the four boxes on the front windows. Disbelieving, she stepped onto the grass and went around the side of the house. One hand holding the mail to her chest, the other automatically rose to cover her mouth. "What the hell!" she whispered, upset and angry as she looked around for signs that the gardeners had been there.

No, wait. They'd been by the previous week. Like most of her neighbors, she had a gardening service to care for the lawns, while she tended to the flowers and planting. And though they might occasionally run the mowers a bit too close to the shrubs and ground cover, they'd never intentionally do damage—especially not anything as bizarre as this.

Clutching the mail to her chest like armor, she retraced her steps, eyes traveling from one end of the front garden to the other. Then, her stomach fluttering and legs heavy, she made a slow tour of the entire property before at last returning inside. She dropped the mail on the kitchen counter and stood thinking. Then she hurried out the mudroom door to check the garbage cans. Empty. The truck had been by that morning.

Back in the kitchen, she picked up the receiver and with an unsteady finger poked out Aggie's number. Four rings and then the message. "You know what to do and you know when to do it. Thank you for your courtesy and intelligence." Rebecca didn't want to leave a message. She hung up, debating whether or not to call her mother.

Bad idea. Mothers worried. It was as Evelyn often said, "Our primary function in life: we worry."

But she had to talk to someone, so, on impulse, she grabbed her address book and looked up Ray's office number. The voice in her head was telling her this was even a worse idea than calling her mother, but she went ahead anyway. She *had* to talk to someone about this, and they were still seeing one another. So maybe she did want to break up, but at least Ray was someone who cared about her, and she badly needed some feedback. She asked for him. There was no inquisition. The woman merely said, "Hold, please," and a few seconds later Ray came on the line.

"It's Rebecca," she said somewhat breathlessly. "Something very weird's happened."

"What's wrong?" he asked. "Are you all right?"

Feeling shaky, her voice sounding too high, she told him. "While I was at school today, somebody cut the heads off every last one of the flowers. All the window boxes, and the entire bed."

"*What?*"

"All the mums, geraniums, the rhododendron, the marigolds, even the last of the impatiens. Every single flower cut off!"

"Why the hell would anyone do a thing like that?" he wondered, sounding appropriately appalled.

"That's what I'd like to know. And you know what else? Whoever did it took away the flowers. It's unbelievable! I even looked in the garbage cans. Imagine going to someone's house and doing a thing like that, then taking them away with you! What for?" She knew she probably sounded ridiculous, but she wanted sympathy and reassurance.

"It's probably a prank," he said a bit doubtfully.

"No, Ray. A prank is putting a cherry bomb in the mailbox, then driving off like a bat out of hell before the damn thing goes off. A prank is not spending a lot of time in broad daylight decapitating flowers at the very front of someone's house."

"Maybe you should check with the neighbors, ask if anyone saw anything," he suggested.

"I doubt they did," she said. "I will do that, though. It's a good idea."

"Fix yourself a drink, Beck, and try not to think about it."

"I'll fix a drink all right, but I'm going to be thinking about it. I'm sorry to disturb you at the office, but I just had to tell someone."

"Don't worry about disturbing me. I want you to feel free to call me. Look, how about if I stop by this evening? I can hear how upset you are. Maybe you shouldn't be alone."

"Would you?" she asked, increasingly eased by the way he was responding.

"Sure. I've got a couple of things to do, but I could be there by, say, nine."

"Okay, that'd be great. Thank you, Ray."

"And don't forget to check with the neighbors. Maybe somebody saw something."

"I'll do that. Thanks again."

"See you around nine."

She phoned her neighbors. No one had seen a thing. Mrs. Pasorelli next door had been out most of the afternoon, and Ellie Thorne across the road had been in bed all day with a cold. Anyway, Rebecca thought, fixing herself a Stoli on the rocks, the Thorne house was way up at the end of that long driveway. Unless Ellie had been going out or coming home, she wouldn't have been able to see a thing from her front windows.

The telephone rang, and Agnes said, "Did you ring a short time ago and fail to leave a message?"

"As a matter of fact, I did. If you were home, why didn't you pick up?"

"Playing possum," she said. "Why didn't you speak?"

"I didn't feel like being courteous and intelligent," Rebecca said.

"You sound a bit ragged. Has something happened?"

Rebecca gulped down some of the Stoli, then told Agnes about her discovery.

"How curious!" Agnes said. "Of course there is a literary precedent."

"What?"

"To Kill A Mockingbird," Agnes explained. "Jem Finch, the brother, lops off the heads of the old woman's flowers."

"That's right," Rebecca said, remembering. "This is a little different, Agnes. For one thing, this is my house, not some irritable old woman's in a book." Why were they discussing this as if it were some far-removed literary event?

Rebecca wondered. Maybe it was childish, but she wanted sympathy, not a discussion of novelized precedents.

"Any of the students acting up more than usual?" Agnes asked.

Rebecca thought about that, then said, "No. And even if it was one of the kids, how would he or she know where I live?"

"Good point. It would seem we have a bit of a mystery. Best forgotten, really," Agnes counseled. "Although it is sad. Yours is such a lovely garden."

"*Was*," Rebecca said bitterly, wishing Agnes weren't quite so detached-sounding. What was wrong with her lately? A couple of months ago Agnes would've been over in a shot. But here she was, chatting away as if this was nothing of any consequence.

"Never mind, poppet. If it's any consolation, someone's done you a service. There'll be no need for you to dead-head the plants, and next summer's growth will likely be doubly abundant."

"I'm not consoled," Rebecca said irritably. She'd never known Agnes to be quite so callous. "Why were you playing possum, anyway?"

"Just felt like it," Agnes said airily. "But I simply *knew* that was you."

"Well, you were right."

"You're not feeling edgy now, are you?" Agnes asked, sounding less brittle and more like herself. "If you are, I'll be happy to come keep you company."

"No, I'm fine, thanks. Ray's going to drop over later."

"Ray?"

"Mister X," Rebecca clarified, realizing she'd slipped for the first time and given away his name.

"Ray," Agnes repeated. "An uninspired name. Sorry. That was sheer bitchery. *Are* you all right?"

"I'm pissed off more than anything else. It's so damned *creepy* that someone would do something like this."

"And so you should be! If I had a garden instead of this ill-bred assortment of herbaceous nastiness, and some little bugger did that to my flowers, I'd be equally infuriated. Drink some of your favorite 'liquid bullet,' my dear, and try not to think about it."

"You think it's one of the students, don't you? Why?"

"It's just the sort of thing they do, really."

"Why is it people always want you to forget what upsets you most? As if that's even possible."

"Merely a sympathetic expression, darling. Do whatever you fancy. I'm off to pick up my pizza. You're welcome to share it if you like, unless Mister X is speeding to your side even as we speak."

"He's not coming until about nine. It's only five o'clock, Aggie. How come you're eating so early?"

Agnes gave one of her booming laughs and said, "Because Teddy and I are hungry, you twit. I'll speak with you during the weekend." She laughed and hung up.

It took Rebecca a few seconds to remember that Teddy was the eleven-year-old teddy bear with the serious face and the light-reflecting brown eyes that Agnes had held to her breast with all the attentiveness of a new mother. Why, all of a sudden, was this toy figuring so prominently in Aggie's life? Or had she only said that to be witty, hoping to distract Rebecca from her upset?

She took another swallow of the vodka, deciding Aggie had been trying to amuse her.

Ray arrived with an armload of cut flowers and a bottle of Portuguese red wine. "Poor old you," he said, giving her the flowers, the wine, and a kiss. "Are you feeling any better now?"

"Doctor Stolichnaya has been a big help. Thank you for these, Ray," she said of the immense bouquet. "This helps, too. D'you want some of your wine?"

"Will you have some?"

"I'd better not. I'm already half in the bag."

"Then we'll save it. How about some coffee?"

"Have you eaten?" she asked as she unwrapped the flowers, deposited them in the sink, then ran enough cool water to cover the stems.

"Have you?" he countered. "Why don't I get the coffee started?"

She leaned against the counter looking puzzled. "Did I eat?" she asked herself aloud, then with a laugh said, "I don't remember. I'm not hungry, so maybe I ate after all."

Very quickly he got the coffeemaker going, then came to stand in front of her, looping his arms around her waist. "You're pretty cute when you're half in the bag." He smiled, kissed the tip of her nose, then leaned away to look admiringly at her.

"You always smell so good," she said, thinking she really was quite drunk. "Many times I've been a victim of aftershave syndrome."

He laughed. "And what might that be?"

"I believe at least fifty percent of all women are seduced by their olfactory nerve. It's this thing that bypasses common sense and goes directly to the central nervous system." Her eyes filling, she said, "Somebody assassinated all my beautiful flowers. And I think there's something the matter with Agnes."

"What?" he asked, stroking her back as she let her suddenly heavy head rest against his chest.

"She's been . . . strange the past few months. Different.

All of a sudden she's absentminded, sort of detached. . . . The coffee smells good."

"Strange how?" he prompted.

"I don't know. Just strange. Why would anyone do that to my garden?" she asked plaintively. "It's so cruel."

He shrugged and tightened his arms around her. "It's a peculiar world, Rebecca. People do cruel things. I'm sorry it's happened to you. I know how much work you put into that garden. It's a damned shame."

"Yes, it is," she agreed thickly.

"You'll have some coffee, then I'll put you to bed," he said, sounding most paternal. "You'll feel better when you've had some sleep. Things always look worse after nightfall. Comes the daylight and bingo! Nothing looks quite as bad as it did the night before." He gave her a coaxing smile, then got two mugs and poured the coffee.

When she opened the door the next morning to get the paper, she couldn't avoid the sight of the neatly severed stalks that had been her garden. Ray was wrong, she thought. Things didn't look any better than they had the night before.

She carried the paper to the kitchen. Removing the rubber band, she slid the folded *Times* from its blue plastic envelope. After dropping the envelope in the trash, she unfolded the paper. Something fell out of it to the floor. What? She looked down. What was that? She stared for a few seconds, then it registered. Lying there on her clean off-white linoleum was a used tampon. Disgusted, she threw the newspaper aside, backing away before going to the sink to wash her hands. God! Why the hell was she washing her hands? She was going to have to get that thing out of her house. Grabbing a fistful of paper towels, she looked over her shoulder at what someone had put in her newspaper. Her stomach was threatening to heave.

"This is just great!" she said aloud, sickened. "Okay. How do I get it out of here? The dustpan? No! Then I'd never be able to use it again." Muttering, she backed up to the stove, trying to think how to deal with this. "Okay," she said, "the rubber gloves. Under the sink." She opened the cabinet door, ducked down and found an old pair of yellow gloves, then stood up, pulling them on. She didn't want to have to look at the thing, but she couldn't help it. Her eyes just went to it, and she gagged. "I won't throw up!" she said angrily. "I have to deal with my own tampons, and worms in the garden, beetles, centipedes. I'll just treat this like another centipede. Pick up the newspaper and use it for a scooper. Now a plastic garbage bag. Get it open. Okay. Put everything in the bag, the gloves, too. A twist tie."

Done, she ran out the back door. After dumping the bag, she slammed the garbage-can lid firmly into place. Then she raced back inside, locked the door, got the Lysol and a bunch of paper towels and cleaned the floor. She went to wash her hands again, decided what she really needed was another shower, and marched upstairs to the bathroom. After the shower, she took the oversized T-shirt she'd slept in and her robe, grabbed whatever was in the hamper, and carried everything downstairs to throw them into the washer. While the machine was filling, she carefully inspected the floor to be sure there was no trace of the nasty little item someone had inserted into her newspaper.

What the hell was going on? Why had someone suddenly decided to start tormenting her? And when had her paper been tampered with? She glanced at the clock on the stove. Seven thirty-two. The paper was delivered sometime between four-thirty and five-thirty in the morning. That meant that whoever had left her that vile surprise had crept right up to her front door after five-thirty that very morning. What did this all mean? Was each day going to bring something more? God! The thought made her shudder.

Angry and puzzled, she poured some coffee, trying to imagine who'd want to demoralize and upset her this way. And why? She looked at the telephone, tempted to call Agnes. But Agnes was so unpredictable lately, and she certainly hadn't been very sympathetic yesterday. What about Ray? she wondered. He'd been very kind last night, and as a result, a small measure of her fondness for him had been salvaged. Better not to call, she decided. She'd be seeing him again tonight for dinner. Two nights in a row, twice in one week. Now that it was too late, he seemed all at once to have more time for her. Was it possible Ray was doing these things so he could play the hero?

"That's ridiculous!" she said, suddenly angry all over again at realizing she'd have to drive up the road and buy another paper. "Damn it!" she cried, snatching up her keys. "Damn it all to hell!"

CHAPTER

Six

He was really getting off on thinking up freaky stuff. The Friday gig was kind of on the nervous side, but he played it like he was supposed to be there, no sneaking around and looking furtive. Just parked the bike, marched right up to the house with scissors and a plastic garbage bag. Whack, bam, done. Then off on the bike to toss the bag of flowers into the dumpster behind the service center on I-95. Which was where he got his next idea, seeing the spilt bag of garbage from the women's toilets. Gross, but too good to pass up. He swung by the drugstore on his way home to buy some disposable rubber gloves he'd wear to pick the stuff up. Perfect.

Five-fifteen Saturday morning he's on his way, flying through town on the bike. Not a thing on the roads. He's got the entire town to himself. It's dark as hell; the streetlights have these misty clouds around them from the cold air, all eerie-looking like a horror flick. He's whizzing toward the Post Road when he has this flash, thinking this is bullshit.

What the hell's he doing? What if he sends Leighton right out of her brain, makes her seriously nuts? He's only after a little pay-back, nothing major; just a couple of numbers on her to even the score. He's thinking maybe he should quit now, bag it. But then he hits the intersection, hangs a left, and he's almost there. The hell. He'll lay this one on her and that'll be the end of it.

It's even worse this morning than the day before, because of the dark and because she's right inside, could come out any second and catch him. He's sweating like a beast, his teeth locked so hard his jaw aches. Two minutes max, and then he's back on the bike and out of there.

Once he's well away from her house, his mouth opens and he lets go this wild-man laugh that's total relief. The gig's over. It was beautiful, fantastic. It's finished. Plus he's off the hook with his mother. He'll be back driving today, make that party tonight at Shell's place.

He's standing in the kitchen putting away a bowl of Total when his mother comes in and goes, "What're you doing up so early?"

She's pissed at him. Every last thing he does drives her nuts. When's she going to get a goddamned life and leave him the hell alone?

"I've got stuff to do," he goes, waiting for her to start the routine drill. What stuff? Where? Who with? But she doesn't say a word, just hits the switch on the coffeemaker, lights up a Marlboro and stands there looking at him while she waits for her first caffeine blast of the day. She's addicted to the stuff, drinks six cups before she even gets dressed in the morning.

"There's this party tonight," he goes. "Is it okay if I use the car?"

"Just make sure you're home before one."

He's blown away. No hassles, no endless questions.

"No biggie," he goes, feeling positively great. Things are definitely looking up. He's scored not one but two numbers on Leighton. He's no longer grounded. He can have the car tonight. And his mother's acting practically human.

"So what's this stuff you have to do?" she asks finally.

Inspired, he goes, "I want to finish cleaning up my room." Which in fact he does want to do. The tapes are half on the shelf and half in the drawer. He's got a couple of pill stashes but can't remember where, and if he cleans up he'll probably find them. Plus he's got this dub he promised to do for Shell. She's finally broken up with Chuck, and if he plays it right, they could maybe get together.

Shell goes, "Oh, thanks," when he gives her the dub, then turns back to Jenny Baker, the two of them yakking about Tyrell, of all people, that gigantic English whack they've got for English. Shell and Jenny think she's hot; they like her clothes and her hair.

Jen goes, "I wish *I* was that tall."

And Shell says, "Don't you just *love* her accent?"

"She was pretty famous in London," goes Jen.

Then that dink Murray Beckworth gets into the act, oohing and aahing with them. It's pathetic. Everybody knows Murray's got the hots for the old broad. The guy's been in every school play they've ever put on. Now he's got this big-deal scholarship to Juilliard Tyrell helped him get. She loves his ass. The guy goes over to her house for private coaching, for chrissake. And in his locker he's got this teddy bear Tyrell gave him.

He can't get anywhere with Shell. And Cal's still pissed off at him for hanging up on him the other night. The party sucks, except he connects with good old Dunc, who's willing to part with a little acid for a fiver. It's only eleven-thirty but this thing's turning into such a downer he decides to leave. He'll go home, do the acid, crash.

For no reason in particular he cruises toward home along

the Shore Road. He happens to glance over at Leighton's house in passing, and nearly drives off the road. Can't be! he goes to himself. *Cannot possibly be!* But to be sure, he hangs a hard right onto the Post Road, goes down a block, hangs two more quick rights and comes back onto the Shore Road. Leaves the car a good way up the road, then jogs toward the house. Takes a good look as he jogs past the driveway, and it's like his head's going to explode. What's the fucking deal here?

No cars coming, nobody around. On the far side of the driveway, where it's good and dark, he slides onto the grass, keeping an eye on the doors, the windows, and creeps the entire way around the house. All the shutters are closed on the downstairs windows. Moving right the way back to the high fencing, he checks the upstairs windows, where the lights are on and the shutters are open. Bingo. He wants to see inside this house, absolutely has to. How?

He could easily make it onto the mudroom roof, but there's no way from there to see into the windows. It's too low. The tree. It's a huge old mother, lots of toeholds, low branches, an easy climb.

He's so freaked he wouldn't even care if he gets caught. Scoots up the tree until he can see in through the corner window. Has a clear view of the entire room and the two people inside.

First he feels like a little kid, all helpless and lost, starting to cry from the terrible hurt. It's this aching injury in his chest that makes his lungs pump like crazy, makes his throat feel as if he's strangling. There's this train rocketing through his skull; the noise is tremendous, deafening. His mouth's hanging open, his tongue all dried out; his eyes feel too big and oily-wet for their sockets. His hands are gripping the rough bark of the copper beech; he's out there in the tree and his goddamned father's inside with that rotten bitch Leighton.

Then the anger comes, and the noise inside his skull

grows even worse. The light from the bedroom is going from yellow to red as his hands grind around the branches tighter and tighter, the flesh on his palms shredding. The train's still roaring through his head, going, hate hate hate hate, *hate hate hate hate,* HATE HATE HATE HATE! Every muscle in his body's pulled tight to the point of snapping; even his skin feels like it'll split and fall off, leaving everything underneath exposed. It's all her fault. It wasn't for her, his goddamned father would be home where he's supposed to be. She'll pay for this, the bitch. No way she's getting away with it. *He'll make her pay.*

When she told Ray about what she'd found in her newspaper that morning, she knew instantly he didn't believe her. It was etched into his features—the slightly raised brows, the barely discernible uptilt to the corners of his mouth. It was evident even in the set of his shoulders and the angle of his head. He thought she was, for some unknown reason, fabricating this story. His reaction was utterly offensive to her. Whatever lingering fondness she'd had for him simply evaporated, leaving her chilled. She felt like a fool. She also felt morally superior to this man who was so quick to pass judgment. He didn't have to say a word; she could tell all too clearly what he was thinking. Well, the affair was definitely over. It wouldn't matter to her if she never saw him again.

"Forget I mentioned it," she said, looking pointedly at her wristwatch. "It's getting late. You should be going."

"Wait a minute," he said. "What's going on here?"

She could scarcely wait to be rid of him, and had to keep a firm grip on her mounting anger as she said, "I've changed my mind. I'd like you to go."

She couldn't believe she'd actually come upstairs with the idea in mind of making love with him one last time, but she was glad at least that she'd told him about the morning's incident before they'd had a chance to get started.

"Why? What's the matter?"

"I'd like you to go now," she repeated.

He stared at her for several seconds, as if prepared to argue. Then, with a sour expression, he said, "Okay. If that's the way you want it."

When he went to kiss her good-bye, she turned her head, presenting her cheek. He said, "I'll talk to you tomorrow. Maybe you'll be feeling better," and started down the stairs.

"I feel perfectly well," she said, keeping a grip on her temper as she saw him out.

"Oh," he said, nonplussed. "Okay. Well, I'll give you a call, see how you're doing."

"Right," she said, starting to close the door as he was going through it.

Disgusted, she put the chain on the door, then started cleaning up the kitchen. She stayed awake for hours, berating herself for having ever become involved with someone so wrong for her in so many ways. There was no question of her seeing him again. It was definitely over.

"Could we make it Friday this week instead of Saturday?" he asked when he called the next evening. "I'm going to have to stay in the city, work all next weekend."

"I'm afraid not. I'm going out with my mother," she told him. It was true. Evelyn had made an appointment with a real estate agent to look at some condos and had that afternoon asked Rebecca to accompany her.

"Couldn't you change it?" he asked, sounding both disappointed and annoyed.

"I couldn't possibly," she said pleasantly. "We're talking about my mother, Ray."

"You're right. I shouldn't even have suggested it." There was a pause, then he said, "Damn! I really was looking forward to seeing you."

"You just saw me last night," she said, but he didn't seem to notice her mild sarcasm.

She could hear him breathing rather heavily. She waited, wondering why she couldn't simply tell him it was over. What was she waiting for? This procrastinating was despicable!

"What's going on, Rebecca?" he asked at last.

"I think we should stop seeing each other. We're not going anywhere. I've decided I don't want to see you anymore."

"But I've explained about the divorce," he began.

"That's only part of it, Ray. I don't want to keep on with this."

"Did I do something to upset you? I mean, if there's some—"

"Let's not get into a postmortem," she said. "Let's just say it didn't work, and that's that."

There was another pause, this one utterly silent. Then, his voice deadened, he said, "I see," and managed in those two words to convey that he blamed her—for what?—and was shattered by her decision.

Refusing to allow herself to be blackmailed, she said, "We had some fun together, but it's over, Ray."

Again he said, "I see," in that tone fraught with recriminations.

She said, "I'm sorry," then carefully put the receiver down and took several steps away, her eyes remaining on the telephone. "God!" she exclaimed. She'd finally done it.

She turned and walked into the living room, stood restlessly looking at the plants for a minute, then went back to the kitchen. She'd done it, and it hadn't even been that difficult. There'd be no more Saturday night dinners in. She'd be able to go out again, be able to plan ahead, without worrying about Ray's changes of schedule. She was enormously relieved.

She worked at her desk in the downstairs guest room/den for an hour, then flopped down on the convertible sofa to watch *Sixty Minutes*. There'd been no nasty surprise today. She'd canceled delivery of the *Times;* she'd stop and pick up a paper on the way to school from now on. The sight of her decimated garden was almost unbearable. The incidents had turned her cautious. Her neck and shoulders felt permanently tight with tension as she waited to see what would happen next. She wanted to believe it was over, that whoever it was had worked the venom out of his or her system and would leave her alone now. But she wasn't counting on that. She couldn't shake the idea that it was only just beginning, and that she was in for more shattering surprises. There didn't seem to be anything she could do about the situation. She could, however, make an effort to get her life back on track. She reached for the telephone to call Agnes.

"Are you booked up for Saturday night?" she asked.

"Has Mister X canceled out again?" Agnes wanted to know.

"As a matter of fact, I did. I called the whole thing off."

"Can it be you're actually reclaiming your independence?" Agnes sounded amused.

"D'you want to do something Saturday?" Rebecca asked, choosing to ignore Agnes's amusement, if that's what it was. "We could eat Mexican, then catch a movie in Stamford I've been wanting to see."

"That sounds pleasant."

"Good. I'll pick you up at seven and we'll go to the nine o'clock show."

"What fun! Just like the old days."

"You're being sarcastic," Rebecca said warningly.

"I do believe I am. Actually, I'm terribly proud of you. It

takes courage to do what you've done. It truly does, my dear. I'm proud of you. Look, my kettle's boiling. I must go. We'll talk tomorrow, shall we? Congratulations." She hung up, and Rebecca put down the receiver to sit thinking. Was she imagining it, or had Aggie sounded as if she was doing a read-through of a third-rate script? What was wrong with her? Clearly, something was going on. Frowning, she switched off the TV and went back to her desk.

Murray watched Agnes talking on the phone, noticing how she wrapped her arm tightly around herself. He guessed she was talking to Rebecca Leighton. He knew she and Agnes were close friends, and he was glad of that because he had the feeling that Agnes was a very sad, lonely person. It was partly what had attracted him to her. He also thought she was beautiful. He liked her softness, and the way she talked. And he was fascinated by how much she knew, not just about the theater, but about all sorts of things. She'd been to so many places, done such a lot, taught him so much.

She finished the call and lit a cigarette, her arm still wrapped around herself. Then she said, "I'd like you please to go home now, Murray." She took a puff on the cigarette and pulled up the sheet, covering herself.

"Is something wrong?" he asked.

"Murray," she said softly, *"everything* is wrong." She held the cigarette and looked at him, feeling, as always, pained by guilt while awed by his beauty. "This must stop. It can't be good for you, and I'm risking everything. I could lose my job, my credentials, every last thing I've got."

"But I'm almost nineteen. I'm an adult," he said with sweet naivety.

"Murray," she said patiently, "I believe people go to jail for this sort of thing. It's only the grace of God and sheer good luck no one's found out so far. I know you don't understand, but it's tempting fate to keep on." Looking away from him, she said, as if to herself, "I can't think why I ever allowed this to happen." She looked back at him. "It's morally reprehensible of me. And aside from everything else, it's stunting your social life."

"I'm not interested in a social life," he protested.

"Please," she sighed. "You're far too young to know what you really want. And I'm far too old . . ." She trailed off, shaking her head.

"Don't!" he said, tentatively placing a hand on her shoulder. "You've said it all to me a hundred times before. I'll be graduating at the end of this semester. Then I'm off to the city and Juilliard. It's a few more months, that's all. I want to be with you for now. I love you."

"Don't talk about love, Murray. You have no idea what it really is. What you are is grateful, and it's a great mistake to confuse gratitude with love."

"How do you know what I feel?" he asked reasonably. "You're not me. You don't know what I'm thinking. I know the difference between gratitude and love. I may be young, but I'm not stupid. You're always telling me that."

"No," she conceded, "you're not stupid." She turned away intending to put out the cigarette, glancing instead at the clock. "It's coming on for eight, Murray. You really must go."

"Why?" he asked simply. "Don't you want to finish this?"

She sighed again and looked over at Teddy on top of the dresser as Murray's hand slipped from her shoulder down over her breast. Madness. Dangerous madness. She had to put an end to it, had to. And when it was over, she'd feel even more lost than she already did. He was so young and so beautiful. For months she'd been defying both the laws and the Fates with this exquisite young man. But he'd allowed her an opportunity to feel desirable and of value. She'd dared to see herself reflected in his eyes. But it was nothing more than illusion, pure treacherous illusion.

She'd chatted with this boy's mother and father on parents' nights, and they'd expressed their appreciation of her interest in and kindness to their son. And while they'd talked, she'd thought about Murray's firm young body and magnificent face, trying to quell the interior tremors that came with her recollections. She'd lost her reason, and one way or another, she'd pay dearly for daring to touch him. The strain was already taking its toll.

"This must stop," she said, covering his mouth with her hand. "I'm finding it more and more difficult to live with myself. Can you understand that?"

He nodded, then waited while she looked off into space for several moments.

Imagine Rebecca sending Mister X packing! A stunning bit of news, considering Rebecca's general tendency to shy away from confrontations. But she'd taken charge and put an end to what had sounded, from the outset, like a mediocre relationship at best. It truly did put one to shame. She'd been far too abrupt on the telephone. Obviously, Rebecca wanted and needed to talk. There was simply too much going on, too many complex emotions demanding attention.

"Then understand that this is the last time, Murray." She removed her hand from his mouth, then said, as if to herself, "It's already too late."

He was such a glorious creation! And still too young to have learned how to make his beauty work for him. He'd learn soon enough. He would embark upon a fascinating and splendid new life. In no time at all he'd forget her; she'd be nothing more than a vague memory. He'd be completely absorbed in the day-to-day details of his exciting new life. And she'd be rid of her old one. But this one final time would be memorable, she decided, putting out the cigarette at last before gathering him into her arms.

CHAPTER

Seven

Rebecca was actually relieved to set off for school on Monday morning. The low concrete building felt like something of a haven; nothing very much out of the ordinary could happen to her here. She was in the midst of some five hundred students and a few dozen staff members. Security in numbers, she thought with grim humor as she pulled into the lot. She made her way to the entrance, head down against a driving wind laden with unshed rain.

Agnes was already in the English office, a cup of black coffee near to hand as she finished reading a student essay, then sat for several moments, pen poised, before marking a grade and writing her comments.

"Extraordinary," she said, reaching for her coffee and looking over at Rebecca. "I can tell exactly what these kids read by the work they hand in. This one," she picked up the paper she'd just graded and fanned the air with it, "is a devout Stephen King fan. Everything he submits has some King element: slavering rabid dogs, living dead, telekinetic powers, cemeteries, the lot. Then," she went on, returning the paper to a stack of others and placing her hand over top of it, "we have one or two with the good taste to read Bradbury; another few who aspire to live in Narnia. As usual, there are at least four who think *Less Than Zero* is a thinly disguised recounting of their lives; one who aspires to reaching the heights of Jay McInerney; and then there's Jenny Baker, who's a complete original. She can actually *write,* my dear. I stand, or should I say sit, in awe of this girl's audacity. She takes the assignments, goes off and finds something from the extreme outer edges of left field and manages to make it fit the topic. Incredible!"

"I know," Rebecca agreed, looking around. "Have you seen my mug?"

"Metaphorically or literally?" Agnes laughed.

"My mug, as in drink from."

"Sorry, my darling, I have not."

"I hate it when this happens. I'm beginning to believe all people are petty thieves at heart. I guess I'll have to go get a paper cup from the staff room."

When she returned with some coffee, Agnes was conferring in low tones with Liz Marley, one of the five other English teachers in the department. Sensing this discussion might go on for some time, Rebecca gathered up her things and went along to her classroom. She stood for a few minutes, hearing the morning's announcements over the PA system echo down the corridors as she drank the flavorless institutional coffee Agnes had long ago dubbed battery acid. Through the window she watched the stand of trees at the rear of the school shiver in the wind.

Why, all at once, had things taken such a wretched turn in her life? True, she'd been growing progressively more dissatisfied with Ray and was glad to have extricated herself from the involvement. But it would take some time before she readjusted back to a solo lifestyle. Then there were the nasty incidents. Again she wondered if it was possible Ray had something to do with them. But it was highly unlikely, especially in view of the fact that he hadn't believed her when she'd told him about the tampon.

Who could be doing these things? And why? Gazing out the window, her stomach knotted, she wound one long strand of hair around her finger as she tried to sort through the possibilities. Nothing came to her. None of it made sense.

With a sigh she turned from the window to look through the various notices and messages she'd collected from her box in the office.

The rain started just after lunch and descended in angry gusts, slanting in streaks across the windows, pinging metallically off the rows of parked cars. The interior of the classroom darkened and the atmosphere became heavy, almost somnolent. Rebecca was grateful to hear the last bell ring and to see the renewed energy of the students as, suddenly chattering with animation, they stacked their books and hurried from the room.

It was four-twenty when she left the building and made a run through the still-driving rain to the Jetta. She started up the car, put it into reverse, and knew at once there was a problem. Leaving the engine going, she got out to have a look, and swore fiercely under her breath at the sight of the flat right-rear tire.

By five past five when she finished putting on the spare, water was running in a steady stream down the back of her neck, her hands were sore and cramped, and she wanted only to get home and sink into a tubful of hot water. But first she had to drive over to the Amoco station on the Post Road and drop off the tire to be repaired. Then she had to make a quick stop at the deli to get something for dinner. There was no way she'd do any cooking tonight. By the time she pulled into her driveway, she felt as if she'd completed a perplexing obstacle course.

She dumped her purse and briefcase on top of the washer in the mudroom, removed her sodden shoes and stepped into a pair of old loafers she kept downstairs. Tiredly she walked through the living room on her way to get the mail, thinking it was unusually dark as she paused to turn on a lamp. Opening the front door, she dashed out to the mailbox, emptied it, and darted back inside. She stood looking through the mail, then thought again how dark the room was, and put her hand out to the table lamp as her eyes lifted to the skylight.

Black. The skylight was black. Instead of the wide-spreading branches of the copper beech, all she saw was a dark reflection of the room, her own image gazing back at her.

"What . . .?" Several steps brought her directly beneath the thirty-six-square-foot expanse of glass. Her heart gave a massive leap in her chest, as if trying to overturn itself, while she tried to absorb the fact that the skylight had somehow become a mirror. Then, thinking of the skylight in the master bedroom, she tore into the kitchen, threw the mail on the island, and raced up the spiral staircase.

This one was also black. Not so much as a speck of light. *"What the hell's going on here?"* she raged, eyes lifted, pulse racing. Unnerved, furious, she ran back downstairs and out the mudroom door to the storage shed.

Ignoring the rain——her clothes were already soaked, so what did it matter?——she climbed the ladder to the living-room roof and touched her hand to the matte-black paint someone had applied to the skylight. For a minute or two she felt so beleaguered she wanted both to scream and to weep. Who was doing this? Why? A feeling of despair swept over her, and she longed suddenly, intensely, to walk away from this house and never come back. She could go home to Greenwich, where her mother would look after her. She could almost feel her mother's arms sheltering her from this ongoing assault.

The hell with that! she thought, her anger returning in full force. She wasn't a little kid anymore, and couldn't go running home to her mother when the going got a little rough. This was her house, her home, and she refused to be victimized. "I won't let you do this to me!" she declared, descending the ladder to find the wide-bladed paint scraper she'd used when redecorating the house.

Wielding the scraper like a weapon, muttering under her breath, she pulled on rubber boots and a slicker, then climbed back up to the roof there and then and began scraping the paint off the glass. "Son of a bitch," she whispered as ribbons of black paint slid off down the rain-soaked surface of the skylight. "You son of a bitch. You can't do this to me!"

Breathing hard, working in a frenzy, she scooped the scrapings from the base of the skylight and tossed them to the walk below. When she was at last able to look down into the living room through the cleared glass, she emitted a choking cry of triumph, then descended the ladder. For a few moments she stood holding the ladder, the rain pouring down on her, in the grip of despair. She wanted this to stop, wanted an explanation of why this was happening. She longed to go back inside and go to sleep, but she couldn't. She had to fight back, and the only way she could do that was by refusing to be defeated, by climbing back up the ladder and finishing the job.

Driven by anger, she got up to the roof of the second story and began working on the skylight there. Her arms ached, and she had to rest for a few moments, sitting back on her heels and relaxing her grip on the scraper. This was crazy! What the hell was she doing? No! This was the right way to handle the situation. Maybe he was hiding somewhere, watching her. She looked around the property, imagining people hidden behind all the shrubberies. God! Was she losing her mind? There was nobody watching. And she was soaked through, chilled, shivering. Get it finished! she told herself. Don't let him win!

Just as she was getting to the end of the filthy job, some two hours after she'd begun, Agnes arrived. Her umbrella preceding her, Agnes slid out of the car and gazed up at Rebecca with a bemused expression.

"At the risk of demonstrating my ignorance," she said, "might I enquire what precisely you're doing up there in the pouring bloody rain?"

Shaking streamers of black paint from her hands, Rebecca stared down at her. Why was Agnes asking when it was perfectly obvious what she was doing? Wasn't it? Suddenly doubtful, she was unable to speak. Was Agnes the one doing all these things? Was she the one who'd been watching from the bushes? That really was crazy, Rebecca told herself. Was she losing her mind? There was Agnes staring up at her, waiting for an answer as to why she was up on the roof in a downpour. And all at once she was able to imagine how she must look. It enabled her to speak. "Why don't you go in and fix us drinks? I'll be down in a minute."

Agnes stared up at her for a few more seconds, then walked to the back door.

Ten minutes later Rebecca came into the mudroom, kicked off the rubber boots, threw her raincoat over the radiator, marched into the kitchen to pick up the Stoli on the rocks Agnes had fixed for her, and tossed it down in one long swallow. She grimaced, shuddered, then said, "The son of a bitch painted the skylights black!"

"Which son of a bitch?" Agnes asked mildly.

"The one who destroyed my flowers and put that revolting thing in my *New York Times*. *That* son of a bitch. Or are you thinking I've got an entire brigade of sons of bitches trying to drive me crazy?"

"Hardly," Agnes said, frowning. "Is that what's going on here?"

"Of course!" Rebecca snapped. "But I'm not going to let him."

"Oh! I thought possibly you were referring to Mister X. And what revolting thing?"

Rebecca told her, gratified by Agnes's expression of revulsion, then asked, "Why would you think Ray had anything to do with this?" as she poured more Stoli into her glass.

"Men have been known to behave rather badly when given the push," she said. "There was one, years ago, who relieved himself on my doorstep. They're a peculiar bunch altogether, men." Agnes raised her Scotch and water as if in salute, then took a drink before lighting a cigarette.

Rebecca automatically opened a cupboard, got an ashtray and set it down on the island in front of Agnes. Then she hoisted herself up to sit on the counter opposite, saying, "I've had enough of this! I'm going to the police."

"Hmm." Agnes looked thoughtfully at the ashtray, then at her glass, and finally at Rebecca. "When were you thinking of doing that?" she asked.

"Right now. Soon as I finish my drink."

"What will you tell them?"

"What d'you mean, what'll I tell them?" Rebecca said, irate. "I'll tell them what's been going on here."

"And they'll say, 'Can you prove it?' "

Rebecca's mouth opened to answer, then closed. "I don't care," she said stubbornly. "I pay taxes in this town. I've got a right to some protection." She climbed down off the counter. "In fact, I'm going over there right now."

Agnes made a doubtful face and shook her head.

"What?"

"I shouldn't, in your present condition," Agnes said.

"What's my condition?"

"Aside from the fact that you're obviously distraught and

not thinking clearly, I suggest you go have a look at yourself. Then you tell me."

Rebecca went into the guest room/den to stand in front of the mirror. Her hair was molded to her skull in snaky tendrils, mascara trails ran down both her cheeks, and flakes of black paint were everywhere—in her ears, on her neck and arms, all down her clothes. It made her want to start weeping. She looked as crazed as she felt.

"All right, I admit I look terrible. But I don't care!" she declared, returning to the kitchen. "I'm going! You're welcome to come with me if you like. Unless you don't want to be seen in public with a lunatic." She paused, then asked, "How come you're here, anyway?"

"You're hardly a lunatic," Agnes said calmly. "I couldn't reach you by telephone, so I thought I'd stop by on the off chance you'd be home and possibly interested in going out for something to eat. Clearly, that's the last thing you'd want to do. If it's all the same to you, I'll pass on visiting the town constabulary. I'm really not in the mood to view the local felons. I see enough of them at school every day."

"I must say," Rebecca said indignantly, "you don't seem especially sympathetic to what I've been going through."

Agnes's face was transformed by hurt. "Oh, my dear," she said, "you mustn't think that. I've been trying to jolly you out of it. Of course I'm sympathetic. It's frightful, truly frightful. And if you really want me to come with you to the station, I will. I'm afraid this is one of those situations where it's impossible to know the right thing to say or do."

Somewhat mollified, Rebecca said, "Sorry if I snapped at you, but this business is starting to drive me out of my mind. It's getting to where all day at school I'm worrying about what I'll find when I come home. And what I find is progressively worse each time. I shouldn't have to live this way!"

"No, indeed you shouldn't," Agnes agreed, stubbing out

her cigarette. "I'm very sorry someone's decided to persecute you." She got up to go, saying, "If you don't mind a word of advice, my darling. A wash might be a good idea before you set off to file your complaint." She came around the island to cup her hand under Rebecca's chin. "Feel free to ring me if there's anything you need. I expect to be in all evening. If you don't want to be alone, I'll be happy to come keep you company. Or you could spend the night in my guest room. All right?" Rebecca nodded. "You really mustn't allow this to do you in." Then, her hand still cupping Rebecca's chin, Agnes gave her a kiss on the cheek and went to let herself out, leaving Rebecca enveloped in the warm vanilla fragrance of Shalimar.

Rebecca remained in the kitchen feeling strangely bereft, and wondering about the real reason Agnes had stopped by.

The reception area of the police station was empty except for a uniformed officer behind the desk and a thirtyish shaggy-haired man wearing a gold earring and tattered jeans, an ancient-looking tweed jacket over a navy Yale sweatshirt, with clean new Nike Airs. He was slouched in a chair over by the far wall and raised his head to watch with interest as Rebecca approached the desk.

After making her wait for some moments, the officer, a man no older than twenty-five, raised his head and simply stared at Rebecca. With closely cropped hair, a wide, red-cheeked, narrow-eyed face, and a neck so thick it seemed the same diameter as his head, he was the type of man she'd always found fairly frightening. Six-two or -three, at least two hundred and eighty pounds, with meaty hands and bitten fingernails, he exuded menace. To find this fellow in a police uniform wasn't in the least reassuring. At first sight, she believed him capable of the kind of gratuitous violence that fueled best-selling mystery novels. In no mood, however, to put up with anyone's rudeness, she said, "Are you ready to speak to me now?"

"Yes, ma'am," the officer said, stone-faced. "What can I do for you?"

"I wish to file a complaint."

"Uh-huh. What kind?"

"Someone is harassing me, vandalizing my property."

"Vandalizing how? What property?"

"Don't you want to take a note of the details?" she asked. "Aren't you supposed to get my name and address?"

"Ma'am, when I've determined the exact nature of the complaint, then we'll get to the details." He gazed steadily, flatly, at her.

Telling herself she wouldn't get anywhere by antagonizing this fellow, she took a calming breath and said, slowly and carefully, "Someone has, first of all, destroyed my garden." She went on to detail what she'd discovered in her *New York Times,* and then the painting of the skylights. "I just spent several hours in the pouring rain scraping off the paint," she said, her anger returning as the officer began slowly shaking his head.

"This happened when?" he asked with a hint of a smirk.

"It started last week," she answered, glancing over her shoulder to see that the scruffy guy across the room was intently following the conversation. Turning back, she said, "I want something done!"

"Let me get this right," the officer said. "Whoever did your garden took the flowers away with him. And you threw out the newspaper with the whatchamacallit in it. Plus you scraped off all the paint. I don't suppose you took pictures of any of this?"

"Pictures?"

"Evidence," he said, making a show of sorely tried patience. "You've got no evidence."

"You can come to my house right now and see my garden. That's evidence," she said hotly, her voice rising into the upper register and her hands beginning to tremble. Had she already lost her mind and failed to realize it? Certainly this encounter felt surreal.

"No, ma'am, it isn't. Anybody could've done that. You could've done it yourself."

"Oh, for God's sake! Why would I do that to my own garden?"

The officer shrugged, the smirk gaining control of his mouth.

"There must be someone else I can talk to here, someone who has a less supercilious attitude."

"You can talk to the entire force if you like, ma'am, but they're all going to tell you the same thing. There's no evidence of any wrongdoing. From what you say, nothing's been stolen or actually damaged. Is that right?"

"My garden's certainly been 'actually damaged.' Why am I paying taxes if you're not prepared to do anything about this?"

"I'll take down the details," he sighed, and with annoyance reached for a pencil and a ruled pad. "Name?"

"Rebecca Leighton."

"Wanna spell that, please?"

"R-e-b-e-c-c-a L-e-i-g-h-t-o-n."

"Address?"

"Two-six-two Shore Road."

"Phone?"

She recited her phone number, feeling acutely frustrated and very aware of her disheveled appearance. She should've listened to Agnes and taken the time to clean up properly instead of merely washing her face and pulling her hair back into a ponytail. One part of her brain was insisting she looked and sounded demented. The other part was saying she was a taxpayer and had every right to ask for help. She glanced again over her shoulder to see the scruffy fellow taking all this in with a look of open fascination and a slight smile that fueled her indignation.

"So, now let me see if I've got this right," the officer said, staring at what he'd printed on the pad for a few more seconds before looking up at her. "Nobody, so far as you know, has been inside your house. Nothing's been stolen. Nothing's really been damaged. No windows broken, no *actual* damage to your property. Oh, yeah. You got a business number?"

"I teach at the high school," she said stonily, wondering why she'd bothered to come. Obviously, she was mistaken in her lifelong belief that the police were here to protect and serve her.

The officer now smiled widely, saying, "You're a teacher, huh? Well, that probably explains it. Some of the kids playing pranks. You should've said so in the first place."

"They are *not* pranks!" she cried, then took another deep, calming breath and tried to respond rationally. "Let *me* be sure I've got this right," she said coldly, her voice dropping to below its normal register. "Because I happen to be a teacher, in your mind it's perfectly logical and reasonable that students might decide to make me a victim of their so-called practical jokes. For the sake of argument, let's suppose that's true. Are you trying to tell me that makes it all right? Is that what you're saying?"

"Well, kids do stuff like that," he defended himself.

"I'm sure *you* probably did," Rebecca said. "I suppose you drove around town stuffing mailboxes with cherry bombs and defecating on peoples' doormats, neat stuff like that."

At this, the man opposite burst out laughing. "She's got that right, huh?"

The officer glared at him, then turned back to Rebecca. "They're pranks, is all. But I'll pass along your complaint. Okay?"

"And, of course, no one will bother to do anything, because no serious damage—at least not by your standards—has been done. Do I have that right?"

The officer thought for a moment, then said, "Well, basically, yup."

"You probably had to do summer school every year just to make it through, didn't you?" she said quietly, angrier than she'd ever been in her life. "Probably never had a grade higher than a C-minus, did you? Well, if you're representative of what my tax dollars are going for, either I'm not paying enough in taxes or the town's standards are down the toilet. You just make sure you keep a record of the fact that I was in here and *tried* to lodge a complaint. And next time I'll *try* to remember to have my camera handy so I can bring you some *evidence.*" With that, she moved away from the desk and started toward the door. As she was pushing through it, she heard the guy across the room say, "You really have one hell of a way with people!"

Thinking he was addressing her, she turned back prepared to argue, only to see he was in fact talking to the desk officer.

"He could win a goddamned congeniality award," she said, grateful for this bit of support, then turned and continued on her way out.

CHAPTER

Eight

She was halfway to the car when the unkempt man from the station house came running after her calling, "Hey, wait!"

"You keep away from me!" Rebecca said over her shoulder, thinking with her luck, she'd probably be molested right in the parking lot of the police station and they'd come out in full force to tell her there was nothing they could do about it because there was no evidence.

"Hang on!" he said, still coming after her.

Inserting her keys between her fingers, she whirled around to confront him. "I swear to God if you don't back off, I'll poke your eyes out!"

"Whoa!" He skidded to a stop, reaching into the inside pocket of his ratty tweed jacket.

"What do you do," she demanded, brandishing her key-studded fist, "hang around police stations looking for victims?"

With a laugh, he brought out his ID and flipped it open,

holding it about six inches in front of her nose. "Plain-clothes," he explained. "Okay?"

She took him in from his new Nike Airs, torn jeans and Yale sweatshirt to the gold earring and longish disheveled hair. "Are you kidding, or what?"

"You watch too many old black-and-white movies," he said, returning his ID to his jacket pocket. "Plain is whatever's comfortable. Nobody wears the shiny suits, the black lace-ups anymore. Listen, why don't you follow me over to Hojo's, let me buy you a coffee, and you can tell me the whole story."

"Why?"

"Maybe I can help."

"Look, you heard that genius tell me to go home and be a good little girl, stop bothering the busy officers."

"Yeah, I know." He glanced over toward the building. "But why not tell me? It couldn't hurt."

"I don't feel like repeating it," she said, pulling her coat more tightly around her.

"You hungry?" he asked. "You want to go to the IHOP for some pancakes, maybe some waffles?"

"Are you serious?"

"I'm seriously hungry. I'm Jason, by the way." He made a kind of dancing step forward, extending his hand.

Still suspicious, she shook hands with him.

"You're Rebecca," he said. "L-e-i-g-h-t-o-n. So, which? Hojo's or IHOP?"

"The pancake place," she said. "And you can follow me."

"Fine, no prob."

As she headed for the restaurant, she told herself this was ridiculous. She should've been on her way home to a tubful of hot water. She had work to do. But she was hungry, and for the moment she just couldn't face going home.

———

Jason ordered three eggs, double bacon well done, whole-wheat toast, and a side order of blueberry pancakes. Rebecca stared at him for a moment, then asked the waitress for waffles and coffee.

"Don't you want some bacon or fries to go with that?" Jason asked her. "A couple of waffles won't hold you for long. Have some bacon. Or how about sausages?"

"All right," Rebecca said. "Bacon."

"Make it well done," he told the waitress, who went off chuckling.

"Okay," he said, settling back in the booth. "So tell me the whole thing, from the top."

"You've already heard me tell it," she said. "I don't feel like repeating it."

"Fair enough. You got any ideas who could be doing this stuff?"

She shook her head. "I wish I did. It's driving me out of my mind."

"Well, that's the whole point, isn't it?" he said with a smile.

"You think it's funny?" she challenged, ready to get up and leave. "Let me see your ID again."

"Don't believe I'm the real goods, huh?" he said, the smile holding as he reached into his jacket and dropped the leather case on the table in front of her. "Feel free."

She looked at the gold shield and the photo card, then pushed the case back across the table, thinking she'd never seen a less likely looking detective. For one thing, she doubted he was even thirty years old. For another, he didn't look, dress, behave, or talk like a detective. He wasn't unattractive, his clothes notwithstanding: around six feet tall and a little on the stocky side, light brown hair, dark brown eyes, straight nose, kind of a quirky mouth that made it seem as if he was always smiling, decent teeth, a cleft chin.

"So?" he said, sitting with his arms spread along the back of the booth. "Finished checking me out?"

"Is that gold?"

"Get real," he scoffed.

"You want me to give you all kinds of details about my life just because you've got that imitation gold shield, but it's off the record or something. Am I right?" Sitting here, trying to talk with this man, felt weird. She was having trouble taking him seriously.

He nodded. "That is right."

"Why?"

"Because maybe I can help."

"Why?" she asked again.

"Why not?" he countered. "You got anything else going for you?"

"Not so far."

"So, maybe," he repeated, "I can help."

"Why?"

"Jesus!" he exclaimed. "You're exasperating, you know that?"

It was her turn to smile. He was a surprising type to be a police officer.

"What? You don't think cops know words like exasperating? See! It's those black-and-whites, and those dumb-ass TV shows all promoting stereotypes. I've got polysyllables you've never dreamed of."

"I doubt it."

"Hey, don't doubt it!" he told her. "We're not all endomorphs like Lenny on the desk tonight. Believe it or not, most of us have degrees; we've even got one guy working on his doctorate in forensic science."

"And what about you?"

He smiled and said, "I'm not telling. You assume things, Rebecca Leighton, and that's a no-no." He brought his arms down and folded them in front of him on the table. "Seriously. Give me background, let me see if I can get some kind of picture."

"What background?" she asked tiredly.

"Where're you from, who're your friends, you seeing anybody? You got enemies, maybe some kid at school you've been riding?"

"How old are you, anyhow?" she asked.

"Why? You don't think I'm old enough to hear the sordid details of your life?"

"This is too weird," she said, discomfited. At moments she found him likable and amusing; at other moments she wasn't sure how to take him.

"Hey, Rebecca. What's going on in *your life* is weird. I'm just trying to get some kind of fix on the situation. Okay? Your hair naturally curly or is that a perm?"

"What?"

"Natural or a perm?" he asked, leaning now on his cupped hand and gazing at her.

"Natural. What's that got to do with anything?"

"Just wondering. So, come on. Tell me something."

"I don't have any enemies. At least none I'm aware of. And I get along well with my students. I'm not in the habit of 'riding' them."

"Don't get riled, Rebecca. They're just questions, not accusations."

"I'm good friends with the head of my department. She's a woman."

"What department?"

"English."

"Figures." He grinned.

She refused to rise to that bait, instead blew her nose and sat back as the waitress delivered their food.

"Go on," he prompted, reaching for the salt and pepper.

"I was seeing someone, but we broke up recently."

"Yeah?" He paused with the pepper shaker poised over his trio of sunny-side–up eggs, regarding her with heightened interest. "Fill me in on that."

She sighed heavily. "This is pointless." No one would do anything, and the nasty tricks would proliferate until her brains were well and truly scrambled, or she got hurt somehow.

"Not to me."

"It lasted for seven months. He was separated. The divorce was taking forever. He was hypercautious about being seen with me in public. It finally got on my nerves and I called it off. Very recently," she clarified. "This past weekend, in fact."

"How'd he take it?"

"I don't know," she said impatiently. "He was disappointed, I suppose. So was I, in a way."

"Think he's the one doing these numbers on your place?"

"I've thought about it," she conceded, watching Jason eat swiftly but neatly. "You always eat like that?"

"Like what?" He looked up at her, down at his plate, then again at her.

"Like it's your first meal in a week."

"Damn nearly is," he said, adding more butter and syrup to his pancakes. "Mine is not your basic nine-to-five desk-jockey gig, with predetermined meal breaks. A lot of the time I don't get to eat at all. You wear tinted lenses? Those your real eyelashes?"

"What?"

"D'you have a hearing problem?" he asked, looking straight at her.

"No, I do not."

"So how come every time I ask you something, instead of answering, you say 'what?' "

"What do my hair and eyelashes and the rest of it have to do with my home's being vandalized, with someone trying to drive me crazy?"

"They don't," he said with a little shrug. "I'm just asking. I like to know certain things. I'm interested. Okay? Your waffles're getting cold."

She turned to inspect the rack of syrup bottles, reached for the maple and drizzled some over the waffles. Narrowing her eyes slightly, she asked, "Are you gay?"

"Nah. I'm just preternaturally cheerful."

For a moment all she could do was gape at him, then she laughed so hard it made her chest hurt. It seemed years since she'd found anything funny.

"Eat," he said, tearing a wedge of toast in half to blot up some of the egg yolk. After swallowing the toast and a gulp of coffee, he said, "The fork goes in your left hand, knife in the right. That's right, like that."

With a smile he watched her cut into the waffle. When she'd taken a bite, he said, "I majored in psychology, minored in English, thought I'd maybe be a shrink or a lawyer, couldn't make up my mind, so I did my Master's in sociology. Yale," he said, pointing his thumb at his sweatshirt. "I come from this long line of bleeding-heart liberals. Right? So I'm set to do something for the good of mankind, some not too esoteric but basically humanitarian gig. Nobody's more surprised than I am that I joined the cop shop. But there you are.

"Six years in Manhattan and I don't have an illusion left to my name. After the city, Nortown's like an extended vacation in Disneyland. Your situation interests me. We've got peepers and flashers and guys who like to whack off over the phone. But we don't have all that many phantom vandals. Matter of fact, this is my first. Kind of arouses my curiosity. So if you don't give me details, it makes it a little hard for me to get any kind of a fix on the situation. Okay, Rebecca?"

"I guess," she said, still considering the information he'd just rattled off.

"I'm thirty-seven," he told her, "and I figure my major problem's going to be convincing you I'm interested in your body, not your mind."

Again she laughed loudly. Then she coughed and sneezed at the same time, her eyes watering in the aftermath.

"You're getting a cold," he said. "And here you sit letting a plateful of perfectly good waffles go stone cold while you try to make up your mind if I'm scamming you and if you should've gone for my eyes in the parking lot like you wanted to."

She finished blowing her nose, then sat looking at him. "Do you mean it?" she asked, thinking this conversation fit in perfectly with the increasingly freakish aspects of her life. She was beginning to wonder if she was in any way equipped to deal with the ongoing, low-level lunacy she kept encountering.

"Mean what?"

"About helping."

"Sure," he said readily. "Sure seems like you could use some."

"I don't wear contact lenses or false eyelashes," she said flatly. "I don't wear false anything, as a matter of fact."

"What? Not even the tiniest polyester blend?"

She couldn't manage a smile and instead took a bite of the waffle. "I can't taste a thing. I might as well be eating Kleenex."

"Trust me, Kleenex sucks. Mind if I light up?" he asked, reaching into his jacket pocket.

"I don't care. Agnes smokes."

"She a buddy at school?" he asked, pushing some tobacco into the bowl of his pipe.

"Uh-huh."

"She on your suspect list?"

"For about twenty seconds. But no. All day today I kept looking at my students, watching for one of them to make a false move. I hate this. I want it to stop. You don't look thirty-seven."

"You don't either," he said, holding a wooden match over the bowl of the pipe and puffing strenuously.

"That's because I'm not."

"Twenty-seven?" he asked.

"Not even close."

"Forty-one, right?"

"Exactly right," she said sarcastically, pushing away the plate of waffles. "I'm thirty-three, for God's sake."

"Perfect. Anything unusual happen before this harassment started?"

"Nothing I can think of."

Pulling a small coiled notebook and a pen out of his pocket, he said, "You want to give me the name of the ex?"

Feeling a pinprick of alarm, she asked, "Why?"

"So we can eliminate him as a suspect."

"I don't know if I want the police turning up on his doorstep."

"I'm not going to 'turn up,' Rebecca. I'll just subtly check it out."

"I feel funny about giving you his name."

"Okay, give me some others."

"Whose?" she asked.

"Got any family in the area?"

"My mother lives in Greenwich. I've got one brother in Nyack and another in Ridgefield. Please don't involve my family. My mother would worry herself sick if she knew about any of this."

"Give me the names and addresses," he said patiently. "I'm not going to rat on you to your mother."

"You promise?"

He smiled at her around the pipe stem. "Sounded like a little kid just then. You're a real cutie. You know that?"

"*A real cutie?* And you talk about me watching old black-and-whites? How do you expect me to take you seriously when you keep coming out with stuff like that?"

"Hey, just because I like you doesn't mean I'm not going to do a good job."

"This is ridiculous. You don't even know me. I think maybe this whole thing's nothing more than a ruse."

"A ruse. That's very good," he said. "Listen," he said sharply, abandoning the humor. "This started off with your garden and there's nothing to suggest it's going to stop any-time soon. I'm trying to keep things light because basically I think what we're dealing with here is a mind that's more than a little right of center, if you catch my drift." He looked at his wristwatch, then said, "I've got twenty minutes left, so give me names and addresses and let's stop fooling around."

Taken aback by the abrupt shift of tone, she recited the family information, as well as Agnes's address and telephone number, and finally, reluctantly, Ray's. Jason printed everything in his notebook, then signaled to the waitress for the check.

"Leave it with me, Rebecca. I'll see what I can do. In the meantime, you need me, here's my number." He turned to a fresh page in the notebook and printed his home number. "I'll put down the direct line to the station, too. They'll beep me if it's urgent." He tore out the page and handed it to her.

"How come on television, detectives always have printed cards?"

He snorted derisively. "Sorry, Rebecca. Nortown doesn't do calling cards. Of course, if you like, I could zip over, put in an order for something embossed on extra-heavy card stock." His grin took the sting out of the sarcasm. "This ain't television, toots. This is just a dinky little force covering a town of twenty-six-thousand miscreants, deviates, and dipshits. Jesus! Even with paint in your ears, you're absolutely gorgeous. You know that? I figure your ex is the heavy, trying to shake you up so you'll come running back to him for comfort."

"Do you mean that?"

"Which?"

"About Ray," she said.

"Who knows? If there's one thing I've learned in nine years of 'protecting and serving,' it's that people are very damned strange." He looked again at his watch, then reached for his wallet. "I've got just enough time to make sure you get home safely, so let's hit the road."

He went to the counter to pay the check and came back to slide two singles under the edge of his plate, saying, "Come on, Rebecca."

In the parking lot he walked her over to her car and waited while she took out her keys. As she was about to open the door, he said, "Listen, it'll be okay."

She looked up at him. "I really doubt it," she said, too worn out to hide her anxiety.

"No, really," he insisted, putting a hand on her shoulder. "Sometimes it gets a little worse before it gets better, but it most always does get better. You want to get together Friday night, do something?"

Too exhausted to react to this surprising invitation, she said, "I'm going condo shopping in Greenwich with my mother."

"Hey!" he smiled widely. "Can I come, too?"

"Get real!" she smiled back at him.

"What about Saturday?"

"Dinner and a movie with Agnes."

"Okay," he persisted. "Sunday."

"Sunday lunch with my mother."

"Wow! You've got a phenomenal social life."

"Right! Phenomenal."

He gave her a brotherly hug and said, "You might not see me and you might not hear from me, but I'll be on this. If anything happens, you've got my numbers, call me. I'll get to you as fast as I can."

He walked across the lot to his car, then followed her home. Pulling up behind her in the driveway, he rolled down the passenger window and said, "Go check it out. I'll wait."

Still bewildered but oddly comforted by his hug, she did as he asked. Returning to the back door, she said, "Everything's okay. Thanks a lot."

"No prob," he said. "I'll be in touch." He rolled up the window, slid back behind the wheel and reversed out of the driveway.

After he'd gone, she went to start the water running in the guest-room tub—her bathroom equipped with only a stall shower—then went upstairs to get a nightgown, her robe, and a pair of heavy socks. In the tub at last, with scented steam coating the mirror and the heat drawing some of the ache out of her muscles, she gave in and allowed herself to cry. It didn't help. In spite of her determination not to, she felt like a victim. It was a terrible, defenseless state, and she hated the unfairness of the situation. Her property and she herself were entirely at the mercy of this monstrously imaginative vandal. And nothing she could do, short of selling the house and moving, was likely to put a stop to this.

It was all fine and well for Jason to say he'd help, but the idea that this was going to go on and on made her want to scream. And, she thought, sneezing three times in succession, to cap a perfect day, she really was coming down with a cold.

CHAPTER

Nine

On her way to the English office at lunchtime the next day, Rebecca encountered a cluster of students in the corridor engaged in a heated but purposefully low-volume argument. As far as she could tell, Michelle Mercoli, Jenny Baker and Murray Beckworth comprised one side. The other consisted of two girls whose names she couldn't recall, Hank O'Connor and Chuck Brewer. The four in opposition seemed to be taking considerable pleasure in the argument, wearing expressions of smug superiority, while the other three appeared sincerely upset.

Rather than play teacher and arbitrarily break up the group, Rebecca smiled, halted for a moment and said, "Jenny, could you spare a minute?"

Jenny said, "Sure, Ms. Leighton," murmured "Assholes" to the four opposing seniors, and fell into step beside Rebecca.

When they were far enough away not to be overheard by the group, Rebecca asked, "What was that all about?"

Jenny rested her chin for a moment on the armload of books she held to her chest with both arms, then said, "Ms. Tyrell. She brought a teddy bear to class this morning." She looked sidelong at Rebecca. "Talked about how important teddys are to people, not just kids. I thought it was *sweet,*" Jenny said staunchly, her pointed chin jutting. "I mean, *I've* still got *my* teddy. I never even knew about Theodore Roosevelt, and teddy being named for him. Roosevelt won the Nobel Peace Prize, for heaven's sake! I mean, he was hardly some wuss. Right?"

"Right," Rebecca agreed, trying to imagine what must have gone on in Agnes's class.

"So anyway," Jenny said, "she had her bear sitting on the desk, with its legs hanging over the edge. It was cute, really. And she said we should all bring our bears to class, that we should take them with us everywhere we go and not concern ourselves with what people might say. I thought it was a metaphor. You know? I mean, it was like she was telling us not to allow other people to decide for us about the things we do. Then . . ." Jenny hesitated, a flush spreading over her cheeks.

Apprehension causing her stomach to drop, Rebecca prompted, "Then?"

"Then she sang 'The Teddy Bears' Picnic,' and wanted us all to sing along." Jenny dropped her head for a moment, and Rebecca could feel the girl's confusion, could picture the other kids' contemptuous reaction. "That," Jenny admitted, "was kind of embarrassing." She looked searchingly at Rebecca, and Rebecca patted her on the arm. "Those four morons," Jenny said with passion, briefly glancing back over her shoulder, "were dumping on her, saying she's lost it. Shell and Murray and me, we were on her side. But most of the others, they were treating the whole thing like this complete *joke*. What should we do?" she asked. "Should we bring our bears to school or what? Was it a metaphor?"

"I don't think you need to bother bringing your bear to school, Jenny. I'm sure she was simply attempting to make a metaphor. Unfortunately, it doesn't seem to have worked." Feeling a sneeze coming, Rebecca reached into her pocket for some tissues. "I think it might be wise just to forget the whole matter. I'll see what I can do."

"I hope she won't be mad at us," Jenny said earnestly. "I mean, I go along with what she was saying. So do some of the others. But we're *seniors,* Ms. Leighton. Sure, we still have our teddy bears, but it's not like we play with them. They're just in our rooms. You know? I've still got my Snoopy," she admitted. "I've even got my Barbie dolls. But it'd be so *uncool* to bring them to class."

"I know," Rebecca said supportively. "Go have your lunch and don't worry about it. And if you don't mind a word of advice, let the matter drop with the others. It'll be forgotten in a day or so."

"Okay. Thanks a lot. I really was kind of worried. I mean, the last few weeks she's been different. You know? Not totally in charge, the way she usually is."

"It'll be all right, Jenny. You go ahead now, catch up with your friends."

Rebecca watched the girl go back down the corridor to where Michelle and Murray were waiting, obviously anxious to know what Jenny and Rebecca had been talking about. From her own experience with the girl the year before, she had no reason to doubt the accuracy of what Jenny had told her. It hadn't been Rebecca's imagination. Agnes actually had been behaving oddly for several weeks. And now clearly the oddness was spilling over into her work, to the extent that even the kids were noticing it.

Holding the tissues to her nose, Rebecca opened the door to the office half hoping Agnes would be at lunch in the staff dining room. But she was there, her feet propped up on the desk, cigarette in hand, and Teddy positioned prominently on the bookcase. Rebecca sneezed, and Agnes said, "You do know how to make an entrance, my dear."

Rebecca smiled, sneezed again, then asked, "Aren't you eating today?"

"In a moment. I felt the need for a cigarette before facing the troops. Caught a cold, have you?"

Rebecca nodded, looked at Teddy, and tried to think how best to deal with the situation. She dreaded saying the wrong thing and upsetting Agnes, but she knew she had to address the problem before it got out of hand. Inspired, she said, "Teddy seems a bit bored with school."

Lowering her feet and sitting up straighter, Agnes said, "You think so?" and looked penetratingly first at Rebecca and then at the bear.

"He really does, Aggie." Rebecca perched on the edge of the desk and also directed her eyes to the bear. "An intelligent fellow like Teddy has to be bored here. It's all so old hat."

Agnes folded an arm on the desk and puffed thoughtfully on her cigarette. Her eyes flicked over to Rebecca as she exhaled what seemed to be a remarkable amount of smoke. "You think I've gone round the fucking twist, Rebecca, and you're patronizing me," she said in a low, almost deadly, tone of voice.

"I don't think that at all. Maybe it was a patronizing remark. I don't know, Agnes. None of this is on the curriculum. I'm kind of thrown, to be honest."

Agnes said, "Aaah!" and leaned back in her chair, studying Rebecca through the smoke of the cigarette she held a few inches from her mouth. "I do appreciate honesty," she said, taking another drag before extinguishing the cigarette. "That I do appreciate. So now, what is the truth?"

Feeling logy and light-headed, Rebecca couldn't decide how to begin.

"Which one of the little buggers did you talk to?" Agnes wanted to know, a hardness redefining her features.

"Agnes, I love you dearly, but could we please have a civilized conversation over something to eat? I crave hot tea, some soup, and about a dozen Tylenols. I feel like hell."

Getting to her feet, Agnes said, "If you will insist on crawling about on your roof in a downpour, what do you expect? Come along, Rebecca, and we'll organize your tea and Tylenol and the rest of it."

"You're just furious with me," Rebecca said, remaining seated on the edge of the desk. "I can see it, for God's sake! You're practically *vibrating* you're so angry."

Agnes began pacing, her jaw working. Rebecca watched her, overcome by a terrible reluctance. She hated the idea of pursuing this discussion; the very thought of it heightened her distress and fatigue. But Agnes was her dearest friend, and she was going to have to see this through.

"I hate my life," Agnes said abruptly, stopping about six feet away and turning to look at Rebecca with an expression of abject misery. "It's a complete washout."

She put such energy into this declaration that Rebecca felt as if she'd been struck physically. "We all feel that way from time to time," she said. "God knows, for the last week I've certainly hated *my* life."

"You don't understand," Agnes said disappointedly, as if she'd expected Rebecca to glean from her statements something other than what the words indicated. "I hate *living* my life, Rebecca. It's been this way for quite some time now. Some time indeed," she said, looking off into space.

"You're overworked, underpaid, and you need a vacation."

"Too simple."

"All right, then. Perhaps you need some help, someone to talk to."

Again Agnes looked over at her. The ensuing silence was so intense Rebecca thought she could hear a clock ticking but didn't dare break eye contact. Then Agnes sighed. Her features cleared, taking on a neutral aspect. "Come along," she said, extending her hand to Rebecca. "You look like the wreck of the Hesperus. I feel duty-bound to push masses of vitamin C into you."

Bewildered by the suddenness of these mood swings, Rebecca held out her hand and got a small shock at the coldness of Agnes's fingers as they closed around hers. Standing together, their hands joined, Rebecca felt for a moment like a child, locked helplessly into her role as witness to a situation she simply did not comprehend. Then, as if able to see that she felt this way, Agnes drew her into a singularly maternal embrace, softly saying, "Poor little Rebecca. It's all a bit too much for you."

"I'm okay," Rebecca said, dizzied by the increasing congestion in her skull and Agnes's fragrant warmth. "I just really need to eat something."

"And so you shall," Agnes said, releasing her with a smile that displayed her fine teeth. "Right now." She got her handbag from the desk, then went to open the door. Her eyes, Rebecca noted, flashed over to Teddy, then away again. Rebecca felt like weeping.

Between swallows of hot soup, Rebecca said, "Agnes, you know how it throws everyone when you deviate from the course outline. You know that." Agnes nodded soberly, and Rebecca went on. "It'd be best for everyone if Teddy didn't become part of the curriculum. It's that simple."

Agnes nodded again and looked down at the sprig of parsley she was spinning back and forth between the thumb and forefinger of her right hand. Rebecca drank a little more soup, then reached for her tea, deeply concerned about Agnes's possible reactions to this truth she'd claimed to want to hear. The silence lengthening, Rebecca felt an awful need to expand further on what was already a satisfactory statement. "You know what kids are like," she said, watching Agnes's every move. "They want things to be the way they expect. No wrinkles, no surprises, unless they're directly related to the course materials."

"You've made your point," Agnes said at last, dropping the parsley on her untouched plate of food. "There's no need to drive it home with a battering ram."

"Don't be angry with me," Rebecca said quietly. "I don't deserve it, and I know you don't really mean it." She opened her bag, shook two Tylenol caplets from a bottle, then swallowed them with some of the tea. "Sometimes we need to talk things out, try to get a different perspective on our lives. And sometimes a conversation with a friend just won't cut it."

"You're suggesting, with the best possible intentions and no implication whatsoever that there's anything wrong with my head, that I see a shrink," Agnes said with a tight smile. "Or did I miss entirely the point of that fatuous remark?"

"Jesus!" Rebecca whispered. "What I'm *suggesting,* Agnes, is that you need someone to talk to. You just *told* me you hate your life, you're not happy. If it were me, I'd want to talk to someone who might be able to help, maybe show me how I could change the things I don't like."

"You're saying—do correct me if I've misinterpreted—a dialogue with some paid professional 'listener' would work wonders for me. A few hours on the couch and I'll be right as rain."

"Now you're making me mad!" Rebecca scowled. "All I'm saying is if you're having problems, it might help to talk about them. Talk to *me.* Or call up my mother and talk to her. She's very fond of you. We both are. Everybody needs to talk at some point or another. It's why God gave us mouths, for chrissake!"

Agnes laughed, a rich robust burst of infectious music that caused the other teachers to look over with automatic smiles.

"You, my darling, believe our mouths are best used for confessional chats intended to achieve conciliation with one's self. Have I got that right?"

"You're being such a bitch," Rebecca said in a near whisper.

"I do it well." Agnes smiled. "Everyone says so."

"Fine, be a bitch. I love you anyway. Where's that vitamin C you promised me?"

"Indefatigable, that's what you are," Agnes said, frowning now.

"Look, give me a break. My head feels the size of a watermelon; my body feels as if the Wallendas used me as a trampoline, and the last thing I want or need right now is to have a battle of wits with you. You'd win, hands down. You're the cleverest woman I know. Will you please give me the vitamin C and stop busting my chops just because I care about you and it makes me feel terrible when you tell me you hate your life?"

Agnes opened her purse, brought out a large bottle of chewable tablets and plonked it down on the table in front of Rebecca. "Why should you care?" she asked with what seemed to be unfeigned puzzlement.

"I just do," Rebecca insisted, taking four tablets before returning the bottle. "Hang me, but I do. Do you trust me, Aggie?"

"Well, of course!"

"Then leave Teddy at home. Don't bring him to school again. It's not a good idea."

Agnes sniffed. Her chin lifted, her head tilted to the side—a gesture of offhandedness Rebecca knew well—and said, "I got the message quite early on, thank you."

"Don't be like that!" Rebecca warned with a smile. "I mean it. Keep it up and I swear I'll murder you."

"I want a cigarette before class," Agnes announced. "Are you done yet with that invalid's repast?"

"You go ahead. I want to finish my tea."

"Right!" Agnes got up from the table, then stood for a moment with one hand on the back of her chair. "I know this wasn't easy for you, my dear. Don't take me too seriously. As you say, we all have these days."

"Go smoke," Rebecca told her. "We'll talk more later."

She dreaded going home, dreaded the thought of arriving to find something more had been done to the house. From the time she got into the Jetta until she let herself in through the mudroom door, she was fairly hunched over with anxiety.

Taking her time, she went from room to room looking for anything out of place. Nothing wrong that she could see. She opened the front door, got the mail from the box, then did a slow tour of the property that brought her back to the front door. Not a thing amiss. She exhaled slowly as she put the kettle on for tea.

While waiting for the water to boil, she went through the entire house, making sure both the front and back doors, as well as all the windows, were securely locked. She closed the shutters and curtains in every room, then changed into the long flannel nightgown she always wore when she wasn't feeling well, pulled on her robe and a pair of heavy wool socks, and returned downstairs to sort through the mail while sipping her tea with honey laced with a small amount of brandy.

Jeopardy was just ending when her mother called.

"What's wrong?" Evelyn asked. "You sound awful."

For a few seconds Rebecca debated telling her mother what had been going on—the vandalizing, Agnes's increasingly aberrant behavior, her wasted visit to the police. A mistake. Evelyn would be needlessly upset. "I've got a cold. It sounds worse than it is. How are you?"

"Oh, fine. You haven't forgotten about Friday, have you?"

"Nope. I've got it written down right here in my diary. Are you having second thoughts?"

"I don't think so. It all depends on how much I like what we see. Some of these new places are just thrown together, you know, Rebecca."

"And some of them are first-class. You'll see."

"You should be in bed, the way you sound."

"That's where I'm headed in about five minutes."

"Two things," Evelyn said, "then I'll let you go. I thought I'd warn you. Sunday your brothers are coming."

"What d'you suppose prompted this?"

"Probably the news that I'm think of selling the place. They're coming to pick it clean like those villagers in *Zorba*. Remember that scene after the woman died when they stripped her place to the walls? One of the most frightening things I've ever seen."

"It ought to be interesting."

"The other thing," Evelyn said. "Those bonds your father bought for the three of you matured last week. You'll be getting a check."

"That's great! How much?"

"You each get just over five thousand. I thought you'd want to know."

"Thank you," Rebecca said. "I'll have to think about what I'd like to do with the money." She looked around the kitchen nervously. Even with everything locked up tight, with the shutters closed and the outside floodlights on, she could all too easily imagine someone creeping around the property, spying on her, keeping track of her comings and goings. "There are quite a few things I could do with that money. It'll come in very handy." She coughed, then sneezed. "Sorry," she said, reaching into her robe for some tissues.

"Go to bed, sweetheart."

"I feel as if I could sleep for a week."

"You probably could," Evelyn laughed. "Champion sleeper of all time, that's my girl."

"I may never forgive you for waking me up all those years by putting an ice cube on my neck."

"If I hadn't done that," Evelyn said, "you'd still be in the seventh grade. Go! I'll see you Friday."

"I love you, Mom." Rebecca tried but failed to suppress a yawn.

"I love you, too. Feel better," her mother said, and hung up.

Putting down the receiver, Rebecca wished for a moment she was still in the seventh grade, safe in her corner bedroom, with her parents in the room across the hall.

CHAPTER

Ten

Stopping into the English office on her way to lunch Wednesday, Rebecca was pleased to discover that her mug had been returned. She picked it up to take with her to the cafeteria, having agreed to substitute for the assistant principal.

"Off to do your stint on Canine Patrol, are you?" Agnes observed. "Well, don't let any of them bite you. They're all rabid."

Both amused and curious, Rebecca studied Agnes's pale but very beautiful face. Exotic wide-set green eyes, a perfectly sculpted nose, her generous mouth defined by clear red lipstick. She didn't *look* any different, but she was, without question. "Why do you talk about them the way you do?" Rebecca asked her. "You love the kids. You love teaching. But lately you make it sound like warfare."

"One must never allow them to get the upper hand," Agnes said, dusting ash from the sleeve of her smartly cut black wool dress. "The moment they realize they've made inroads, your usefulness is over."

She was being facetious, Rebecca decided, completely lacking the energy to pursue the discussion.

"I see you've found your mug," Agnes said.

Rebecca held it up with a smile. "The thief was obviously overcome by guilt and returned it. Even washed it, too."

"Hah!" Agnes scoffed and reached for several message slips. "Joy of joys! I must," she stated, "communicate with a few parents."

Watching her reach for the telephone, Rebecca had the alarming notion that this wasn't the Agnes she'd always known and enjoyed and admired. Someone brittle and caustic and hard-edged had, like an unpleasant doppelgänger, stepped in to replace her. From moment to moment there were glimpses of the familiar woman, but she seemed to surface less and less often. Suddenly very frightened, Rebecca had the idea that if she didn't say or do something, the Agnes she loved would cease to exist. But what could she say? What was there to do?

Agnes finished dialing and held the phone to her ear with an upraised shoulder as she reached for her cigarettes, glancing up at Rebecca. Her eyes widening, she was about to speak when someone picked up at the other end. Her eyes clicking away from Rebecca, her voice dropping to the deep, plummy register she used on parents, she said, "Oh, hello. Agnes Tyrell here, returning your call."

Holding a fistful of tissues to her nose, Rebecca went off to the cafeteria, worried.

It was just too difficult trying to chew and breathe at the same time, so Rebecca gave up after eating only half a sandwich. She took two more Tylenol caplets and an antihistamine, filled her mug with hot tea and returned to the classroom. All she wanted was to get through the afternoon, then go directly home to bed. She hated being sick. She was also admittedly angry, apprehensive, and impatient, and had to keep reminding herself not to take it out on the students.

The tea soothed her raw throat, and she drank it slowly throughout the first fifteen minutes of the class. She was leaning against the front of the desk, her eyes moving over the faces of the kids, her mouth open to speak, when her head seemed to swell suddenly, terrifyingly. Her thoughts shrank and fell to the bottom of the immense balloon that had become her head. She could hear them rattling like gravel as they settled at the base of her skull. Her eyes swiveled and, with astonishment, she could hear them rotate on their stalks; like greased ball bearings, they made a smooth, wet sound as they turned.

Confronting her were neat rows of stick dolls with immense flower heads of all varieties and colors. The flowers were centered not with stamens and filaments or ovaries, but with doll-like eyes and fleshy mouths. Some of these flowers were bisexual, some visibly monoecious, others dioecious. Golden grains of pollen floated in the air, drifting between the flowers, landing on the outthrust tongues of poppies, roses, daisies, buttercups, dahlias, lilies—an entire world of luscious blooms too numerous to count. Colors flared in dazzling coronas, each corresponding to the blossom it encircled. She blinked several times, hoping to dispel the eerie images. Had she gone mad finally? Was this the way it happened?

Her heart was beating rapidly against the front of her sweater. She could actually see it moving the wool, and tried to lift her hand to cover it so the flowers wouldn't see. But she couldn't seem to lift her hand, and she was distracted by a low distorted rumbling that emanated from somewhere in the midst of the flowers.

It's the antihistamine, she thought. She was having some kind of toxic reaction to the pills. She wanted to explain. She wanted to sit down. But she seemed to be tied to the desk, and her hands wouldn't respond to her mental commands. She tried to shake her head, anxious to clear it, but it merely wobbled top-heavily on the thin stem of her neck, and she knew if she shook it too hard, it would tumble off and fall to the floor. If that happened she'd really be in trouble. There was no way she could possibly reattach it with hands that refused to work. She was losing her grip on reality; she could almost feel it slipping away from her.

There was a tremendous noise at the windows, and her eyes slid around to see yellowed leaves striking against the glass like the outstretched hands of evil creatures in some horror movie, clattering as they collided, scrabbling to maintain a hold before slipping away as more, then more, of them came hurtling through the air. She forced her mouth to open, anxious to cry out for help, but the air was so thick now with pollen she could scarcely see the stick dolls, and she feared swallowing any of the potent amber buds. They'd make her pregnant; she'd give birth to a cross-pollinated hybrid with yellow talons instead of hands. People would talk about her as she wheeled her offspring up and down the aisles at the supermarket. They'd whisper about the madwoman with her deformed children. More of that bass metallic rumbling was coming from somewhere in the depths of this overwhelming and magnificent garden.

A dream. She was dreaming. None of this was real. If she concentrated, she could make herself wake up. Her greasy lids slammed shut and she told herself to wake up. Wake up! You're in control of this. You can end this. Up rolled her eyelids to reveal the flowers unchanged, their furred and feathery leaves lolling on unseen air currents. It was all so beautiful, these extraordinary flower faces with their provocatively tinted petals, their delicate acts of pollination pushing unearthly fragrances into the already weighted air.

Was she having a stroke? It was so hard to think with the

noise of the leaves crashing against the windows and the increased bass-heavy rumbling that had the flowers vibrating and made their luminous auras diminish and flare repeatedly. Some of the stems were uprooting themselves, to drift up to the ceiling; they bounced to the floor, to the ceiling, then away out the door. She wanted them to stay, wanted to feast her senses on their magnificent improbability.

It's a metaphor, she thought, recalling, as if from the far-distant past, talk of wild beasts and metaphors, and understanding suddenly the wisdom of metaphors, their validity, their value. There was nothing to be afraid of. All these exquisite creations, each so unique, so compelling. Beautiful beautiful. A heavenly lassitude was settling in her limbs, in her weighty, misshapen head. An illustrated metaphor. She'd have to tell . . . someone. Who was it who'd spoken of metaphors? Somebody, a long time ago. No matter.

Her heart wouldn't stop pushing against her sweater. Irritating, distracting. She wished it would stop. It was interfering with her pleasure in the miraculously evolving panorama. And if she didn't have to pay attention to her racketing heart, she'd be able to narrow down her focus and glean the precise message of this singularly unique metaphor.

White-faced and frantic, a girl burst through the door to Agnes's classroom. Dumbfounded, Agnes held up a hand to still the class as the girl signaled urgently to her to come. Agnes walked over to the door.

"Something's wrong with Ms. Leighton," the girl said in an edgy whisper. "I think she's tripping out or something."

"Tripping out?"

"Please! You've got to come."

Agnes said, "Just a moment," and stepped back into the room. Quickly scanning the faces, she said, "If there's so much as a single pin-drop of sound from this class, the lot of you will have detentions. Get on with the reading. I'll be back in a few minutes."

"What precisely do you mean by 'tripping'?" Agnes asked as she and the girl hurried along the corridor.

"Like an acid trip. You'll see."

There was a nervous murmuring that stopped abruptly as Agnes opened the door. She cast a warning glance at the students, then looked over at Rebecca, who was sitting on the floor with her back against the desk, her eyes wide and lips moving.

"See?" the girl whispered. "She's completely out of it. Everything was fine and then all of a sudden she just lost it. It was kind of like she blissed out on us. D'you think she'll be okay?"

Agnes bent to look at Rebecca, noting that her pupils were hugely dilated. Straightening, she turned to the girl and quietly said, "I want you to take your books, ask Mr. Gianelli to come here, then tell my class to go to the cafeteria for the remainder of the hour." Raising her voice, she spoke to the others. "I'd like you all to collect your books, please, and go to the cafeteria. Do it quickly and quietly, now!"

With obedience born of bewilderment, the kids filed hastily out of the room while Agnes dropped down to try to talk to Rebecca.

An immense portrait all at once filled Rebecca's field of vision, a portrait of a woman with flawless milky skin, glowing emerald cat's eyes with flecks of amber, full scarlet lips, and a nimbus of sleek fiery hair. She lifted her hand to touch the expanse of porcelain flesh, only to have her fingers disappear below the surface to touch the liquid underneath. With a cry she drew back her hand to examine it front and back, then looked with wonderment to see that the skin was already closing over the indentations caused by her touch. The cat's eyes glowed, sending out rays of green and gold, and the lips parted, reshaped themselves, then began pushing out discordant sounds in a minor key. Rebecca laughed. The lips moved, and inside the cushiony red interior of the portrait's mouth, the tongue, like a serpent, squirmed to life, moving too. Absurd.

The portrait receded slightly, the enormous mouth drawing closed like the doors to a medieval castle. All around the portrait were circles of pale pulsing light, not vibrant and strong like the coronas of the flowers, but thin and leached of color so that they were barely discernible. Poor portrait, Rebecca thought, stricken by the poverty of those sad circles. So sad, these fading aureoles.

Gianelli came on the run. He was the head of the math department and, in Agnes's opinion, the most reliable staff member and the least likely to gossip. They'd worked together for twelve years, and in that time she'd found him to be eminently rational and highly likable. After his divorce a couple of years earlier, she'd debated inviting him over to dinner. Then she'd reconsidered and decided it was a bad idea. Given all the options available to unattached men, she was very probably the last woman on earth he'd find of any interest.

"What's happened?" He dropped to his haunches beside Agnes to look at Rebecca.

"The kids seem to think she's having a bad trip," Agnes said worriedly. "It seems a reasonable diagnosis. We've got to get her out of here."

Gianelli stroked his mustache a moment, then said, "Where to?"

"I think I should try to get her home," she told him. "First off, we should see if she's able to walk."

Between them, they hauled Rebecca to her feet. She stood smiling, her unfocused eyes crowded with visions.

"Do you have a class last period?" Agnes asked Gianelli.

"Calculus," he answered, eyeing Rebecca as if fearful she'd fall.

"Look," Agnes said, "help me get her to the office and then out to the car. I believe I can manage her from there."

"Sure," Gianelli agreed, and took Rebecca's arm.

"We're going to walk, Rebecca," Agnes said, taking her other arm.

"Walk," Rebecca repeated dumbly.

In the office, Gianelli got Rebecca into her coat while Agnes collected her own handbag and Rebecca's.

"D'you think one of the kids dropped some acid on her?" Gianelli asked when they'd maneuvered Rebecca into the passenger seat of Agnes's car. "The stories about this happening are legion, but I'll be damned if I've ever actually seen a case." Again, thoughtfully, he stroked his mustache.

"Louis," Agnes said, "at this point, I'm willing to believe almost anything. Would you do me a favor and stop by the main office, explain?"

"Glad to," he said, still eyeing Rebecca doubtfully. "You sure you're going to be able to manage?"

Agnes now looked at Rebecca, saying, "Given that I'm roughly twice her size, I think so. Thank you, Louis."

"Are you going to stay with her?"

"I most certainly am."

"Okay. I'll give you a call later, see how it's going. In the meantime, I'll put out some feelers, see if anybody knows anything."

"Do that," she said, opening the door on the driver's side. "I'd be most interested in hearing whatever you might learn."

———

So this was what it was like to lose your mind! She was strapped into her seat on a rocket, shooting through dazzling silver comet clusters to the far reaches of space. It wasn't bad at all. Breathing deeply, she could taste the rocket fuel, smell the residue of the ignition burn. Enclosed in her capsule, she went soundlessly soaring through layer after layer of ever-deepening blue, into the primordial darkness of the cosmos. Turning to absorb the full impact of the spectacular panoptic view of infinity, she saw that the portrait was with her. Yes, of course. That was her mission: to see this astonishing portrait safely to its destination.

It was a great and sacred privilege to have been entrusted with this valuable work of art. It had its own life-force, which was doomed to be extinguished if Rebecca failed to return it to its rightful place on the all-enclosing wall of the universe. "I'll get you there safely," she promised the rare composition. "Don't worry. I'll get you there."

"I'll get you there safely. Don't worry. I'll get you there."

Agnes turned to stare for a moment, wondering what on earth could be traveling through the spiraling chambers of Rebecca's mind. Then she simply had to laugh at the preposterousness of it. "Poor darling," she said. "Someone's playing hell with your life, aren't they?"

Naturally, Rebecca didn't respond. The laughter emptied out of Agnes's chest, leaving an exhausted remainder of despair. Nothing very amusing about this situation. Nothing very amusing, really, about anything.

Lou Gianelli, true to his word, telephoned just before seven that evening. "How's she doing?" he asked Agnes.

"I'd say she's slowly starting to come out of it. I've been

pouring coffee into her, walking her up and down. Can't really think of what else to do."

"One thing," he said. "I noticed her mug on the desk when we were in there. Well, I was thinking about it, and I decided maybe I'd get Gerry to test the residue. He's pretty good at that kind of thing. Anyway, when I went back to her classroom the mug was gone. I checked the English office and the staff room. It's just vanished."

"Which very likely proves something was indeed put in her tea."

"Sure looks that way. You going to be able to cope on your own, Agnes?" he asked. "I'd be happy to swing by, give you a hand."

"Louis, you're very dear. We'll be fine."

"Okay, if you're sure. I really don't mind."

"I'm sure I'll be able to manage."

"You've got my number if you need me?"

"I do indeed. Thank you." How very considerate he was, she thought.

"I'm in for the rest of the evening," he said. "Don't hesitate. Okay? Really. Anything at all I can do to help."

Agnes thanked him again, then hung up, wondering if perhaps she shouldn't have invited him to dinner after all. He really was very sweet.

Very gradually Rebecca began to have glimpses of an alternative reality, one that struck her as infinitely more viable. It was like coming out of an anesthetic stupor, struggling up to the surface of consciousness and fighting to stay there for long minutes before once more slipping down into the subterranean depths. It was exhausting and frightening trying to battle her way free, but she was desperate to escape from what felt like an ocean of hot, congealing glue that threatened to drown her.

During one of her increasingly prolonged sojourns in what she knew to be the actual reality, she became aware that Agnes was holding her, gently, rhythmically stroking her hair as she talked softly about someone, almost crooning. It was wonderfully comforting, almost too much so. Her perfume and the motion of that stroking hand were sending her back down into the sticky glue, and Rebecca didn't want to go. Agnes was talking about someone.

". . . and so I was thinking it might actually be a good idea to send Teddy off on holiday to visit people I know in Sydney," she was saying. "Teddy's always wanted to travel, and now seems as good a time as any."

It wasn't a someone, Rebecca all at once understood, but a *something*. Agnes was talking about the damned teddy bear, quite seriously holding forth on the idea of sending it to Australia.

"Don't do it," Rebecca said, her mouth full of the glue, her tongue thick. It took all her strength and powers of concentration to think the words, then get them out. "You'd be unhappy without Teddy." She could see the bear sitting against Agnes's thigh and longed to get it away from her friend. The thing was destroying Agnes's rationality; it was responsible for the doppelgänger effect.

Agnes tilted her head and looked at her. "Where are you, Rebecca?" she asked uncertainly.

"I was here," Rebecca answered, feeling herself starting to go again. "I don't think you should talk about Teddy like . . . as if he's real . . ." She couldn't complete the thought; she was rabbiting back down the corkscrewing passage brilliantly alight with multicolored neon coils. She fought furiously but couldn't save herself.

Rebecca opened her eyes. She was in her bed. Light from the kitchen showed at the top of the spiral staircase. Was someone

in the house? Her heart constricted. She sat up, afraid, trying
to orient herself. God! She could hear someone moving quietly downstairs. Her heart was now climbing into her throat.

"Who's there?" she called, her voice hoarse, nearly sick
with fear.

"Queen Marie of Rumania," Agnes bellowed, to Rebecca's immediate relief, and came quickly up the stairs from
the kitchen to stop at the top, her hand on the railing. "Are
you all right, my dear?" she asked solicitously.

"I guess so," Rebecca said, taken off guard by the sight of
Agnes in a black slip, with her hair down, her arms and legs
bare. She looked positively magnificent, her skin glowing as
if polished. "Aren't you cold in just your slip? There's a spare
robe in the downstairs bathroom if you'd like to use it."

Agnes came over to sit on the foot of the bed. "You're
forgetting I grew up without the luxury of central heating.
I'm not in the least cold. Are you?"

"No. I'm fine, except my mouth feels as if I've been
eating library paste and my ears are all blocked up."

"I'll get you something to drink. Hot or cold?" Agnes
asked.

Rebecca swallowed experimentally. Her throat felt as if
she'd swallowed a razor blade. "You don't have to wait on
me, Aggie. I'll come down and we'll have some tea. What
time is it, anyway?"

"Just gone eleven. Are you sure you're up to it?"

"Eleven?" Rebecca could scarcely believe it.

Rising, Agnes said, "From what I've been given to understand, you're lucky. It sometimes takes as long as eighteen
to twenty-four hours before one comes down off a trip."

"A trip?" Rebecca felt about on the floor for her slippers.
"God! Of course! I didn't want to believe it, but I'd say this
proves it's one of the students."

"If you're referring to whoever it was who doctored your

tea, it would seem so," Agnes agreed, going first down the stairs to the kitchen.

"I think it's the same one who's been doing all of it. It's got to be one of the students."

Rebecca filled the kettle, put it on the stove, then automatically got the teapot and cups down while Agnes settled in at the island and lit a cigarette. Open facedown beside the ashtray was one of the volumes form Rebecca's set of the *Encyclopedia Britannica*.

"Reading up on LSD?" Rebecca asked.

Agnes guiltily closed the volume, got up and carried it back to the bookshelf in the living room. "No, actually," she said on her return. "Merely browsing. Do you suppose there's a section on LSD? Perhaps we should look it up, see what we're dealing with."

"Not much point," Rebecca said. "It seems to be over now. And unless Timothy Leary wrote the entry, my guess is whatever the *Britannica* has to say would pale in comparison to my personal experience today."

"I'm sure it was dreadful. In view of the fact that you very nearly wrestled me to the floor earlier this evening, I expect you had visions of a fairly ghastly nature." Agnes retrieved her cigarette from the ashtray and turned to look expectantly at Rebecca.

"God! I did that?"

Rather nonchalantly, Agnes said, "From what I could gather, you thought I was attempting to drown you. I had no idea you were so strong."

"I'm sorry," Rebecca apologized, mortified. "I didn't know what I was doing. I thought I'd lost my mind, that I'd finally gone crazy."

"How alarming," Agnes said with heartfelt sympathy.

"Having no control was the worst part of it. At the beginning, I was terrified. Fortunately, that didn't last very long. Then I began seeing all these incredibly beautiful . . . hallucinations, I guess. Let's say it hasn't been one of my favorite experiences. Especially having it happen smack in the middle of my junior English class. How did the kids take it?" she asked with misgivings, thinking that yesterday Agnes had upset the senior English class. Today she'd had her turn upsetting the juniors. The kids would start being afraid to come to class.

"They were a stalwart group, really. I took a good look at them and they all seemed thoroughly rattled. I didn't see anyone who appeared to be deriving the least bit of satisfaction from the situation. So," Agnes wound down, "I think it's safe to say it's unlikely our culprit's in that class. Or else he or she has award-winning acting talent."

Pulling herself up to sit on the counter opposite, Rebecca said, "Thank you for taking care of me, Aggie. You're a good friend."

Agnes leaned on her elbow and gazed over at her. "Do you remember all of it?" she asked.

"Only bits and pieces. I kept tuning in and out. Why the hell is this happening? I wish I knew that. I feel as if I'm battling shadows." She was close to tears. To cover it, she slipped down off the counter to pour boiling water into the teapot, saying, "I can make up the bed for you in the guest room."

"Already done it," Agnes said. "I wasn't about to go off and leave you on your own."

"I really do appreciate it," Rebecca told her, putting the lid on the teapot, then again looking over at her friend. Aggie really was remarkably beautiful, with her long flamboyant hair and opalescent skin, her lean elegant limbs.

"Stop thanking me," Agnes said quietly. "You'd have done the same for me."

"Yes," Rebecca agreed, "I would. But be gracious and let

me thank you. I was so scared," she said thickly, "and you were there to help."

Abashed, Agnes lowered her eyes and said, "It was the least I could do." What she wanted to say, but couldn't, was how good it had made her feel to be needed.

Rebecca awakened just after three. One moment she was asleep, dreaming vividly, the next she was wide awake, and extremely hungry.

Tiptoeing downstairs in her heavy socks, she grabbed a handful of crackers and cut herself a wedge of Jarlsberg. The light was still on in the guest room. Poking her head around the corner, she looked in to see that Agnes had fallen asleep while reading. The book lay across her lap. And held tightly to her breast was Teddy. For some reason, Rebecca found the scene upsetting. The bear looked as if it were nursing, one paw resting possessively, somehow obscenely, on the swell of Agnes's breast.

For a few seconds Rebecca was overcome with loathing for the toy, seeing it as the embodiment of everything that had gone wrong—in both their lives. Then, deciding she was being ridiculously melodramatic, she turned out the light and crept back upstairs, to sit on the side of her bed for quite some time, staring at the floor, eating without tasting the food, and trying but failing to decide who was trying to drive her mad, and to pinpoint what was wrong with Agnes.

At last, her hunger satisfied but all her questions unanswered, she climbed back into bed and switched off the light. In the dark, she lay gazing up through the skylight at the twitching branches of the copper beech, tears trickling irritatingly down the sides of her face, coughing intermittently, and fervently wishing this nightmare were over.

CHAPTER

Eleven

As she readied herself to go to school the next morning, an agitated Rebecca wondered aloud about what, if anything, she should say to the junior class.

"Don't attempt to explain," Agnes counseled. "At this point, there's not a thing you could say."

"Maybe you're right. Although if I'd been one of the kids watching that display, I'd kind of like some sort of explanation. You're sure I didn't do anything too terrible?"

"Given the circumstances, you were remarkably well-behaved. It's up to you, of course, what you choose to say to anyone." Agnes shrugged and poured herself more coffee. "I do like this house," she said, admiring the fine birch paneling and tall narrow windows at each of the far corners of the kitchen. "It's so charming."

"I used to like it," Rebecca said glumly, thinking of the pleasure she'd taken in the renovations and decorating that had been done during her eight years of occupancy. Now her home felt like the scene of an ongoing crime. She couldn't get past the idea that there was more, and worse, to come. Watching her friend finish her coffee, she wondered what Agnes had done with the teddy bear. The damned thing seemed to disappear and then materialize like the end product of some esoteric conjuring trick. She wished she knew why Agnes had taken to treating it like her newborn infant, wished she could come right out and ask her about it. But she couldn't. In the overall scheme of things, the bear was a minor irritant.

Upon arriving at the school, she was relieved to see that the Jetta hadn't suffered any damage during its night spent in the parking lot. She realized, after inspecting the exterior, that she no longer took for granted her own well-being or that of her property. She was now waiting to see what new malevolent act each day would bring.

Someone had left a package for her in the English office. It was done up in gaily printed wrapping paper and topped with a large yellow bow. A plain white card tucked under the ribbon had her name printed on it.

"What do you suppose it is?" Agnes asked with a smile.

"I know it's silly," Rebecca said, moistening her lips, "but I'm afraid to open it."

"Shall I?" Agnes offered.

"God! I think we should just throw it away without opening it." Rebecca stared doubtfully at the box.

"Rubbish! I'll open it." Agnes picked up the package and looked it over, then began removing the wrapping.

"I really think we should throw it away," Rebecca repeated. "I've got a bad feeling about this."

Agnes set aside the gift wrap, saying, "It's quite heavy."

"Please don't open it!" Rebecca told her, but it was too late. Agnes was lifting off the lid.

"This is curious," Agnes said, setting the box down on her desk. "Some sort of plastic all pushed in on itself." She plucked at what seemed to be a heavyweight transparent food-storage bag and opened the top of it. Bending forward, she looked into the bag.

As Rebecca watched, Agnes's eyes went wide, her head jerked back, and she threw her hands out to the sides.

"Good Christ!" she gasped, straightening abruptly.

"What is it?"

Agnes couldn't speak for a moment. She had to close her eyes, trying with all her might not to vomit.

"What?" Rebecca repeated, looking fearfully from Agnes to the box.

Agnes opened her eyes and said, "For God's sake, don't look! It's utterly disgusting." Steeling herself, she pushed the top of the plastic bag back inside, then jammed the lid on the box.

"What *is* it?" Rebecca asked, making a mental note to tell Jason about the LSD, and now this.

"Some sort of rotting animal innards, crawling with maggots." Agnes shuddered, grabbed for her cigarettes and lit one, inhaling deeply. "What a *filthy* thing to do!" she said as her telephone rang. She picked up the receiver and, eyes on Rebecca, said, "Yes?" then, "I'll tell her," and hung up.

"What?"

"There are flowers for you at the front office."

"Flowers?"

"That is what Eileen said. You go along, and I'll get rid of *that.*" She pointed one long manicured finger at the package on her desk.

"God!" Rebecca said, thoroughly rattled and unable to think clearly. "What if it's another box that only looks like something that came from a florist?" There was too much going on. Should she call Jason now?

"She said very specifically flowers. Go ahead, Rebecca."

"All right," Rebecca said reluctantly, casting a final glance at the package on the desk before heading off to the office, wondering as she went if they ought to hang on to that box. It was evidence, after all.

A dozen pink carnations in a vase stood on the counter in the front office. Rebecca looked at them, rubbing her arms as if chilled.

"What's wrong?" Eileen wanted to know.

"I hate carnations. They remind me of funerals." She reached into her pocket for some tissues and held them to her runny nose.

"Aren't you going to read the card?" Eileen asked.

Looking again, Rebecca saw a gift card tucked under the side of the vase. She picked it up. It read "Have a nice day" in small, neatly printed letters. "Great!" Rebecca made a face. Then, aware Eileen was watching, she asked, "Did you happen to be here when they were delivered?" She wondered if Ray might have sent the flowers. Then she decided it was out of character. He wouldn't have done it. More likely it was the same person who'd sent the package.

A pleasant, heavy-set woman in her early fifties, Eileen was, after more than twenty years at the school, prepared for all contingencies, and basically unflappable. She dealt with every conceivable teenage drama—from pregnancy to drug overdoses—and was the one to whom both staff and students turned with problems. "They were here when I got in this morning," Eileen told her.

"Why don't you keep them?" Rebecca suggested.

"You don't want them?" Eileen's eyebrows lifted.

"Please, have them," Rebecca insisted.

"Are you sure?" Eileen asked. "They're just gorgeous."

"I'm absolutely positive."

"Well, thank you, Rebecca. They sure will brighten up the place."

"My pleasure," Rebecca said from the door.

She hurried back to the English office, the morning announcements booming out of the PA system, the kids as usual paying little if any attention.

Agnes was gone. So was the box. With only a few minutes left to get to her classroom, Rebecca collected her things and hurried off.

Agnes was right about not attempting to offer any explanation to her junior class. Several of the kids approached to ask how she was feeling, and to say they hoped she was okay now. Touched by their concern, she assured them that aside from her cold, she was fine. But throughout the day she was studying every face, looking carefully to see if one of them betrayed any sign of guilt or pleasure. They all looked the same as ever, and she felt simultaneously paranoid and entirely justified. It was hopeless. There was no possible way she could guess, just from looking at people, which of them might be responsible for the ugly invasions into her life and sanity.

At lunchtime Agnes said, "I've got an errand or two to run. I'll ring you this evening and we'll talk."

"What did you do with that box?"

"I've taken care of it. The less said about it, the sooner I'll be able to contemplate eating again."

"Well," Rebecca said awkwardly, "thank you."

"Don't mention it," Agnes said, then smiled and added, "I mean that literally. *Please* don't mention it."

After school when she was on her way out to the parking lot, Jenny Baker caught up with her to ask, "Are you okay, Ms. Leighton? We heard about what happened. I mean, there's some rumors. You know. I was a little worried."

"I'm fine, Jenny. What kind of rumors?"

"Oh, stuff. You know."

"No, tell me."

"Well, the major one is that somebody dropped acid in your tea."

"Amazing," Rebecca said with a shake of her head.

"I knew it was bull," Jenny said with satisfaction.

Rather than clarify, Rebecca decided to let the girl go with her own interpretation. "Thanks for your concern, Jenny."

"Hey! I'm just glad you're okay. You know?" Jenny went off across the lot to the new Saab her parents had given her as an advance graduation present. The girl waved before climbing into the car. Rebecca waved back, then unlocked the Jetta.

She drove slowly, realizing she didn't want to go home. The school had ceased to be a haven, and her house had become the arena where arcane, unsettling games were being played. And Agnes talked about hating *her* life! Agnes's life was a veritable garden party by comparison.

She hadn't had a thing to eat or drink at school; she'd been reluctant to touch anything she hadn't prepared herself, deeply afraid of going off on another unscheduled "trip." LSD had no taste or color. It could be put in anything and she'd have no way of knowing. God! she thought, signaling the turn into her driveway. When was this going to end? On top of everything else, she was going to have to start packing a lunch each day.

As had now become her habit, she made a tour of the outside of the house and got the mail before letting herself in the back door. Her stomach was gurgling and she felt a little light-headed from hunger, so she at once put on the kettle, then studied the contents of the refrigerator. Baked ham and imported Swiss on pumpernickel with honey mustard, and a cup of Earl Gray tea. She ate sitting at the center island and sorted through the mail. No check. Probably too soon to be looking for it. While she finished the tea, she thought of using some of the money to go off for a week at Christmas to some Caribbean island, where she'd laze in the sun and read, take long walks to collect seashells, and in the evenings sit out of doors and listen to a steel-drum band. Impossible. She hated traveling alone.

With a sigh, she started up the spiral staircase to her bedroom. At the top she stood, holding fast to the handrail, shaking her head back and forth in instinctive denial. It couldn't be. She'd checked this morning before she and Agnes had left for school, and all the doors and windows had been locked. A tremor of fear started in her legs. Her knees wanted to buckle. Her grip on the handrail tightened as her stomach muscles clenched. She took a long, slow look around the room, then turned and went woodenly back down the stairs and through the kitchen to look first in the guest room and then in the living room.

Her head still shaking back and forth, she sat down on the floor just inside the living room and started to laugh. She howled with it, feeling her self-control dissolving. Then, a catch in her chest, and she went from laughing to sobbing. Crossing her arms over her knees, she let her head rest on her arms and cried miserably until she began to cough. Once the coughing fit had subsided, she sneezed three times in succession. At last she got up and went into the downstairs bathroom for a fistful of fresh tissues. She dried her face, blew her nose, then stood in the living-room doorway, looking in at the room in despair.

With the exception of the kitchen and the two bathrooms, the furniture in every room had been rearranged, including the pictures and plants. *Someone had been inside the house*. But how? No broken windows, neither of the doors had been forced.

"Oh, my God!" she whispered, looking down at the trapdoor beneath her feet.

A low-grade panic squeezing her lungs, she ran out the

back door and around the side of the house to test the storm doors. They were unlocked, lifted open easily. How could she have forgotten them? Returning inside, she looked at the trapdoor. Maybe the vandal was still down there, hiding in the cellar. No. There was nowhere to hide. Wait! What about the crawl space under the kitchen extension? She hesitated. The opening to the crawl space was perhaps eighteen inches high and two feet wide, big enough for someone to climb through. Nobody was down there now, she told herself. Even if someone had been there when she'd come home, he'd have heard her walking around. Not wanting to be caught, he'd have crept out quietly through the storm doors.

"You can't scare me away!" she whispered, battling down her fear. "And I won't let you drive me crazy. I won't!" Getting the flashlight from the shelf in the mudroom, she raised the heavy trapdoor and with legs rubbery with fear, climbed down the ladder, reaching for the light pull. She almost never came down here. Once a year the oil company sent a man to clean the burner, change the filters or whatever. She'd had few occasions over the years even to think about this small area that housed the furnace, the hot-water tank, and the sump pump that dealt with the occasional seepage from heavy rains.

Brushing aside cobwebs, she aimed the flashlight at the entry to the crawl space. Empty. Letting out her breath, she went to the far end and reached up to turn the metal rod that locked the doors from the inside, then gave an experimental push to make sure they were secured. Satisfied, she dusted off her hands, checked to see nothing else had been disturbed, then turned off the light and climbed back up to the kitchen.

"There!" she declared, proud of the bravery she was displaying. "You think you're getting to me, but you're not!" Allowing the trapdoor to slam closed, she studied it, wishing there were some way to lock it. There wasn't. The door fit snugly into the tiled floor with a thumb loop that allowed it to be lifted open. With the storm doors locked, though, she'd now cut off all legitimate access to the house. If the bastard wanted to get in again, he'd have to break in. This fact didn't console her in the least.

It didn't take long to return all the furniture to its original positions. But as she pushed and shoved everything back into place, pausing to sneeze and blow her nose, her anger swelled in direct proportion to the amount of energy she expended. When the last of the pictures had been rehung, she washed her hands and face, tidied her hair, shoved a fresh supply of tissues into her pocket, and sat down at the island to telephone Jason Blondell.

By the time the ringing started on the other end, she was geared up to do physical battle if necessary. Her anger had grown so large it was like a guest in the house, something animate taking up air and space. She sneezed, blew her tender, reddened nose, then heard him say hello.

"This is Rebecca Leighton," she said. "I thought you told me you were going to help me."

"Hey, Rebecca," he said happily. "This is swell."

"This is not a social call," she said irritably.

"Oh, too bad."

"Listen, this situation is getting out of hand. Yesterday somebody put LSD in my tea at school. I went into space for roughly fifteen hours. Today not only was I sent a box of maggot-ridden offal at school, but there were also flowers with a note saying have a nice day. Then I got home from school this afternoon and did my now-routine check of the property before I came inside to find that the ghoul got inside my house through the storm doors and rearranged all my damned furniture."

"They're locked up tight now, right?" he asked.

"Of course!" she snapped.

"And dollars to doughnuts you threw the box of gunge away. Right?"

"Naturally!"

"Was anything stolen?"

"I don't know. I mean, there's nothing obviously missing. I might go to look for something next week and find it's gone. But for now, I have to say no."

"Too bad," he said.

"What do you mean 'too bad?' It took me more than an hour to put everything back."

"Jeez, Rebecca. You've got a bad habit of destroying evidence. Very naughty. From now on, you don't throw anything away and you don't put back anything that's been moved. Remember that! Okay? Now you're sure he got in through the storm doors?"

"Positive. Everything else was locked."

"Much as I hate to say so," he said, "there's nothing the force can do. Whatever evidence there might have been was disposed of one way and another. And since nothing's been taken from the house, there's really no way of proving a break-in. About the best they'd do is have a patrol car swing by your house a couple of times a day, keep an eye on the place."

"But he's been inside my house!" she protested. "There must be something you can do. You *said* you'd help me! Do I have to be injured before you'll do anything? What do I have to do to convince you this is no joke?"

"I know you're upset," Jason said. "And you've got cause. The thing is, they don't have the personnel to keep a full-time watch on your property. I know that's not what you want to hear."

"You're damned right it isn't!"

"Hey, Rebecca," he said in a cajoling tone, "ease up a little, okay?"

"What am I supposed to do?" she cried.

"I'll keep an eye on your place," he promised. "That's about all I can do."

"This is just like those stories in the papers about women whose husbands threaten to kill them, and they call the police for help but nothing's ever done until the women get killed."

"Come on," he said quietly, stung. "It's not that bad."

"How would you know? You don't have to live with this. I do!" She gave up, saying, "Thanks anyway," and put the receiver down, breaking into tears. No one was going to help her, and she'd wind up locked away in some mental institution.

Reaching into her pocket, she pulled out some tissues to mop her face as the telephone rang.

It was Jason. "Why'd you hang up on me, Beck?" he asked as if they were old friends who'd had a minor misunderstanding.

"What?"

"You didn't give me a chance to finish," he said. "And how come you didn't call me *before* you started moving the furniture around?"

"I . . . I don't know," she said helplessly.

"Next time, call me. Okay?"

"What for? So you can tell me everything I've done wrong?"

"No, so I can help. You want me to swing by?"

"No, thank you," she said stiffly. "I'm going to get into bed and try to sleep."

"Take some tea with honey and lemon. It'll help your throat."

"I'll do that, Doctor. Anything else?"

"You can be real mean," he said, again sounding wounded.

"I get that way when someone breaks into my house," she said sullenly.

"I do want to help, Rebecca."

"Thank you very much," she said, worn out. "I'm going to say good-bye and hang up now. Is that all right?"

"Don't be mad at me. Okay?"

"I'm not mad at you. Okay?"

"Take it easy, Beck."

"I'm hanging up now."

"Hope you feel better," he said.

"Good-bye," she said, and put the receiver down. Sitting with her head in her hands, she cried some more, then tiredly got up to put on the kettle, the feeling she was being watched more pronounced than ever.

CHAPTER

Twelve

Rebecca stood looking out at the dozen or so boats moored at the condominium's private marina three stories below. The majority of the slips were vacant, the boats undoubtedly already in storage for the winter. Turning, she surveyed the large airy living room: a black marble fireplace, nine-foot ceilings, pristine off-white carpeting, and matching verticals, now drawn open, on the two glass walls that afforded a spectacular view. From where she stood, she could see through the dining room to the eat-in kitchen.

She and her mother had made one tour of the place with the real estate broker; now the woman had wisely taken herself off to the lobby to wait, and Evelyn was having a long look at the master suite with its huge mirrored bathroom and enormous dressing room/closet.

Rebecca turned back again to view the dark choppy waters of the Sound beneath the heavily overcast early evening sky. How long was she going to be able to continue the routines of her life while pretending to everyone but Agnes that nothing out of the ordinary was happening? She was laboring to maintain a surface of normalcy while afraid every morning just to open her eyes. Her sleep was ravaged by increasingly grotesque dreams. Her suspicion was miasmatic, insidious. She couldn't stop studying the kids at school, trying to determine which of those bland young faces was the clever mask concealing a decaying mind. Sudden laughter in the staff room had her examining her associates; loud noises caused her heart to thud sickeningly.

"So what do you think?" her mother asked from the foyer.

"What do *you* think?" Rebecca countered, plastering a smile on her face.

"I asked you first." Evelyn stood with her eyes fixed expectantly on Rebecca, hands in her jacket pockets, small feet firmly planted close together on the springy, luxurious carpet.

"I think it's fabulous. I love it. But they're asking an awful lot of money."

"Nobody pays the asking price, sweetheart."

"Does that mean you're going to make an offer?"

"Well," Evelyn said, "it's definitely the best of the ones we've seen."

"That is absolutely true."

"I could fit most of my furniture in here."

"That is also true." Rebecca's smile was now entirely spontaneous and filled with affection.

"Naturally, I'd have everything done over, reupholstered."

"Naturally," Rebecca agreed.

"The second bedroom would make a nice den."

"With the sofa bed so the grandchildren could sleep over."

Evelyn shook her head. "You'll probably sleep over," she

said. "Or Bertha, after one of her hot dates with another decrepit old poop from the Singles Club. But grandchildren? Risk exposing those babies to someone who hates alfalfa sprouts and who buys senior's tickets at the movies? Uhn-uh. Don't hold your breath."

"Buy this place, Mom! You'll love it here. Even the garage is nice. Hot- and cold-running doormen, valet service, a built-in Jacuzzi. It's heaven."

"I'll think about it," Evelyn said, pushing her toe into the carpet as if examining its depth. "I will definitely think about it."

Rebecca looked over at her mother, wanting all at once to run and throw herself into her mother's arms, tell her what was happening to her life. For a few moments she had the completely arbitrary idea that her mother could rescue her, could make everything right. Instead, she said, "I met kind of an interesting guy this week."

"So you finally got rid of the married one," Evelyn said brightly. "Let's go eat, and you can fill me in."

"What're you going to tell the broker?" Rebecca asked her in the elevator.

"I'll tell her I'm going to think about it. What does this new one do? And please don't say he's in the middle of a divorce."

"I don't know what he's in the middle of," Rebecca said. She'd assumed he was single, and she could just hear Jason saying assuming was a no-no. "He's a detective, if you can believe it."

"Now you're going out with Sam Spade?" Evelyn looked askance at her.

"More like Sam Spade's whacky great-nephew. And I didn't say we were going out. I just said I met him."

"From meeting to going out is a hop, skip, and a jump."

"Nobody's doing any hopping or skipping. Not yet anyway," Rebecca said as they arrived in the lobby, where the real estate broker was waiting.

"You get a certain look when you're interested in someone," Evelyn said, scanning Rebecca's face as the broker came hurrying over.

"A lovely place, isn't it?" the woman asked eagerly.

"Lovely," Evelyn agreed. "Overpriced, but lovely."

"They'll negotiate, of course."

"How long has it been on the market?" Evelyn wanted to know.

The woman referred to the listing. "A while," she said. "Close to six months."

"So I'm not the only one who thinks it's overpriced."

"Look," the woman said reasonably. "Make an offer. They can only say no, or make a counteroffer. I doubt very much they're going to give you a flat-out no, not in this market. Anyway, it's only an offer, not a final commitment. Take your time, think about it."

"Make an offer, Mom," Rebecca urged, liking the broker's soft-sell, commonsense approach.

"I'll think about it," Evelyn said again.

Rebecca and the broker smiled at each other.

"I'll run the two of you back to your car," the woman said good-naturedly. "Take your time. If it's been on the market for six months, it'll stay on a while longer. It's a big decision, I know. Don't rush into anything. If you want to come back for another look, just call me."

"What's going on, Rebecca?" her mother asked.

"What d'you mean?"

"You hardly ate a thing," Evelyn said, tucking her legs under her on the sofa. "That's always a sure sign something's up with you."

"I've got a cold—"

"You've had worse and still managed to eat. You also look completely worn out. I've never seen you like this."

"Well, I *am* tired," Rebecca admitted.

"Don't waltz me around, sweetheart. Nobody's ever going to know you better than I do. And the Rebecca I know doesn't mope around, staring out the windows of overpriced condominiums; she doesn't go out for dinner, order nothing but an appetizer and then not even eat it. And where does my daughter go to meet a *detective,* of all people?" she asked with a smile that invited an exchange of confidences.

"I've got a lot on my plate at the moment," Rebecca said, torn between a desire to unburden herself and an aversion to placing that burden on her mother.

"Show me anyone who doesn't," Evelyn said dismissively.

"I think Agnes is having some kind of a breakdown," she began, thinking she might slowly work up to the rest of it.

"What if I tell you that it doesn't surprise me," Evelyn said.

"It doesn't?"

"Listen, sweetheart. Much as I like the woman, she's always struck me as someone who would rather walk naked through a fire than discuss her true feelings. She . . . performs. It's charming. But I don't know how many times I've been tempted to say, 'So, Agnes, how are you really? *Who* are you really?' It's as if a long time ago she decided her primary asset was her ability to be entertaining. So that's what she does. She looks wonderful; she's very clever. But if you asked me to define Agnes for someone who'd never met her, I couldn't do it. Eight years she's been coming with you to visit once a month or so, and I couldn't begin to guess what the woman's thinking or feeling. So when you tell me she seems to be having a breakdown, I have to say, in all honesty, Rebecca, it doesn't come as a great surprise."

"Well, *you* sure surprise *me*," Rebecca said.

"That's because you only think of me as your mother and not as a person who's been alive in the world for sixty-seven years. Nobody who has her eyes closed could keep a marriage afloat for thirty-eight years, and raise three children, too. Besides, people like Agnes are intriguing. You live in Connecticut long enough and you forget there's a whole other world out there"—she swung her arm in an arc—"filled with peculiar characters. When Agnes comes through my front door, she brings that world with her. She may have lived in this country for a long time, but she's always going to be foreign, and she's always going to be different. I enjoy her. I like her. I know she's very fond of you. And I don't think she's got a mean bone in her body. I'm sorry to hear she's in trouble, but as I said, I'm not surprised. Now, tell me what's really bothering you."

"Well, I am very worried about her," Rebecca insisted, struggling not to yield to her mother's invitation.

"Are you pregnant?" Evelyn asked.

"God, no!" Rebecca laughed.

Evelyn shrugged. "Don't make it sound impossible. It's been known to happen."

"It's not happening to me. Okay?"

"What *is*, then?" Evelyn persevered.

"Someone's been vandalizing the house," Rebecca confessed, too worn down to resist any longer.

"So you went to the police and that's how you met the detective," Evelyn filled in. "What kind of vandalism?"

Rebecca pushed off her shoes, drew her knees up to her chest and wound her arms tightly around them. "It started with this person, whoever it is, cutting off every last flower in my garden. It's gone on from there."

"Gone on to what?" Evelyn asked, registering some alarm.

"Almost every day there's something else. He painted the

skylights black, sent things to me at school. He's probably the one who let the air out of my tire, too, now that I think about it." She paused, deciding it wouldn't be wise to tell her mother about the LSD or the fact that he'd managed to get inside the house. "I've been to the police and been told there's nothing they can do. The officer I talked to looked at me as if I'm crazy, the implication being that I'm doing these things myself to get attention."

Evelyn looked appalled. "How long's this been going on?"

"A week or so."

"And the police won't do anything about it?"

"There's no evidence," Rebecca said wearily. "Nothing's been stolen. I can't prove any of it. I made the mistake of throwing away the things that were sent to the school. And I also cleaned the paint off the skylights. From their point of view, it's all stuff I could easily have done. Except, of course, that I'm never there when it happens."

"Maybe it's your married boyfriend," Evelyn suggested.

"Separated," Rebecca corrected automatically. "It's possible. Except this started before I broke it off with him."

"He could still be the one. How much do you actually know about the man?"

Rebecca rested her chin on her knees and gazed at her mother. "How much does anybody ever actually know anyone else?"

"Okay. You've got a point. But what do you know about him?"

Embarrassed, Rebecca had to admit, "Not a whole lot."

"Just what I thought. So, tell me. What's this detective going to do about it?"

"I don't know. He promised he'd look into it. Talk about characters! You should meet Jason," she laughed. "He actually wanted to come along tonight."

"So why didn't you bring him?"

"Mother, I could hardly bring along someone I just met."

"So bring him on Sunday," Evelyn said. "I want to have a look at this one. He sounds like fun."

"You mean it?"

"Sure. Why not?"

"I'll think about it. I really should be going. I'm tired, and this cold's moved into my chest. You know, when your lungs feel as if they're slowly filling with wet cement?"

"Maybe you should pack a bag and move in here with me for a while, let me look after you. For all you know, you could have pneumonia."

"I'm sure it's not pneumonia. And I'd love to have you look after me, but it's impossible."

"Now I'll be worrying about you," Evelyn said unhappily.

"That's why I didn't want to tell you."

"I want your promise that you'll get out of that house and come stay here with me if this doesn't stop soon."

"I wish I could buy one of those condos we saw this evening, one of the smaller ones in that last building with the gorgeous view. I'd love it."

"Put the house up for sale and buy one."

"Let's get you organized first," Rebecca said, crossing the room to give her mother a hug. "Make an offer on that apartment, Mom. It's perfect for you."

"I told you I'll think about it. And while I'm thinking, you do some yourself. I could always help you out if you decide you want to move. Besides, I wouldn't mind having you right in the same building."

"You'd have to vow never to come to my place without phoning first."

"So you would consider it." Evelyn beamed at her.

"Yes, ma'am, I sure would."

"You bring that Jason on Sunday. I want to meet this detective."

"I'll see," Rebecca told her. "He's pretty strange, you know."

"That won't be anything new. You have a long-term affinity for strange people."

Rebecca laughed and gave her mother another hug.

She pulled into the driveway and sat, keeping the motor running and the headlights on, while she reviewed her actions before leaving the house that morning. "Damn it!" She pounded her fist on the steering wheel. She'd forgotten to leave the outdoor floodlights on. The house and grounds were completely dark, and she couldn't bring herself to get out of the car. She knew it was probably ridiculous, but she had the idea that she'd be in terrible danger the moment she left the relative safety of the Jetta. She sat for several minutes, telling herself to turn off the engine and go into the house, but she couldn't do it. The longer she sat there, the more frightened she became, her pulse quickening, her mouth going dry.

Finally she reversed out of the driveway and drove back up the Post Road to the pay phone outside the convenience store.

The answering machine picked up on the second ring. "This is Jason. Either I'm not home or I just don't feel like talking. You pays your nickel and you takes your chances."

At the beep, Rebecca said, "I'm taking my chance. This is Rebecca. I hope you're home, because—"

"Hey! You're calling. I knew you liked me," Jason overrode the machine.

"I'm calling," she said, praying he'd take her seriously, "because I forgot to leave any lights on when I left the house this morning, and I know it's stupid but I'm actually afraid to go in there."

"Where are you?"

"At the pay phone outside the convenience store on the Post Road."

"No prob. Give me ten minutes. I'll meet you at your place."

"God!" she said tremulously. "Thank you."

He arrived in exactly ten minutes.

"You stay in the car," he told her. "Give me the keys. I'll do a check, make sure everything's okay."

She did as he asked, watching as he let himself in, then went through every room turning lights on. Three minutes and he was at the back door motioning to her to come.

"Nice house," he said as she hung her coat in the mudroom. "Couldn't find the switches for the outside lights."

"They're in here." She pointed out the switches in the mudroom.

"You want to look around, see if there's something I missed?"

"Whoever's doing these things isn't that subtle," she said. "I really appreciate this, Jason."

"Courtesy of the department," he said with a mock bow.

"Would you like something to drink, coffee or a Coke?"

"Sure. Coffee would be swell."

"You talk like an old black-and-white," she accused with a smile, overwhelmed by relief, and grateful to him.

"They made great flicks back then. You look kind of wilted, Rebecca."

"I feel wilted." Ongoing fear kept her on the edge of exhaustion.

"So, how was the condo shopping with your mother?" He sat down on one of the stools at the center island.

"I think she's going to make an offer." She finished measuring grounds into the paper filter, poured water into the coffeemaker, then leaned against the counter and with sudden boldness said, "My mother's invited you to come to lunch on Sunday."

"Hey!" he grinned. "You told your mother about me. This is real progress."

He was wearing gray sweats, the Nike Airs, and an ancient leather bomber jacket. It was odd, but he already seemed very familiar to her, as if they'd known each other for years.

"Do you own any shoes?" she asked, thinking how much safer she felt with him in the house.

"I certainly do. I have a pair of Topsiders, and I also have a pair of black-patent evening shoes. They were my dad's. They've got nifty little bows on the front. I'm waiting for just the right occasion to wear them. You got any good shoes?"

She laughed. "Nothing as good as that."

"The message is, I should show up looking spiffy for Sunday lunch. Right?"

"You actually want to come?"

"Absolutely. Sunday lunch with Mom? I wouldn't miss that on a bet."

"There'll be my two brothers and their families, too. What writers do you like?"

"I read strictly mysteries. You want names?"

"How do you feel about South American authors?"

"They don't write mysteries, I don't read them."

Again she smiled. "Good."

"You've got some problem with South Americans?"

"You honestly want to come on Sunday?"

"Definitely. Mom wants to check me out, huh?"

"It doesn't mean anything, so don't get your hopes up."

"It does so mean something," he disagreed. "You like me."

"You're not married or anything, are you?"

He stared at her for several seconds, then said, "Nice people you've been hanging out with, Beck. I don't do shit like that."

"Good." She turned to watch the coffee drip into the pot. "You'll like my mother."

"I already like your mother." With both elbows propped on the counter, his chin cupped in his hands, he said, "I figure if the kids get your hair and eyes, my height, and an average of our combined intelligence, they'll be dynamite."

"What?"

"You're doing that deaf thing again," he said in a warning tone.

"What?"

"Hey! When you came charging into the station and verbally laid out old Lenny, I knew you were the woman for me. 'I suppose you drove around town stuffing mailboxes with cherry bombs, and defecating on peoples' doormats, neat stuff like that,' " he quoted.

"It was good," she smiled, "wasn't it? I get very articulate when I'm angry. Do I have anything to say on the matter?"

"You have something to say about everything, so far as I can tell," he said equably. "I like that."

"You get one cup of coffee, then you're out of here," she declared.

"You're crazy about me. You can't wait to see me in my black-patent dancing shoes."

"Right! I've been waiting all my life for that," she laughed.

"Yes, you have," he asserted.

"Yes. Well, before I forget, thank you for coming over. I really am very grateful. It's stupid, but I was scared to get out of the car."

"It's not stupid. What you want to do is get an electrician to put your outside lights on a timer. That way you won't have to worry about coming back to a dark house."

"Good idea. I'll do that."

"I've got more good ideas than you ever dreamed of."

"I'll bet."

"You sure are the prettiest woman I've ever seen."

"You've obviously had limited life experiences." Surprised to find her hands unsteady, she poured coffee into a mug, then opened the refrigerator, saying, "You take cream and sugar, don't you?"

"See!" he said. "If you weren't crazy about me, you wouldn't have remembered something so significant."

"Drink this and go home!" She put the mug down in front of him.

"What if I drink it v-e-r-y slowly?"

She closed her eyes for a moment and gave a little shake of her head, thinking he was right. She really did like him. How the hell had this happened? She opened her eyes and said, "I'm a tired little camper, Jason. Be a good scout and drink your coffee, then go home."

"Can I come to dinner and the movies with you and Agnes tomorrow night?"

"No, you cannot. God! You and my mother, you only have to hear a name once and you remember it for life."

"Ah! You told her my name, didn't you? You really really like me. It's going to be rough waiting until Sunday."

"You'll survive somehow."

"Like to play it tough, don't you, cookie? But underneath, you're a marshmallow."

"Right." She rolled her eyes, marveling over her ability to react normally to the things he said and did while just below the surface, fear played hellish games with her nerve endings.

"Good coffee. Can you cook, too?"

"Yes, I can cook. Finish that and go home!"

Before he left, he gave her another wonderful hug. She thought she could easily develop a dependency on his willingness to give them. She put his cup in the sink, then went upstairs, leaving all the downstairs lights on.

Pete stayed flat on his belly in the crawl space, listening to the muffled voices overhead, convinced any second they'd twig to the fact he was down there. Sweating, imagining spiders were climbing all over him, he buried his face in his arms wishing he'd never been dumb enough to think of coming into the bitch's house when he couldn't be sure she wouldn't walk in on him. Goddamned lucky he'd heard the car pull in, otherwise he'd have been nailed. Opened that trapdoor and dived down the ladder like a shot, being careful not to let the heavy mother slam.

He was totally freaked, lying in the dark in the god-damned dirt with the bitch and some guy up there yakking away. Too bad he couldn't make out what they were saying. Shit! He could be stuck in this creepy hole for hours and his mother would go off her head, wanting reasons for why he didn't phone in. Pitch fucking black down here. The furnace rumbling away. It felt like forever, and he hated the dark, totally hated it. Man!

Footsteps. He raised his head, listening. The guy was going. About goddamned time. Straining, he heard a car engine start up outside. Then more footsteps in the kitchen. What if she decided to sit up and catch the late show? The bitch had a cold. He willed her to head upstairs and sack out. If he had to, he could sneak out through the storm doors. But then if she checked and found them unlocked, she'd know he'd been in the house. She'd figure it all out, and he didn't want that. He wanted to hang on to his little secret element. Jesus! He couldn't hear a thing now. Where the hell was she?

His neck was getting all kinked, so he dropped his head back down on his arms. He'd just have to wait a while longer. Couldn't even see the face of his watch to check the time. Maybe he'd plant a few handy items down here in a corner where nobody would see them. A box of matches, a flashlight, some tools, stuff that'd come in handy.

Finally, after what had to be at least an hour, he had to chance it. He didn't need his mother getting all bent out of shape and grounding him again. That'd totally wreck the pay-back. He squirmed out of the narrow opening and lowered himself to the floor, feeling his way past the hole for the sump pump. Last thing he needed was to fall into a god-damned hole full of water.

He cautiously pushed the trapdoor open a crack, then closed it at once. All the fucking lights were on! Man! He felt like he was going to have a heart attack or something, he was so freaked. She was supposed to be in bed, for chrissake! What the hell were all the lights doing on? Shit! He squatted at the foot of the ladder, trying to think. His heart was going like crazy. He needed to cool out, get it back together. Where'd he put that last Valium? He patted his pockets, started checking each one, found the pill almost lost in the corner of his shirt pocket. He dry-swallowed the little sucker, then leaned against the ladder, waiting.

At last he felt okay again, calm and in charge. Back up the ladder to crack open the trapdoor. The lights still on, but he couldn't hear a thing. Nothing. The bitch was trying to fake him out. She'd hit the sheets, but left all the lights on. He climbed up into the kitchen, then very slowly lowered the trapdoor. Keeping down, he crept into the kitchen, his eyes going back and forth from the spiral staircase to the living room as he crept to the bottom of the staircase and looked up. No lights on up there. Bingo.

Nothing planned, he inched up the staircase until he could see into the bedroom. There she was, out like a light. He could do any fucking thing he wanted downstairs and she'd never know. Remaining motionless, he listened to the wheezy sound of her breathing, slow and steady. He was halfway tempted to go right the way up there, do a number on her while she was sleeping. But then he thought about his mother going out of her head and decided the timing sucked.

Back down the stairs, he crept into the mudroom and made for the door. Using his shirttail, he turned the spring lock, then got hold of the knob, turned and pulled open the door, looking over his shoulder every other second at the kitchen.

He used his shirt again on the outside knob and very, very slowly got the door closed. The lock clicked and his goddamned heart started going nuts again. For all he knew, the least little sound could wake up the bitch. He slipped around the back of the house, making for the shrubberies, where it was darkest. Then, keeping low, moving like a fucking Indian scout, he hauled ass out of there, running fast and silent to the road. A few hundred yards and there was the wagon, right where he'd left it. He scooted into the front seat, jammed the key into the ignition, threw the sucker into gear and cruised away.

He couldn't believe it when he checked the time on the console clock. It wasn't even midnight! Here he thought he'd been in that rotten crawl space for hours and it'd been maybe forty minutes max. He tooled up the Post Road to the Mc-Donald's drive-thru, grabbed a coffee and drank it as he headed for the service center on I-95. He'd crank up on some uppers, get some amphetamines from the long-distance guys. Then he'd work out what he wanted to hit the bitch with next. Shit! All that time in the goddamned crawl space with bugs and spiders all over him. His skin felt itchy. He rubbed his face hard with his free hand.

CHAPTER

Thirteen

Early Saturday morning after seven and a half hours of sleep that in no way eased either her nervousness or her feeling of debilitation, Rebecca went out to get a newspaper, then came back to the house and called the electrician. She made an appointment to have him come Wednesday evening to put the outdoor lights on a timer, then hung up and was about to pour a fresh cup of coffee when the telephone rang. It was Ray.

"I've been thinking about you," he said with effusive warmth, "missing you. How are you, Rebecca?"

"I'm fine," she replied stiffly. "Thank you for the flowers. How are you?"

A pause, then hesitantly he said, "That was a while back, but you're welcome. How am I? I'm bored, lonely for you."

In the ensuing silence she once again wondered if he could possibly be responsible for the ongoing incursions into her life. He certainly sounded as if he was lying about the flowers.

"I'd really like to see you," he said at last. "I *need* to see you."

"I don't think so, Ray. There's no reason for us to see each other. I'm not going to change my mind."

"How do you know that?" he asked plaintively. "How can you decide from one day to the next to throw away everything we've got going?"

"It wasn't an overnight decision," she said, trying to sound calm in spite of the awkwardness he was making her feel. "In my opinion we don't have anything going."

"Why are you being such a bitch? You're not giving me any kind of a chance."

Heat and anger swept over her. Having temporary difficulty breathing, she firmly put the receiver down.

Grabbing her mug, she crossed the kitchen to get more coffee, then leaned against the counter looking over at the phone. Maybe Ray *was* her tormentor. Maybe, as Jason had suggested, he'd intended to create some drama with the idea in mind of playing the hero. It wasn't working, so now he was trying to heighten the drama and thereby punish her for failing to act out her assigned role. Except . . . he hadn't believed the episode with her morning paper. He couldn't have faked that. And he had sounded genuinely confused about the flowers. Plus there was no way he could have got into the school. She didn't know what to think.

The telephone rang again and she tensed, afraid it was Ray calling back. She didn't want to get into a telephone battle with him, and wished she had an answering machine so she could screen her calls. She was probably one of the few holdouts in all of North America.

She said a wary hello, and relaxed at the sound of her mother's voice.

"Are you any better?" Evelyn asked.

"Oh, I'm much better," she lied. "I had a good long sleep. What're you up to?"

Evelyn gave an edgy, excited laugh and said, "I spoke to that broker, Mrs. Dunbar, this morning."

"Did you make an offer on the condo?"

"I did," Evelyn said, sounding girlish and somewhat dazed. "I thought the woman was going to have a heart attack, I came in so low. But if there's one thing I learned from your father, it's to come in at the bottom." Evelyn laughed again. "Nothing to lose, right? The broker hemmed and hawed, then said what the hell, and phoned the people."

Rebecca looked over at the clock on the stove. It was almost nine-thirty. "Nothing like wheeling and dealing first thing in the morning. So what happened?"

"They counteroffered, then I did. Back and forth. They finally accepted my last offer."

"You got it! That's fantastic!"

"Now I'm a nervous wreck. In the meantime, Mrs. Dunbar's already been over with a binder on the offer. This is all going so fast!"

"That's probably best," Rebecca said. "Knowing you, if you have too much time to think, you won't do anything. This is great, Mom. And by the way, Jason's going to come with me tomorrow."

"Well, well. It ought to be quite an afternoon. You really like the apartment, Rebecca? You don't think I'm crazy?"

"I *love* it, and you're the least crazy person I know."

"Okay," Evelyn said doubtfully. "Listen, I've got to run. I have to call Ned Givens. I just hope he hasn't changed his mind. I'll see you and Sam Spade tomorrow."

After the call, Rebecca tried to read the newspaper while she finished her coffee, but couldn't concentrate. Things *were* happening very quickly—not just her mother's selling the house and buying a condo, but also with Jason. Yet there was an ease and spontaneity to her dealings with him that she'd never experienced with other men. When she was with him, she felt completely safe, and entirely sane.

She sighed and gave up on the newspaper. Once her mother sold the house, any possibility of ever going home again would be sold with it. Not that it was something she was likely to do. But always in the back of her mind was the knowledge that she had a place to which she could return. Now that place would belong to others. The sale of the house meant the end of an era. She couldn't help feeling a pang, reviewing the eighteen years she'd spent growing up in that enormous old clapboard colonial.

Still, this was right for her mother. Things did change, whether or not you wanted them to, and everyone adapted. Plus, she reminded herself, she was the one who'd been urging her mother to move. She just wished she could also be moving into a bright, secure condominium.

She tried to reach Agnes to confirm their plans for that evening, got the answering machine and hung up without bothering to leave a message. Going out to do some shopping, she smiled at the storm of golden leaves swirling in gusts in the sunlight. So much for the meteorologists and their gloomy predictions. The sky was a perfect cloudless blue; not a hint of rain. The air was tangy with wood smoke, crisp and refreshing. Out of doors, relishing the sights and smells of autumn, she was able to be optimistic. Ray would soon leave her alone. The attacks on her rationality would stop. And she'd met a man who could make her laugh and who wanted to be seen with her in public. Her life would be just fine if it weren't for the fact that someone was trying to drive her insane. *Leave me alone!* she begged silently. *Just leave me alone!*

Pete woke up and went reeling into the bathroom. He felt lousy, head pounding and a rotten taste in his mouth, cramps in his gut. He needed some coffee, a blast of caffeine to get him going.

He goes into the kitchen and his mother's sitting there

dressed to the teeth, with her smokes. The ashtray's already crammed with butts. She's doing the crossword puzzle in the *Times* magazine. In ink. It's the highlight of her week. Every Saturday morning she's like a kid at Christmas, over a god-damned puzzle. It's pathetic. He grabs a mug and pours some coffee, chugs a big mouthful, then stands by the counter waiting for it to kick in.

His mother puts down her pen. She's got this look, and he thinks Oh, shit! What did he do now?

She goes, "Do you know what time it is?"

And he goes, "It's Saturday. What's the big deal? Five days a week I'm up before it's even light. Weekends I get to sleep in."

"Not till one in the afternoon," she goes, like it's the first time he ever slept late and it's this personal injury he's in-flicted on her. She's still giving him the look and he plays it innocent, chugs some more of her wicked brew. Man! How can she drink six, eight cups of this stuff a day?

"I'm fed up with it," she goes, firing up a cigarette and squinting at him through the smoke. "You stay up half the night, then sleep the day away. Your room's a pigsty. And when do you plan on doing your homework?"

"Hey!" he goes, offended. "I cleaned my room. And I've got all day tomorrow for homework. What's your problem?"

Her voice gets all deadly, and she goes, "Don't you *dare* talk to me that way! Who the *hell* do you think you are, talking to me that way?"

"What way?" he goes, wishing he'd wake up one morn-ing and find her dead. He wants it so badly he can even picture the funeral.

"I'm sick of your attitude. I'm sick of you."

"What's the deal here?" he goes. "I didn't do anything."

"Where were you last night?"

"What d'you mean, where was I? I was out. I checked in with you, or don't you remember?"

She freaks. He's standing there with his coffee, trying to have a conversation with her, and she totally freaks. It's just like the time with the knitting needle. She snaps, and flies at him like some kind of goddamned lunatic. Just hauls off and whacks him hard across the side of the head. The coffee sloshes all over his hands, but he hangs on to the mug like maybe he'll crush it.

"I'm sick of you!" she shrieks, standing there with her face jammed into his.

He can't believe she walloped him. His head's on fire. "You don't hit me," he goes, putting the mug down on the counter, coffee dripping everywhere. "You don't *ever* hit me!" He could kill her, he hates her so much. "I'm not a little kid you can hit."

"Where did you get these?" she goes, pulling a Baggie out of her pocket. She's been in his room again, nosing around, and she's found a stash. Now he's really mad.

"None of your goddamned business," he goes, daring her to try to hit him again. Just let her try. He'll deck her. His fists are all ready for it. "Where d'you get off anyway, going through my private stuff?"

"As long as you live in *my* house, it's my *right!*" she yells, waving the bag in his face. "What *are* these anyway?" she goes, holding the bag up. He glances at it, sees a couple of Valiums, some speed. Maybe eight pills max.

"Vitamins. Okay?" He goes to grab for the bag and she spins around, dumps the pills in the garbage disposal and hits the switch. "Oh, right!" he goes. "Good move. Jesus H. Christ!"

She swings around like she's going to wallop him again, and he goes, "Don't even *think* about it! You try it again and I'll flatten you."

Her eyes go all big like she can't believe what she's hearing, and she turns off the disposal. "You're a monster," she goes.

"Right. Whatever." He starts off back to his room.

"You're an animal!"

"Whatever," he goes, under his breath. "And you're a fucking head case."

"What did you say?"

He turns back and goes, "Nothing. I'm going to my room now. Okay?"

She gives him this look like she wishes he'd die, and he thinks that's fine. It makes them even. "You want to ground me for life?" he goes. "Go ahead. I don't give a shit." He's actually getting a headache from that whack she gave him, and he'd like to hit the sheets again, but he knows there's no way she'll let that happen.

He's waiting for her to say he's grounded, but she doesn't say a thing, just stands there with her face all twisted up and her mouth open. "Get out of my sight!" she goes. "And clean that room, or I'll burn everything in it."

"Yeah, right! Like you'll burn the place down. Sure." He goes back to his room, slams the door. Burned his goddamned hands with the coffee. Son of a bitch! Imagine thinking she can go hitting him! He's so mad he'd like to break stuff, smash the place to shit. His pillow's on the floor and he drop-kicks it across the room, then locks himself into the bathroom. He's got this killer headache, he needs a Valium and some goddamned aspirin. He feels like killing someone and has to force himself to unclench his fists to open the medicine cabinet.

While he's in the shower, he decides he'll cruise the bitch's house tonight. If she's not there, he'll leave her a big surprise. He's in a mood to do serious damage. He wishes now he'd pulled a number on her while she was sleeping. He can see himself doing all kinds of shit like tying her up, stuffing a load of Kleenex in her mouth, then ripping off her fucking nightgown.

Back from her shopping, Rebecca inspected the house inside and out, then spent fifteen minutes hooking up the answering machine. Trying to think of a suitable outgoing message took longer. At last she recorded a typical wait-for-the-tone message, then stood back, willing the phone to ring, anxious to screen a call. Of course, nothing happened. Standing in the kitchen looking at the machine, she wished she had some kind of system—some esoteric, hi-tech gizmo—that would not only tell her when somebody had been in the house but could also identify the intruder.

God! She was becoming completely paranoid. She didn't dare even open the shutters or curtains in broad daylight for fear of being spied upon. Somewhat enervated by the unavoidable fact that she was being forced to behave in ways that were counter to her instincts, she went to the guest room to make a start on the work she wouldn't have time to do on Sunday.

Mercifully, she was able to lose herself in her work. When the phone rang at ten to two, she got up automatically to answer, remembered the machine, and waited to hear who was calling. It was her mother. She picked up, saying, "Hi. I'm here."

"Since when," Evelyn asked, "do you have an answering machine?"

"Since today. It's great. Maybe I'll buy one for you, too."

"That's the last thing I need, thank you. My God!" she exclaimed. "This is turning out to be quite a day."

"What now?"

"You won't believe it."

"You sold the house!" Rebecca guessed.

"Sweetheart," her mother said, "when we bought this place in nineteen forty-five, your father and I paid twenty-seven thousand. This afternoon I sold it for an absolute fortune. I'm in a state of shock."

"I'm sure you are. When do you close?"

"Thirty days. How am I going to get everything done in so little time?"

"Easily," Rebecca assured her. "You'll see."

"Ned Givens is paying cash," Evelyn said wonderingly, "and giving the kids a personal mortgage, with almost no down payment."

"It's basically what you and Dad did for us," Rebecca reminded her.

"I'm going to sit down and have a drink," Evelyn said. "Maybe a double. Then I'll call your Aunt Bertha to give her the news. It might take her mind off men for a few minutes. Tell me I'm doing the right thing," she said nervously.

"You're doing exactly the right thing. I'm very happy for you." It was true. She was happy for her mother. So why did she feel like breaking into tears? Why was she so choked she could hardly speak?

"I don't know," Evelyn sighed. "I keep remembering when newspapers were three cents and steak was fifty-nine cents a pound. It's ridiculous."

"It's great," Rebecca insisted staunchly. "Go have your drink. And congratulations."

The phone rang again just before four. Rebecca listened from the guest room as Ray sputtered for a moment, then said, "I didn't know you got a machine. Listen, I want to apologize for this morning. I was way out of line. I, uhm. Jesus! I hate these machines. I just want to say I'm sorry. We really have to talk, Rebecca, at least say good-bye properly. I'm off to St. Louis, but I'll call you Monday night. I'm sorry as hell about this morning. Don't hold it against me, please."

She erased and reset the tape, then tried once more to call Agnes, but again got her machine, and again she didn't bother to leave a message. Just as she was sitting back down at the desk, the telephone rang once more. This time it was Jason.

"We still on for tomorrow?" he asked. "Because I've got my shoes all ready to go."

She laughed, taken off guard by how happy she was to hear from him. "We're still on."

"Swell. What time should I pick you up?"

"Twelve," she said. "What's all that noise?"

"Cops, radios, citizens, suspected felons. The usual stuff. You have a great telephone voice. You know that?"

"Thank you."

"I've gotta hit the road now. See you noon tomorrow, toots."

Rebecca turned on every light inside and outside of the house, then picked up her keys. She was actually reluctant to leave. As long as she stayed indoors, nothing would happen. But the moment she went out, she was open to a fresh attack. She had to get a grip on herself. She couldn't and wouldn't become housebound, but she now had a new understanding of why some people, particularly the elderly, chose to stay cooped up inside their homes. Fear was an insidious crippler. It could incapacitate you if you let it.

"You're not going to turn me into a recluse!" she declared, and marched purposefully to the back door.

She was feeling quite pleased with herself as she knocked at Agnes's door, then waited. She was about to knock again when the door opened and Agnes revealed herself, naked under a heavy black-silk Chinese robe hanging unbelted from her shoulders.

Wondering if the madness she'd been experiencing wasn't somehow contagious, and resisting an impulse to glance around to be sure no one else could see, Rebecca forced a smile, saying, "We had a date. Did you forget?" She felt scared. Was Agnes having a breakdown? Or was she?

"Did we?" Agnes looked blankly at her for a moment,

then turned from the door, the robe swirling away from her long bare legs.

"We did," Rebecca confirmed, stepping inside and closing the door as Agnes went through the living room toward her bedroom.

Rebecca left her coat and bag on the couch, then proceeded uncertainly to the bedroom, where Agnes was standing studying herself in the full-length mirror on the back of the closet door. Temporarily speechless, Rebecca watched as Agnes turned first one way, then the other, critically inspecting her image. She hardly seemed aware of Rebecca. It was scary.

"It's all shot," Agnes said flatly, gazing at herself. "It's truly ironic," she said, executing a turn, then looking back over her shoulder at the mirror, "that one never appreciates what one has until it's gone forever."

Feeling oddly distanced from the scene before her, Rebecca wondered if it was possible to become inured to abstractions, to the bizarre. "You're wrong," she said critically. "You have a beautiful body."

It was true. Agnes's limbs were graceful and lean, her waist and hips narrow, her breasts full and well shaped. She had the body of a much younger woman. Rebecca was fascinated by what was happening. It was almost like watching a foreign film without subtitles, so that she was obliged to guess at the meanings.

"This is strange," she thought aloud, hearing her words bounce off Agnes's resistance like dandelion fluff. All the old rules and codes of behavior no longer applied. Anything could, and evidently would, happen now.

"It is strange," Agnes agreed. "And *you're* wrong. I *had* a beautiful body, firm young flesh. Of course, at the time I didn't realize it. I can see that now, because I do remember very clearly any number of occasions when I accepted a form of . . . homage, I suppose. I mistook it for something else

entirely. I thought it had to do with me, that it was personal."
Slowly she came around, allowing her arms to fall as she once
again faced the mirror.

"How can you be sure it wasn't personal?" Rebecca
asked, catching sight of Teddy seated atop the dresser, his
shiny black eyes seemingly directed at Agnes. She was beginning to hate that toy. It somehow represented everything that
was going wrong.

"Don't be naive, Rebecca." Agnes's eyes met hers in the
mirror. "I find it difficult trying to match up who I was then
with what I've finally come to be. I can't think what happened. Then it comes back to me, and I say to myself, 'Ah,
yes. That's right. That's what it was. Now I remember.' Then
it seems I'm straddling my two lives, not truly committed to
either of them; locked up with the past and struggling not to
let it interfere with my dismal present. I'm sorry I neglected
to make a note of our date." At last she moved away from the
mirror and looked over at Rebecca. "What was it we were
going to do?" She delivered the words distractedly, as if
experiencing great difficulty in returning from her contem-
plation of the past.

Rebecca thought she knew exactly how Agnes felt at that
moment. It was an intuitive comprehension, based completely on her own recent excursions into madness. There
was something strangely comforting in the notion of madness
as a place you could choose to go to seeking sanctuary.
"Nothing major," she answered calmly. "Dinner and a
movie. We can eat in, rent a video if you like. I could pick
up a pizza."

"You seem so young to me," Agnes said with a sad smile,
her head tilting to one side as if viewing Rebecca for the first
time.

"You're not that much older than I am." Rebecca
managed another smile. "And you definitely don't look any
older than I do."

"I've always found your kindness extraordinary. Always. It's why you're such a good teacher, why the kids respond so well to you. You care. You actually care about people. You invariably look for the good in others. It's a wonder you're not disappointed more often."

"You care too," Rebecca said.

Agnes shook her head. "It's been a very long time since any of it mattered."

"There's a big difference between caring and having things matter."

Agnes smiled. "I'm glad you're here," she said, then looked down as if surprised to discover she was exhibiting herself, and belted the robe. "Drink?" she asked.

"Sure." Rebecca stepped aside to allow Agnes to pass. "Are you in the mood for a pizza?"

Agnes stood with the vodka bottle in one hand, Scotch in the other, deliberating. "I suppose so."

"Okay. I'll phone in the order, then zip over and pick it up."

"Seems like a great deal of trouble."

"All right. I'll cook something. What've you got?"

"No idea," Agnes said, headed for the kitchen. "Have a look-see."

The refrigerator was crammed with food. "You've got enough here to feed an army," Rebecca said in awe.

Agnes finished pouring the drinks, saying, "Do you know how few people demonstrate kindness? For the most part it's performance, behaving in a specific fashion because we've heard or read that a given situation requires it. But you are kind, Rebecca."

"I'm just practical, Aggie. You're overstating the case." Rebecca selected some thick-cut loin pork chops from among the many packages of meat. She then pulled out salad vegetables, and some green beans. In the cabinet beside the stove she found a five-pound bag of rice and a bottle of Worcestershire sauce.

Agnes sat down at the table by the window, lit a cigarette, then sipped steadily at her Scotch as she watched Rebecca begin preparing the meal. "I'm forever buying food," she said, "then not bothering to cook it. Do you ever do that?"

"Rarely. I can't afford it. If you don't cook, what do you eat?"

Agnes thought for a few seconds. "Bits and pieces. Cheese, bread, some lettuce, a tomato, tins of soup. Typical single-person fare. I go to the market faithfully every week and load up a basket, promising myself I'll fix a roast, cook up a pot of Bolognese sauce and freeze what I don't eat. I run through a dozen menus in my mind as I go up and down the aisles. A week later I'm filling the trash cans before I set off again for another trip to the market. This is the first time in ages any of what's in there will actually be consumed. Quite a departure from routine."

Rebecca got a baking tray from the drawer under the stove and straightened in time to see Agnes's features melt by degrees from laughter into sadness. Her eyes lowered, and she gazed at the tabletop as if able to see there a chart depicting the route of her life.

"What is it?" Rebecca asked, crossing the room to place her hand over her friend's. "Tell me what's wrong," she coaxed, sliding into one of the chairs while maintaining her hold on Agnes's hand. Her sadness was palpable. Rebecca could feel it enveloping her. Maybe they'd both be suffocated by it. "Talk to me, please," Rebecca begged, resisting the temptation to join Agnes in her misery. It was somehow too easy to surrender. Her every instinct was dictating that not only should she fight to keep a firm grasp on her own emotions, but that she was also obligated to do everything in her power to rescue Agnes.

Agnes seemed not to hear. The cigarette burned down in the ashtray. The ice cubes in her glass made a sudden crackling noise. Then, as if reaching deep into herself to find some buried reserve of strength, she raised her head, looked for a long moment into Rebecca's eyes, and finally smiled. "Ignore me, will you?" she said. "I'm being self-indulgent. It's unforgivable, but try to forgive it. I'm actually hungry," she said, reaching for her drink.

Rebecca stroked the back of Agnes's cool hand, noting the satiny texture of the skin, the length of her fingers, the well-tended nails. She had no clear idea of what to do. She could only wait and hope Agnes might feel more like talking later. "All right," she said. "I'll feed you." She took a swallow of Stoli, got up and went back to the counter. "We'll talk after dinner," she said, peeling the wrapping from the chops.

"If you like," Agnes said, lighting a fresh cigarette. "Although there's really nothing left to talk about."

"There's everything to talk about," Rebecca disagreed, placing the chops in the baking tray. "I haven't told you about Jason yet."

"Oh?" Agnes pushed her hair back behind her ears, crossed her legs, and picked up her glass. "Who is Jason?"

Rebecca began slicing an orange into rings. "He's a detective, of all things."

"You don't say." Agnes gave her a sudden, mischievous smile. "Do tell!"

Rebecca smiled back, amazed that her hands could go about their business fixing the food, and that her face could offer up appropriate expressions, while she was experiencing tremendous apprehension. Agnes was in trouble. They both were. The difference was that in Rebecca's case, the causes were all external. So far as she could tell, the causes in Agnes's case were all internal. God! The way she'd scrutinized herself in the mirror, studying her flesh as if on a tour of an abattoir. Things were out of control here. Rebecca wanted badly to help, but felt utterly unqualified. She was proceeding on pure instinct, trying her best not to say or do anything to throw Agnes further off balance. She was, she suddenly understood, engaged in the performance of a lifetime here. And it was such hard work that every muscle in her body was pulled taut. She wished there was someone she could call to come help, but she couldn't think who. No one she knew was any more qualified than she to deal with this situation. The best and most she could do was go on pretending that nothing out of the ordinary was happening; that it didn't bother her to see Agnes slipping in and out of character, recognizable one minute, a complete and alarmingly detached stranger the next. Why was everything going haywire all at once?

CHAPTER

Fourteen

The rain started shortly before seven that evening. Jason completed the last of the day's paperwork, left the station and picked up coffee and a Whopper at the Burger King drive-thru. As he was approaching Rebecca's house, he saw a late-model Ford station wagon pulling away. What with the rain and the distance, he wasn't able to make the plate number. He also couldn't be sure the wagon had actually been stopped at her house. Half the families in town had station wagons. Still, it was irritating. If he hadn't stopped to grab some food, he might've been in time to see something.

He parked on the Post Road long enough to eat, then drove around the block and left the car in the driveway at 290. The owners were away, had notified the station so the patrol cars could swing by and check out the unoccupied house. Jason had run down the list of absentee owners before leaving the station.

Reaching over to the back seat, he grabbed his black

slicker and struggled into it before climbing out of the car. Then, pulling the collar tight around his neck and keeping close to the fences and shrubbery, he made his way down the road to the edge of Rebecca's property.

Initially he was ticked to find the place in darkness, not a single one of the outside floods on. But when he fished out his Mini-Maglite, he discovered that all the bulbs had been either smashed or, in the case of the lower ones, removed. The carriage lamp by the back door had been ripped right out of the wall and hung dangling by its wires.

As he did a slow careful search of the property, he decided he'd probably missed the son of a bitch by seconds. He wished he'd thought to ask Rebecca for a spare set of keys so he could get inside and have a look around. He hadn't asked because for some dumb reason he hadn't wanted to say he was planning to keep an eye on her house during his off time. Anyway, it was strictly out of line—for all kinds of reasons—to go asking the woman for keys to her house.

She had closed the shutters, drawn the curtains on the downstairs rooms, but not those on the second floor. She'd obviously assumed no one could see in through those windows. Big mistake, he thought, scanning the big copper beech at the rear. Anybody could be up that tree in no time flat to have a good long look through the bedroom windows. He made a mental note to tell her to cover all the windows at night, not just the ground-floor ones.

He directed the small flashlight to his wristwatch. Seven thirty-five. Caldor's was still open. He could zip over, get some floods and be back in half an hour. He stood by the tree looking at the house, debating whether or not to slip the back-door lock and look inside. B and E. He could get busted down to a patrol car for doing it. He was tempted, for Rebecca's sake, but couldn't see risking it. He returned the flashlight to his pocket and worked his way back to the car.

Pete was in the kitchen when a light winking through the shutters caught his eye. He froze, thinking, What the hell? Was it the bitch? A glance to his left showed him the empty driveway. For a second he almost laughed, thinking maybe some crack addict was going to try breaking in. What a howl that'd be! The guy breaks in to find he's got company. Sobering, he watched the light move around to the side of the house. He dropped down behind the center island, calculating the distance to the trapdoor. Ten feet, tops. He can make it in maybe five, six seconds if he has to.

Poking his head around the side of the island, he sees a figure—can't make out if it's male or female—examining the back-door light that he'd ripped out of the wall. He's sweating. Any second the door could open, but if he makes a move, whoever's out there might see him. He's stuck behind the goddamned island. Another peek and the light's gone, the figure's vanished. Man! What's the deal here? There's still stuff left to do but he better not hang around. In some ways he could care less about getting caught, but he wants to be able to come back, keep this thing going, and if he gets caught, that's the end of it. So he scoots across the kitchen, lifts the trapdoor and shinnies down the ladder, one hand letting the door down nice and slow.

He's furious. The job's only half done. He didn't even get to the really good stuff. But he's got to get his ass out of here. No way he's going out the back door. That'd be begging to get nailed. He creeps over to the storm doors and lights a match to see the time. Ten minutes, then he'll get the hell out.

He squats there, listening to the rain pinging off the metal doors, mentally counting off the time, thinking about that scene today with his mother. He gets this totally murderous feeling thinking how she hit him. Unfuckingbelievable!

When the hell was it that things turned to shit at home, how long ago? Years, maybe five or six. A long time ago, for fucking sure. It was kind of gradual, not like from one day to the next or anything. Just this slow kind of changing, with nobody saying anything, but all of them eyeing each other, as if trying to see if everybody knew or was it just them?

This slow change, where they went from talking at breakfast and at dinner to zero conversation. Then to nights when his Dad never made it for dinner. He'd get back late from the city, go tiptoeing through the house like he didn't want anybody knowing what time he got in. Fights, arguments. They kept their voices down so he and Lee wouldn't know they were at each other's throats. Neither one of them saying a word about any of it, not to him or to Lee. Then Lee went off to college and his dad started pushing money at him all the time, and his mom stopped playing tennis, stopped doing much of anything, just did her goddamned knitting while she played couch potato, all dressed up with high heels and shit, glued to the tube.

Was it Leighton who made it all happen? How long had his dad been boinking the bitch, anyway? That hypocritical old fuck! Did his mother know? Was that why she turned into a goddamned head case, taking all her shit out on him? She was lucky he didn't let her have one back, whacking him that way. Man!

He counts to three hundred, then lights another match. Only four minutes. Ah, fuck it! No way he's staying in this dingy goddamned basement with the spiders and shit. He turns the lever to unlock the storm door, raises one side maybe six inches and takes a deep breath of wet air. Doesn't see anyone. Two seconds max and he's out, the door's down, and he's running for the road, wondering who that was back there with the flashlight. Then he thinks, Who gives a shit? And he really has to laugh, imagining the bitch freaking out. It's just too bad he didn't get to finish the gig. But there's all kinds of time. Right now he's losing his high, and he wants the other couple of Dexes he's been saving as a reward for tonight's efforts.

Agnes said several times the meal was delicious, but she ate very little. She seemed more interested in watching Rebecca, and sipped steadily at her Scotch, ignoring the wine Rebecca poured. Rebecca found it difficult to eat, but persevered, determined not to reveal her concern. Between mouthfuls of food she could scarcely swallow, she told Agnes about meeting Jason and about her mother's purchase of the condo. She kept up what amounted to a monologue, thinking she sounded vacuous but lost in terms of what else to do, wondering for a moment if Agnes wasn't perfectly sane and it was she herself who'd slipped over the edge.

Agnes at last pushed her plate aside and toyed with her pack of imported Dunhill cigarettes until Rebecca said, "I don't mind if you smoke. Go ahead."

Agnes continued to turn the red package this way and that, her eyes never leaving Rebecca.

Recalling her mother's comments, Rebecca asked, "Who are you, Agnes? You've never told me anything about yourself or your family."

Agnes continued to gaze at her, but assessingly now. "My father was a politician," she said at length. "Have I never told you that?"

"No."

"Odd," she said. "I thought I had. Never mind. I'm given to understand he was a very good politician. It never interested me. He did, however, greatly interest my mother." The corners of her mouth turned down and her hand went to the glass of Scotch, but she didn't pick it up. "I was an unpleasant surprise to her. A baby at the age of forty-one was the last thing she wanted. His career was the only entity she was inclined to nurture, and she went at it with a vengeance.

"The highlight of my mother's life was the announcement when I was nine of my father's knighthood. To his credit, he wasn't especially taken with himself. I believe he was a sincerely committed man who had faith in the work he did for his constituents. But that woman! She became Lady Benton-Tyrell and never missed an opportunity to let it be known she was 'someone,' even if only by association. An appalling creature." She picked up the glass, took a good swallow, then put it down and lit a cigarette, her eyes once more on Rebecca's.

"You were an only child?" Rebecca asked.

Agnes nodded. "My father was sixty-three when I was born. Too old, really, to take any active sort of role in my upbringing. He was always very kind, very interested in whatever I had to say. I was very fond of him. And he of me. Mother, however, was an ambitious, pretentious megalomaniac. I despised her. She shipped me off to boarding school at nine so I'd be out of the way."

"That's awful." Rebecca set aside her own plate and reached for the wine Agnes had ignored.

"Actually, I was quite happy at school, especially the year I turned thirteen and began having sex with the French master."

"Thirteen?" Rebecca couldn't conceal her shock. "With one of your *teachers?"*

"Do you think it was too young?" Agnes asked, her expression suddenly uncertain and almost childlike in its eagerness for Rebecca's approval.

"Don't you?" Rebecca countered.

"I didn't at the time. I was most anxious to know what it was all about." She puffed thoughtfully on her cigarette. "I suppose perhaps it was rather young. Although I've encountered any number of pregnant thirteen-year-olds during the years I've been teaching. The thing of it is, you know, it gave me a great sense of power. There was something I possessed that could make a thirty-five-year-old man beg. I suddenly understood one of the fundamental dynamics of how the world operates. It was, all in all, a most valuable experience."

"How?" Rebecca asked, the food lumping unpleasantly in her stomach.

"For one thing, it enabled me to understand how my mother could persuade a confirmed bachelor of almost sixty to marry her. It also enabled me to deal with her thereafter with the contemptuous disregard she so deserved."

"God!" Rebecca said softly.

"You're shocked."

"No, I'm . . . I don't know. Sad, I think."

"Don't be," Agnes said with a smile. "I wanted to do it, you know. I remember every last detail of that first time."

"People always remember their first," Rebecca said, convinced that what she was hearing was a classic narrative of child abuse that Agnes had reworked to suit herself.

"There was a moment," Agnes said, looking off into space as if viewing a film of that long-ago event, "just as he was entering me when he stopped and asked if I was sure. I said of course I was sure. It was monstrously painful." She returned her eyes to Rebecca. "I've truly never regretted any of it. My father left me a substantial amount of money when he died, actually more than he left my mother. Which maddened her, but which proved to my satisfaction that he had cared about me. Eventually that money paid for my emigration to America and for my education, helped me establish myself in this country. And once I left England, I became quite an upstanding citizen." She paused, then, averting her eyes, added, "Until recently."

"What do you mean?"

"Nothing." Agnes abruptly got up to refill her glass with Scotch. "Shall we move to the living room?" she suggested. "I'll light a fire."

"Sure. I'll just clear the dishes."

"Don't bother," Agnes said from the doorway.

"It'll take me only a minute."

While she scraped the plates, then rinsed and put them in the dishwasher, Rebecca reviewed what Agnes had told her, trying to decide if that experience of thirty years ago had finally had its delayed but inevitably profound effect. And what had happened recently to undermine Agnes's confidence? "God!" she whispered, working quickly in order not to leave Agnes alone for too long. She wished she knew more, wished she were better equipped to deal with what she could only see as the unraveling of the fabric of her closest friend's equilibrium.

Jason found a ladder in the storage shed, made another mental note to tell Rebecca to get a lock for the shed, then with the Mini-Maglite gripped between his teeth to help him see what he was doing, he began installing the new floodlights.

There was nothing he could do about the carriage light. It would have to be replaced. After stowing the ladder back in the shed, he tested all the doors and windows to be sure they were locked. When the storm doors pulled open, he was surprised, then angry. She'd told him she'd locked them, but here they were, open. He really was going to have to talk to her, he thought, switching the Mini-Maglite on again as he climbed down into the cellar. First he made sure he could open the trapdoor from below, then he locked the storm doors and climbed the ladder. Carrying his wet shoes, he took a quick look through the house. Everything seemed okay. He debated leaving her a note to explain that he'd changed the lights, but decided against it. He didn't want her to know he'd been inside the house, and he didn't want to upset her by telling her the bulbs had been smashed.

In the mudroom he pulled on his Nikes before letting himself out the back door. Convinced the vandal had completed his night's work and was unlikely to return, he trudged back to his car and sat waiting for the heater to warm him. He'd done all he could. But tomorrow he'd talk to her about beefing up her precautions.

As he backed out of the driveway, he again berated himself for making that stop at Burger King. If he hadn't, the chances were he could've nailed the sucker in the act.

"When was your first time?" Agnes asked, jabbing at the logs with a poker. She was sitting on her knees to one side of the fireplace, half in darkness, half lit by the flames.

"Nineteen, when I was at college," Rebecca told her. "Neither one of us knew what we were doing. It was pretty awful. We stopped seeing each other after that night. I think it was because we were both so embarrassed." She wound her arms around her knees and looked at the fire. "We'd really liked each other up till then. Going to bed together killed the friendship. And I was so turned off I didn't make love again for three years. Then it was all right. I discovered I liked it a lot."

Agnes nodded. "Dangerous thing, sex. Especially if one perceives it as a tool, something to advance one's ambitions."

"Is that what you did?" Rebecca asked, maintaining the hushed confessional mood Agnes had established.

Agnes sat back off her knees and carefully arranged the black silk of the robe to conceal her legs. She reached for her cigarettes and sat holding the pack with both hands. "I finished school at sixteen, left home and got a bedsitter in South Kensington. My father gave me an allowance of ten pounds a week which, in nineteen sixty-six, was ample to cover my expenses. Mother knew nothing of it or she'd have forbade him to subsidize me." She sighed, opened the pack and lit a cigarette.

Rebecca remained silent, waiting.

"I was lucky, or talented, or both. Or perhaps I simply slept with the right men. Who knows?" Agnes shrugged, the silk of her robe reflecting the firelight. "I got acting jobs, did some modeling, attended theater classes several times a week. In retrospect, I'd have to say I was lucky and talented, and in fact slept with the right men. I landed a good supporting role in a West End production within a year. Imagine it! There I was, at seventeen, appearing in a hit play, onstage eight times a week. Senga Tyrell," she laughed. "Frightfully exotic. No one ever connected me to Sir John and Lady Benton-Tyrell. And mother certainly wasn't about to acknowledge me, although father wrote congratulating me. I believe he was secretly proud of me."

"I'm sure he must have been."

"He died a few days after my eighteenth birthday. She didn't tell me. I had to read about it in the newspaper. She did have the decency to mention me in the obit." Her voice brimming with bitterness, Agnes picked up the poker and gave the logs a jab that sent sparks shooting up the chimney. "She could scarcely bring herself to speak to me at the funeral. Made a great show of being the gracious, grieving widow to the hundreds of people who came to pay their respects, but intentionally left me in the background. All these people darting looks at me, wondering if I was the daughter or merely another mourner. She would *not* acknowledge me." She took a hard drag on her cigarette, visibly stricken.

"I'm so sorry," Rebecca whispered, placing her hand on her friend's arm.

"It was humiliating," Agnes said hoarsely. "I had every right to be there. He was my father. He cared about me; he was proud of me. He didn't think I was a slut." She cleared her throat, took a final puff of the cigarette, then threw it into the fire. "After the funeral, she said she'd prefer it if I returned directly to London. 'You have no place here,' she said. My bloody *mother*. I had two abortions rather than risk becoming remotely as heartless a parent as that woman.

"The last time I saw her was at the solicitor's office for the reading of the will. She lost control when she heard I'd been left the bulk of the estate, accused me of manipulating the old man. The solicitor was scandalized. Nice man. He apologized to me after she went storming out vowing to break the will. Shook his head, saying he'd never in his life seen anything quite like it. Assured me the will was ironclad and unbreakable, and told me how very much my father had cared for me." She bent her head to her knees and breathed deeply, working hard not to cry. "Why am I dredging all this up now?" She turned to give Rebecca a distorted half smile.

"Does it help?"

"Not one bloody bit. I feel a positive fool telling you this nasty little story."

"Don't," Rebecca entreated, instinctively putting out her hand to smooth Agnes's hair. "You're not a fool. I've always admired you."

"You've admired an illusion, my dear, a role I've played out rather well. I've had the privilege of knowing you while you, I'm afraid, haven't ever had the opportunity of making my acquaintance."

Without thinking, Rebecca said, "My mother said that."

"Your mother's a very perceptive woman. Perhaps more than you realize. I wonder if you have any idea how much I envy you your mother."

"After what you've just told me, I think I can imagine."

"Perhaps," Agnes said consideringly. "Perhaps you can. Cherish her, Rebecca. She's remarkable."

Without warning, Rebecca's eyes filled. She was suddenly overwhelmingly afraid, floundering in territory so unfamiliar she felt totally resourceless. Agnes's past was a nightmare, and so was Rebecca's present.

Agnes regarded her with a mix of compassion and curiosity, and after a moment drew her into her arms, murmuring, "Dear little Rebecca. You're so big-hearted."

Everything was skewed. Here was Agnes comforting her, when it should have been the reverse.

"I do know you," Rebecca said, sitting away but keeping her hands on Agnes's arms. "I know you, and I care about you. It kills me to see you so unhappy. I wish I knew what I could do or say to help."

Agnes took the back of her hand over Rebecca's cheek. "You've been the dearest friend I've ever had. There's no one I've been closer to than you."

"I know you," Rebecca insisted, confronting Agnes's eyes. "I *know* you."

"Very soon now you will be your mother's daughter," Agnes said enigmatically.

"Oh, what the hell does that mean?" Rebecca asked with a croaking laugh. "Please don't go all mystical and prophetic on me. I'm so worried about you."

"There's no need to be. I apologize for boring you with the grizzly details of my upbringing. But you did ask, and the truth is, I was tired of keeping that tainted history all to myself. I did warn you I was feeling self-indulgent."

"Will you tell me something honestly?" Rebecca asked. "Did you really want to be involved with that French teacher?"

"Honestly?" Agnes repeated, stretching out on her back on the carpet. Her head turning toward the fire, she looked into the flames, then up at the ceiling. "Did I honestly want him to lock the door, then put his hand under my uniform and touch me in a way that made me squirm and want to scream? Did I want that? I don't know. I remember standing there trembling. He put both hands up my skirt and pulled down my underpants. Then he sat me on the edge of his desk, folded back my skirt, spread open my legs and kissed me on the mouth while he touched me again in that unimaginable fashion. Then he directed me to touch him." She grimaced, closing her eyes for a moment. "The next thing I knew, I was looking at the ceiling and he was asking me—in French, mind—if I was sure I wanted to be doing this. Doing *this*. I thought of my mother and felt a numbing hatred, and promised him I was quite sure. I hoped he'd kill me. It felt as if he might. But I discovered something else that afternoon." She sat up, again arranging the dressing gown over her legs. "I discovered one can't die merely by wishing it. Don't look so distressed, Rebecca. It was all a long time ago and very far away in another world. It's getting late, and you look tired. I expect you're not completely recovered from your cold."

"Would you like me to stay here with you? I'd be happy to keep you company."

Agnes shook her head. "Thank you for letting me ramble on, and for not judging me."

"Why would I judge you?" Rebecca asked hotly. "You didn't do anything wrong. Your mother did. That French teacher did. But you didn't."

"I'm afraid I've done quite a number of very wrong things, my dear. But I am grateful for your absolution."

"Are you being sarcastic?"

"Not in the least," Agnes said with her normal energy. "I've wondered for years how people might respond to hearing of that episode. I have to confess I felt guilty. You've given me a different perspective. Go along home now. We're both tired."

"You're sure? I wouldn't mind bunking down on the sofa."

"You have an important date tomorrow," Agnes reminded her. "We want you well rested, with roses in your cheeks."

She had no choice but to go. Before she left, she gave Agnes an emphatic hug, saying, "I'll call you tomorrow afternoon, give you a postmortem on Jason's introduction to the Leightons."

"Please do that."

Agnes remained in the doorway until Rebecca reversed the Jetta into the road. Then she waved, stepped back into the house and closed the door.

She saw that the carriage lamp by the back door had been ripped from its moorings and was afraid to enter the house. She stood with the key in one hand, the other on the doorknob, thinking she should call Jason and ask him to come over and check that it was safe for her to go inside. She took a step away from the door and looked over at the Jetta. All the lights were on inside. She'd made sure of that before leaving. God! She couldn't call him every time she was afraid. He'd think she was some kind of idiot, or that she was making a big play for him.

Going back to Agnes's was out of the question. She'd made it very clear she preferred to be alone. Driving down to Greenwich was also out of the question. Aside from the lateness of the hour, her mother would insist on an explanation Rebecca didn't want to give her. She had no choice but to brave it out.

Holding her breath, she let herself in. Her heart drumming in her ears, she went from room to room, even looked in the closets. Nothing appeared to have been disturbed. Exhaling painfully, she left lights burning in the living room and kitchen, then went upstairs. The combination of her concern for Agnes's well-being, her horror and anger at that tale of sexual abuse, and her fears for herself had drained her. After a quick wash, she pulled on a nightgown and climbed into bed.

CHAPTER

Fifteen

Rebecca plunged into a sleep fraught with agonizingly explicit dreams of a thirteen-year-old Agnes being ravished on a desk top. The close-ups of the child's contorted face were accompanied by raucous music, discordant mechanical whirrings, grinding noises. The accelerated surging of her heart and the horrendous din combined to rouse her to the horrifying realization that the sounds were real. Someone was in the house and had turned on the stereo. The whole place pulsed with it. Was the blaring music intended to drown out any cries for help she might make?

Trembling, she turned on the bedside light and reached out to the telephone to call the police. But wait! What if they came and all they found were some appliances running? She didn't know for certain anyone was in the house. God! She didn't know what to do, and the tumult made it almost impossible to think. She put down the receiver. She had no choice but to investigate. Otherwise, a second call for help to the police would likely destroy her credibility altogether.

Feeling the din cutting into her sanity, she looked for something to use as a weapon, found a flashlight in the closet, and stood clutching it with both hands. She wanted this to stop. She couldn't take very much more. Her ears throbbing painfully, whispering, "Please stop doing this, please, please," she went barefoot slowly down the spiral staircase.

Quivering uncontrollably, she looked around. The room was empty. The Cuisinart and blender danced madly on the counter. The TV set played at full volume in the den, as did the radio in the living room. Giddy with dread, repeating, "Please stop, please stop," she crept to the miniscule hallway separating the three rooms. A moment's pause; then, breath held, she darted into the guest room, fumbled for the switch on the table lamp and nearly knocked it over. Frantically righting it, she got the light turned on. Another empty room.

Breathing hard, firming up her hold on the flashlight, she confronted the living room. No one. Air entered and left her lungs in shuddering gasps as she extended a palsied hand to cut the power to the radio. Then back through to the mudroom, where the washer and dryer were churning away. She crept from room to room turning everything off, and at last stood shaking in the kitchen in a silence that battered her eardrums, the only sound the water draining from the washer.

She wiped her runny nose on her sleeve, thinking he'd been inside the house again. How? She'd locked the storm doors. Hadn't she? She'd lost confidence in her ability to distinguish between what was real or simply imagined. Raising the trapdoor, she descended the ladder, got the light on, then crossed the damp cement floor to test the storm doors. Solidly locked. He'd got inside some other way. Oh, God! How did he get in?

Back up the splintery ladder to the kitchen to stand with her arms wrapped around herself, still holding the flashlight, desperately afraid, but glad she hadn't called 911. She couldn't have handled another humiliating encounter with the police.

And there seemed no point to calling Jason now. She'd tell him all about it when she saw him.

The clock on the stove read twenty to four. It was an effort to keep her eyes open. Yet she was afraid to go back to sleep. She could call Jason. No. She didn't want to cry wolf every five minutes. But she hated this house, despised it. It provided no security or privacy whatsoever.

How had he made everything go on at once? She looked at the food processor, the blender, then at the wall socket. There should have been two plugs in the outlets, but there was only one. She removed the plug from the socket and pulled on the cord. From behind the refrigerator came a timer into which were plugged the cords from the countertop appliances.

Further investigation revealed a total of seven timers. Satisfied she'd found them all, she considered what to do. First, she'd get a locksmith to change the cylinders on both doors. And maybe some kind of alarm system. When that check for the bonds arrived, she'd have the money to do it. Quaking from cold and fear and lack of sleep, she gazed at the timers on the counter, wishing she could leave this house and never come back. She wanted to live in one of those condos in Greenwich, with the twenty-four-hour security staff and the surveillance cameras everywhere. She wanted this persecution ended.

Her bare feet cramping, she put the kettle on for tea before going upstairs for some heavy socks and her robe. Her eyes gritty and swollen, she carried the mug of tea to the guest room. Crouched in the corner of the sofa, she pulled the afghan over her and used the remote to turn on the TV.

She stared at the images, every few minutes looking around with a start, convinced she'd heard something. The furnace and refrigerator went on and off at regular intervals. Just after five, she heard gurgling and growling, and sat up sharply to look over at the doorway. What *was* that? The animal-like sounds continued for another minute or two, then abruptly ceased. The sump pump, she thought, sagging back onto the sofa. God! There'd be no more quaint "unusual noise" stories to tell her mother.

Gradually she uncurled and allowed her head to rest on the arm of the sofa. With the robe, the heavy socks and the afghan, she was finally warm again. The back and arms of the sofa cradled her protectively. Several times she jerked awake to look around wildly, her heart pounding. At last she stopped fighting, let her eyes close, and sank again into sleep.

"Why didn't you call me if you were nervous about coming into the house?" Jason asked.

"I thought about it, but I didn't want to waste your time," Rebecca told him. "Everything looked okay once I was inside."

"Next time, don't just think about it, do it. That's what I'm here for, toots." He looked at the timers, saying, "These are all set for three A.M. What time did you say it was when you looked at the clock?"

"Twenty to four."

"So," he said, "allowing for, say, twenty minutes to find all these and disconnect them, that means everything was going for a good half hour before you woke up."

Apologetically, she explained, "I'm a very heavy sleeper."

"I would say so." He remained quietly thoughtful for another few moments, then gave her a smile. "Poor Beck. This is getting rough. There's a thing or two you should do. First off, I want you to get the locks changed. Right away, okay? And while the locksmith's here, have him throw a lock on that shed out there."

"The shed?" She was about to ask why, reconsidered, and simply nodded.

"And at night close all the curtains and shutters, not just the ones down here."

Again she nodded, then asked, "What'll I do with those?" indicating the timers.

"You got something to put them in? I'll take them with me."

She got a supermarket bag, then watched him pick up each timer by its prongs and deposit it in the bag. "What're you going to do with them?"

"I'm not sure. I want to think about it." He knotted the top of the bag, then set it down on the island and gave her another smile. "You look pretty terrific for someone who didn't get a whole lot of sleep last night."

Her eyes traveled over him. He had on tan cords, a white button-down shirt under a red-Shetland crewneck, a new-looking navy blazer, and heavy white socks with his Topsiders. He looked well-rested and healthy, very wide awake. In contrast, she felt faintly dizzy and haphazardly put together. "You look pretty terrific yourself," she said at last, "for a major league liar."

"Hey! What did I lie about?"

"I look like hell."

"You look terrific. Who's out here looking, me or you?"

She didn't say anything. She couldn't shake the feeling that someone was watching them, even though she'd kept all the windows covered.

"So," he said, "you want to get the first kiss out of the way now or wait till later, build up some serious steam?"

"What?"

"Don't go deaf again!" he warned. "You heard me."

"What makes you think I'm interested in kissing you?"

"Ah-ah!" He waggled a finger at her. "Now who's a liar? You know you're dying to kiss me."

"You're assuming, and you told me that's a no-no," she

said, looking at his mouth. She was finding him more and more attractive.

"Okay, fine. We'll let the steam build. You ready to go?" He glanced at his watch.

"I just have to get my coat." She picked up her purse and the bottle of wine she'd bought for her mother and moved into the mudroom.

"Yellow's a good color for you," he said, following right behind her.

"Thank you." She reached for her coat as he lifted her hair and kissed her lightly on the back of her neck. The reaction traveled down her legs, turned her knees rubbery. Her hand still outstretched, she hesitated, then shifted to face him. "You know it's really my mind you're after," she said, her eyes again on his mouth.

"The hell it is," he laughed, sliding his hand under her hair and over the nape of her neck. "Steam's already building," he said, and bent to kiss her.

Pulling away, her palm flat on his chest, she said half-seriously, "If I was in my right mind, I wouldn't be doing any of this. You're taking advantage of my weakened condition."

"Shame on you! I don't take advantage of people. Cashmere, huh?" His hand glided down her back.

"My mother gave it to me for Christmas last year."

"Nice." Now his hand slipped up under the sweater. "And silk. Your mother give you this, too?"

"No. I bought it myself. Kindly remove your hand."

"In a minute."

She felt drugged. Her eyes wanted to close. Too much was going on, and she wasn't sure she could cope. He stroked up and down the bare flesh of her back between her shoulders and the top of her slip. She couldn't move. An urgency was building low in her belly.

"My life's completely weird," he said, "but I want you in it."

"What?"

"Give me another kiss and let's get going."

"You smell very good," she said.

"Obsession. My mother gave it to me for Christmas last year."

"Is that true?" she asked lazily, lulled by his caressing hand.

"No. Actually my dad gave it to me."

She looped her arm around his neck and kissed him, tasting traces of pipe tobacco on his lips, minty toothpaste on his tongue. His return of the kiss was leisurely, sweet, wonderfully affectionate.

"You're a swell kisser," he said, his cheek against hers.

"You, too." Her palm was directly over his heart and she could feel its strong, steady rhythm.

He took her coat off the peg and helped her into it, then smiled at her as he fastened the buttons. "You okay? Think we graded well on the first kissing?"

"I'm fine. We're A-plus. The timing's all wrong. And living here scares the hell out of me now. I feel as if I'm losing my mind. I don't know how much more of this I can take."

"I'm looking out for you. Okay?"

Her hand went again to his chest. This was different. Would he make love in the same friendly unhurried fashion as he kissed? The idea was acutely attractive. If he pushed, even slightly, she'd be willing to let it happen right there. Her defenses were shot. She wanted him to hold her, to place his body protectively over hers, to act as a living shield that would keep her safe from further harm.

"Okay, then. Let's go."

"I do like you," she told him, reluctant to end the closeness.

"I already knew that."

"Don't be smug." She traced his mouth with her index finger.

"Me? Never. I might start whooping or something like that, because it's good to have you come out with the words and admit you like me. But smug's not my style. You know how many times in your life it happens you like someone and they like you, too? Maybe once, if you're lucky. I'm high, 'cause I just got lucky."

Rebecca introduced them. Jason presented Evelyn with a bouquet of a dozen long-stemmed yellow roses. Smiling, the two of them exchanged a long look, then embraced like old friends.

"I hope you like to eat," Evelyn addressed Jason before turning to Rebecca. "Artie called last night to say Michael's come down with chicken pox. And Bill called an hour ago to say Wendy's got a migraine. So it's just the three of us with a roast that could feed a dozen easily."

"No prob," Jason said, trailing Evelyn into the kitchen. "Count me as at least three adults."

Rebecca came in from hanging away her coat to find Jason settled at the kitchen table while Evelyn searched for a vase for the roses.

"Open your wine, sweetheart," Evelyn said, "unless Jason would prefer something else."

"No, the wine would be great," he said. "So, are you buying a condo? Rebecca didn't say."

"I *bought* one. And yesterday I agreed to sell this place to my next-door neighbor, who's been after it for ages." Evelyn placed the roses on the cutting board by the sink, picked up a pair of scissors and began trimming the stems. "Have you been married?" she asked him.

"Nope."

"Mother!" Rebecca groaned.

"I've been saving myself for the right woman," Jason said. Rebecca laughed nervously. Evelyn put another rose in the vase, then looked over her shoulder at Jason, and the two of them smiled with immediate complicity.

Rebecca put a glass of wine down on the counter beside her mother, handed one to Jason, and said, "I'm going to call Agnes, make sure she's okay. Be right back."

She got the answering machine, waited for the tone and said, "Hi, it's me. Just thought I'd see how you are. I'll call back later."

Jason and her mother were laughing, visibly enjoying each other. Evelyn had finished arranging the roses and was standing holding her wine, saying, "I hope you're going to be better about visiting than Rebecca's brothers."

"Guaranteed," Jason said happily. "Every Sunday, if I'm not on duty. Otherwise, we'll make it Friday night or Saturday. And who knows? You might have me popping by at all odd hours."

"Good. Finally something I can count on. So, tell me," Evelyn said. "Where are you from? You have brothers and sisters? We could move to the living room. We've got at least another half hour."

"I like it here," he said easily. "Come sit down."

"I like kitchens, too," Evelyn said, joining him at the table while Rebecca got her wine but remained by the counter, fascinated by how readily her mother had accepted Jason and by how open and accessible he was.

"I'm from New Haven. Mind if I light up?" he asked.

"Be my guest."

Rebecca opened the cupboard for an ashtray, carried it over to the table, then returned to her place by the counter to continue watching this man and her mother establish a rapport. Evelyn's eyes were bright with interest, her face slightly flushed, as she listened to Jason talk. And again, as so many times before, Rebecca admired her mother's enviable ease with people and wished she herself had inherited it.

"My parents divorced when I was fifteen," Jason said,

pushing tobacco into the bowl of his pipe. "Dad got custody of me and my kid sister. My mother married my dad's law partner, which, of course, broke up the practice. Say, you want to meet a swell guy? My Dad's a nifty dancer. You like to dance, Evelyn?"

"Do me a favor," Evelyn laughed. "Don't matchmake. He's a lawyer?"

Rebecca chuckled and took a sip of wine, relaxing for the first time in what felt like months.

"Retired," Jason clarified. "He spends most of his time on his boat. You like boats? His is a beauty. My sister's divorced with two kids, lives in Vermont, teaches math and computer sciences"—he grinned over at Rebecca—"at the local high school up there."

"And you're a police officer," Evelyn said. "You like it?"

"Most of the time. Definitely more than I did in the city. That was appalling. Nortown's fine, pretty quiet. It's like an extended rest cure after six years on the NYPD. And I get to meet nifty people, like you," he told Evelyn with another big grin, "and your cute kid."

"She is cute, isn't she?" Evelyn agreed. "When she was born, I had to fight the nurses to get my hands on her. They'd stand outside my room playing with her, never bring her in."

"Go ahead," Rebecca said. "Talk about me as if I'm not here." She felt all at once absurdly happy, elated to see how well her mother and Jason had hit it off. She savored this temporary respite from the ongoing madness creeping closer to her every day. In this house, with these people, nothing bad could happen to her. The kitchen was warm, fragrant with the aroma of roasting meat, and the wine was spreading a delicious lassitude through her limbs. She thought about how they'd kissed in the mudroom, looked at him sitting now at the table, the ankle of his right leg propped on his left knee, the pipe in his hand, his full attention on her mother, and without actually moving, felt herself leaning toward him. Her desire to touch him was intense. She imagined making love with him and again felt that urgency in her belly.

"Seriously," Jason was saying, "my dad gets one look at you, he'll go crazy. Two gorgeous women in one family."

"Go easy on the flattery," Evelyn said. "A person my age could go into hyperglycemic shock from so much sugar."

Jason laughed hugely, then leaned over and kissed her on the cheek. "I'm crazy about the women in this family. This one"—he tilted his head at Rebecca—"goes deaf every time I say something nice to her. And you peg me as a flatterer. Nice. I'm going to have to get the two of you whipped into shape so when someone comes along and starts stating some simple truths, you'll be able to say thank you and accept a few compliments with appropriate grace."

"Who's Grace?" Evelyn asked. "Sweetheart, do we know a Grace?"

Rebecca laughed so hard she had to put her glass down.

"I get it," Jason said. "It's a routine you two do. Fine. I can live with it. No prob."

During lunch, Evelyn said, "Jason, talk her into selling that house and buying a condo down here."

"Hey!" Rebecca declared. "I'd do it in a minute. It's not as if I'm liking what's going on. But those condos are way out of my league, Mother. Even if I put the full sale price of my house into one, I'd still wind up with a hefty mortgage. I can't do it on my salary, and I'm not about to go into heavy debt."

"Your mom's got a point, Beck," Jason said.

"I agree. It's just, unfortunately, not possible right now. You should see the place my mother's bought. Right on the water, with a view that goes for days. They've even got their own boat slips."

"They do? Wow! Wait'll I tell my dad. He can shoot on down from New Haven and pick you up for a date in the boat."

"Jason," Evelyn warned again, "no matchmaking."

"You'd like him, Evelyn. You might be kind of on the young side for him, but you'd definitely like him."

"How old is your father, anyway?" Rebecca asked, curious.

"Dad's sixty-seven," he answered, then frowned as the two women bent over their food, laughing. "Okay. What's the giggle?"

"My mother's the same age," Rebecca told him.

"Would you like a megaphone?" Evelyn said. "You could tell the whole neighborhood." She smiled at Jason.

"This is the finest meal I've had in years."

"Next Sunday I think I'll cook Italian for a change."

"Great! I love Italian," Jason said.

"I see. Am I invited, too?" Rebecca asked.

"Standing invitation." Evelyn held her glass in both hands, elbows on the table. "It'll probably be the last sit-down meal I cook in this house." She looked around the mahogany-paneled dining room. "It's hard to believe I'm leaving here."

"Dad had a rough time when he sold the old house," Jason sympathized. "He's in a condo on the Sound, and he loves it now. It took a while, but he keeps saying he doesn't know why he hung on to the house for so long."

"Where do you live, Jason?" Evelyn asked.

"I rent a place in Nortown, halfway to the Merritt. Garage apartment I've had for a couple of years now. I was in a building in Stamford for a while, but it was too institutional—little boxy rooms, long ugly corridors. The garage is pretty decent, okay for one person."

"I'm going to try Agnes again." Rebecca pushed back from the table and went to the telephone in the hall.

She got the machine and said, "It's me for the second time. I'll call you later when I get home." She hung up wondering where Agnes could be. Sunday was the day she did her marking, made course notes, and caught up generally. She almost never went out on Sundays. Rebecca was beginning to get worried.

Jason was helping Evelyn clear the table when Rebecca got back to the dining room. She automatically picked up the gravy boat and the serving dish of broccoli. Just before pushing through the swing door into the kitchen, Jason turned, ducked his head and kissed her. "This is fun," he whispered. "I'm going to fix your mom up with my dad."

"She'll murder you," Rebecca whispered back. "She hasn't dated once in the eight years since my father died."

"Then it's time she started." He pushed through the door, deposited the dishes on the counter and said, "We can do a double date. Somewhere with dancing. I'll bet you're a wicked dancer, Evelyn."

"Rebecca, take Sam Spade here back to the dining room before I do him an injury with the coffeepot."

"Come on, Sam," Rebecca grabbed his hand. "She means it."

The instant the kitchen door swung closed, he pressed Rebecca against the wall and leaned into her. "How's the steam doing?" he asked, gazing into her eyes at such close range she could scarcely focus. Her body automatically aligned itself to his.

"Please, don't tease her," she said quietly. "She really won't even consider meeting men."

"That's only because she hasn't met my dad yet. He's pretty much the same way. So I figure we'll have to trick them into it. Trust me, Beck. It'll be good." His hips shifted subtly against hers, and her mouth went dry. "I want to kiss the backs of your knees," he said almost inaudibly, "and the little hollow right here." He pressed his forefinger gently into the base of her throat. "I feel the same way about you that I used to about grape lollipops when I was a kid: I wanted to make them last forever because the taste was so good."

"Wait till you get home to do that," Evelyn laughed, coming through the door with the dessert. "You want to give an old woman heart failure?"

"Why does she talk about herself that way?" Jason asked Rebecca, taking the tray from Evelyn and carrying it to the table.

"I don't honestly know," Rebecca said. "Maybe you can get her to quit." She went into the kitchen to get the coffee. Jason came along right behind her.

"Just one question," he whispered as she got down the cups and saucers. "Do we need to make a stop at a drugstore on the way back to your place?"

"God!" She felt herself blush and had to close her eyes for a moment. "You're making me very nervous." She gave a constricted little laugh.

"That's nothing compared to what you're making me. Do we need to stop, yes or no?"

"No," she whispered. *"God!"*

He picked up the sugar bowl and the creamer, saying, "Are you scared of guns?"

"What?"

"Are you? It's a for-real question."

"Yes!" She wet her lips and looked at him.

"Okay. I needed to know."

"Jason, what the *hell?"*

"I'm a cop, Beck. Gun, bullets, cuffs, beeper, the works. I just don't want to scare you."

"Everything about you scares me."

"Yeah," he said softly. "Ditto. But we'll be okay."

Pete was getting more and more pissed off with Leighton. Things at home were shit, and the way he figured it, it was totally her fault. Four or five years she'd been his dad's little playmate, which was why the family scene was completely fucked. He wanted to kill her.

Planning the gigs, getting into her place mostly during school hours when it was guaranteed she wouldn't turn up, was like this major power trip. It was all he could think about. He just wished he could've finished the whole scene he'd had planned for Saturday night. And what was the deal there? If it was some guy looking to break in, that was fine. He could give a shit. But if it was like a cop, or maybe someone she'd hired to keep an eye on the place, it could really fuck him up. He needed to finish what he'd started. He needed to even the score.

His mother just wouldn't quit now. She had this endless list of sins he'd committed, and she'd start complaining the minute he set his foot in the stinking house. He had this dream of walking through the front door and finding the place empty. Some money and a note saying the house and the car are all yours. Mom and dad are history. House'd probably be in better shape, it was his. He'd open the damned curtains, let some light in, air the place out. It was like a fucking dungeon the way she kept it closed up so the light wouldn't shine on the TV screen. As if the entire civilized world was depending on his mother's being able to watch *Unsolved Mysteries*. Jesus!

He was saving up pills so he could drop a few when he was safely home after one of the gigs, but he couldn't seem to get any kind of high going. It was like no matter what he did, his brain was on overtime, churning away, coming up with guilty, anxious shit he really didn't need. Like he didn't have enough of that already, what with his mother on his case night and day, and the teachers giving him grief because he didn't know what the fuck was going on in class. His life was one major pain.

Pay-back with the bitch was about the only thing that mattered anymore. But he was spooked now, because of this other person creeping around the bitch's place. When he drove by on Sunday afternoon and saw the Jetta in the driveway, he just kept going. He headed for I-95 to cruise a while, get his thoughts together. He popped the tab on a Bud, fished in his pocket for the little yellow jobs he'd scored a couple of nights before from one of the road hags who hung around the service center to do the truckers, and threw them down with a swallow of the Bud.

The hell with everything, man. He'd just drive. Driving always helped get him centered. His life was totally fucked. His mom and dad were a perfect pair of loons, all over each other every time one word got said. Lee was smart, man. She stayed up at college, kept away. He wished he could get the hell away. But, no. They can't wail on each other the way they'd like to, so they're all over him instead. And whose fault is that? Leighton's, totally. He'd get her for it, too.

One hand on the wheel, the other holding the Bud, he cruised down the center lane. The only time he felt free was when he got behind the wheel and took off. Going nowhere, just going.

Cruising at sixty-five down the center lane, he remembered way back when he was little how his mom and dad used to get into it in the kitchen. He and Lee would catch them at it, the two of them giggling at mom and dad kissing by the stove. His dad would break away and come after them roaring like a lion, catch them in the living room and tickle them, wrestle around, while their mom stood in the doorway all red in the face and laughing. Where did it all go? What the fuck happened?

CHAPTER

Sixteen

I love your mother," Jason said as he divested himself of his hardware and locked it in the glove compartment. "I mean it. One look at her and that was it for me. Your dad was a very lucky man."

"Do you see your mother?"

"Not in years. After the divorce, she and Roger moved to Los Angeles. Mimi, my kid sister, went out there a couple of times to visit, but she couldn't stand Roger either, so she stopped going. I remember we took the train into the city to see our mother when Mimi was about sixteen. They were staying at the St. Regis, and we had lunch in the dining room, the three of us. Roger baby was off doing business. Quietest lunch in history. We had nothing to say to each other. It was tough on Mimi. Mothers and daughters, that thing, you know?"

"I know."

"I have to report in at six," he said, pulling the keys from the ignition.

"Oh," she said dumbly, feeling let down. She'd assumed they'd spend the rest of the day and evening together. He had cautioned her about assuming, and she was beginning to see she did quite a lot of it. "I didn't know."

"I told you my life's weird, Beck. Cops aren't like civilians. Not only the shifts. Plenty of people work shifts. It's the stuff we deal with day to day."

"I can imagine."

"Listen, nothing has to happen right now, today, with the two of us. I'm not going anywhere. There's no big rush."

She got her door open, saying, "There is if we've only got an hour and a half." Fairly amazed at herself, she climbed out of the car and headed for the back door.

"I want to take a quick look, make sure everything's okay," he said, locking the door before going past her to do a quick inspection of every room in the house. He looked in the closets and even went down to the cellar to make sure the storm doors were locked.

Her legs unsteady, she took off her coat and hung it on the peg in the mudroom. She was convinced there were probably half a dozen new nasty surprises somewhere in the house. She imagined lifting the bedclothes to find animal entrails swimming in a sea of blood, or opening her closet to find her clothes razored to shreds. The images set her on edge, made her muscles tighten. Jason reappeared in the doorway as she was about to go into the kitchen. She stepped back into the mudroom.

"It all looks okay, so far as I can see."

"Good," she said, barely able to speak.

"Message light's flashing on your machine," he said, moving into the room.

"I'll listen to it later."

"Whatever you like." He came closer.

"Would you care for a drink or anything?"

"Or anything," he said with a smile.

"What?"

He shook his head and shifted even closer.

She tried but couldn't manage to take a breath.

He was standing directly in front of her now, and ran his hand from her shoulder down over her breast to her waist. She had to lean against the washer for support as he lifted the bottom of her sweater and eased it off over her head. She watched his eyes as he lowered the top of her slip, oddly able to read his emotions. They seemed, right at this moment, to match her own, and she knew he too was suffering from first-time nervousness. She closed her eyes as he covered her breasts with both hands and kissed her shoulder, the side of her neck, and finally her mouth.

"How did this happen?" she wondered aloud, pulling his shirt free from the waistband of the cords, anxious to feel the warmth of his bare skin. Then, suddenly remembering where they were and that they could be seen through the glass-paneled back door, she said, "We can't stay here."

"Come on." Knowing it was closest, he led her by the hand into the guest room.

Experiencing a sudden loss of coordination, she struggled with the zipper on her skirt while stepping out of her shoes. What if something happened while they were making love? The ceiling might fall on them, or the doors would drop from their hinges, the mirrors might shatter.

He dragged his shirt and sweater off, threw them on the floor, then reached for her. Her eyes closed again, heart hammering, she absorbed heat from his body in dizzying waves. Nothing awful could happen to her as long as she was with him, she told herself, reveling in the newness of the shape and feel of him.

"I'm trying to slow it all down," he said, one hand going again to the back of her neck, "but I'm not having much luck."

She pressed her lips to the base of his throat and reached

to slide her hand down his thigh. "I have to use the bathroom," she whispered. "I won't be a minute." Separating from him, she felt the shock of cool air enveloping her overheated flesh as she went reeling into the bathroom. Leaving the light off, she opened the medicine cabinet, then peeled off her slip and pantyhose. She stood by the sink for a moment, the porcelain cold under her hand, her thoughts jumbled, overlapping. It was a waste of time trying to think. Straightening, she took a condom from the medicine cabinet. He was right. It was all going very fast. But she didn't want to slow things down.

He'd taken off the remainder of his clothes and stood smiling at the sight of her. "Full head of steam," he declared as he lifted her off the floor to kiss her, then turned in a slow circle as she wound her arms around his neck and her legs tightly encircled his hips.

The telephone rang. They both looked over at the door.

"Forget it!" she said, hungrily opening her mouth over his as she heard the answering machine click on.

They lay crowded together on the unopened sofa bed, lazily stroking each other.

"I have to go," he murmured, drawing circles around her nipple with a fingertip.

"I know." She ran her hand down over his haunch, then up the length of his spine.

"We need more time for this," he said, replacing his fingertip with his mouth.

"Uh-huh," she agreed, ready right then to make love to him again. She'd never experienced lovemaking so heated and intense.

"I'm covering half a shift tonight for a buddy. Otherwise, I'd be free till midnight. I won't be off again until eight tomorrow morning."

"That's a shame." She laced the fingers of her right hand through his and squeezed gently.

"I'd grade us a definite A. What's the teacher's feeling on that?"

"A-plus."

"No lie?"

"Why would I lie? I wish you didn't have to go. I hate being alone in this house now."

"If I wasn't covering for Frank, there's no way I'd be going in tonight. I'd be staying right here, nibbling on your toes, keeping an eye on you. I'm crazy in love with you."

"What?"

"Rebecca, now is not the time to play deaf." He lifted her so they were kneeling facing each other. "I'm out of my mind, gone, whacko, blitzed, zonked, crazy for you. You are the cutest, smartest, and sexiest hearing-impaired woman I have ever known."

She smiled and threaded her fingers through his soft shaggy hair, then tugged gently on his gold earring. "I think I'm pretty crazy about you, too."

"You *think?* You don't *know?*" His hands closed either side of her rib cage and moved slowly upward to cup her breasts.

"Okay. I know. I think I know."

"Don't rush to commit yourself or anything." He made a comically sad face.

"You're going too fast," she told him. "I need more time."

"Been stung a time or two, huh?"

"Haven't you?"

"Hasn't everyone?" He leaned to one side to pick up his wristwatch from the floor. "Hell! I've really got to go. How's tomorrow for you? I could swing by around six. We could grab a bite before I have to clock on."

"That would be fine."

"Listen. Don't misunderstand, okay? D'you happen to have a spare set of keys? I'd like to be able to check the house, make sure everything's okay if you're not here."

"Sure. I'll go get them for you." She got up, ducked into the bathroom, emerged wrapped in a towel and went to the kitchen to look in the drawer where she normally kept the spare keys. They weren't there. She searched every drawer, then went through the pockets of all the coats and jackets in the mudroom. "They're not here," she told him, distraught. "He's out there with a set of keys to my house. He can come and go at will. *God!*"

He could see and feel her distress and nodded soberly. Stepping into his boxer shorts, he said, "Until the locksmith comes, I want you to keep the lights inside and out on all night, and the chains on both doors. The storm doors're locked. I made sure of that. Soon as I leave, get on the phone and set up an appointment to have those locks changed."

"Okay."

"If you need me, call the station. They'll beep me. Okay? And I'll have a patrol car swing by every hour."

"Yes, okay." He'd become very businesslike, and it heightened her fear. They scarcely knew each other, and not only was her safety at stake, but she was also putting herself emotionally at risk by having so willingly taken him into her life.

He quickly finished dressing, then smoothed his hair with both hands and crossed over to her. "What's wrong?"

She raised one shoulder in a partial shrug, feeling she'd completely lost her bearings.

"You're worried," he guessed. "What about? The keys?"

She shrugged again, feeling inept and childish. How could she explain how close she was to the edge? He'd think she was an emotional weakling.

"Me? It's me, right? You think I *want* to leave? You don't think I'd like to stay here with you?"

"I don't know you. I have no idea what you want or don't want, think or don't think."

"I've made some hell of an impression on you," he said unhappily. "I just finished telling you I'm gonzo for you, toots, and you think it's a *line?*"

"Gonzo?" She started to smile.

"Yeah!" Tugging open the towel, he looked at her with evident pleasure, then gave her a long hug, saying, "I'll be having trouble keeping my mind on business tonight, that's for sure. Are you going to be all right?"

Reassured, at least about him, she said, "I think so. I've just got to tough this out."

"Afraid so. What about us?" he asked. "It was A-plus and you're a happy little camper?"

"Yes," she answered truthfully. "Go to work now. I'm going to call Agnes again, then try to get some of my course reading done."

"I really do hate to leave."

"You'll be back tomorrow."

"Six on the button. You ever seriously want me gone, you'll have to use pretty powerful repellent."

She laughed and kissed him on the chin, linking her hands with his.

"Don't forget to close *all* the shutters and curtains," he said, as he went out the back door. "And put the chains on."

She called out, "Phone me if you get a chance. Okay?"

"Definitely." He grinned, sliding in behind the wheel. "You be careful. Okay?"

She nodded, then shut the door and watched him go.

Her mother had obviously left the first message while Rebecca and Jason were en route to Greenwich, and had wanted to let Rebecca know that her brothers had canceled. The second was Evelyn, saying, "I'll bet I know why you're not answering the phone, sweetheart." She laughed. "Finally," she said, "you've found yourself a man a mother could love. Call me later, dear."

The final message was Ray, saying, "Did you get a machine so you could avoid talking to me? I really hope that's not the case. Call me, please."

A bit thrown by Ray's somewhat menacing tone, she reset the tape and dialed Agnes's number. For the third time, she got the answering machine.

"Agnes," she said, "if you're standing there listening, pick up. Otherwise, I'm going out to my car right now and I'll be at your door in ten minutes."

"Are you threatening me, my dear?" Agnes came on the line, her voice even deeper than usual.

"I wouldn't say that. I wanted to be sure you're all right."

"I am perfectly well, thank you. How was your afternoon with the family and the detective?"

"My brothers canceled, so it was just the three of us. It was great."

"You sound decidedly *insouciant*. Have you been a naughty girl?"

Rebecca laughed and touched the back of her hand to her cheeks and forehead. She was very flushed. "I'm admitting nothing."

"You don't have to. Your voice alone is practically melting my receiver. I'm delighted you've had such a rewarding afternoon."

"What have you been doing?"

"You wouldn't want to know."

"Yes, I would."

"Very well, if you insist. I've spent several hours working on the budget, looking through catalogs, and reviewing the curriculum. A thoroughly thrilling time."

"Have you eaten?"

There was a pause. Rebecca could hear Agnes lighting a cigarette.

"Have you eaten?" she asked again.

"Darling, have you decided to take on the role of my personal dietitian?"

"If I have to, I will. You're welcome to come over and eat with me."

"That's very sweet. However, I'm afraid I've one or two things still to do."

"I could pick up some heroes and bring them over," Rebecca offered.

There was another pause and the sound of liquid being poured. "I'm not fit for human consumption tonight," Agnes said at length. "But thank you anyway."

"I don't need to be entertained, you know. I could bring some food and we could watch TV."

"Not tonight, my dear," Agnes said more firmly. "I have other plans."

"Well, if you change your mind, call me. I'll be in all evening."

"If I change my mind, I will indeed call you."

"Please think about it," Rebecca entreated. "It's still early."

"If I change my mind," Agnes said, "I will call you. Good-bye, Rebecca."

Rebecca hung up, bothered by the whole tone of the conversation. But there was only so much she could do. She couldn't force herself on Agnes when the woman had made it clear she wanted to be left alone.

Resigned, she found a listing in the Yellow Pages for a twenty-four-hour locksmith and dialed the number. When a taped message clicked on, she groaned but waited for the beep and gave her name, address, and telephone number. "I need to have the cylinders on two locks changed as quickly as possible. I'd appreciate a call back tonight any time until eleven, or first thing tomorrow morning. Thank you."

That done, she collected her clothes and went upstairs. While she was in the shower, she went back over her conversation with Agnes, trying to determine what—aside from the fact that Agnes had obviously been drinking—had left her with such a pronounced sense of uneasiness.

There was all that silly, irritating business with Teddy, and Aggie's failure to remember their date the night before. There were also remarks she'd made that, upon consideration, were somewhat alarming, like her insistence that Rebecca didn't know her. Then there was her description of her sexual initiation by the French teacher, and her somehow innocent concern that Rebecca would not approve. She'd talked as if she were the one responsible when, in fact, she'd been far too young to have engaged voluntarily in something that sounded sordid and damaging. Just thinking about it made Rebecca ache with sympathy for that child.

And why, Rebecca wondered as she toweled dry, had Agnes's mother refused to acknowledge her at the funeral? Agnes hadn't given a reason.

Pulling on her robe, she went to the telephone in the bedroom. When Agnes's machine came on, she waited impatiently for the tone, then said, "Pick up and talk to me for a minute. There's something I need to know."

A weary-sounding Agnes said, "Are you planning to phone every half hour?"

"No. I only want to ask you one question. You said your mother refused to acknowledge you. Why?"

"Aaah!" Agnes audibly drank from a glass with ice cubes Rebecca could hear rattling. "Why," she repeated tiredly. "So many reasons. Firstly, I was insolent and, at a certain point, ungovernable. And, secondly, because I made the mistake of confiding to her—with the thought in mind that she might have some small secret cache of feelings for me—some of the less graphic details of my, shall we say, affiliation, with Monsieur Roche. She chose to view this confession as yet another example of my intractability. I was, among many other things, a vicious liar who would go to any lengths to draw attention to herself. I compounded my many sins by daring not only to go on the stage, but to bare my breasts to the general public."

"In the play," Rebecca said.

"That is correct. I was by no means the first to do such a thing. As I recall, Peggy Ashcroft did a semi-nude scene in the West End back in the thirties. Not that I put myself quite in her league. But the reviewers did make mention of the scene. And that confirmed what my mother had always believed: that I was, once and for always, an utter slut." Again the ice cubes rattled. "Does that answer the question to your satisfaction?"

"I guess so," Rebecca said quietly. "I'm really sorry, Agnes."

"Whatever for?" She sounded surprised.

"For all of it. None of it was your fault, but you make it sound as if it was. You were just a child, for heaven's sake."

Agnes tried to say something, but what came over the line was an indecipherable guttural sound she covered quickly with a cough.

"Are you all right?"

"Just swallowed wrong," Agnes said. "I must go now."

"Sure," Rebecca said understandingly. "I'll see you in the morning."

Agnes put the phone down.

Rebecca sat on the side of the bed, drying her damp palms on her robe. She had her explanation. So why did she still feel something was very wrong?

At twenty after ten, Jason called.

"I'm just grabbing a burger and thought I'd see how you're doing."

Gratified, and aroused simply by the sound of his voice, she said, "I'm on edge, waiting for whatever's going to happen next, but I'm surviving. How're you doing?"

"You've got the hottest telephone voice. You know that?"

She laughed. "You're pretty hot yourself."

"You know what, Rebecca?"

"What?"

"I love you."

"God! Don't say that!"

"Why not?" He sounded mystified.

"I don't know."

"Scare you?"

"Yes. No. I don't know."

"Okay. As long as you're not confused," he chuckled. "You're stuck with me. Gotta run, toots. Tomorrow at six."

"I'll be here."

"I can hardly wait."

Rebecca couldn't sleep. Every time she closed her eyes she thought she heard someone moving around downstairs. Plus she'd forgotten to call her mother back. She sat up and turned on the light. A quarter after one. She went down to the kitchen to get a glass of water, then sat at the island drinking it, thinking once again about that conversation of the night before. Those references to sleeping with the right men struck a jarring note. There was some kind of message there, but Rebecca just couldn't get to it. What did it all mean?

Suddenly, terrifyingly, it pulled together: Agnes's comment about hating living her life, the revelations about her sadly distressing childhood, her frequent air of distraction, her

statement that she was straddling her two lives and not committed to either of them. She had said "Good-bye, Rebecca."
Not see you tomorrow, but good-bye. "I hate *living* my life."

Rebecca snatched up the receiver, dialed Agnes's number
and as she'd expected, reached the answering machine.
Maybe she was crazy, she thought, racing back upstairs to
throw on some clothes, but something was very, very wrong.

Overwhelmed by urgency, she grabbed her bag and keys
and the first coat that came to hand, and pausing only long
enough to be sure the back door was locked, tore out to the
car.

Speeding along the deserted streets, her hands slick on the
wheel, she tried to tell herself she was being overimaginative,
there was nothing wrong. Her emotional life of late was
tumultuous. Too much going on, too constant a level of fear.
Things had a way of sliding out of focus when viewed
through a haze of ongoing dread. But still, her every instinct
was telling her to go faster, to get to Agnes before it was too
late.

CHAPTER

Seventeen

The house was completely dark, and Rebecca got no response to either the doorbell or her knocking. Certain now that her hunch was right, she searched the ground by the front steps, trying to find the fake rock that held the spare key.

Several minutes passed before she found it. And her hands were so unsteady she couldn't get the thing open. She told herself to slow down and managed to release the plastic base. The key fell to the ground. Dropping down, she felt around for it, cursing under her breath. At last her fingers touched metal. She snatched up the key and ran to the door, jabbing it at the lock. Getting the door open finally, she called out. Her voice bounced back at her off the walls and ceiling like a Ping-Pong ball. Swallowing hard, she turned on the hall light, then hurried to look in the living room.

Everything was unusually tidy: the chair and sofa pillows fluffed up, magazines in neat rows on the coffee table, ashtrays clean, the carpet vacuumed. Racing through the house, she glanced into the kitchen, noting the careful order there, too. She approached the closed door to Agnes's bedroom and put her hands out to it with the irrational feeling that the wood might burn her skin.

She knocked. No reply. Swallowing again, she turned the knob. For a few seconds she could only stare, her eyes quickly taking in the details: two envelopes on the bedside table next to a half-empty glass of what looked like Scotch, an empty plastic prescription vial. Fully made up, clad in her black-silk robe, Agnes lay atop the neatly made bed. And on the floor, pulled to pieces, was Teddy.

With a cry, Rebecca ran over to touch her hand to Agnes's breast. No heartbeat. Yanking open the robe, she pressed her hand to the pale, still warm flesh. A faint heartbeat. Frantic, she lifted Agnes's eyelids. Her pupils were almost fully dilated; in a few more minutes she'd be dead. God! What to do? If she called an ambulance and the medics arrived in time to save her, Agnes's career would be ruined. There was no room in the school system for anyone who deviated from the accepted norm, not homosexuals, or political activists, and most definitely not a suicidal department head.

Rebecca grabbed the empty prescription vial. "Take 1–2 tablets when necessary at bedtime." Sleeping pills. A prescription for thirty. How many had she taken?

"Wake up!" she shouted and slapped Agnes's face hard. Nothing. A slap wasn't going to do it. She needed help. No time to waste. Snatching up the phone, she punched 911. The instant she heard a voice on the other end, she said, "This is Rebecca Leighton. Page Jason Blondell. It's an emergency. Tell him to get to Agnes Tyrell's place right away. He's got the address. *Hurry!*"

She threw down the receiver, then flew into the bathroom to turn on the cold water in the shower stall. Shrugging off her coat as she ran back to the bed, she maneuvered Agnes to the edge, looped her arms around her and dragged her off.

Agnes landed on the floor with a terrible thump. "A couple of bruises won't matter," Rebecca panted, sweating as she towed the bigger, heavier woman toward the bathroom.

"You are *not* going to die, Agnes!" she cried furiously, making painfully slow progress. "I'm not going to *let* you die. This is so goddamned stupid! *Why* did you *do* this?" She had to rest a moment, catching her breath, Agnes's head and shoulders propped against her shins. *"How could you be so stupid?"* she railed, angrily wiping away her tears before continuing the trip to the bathroom. "You're going to be black and blue, and it's your own fault! Don't you dare die!" She was so scared. What if she was doing the wrong things, wasting precious time? But sometime, somewhere, she'd seen or read or heard of treating an overdose this way.

Once inside the glaringly bright bathroom, she managed to push and pull at her until Agnes's upper body was inside the stall. Directing the gelid spray into Agnes's face, she was gratified to see her stir slightly. *"Serves you goddamned right!"* she shouted. Leaving Agnes there, she blotted her arms on a towel as she tore back to call 911 a second time.

"This is Rebecca Leighton again. Did you reach Jason?"

"He's had the message. Do you need other assistance, Miss?"

"No. Thank you." She hung up and hurried back to see that Agnes had slid down out of the direct path of the spray. She lowered the shower head so it was again aimed at Agnes's face, then ran skidding in her wet sneakers to the kitchen, looking for the baking soda. She poured about an inch into a glass, added water, and stirred as she opened drawers and cupboards trying to find the funnel she'd seen the night before.

Carrying the baking-soda mixture and the funnel, she returned to the bathroom. The force of the spray had reddened Agnes's face and chest; her fingers were moving.

Rebecca said "Good!" and set the glass and the funnel to

one side as she knelt on the wet floor and hauled Agnes toward her. It took considerable effort to get Agnes's mouth open and the funnel in place. She had to hold Agnes's head steady in the bend of her arm as she poured in the mixture. Then quickly putting aside the glass, she massaged Agnes's throat to get her to swallow. Please work, she prayed, hoping it was a viable antidote. *"Agnes, wake up!"* she bellowed directly into her ear, working herself up to her knees and trying to shift Agnes to a sitting position. "You're going to vomit your heart up, Agnes. I swear to God, you're going to be sick as a dog."

When she felt again between Agnes's breasts, it seemed the heartbeat was fractionally stronger. She held Agnes's head upright. "You just drank a load of baking soda that's going to turn your stomach, Agnes. It's going to make you very, very sick. Feel that?" she demanded, prodding Agnes's stomach.

Agnes actually made a feeble effort to defend herself. Her shoulders twitched, and her hand lifted several inches before falling back to the floor.

"Okay! Good!"

With a heave and strength born of pure fear, she got Agnes back under the blast of freezing water and held her there by the shoulder.

Where was Jason? *"Wake up, Agnes!"* she yelled over the noise of the shower, pinching Agnes's cheeks, then slapping her again.

"I rang the bell. The door was open. What the hell's going on?" Jason said from the doorway.

"She took sleeping pills, with booze. I made her drink a baking-soda solution. What else should I do?"

"I'm calling an ambulance." He turned to go.

"You can't! Jason, she'll lose her job, and it's all she has. *Please don't!"* she pleaded. "If you call an ambulance, it'll be the same as if she did die. *Just help me!"*

"Okay," he relented. Peeling down to his shirt-sleeves,

he threw his holster and gun, cuffs, bullet pouch, clip-on ID, badge, pager, and wallet on the bedroom floor. "I'll take over here. You go make a pot of the world's strongest coffee, then come back."

"What else should I do?"

"Pray the baking soda works! We've got to get that crap out of her system. Go make the coffee!"

She poured at least a quarter-pound of grounds into the filter and got the kettle going, then ran back to the bathroom. Jason had taken Agnes out of her robe and was performing what looked like the Heimlich Maneuver on her. He had her back in the stall and was standing behind her, his arms around her midriff, his joined hands rhythmically thrusting upward into her stomach.

"C'mon, c'mon," he muttered, his muscles straining as he kept Agnes from slipping away out of his arms.

As Rebecca watched, Agnes's flesh seemed to ripple, reacting. Suddenly her entire body jerked violently, her head flew up, and liquid spewed from her mouth.

"Good girl!" Jason said, keeping her upright with one arm while using his free hand to lift the hair out of her face. "We're gonna do it some more now, Agnes," he said, and repeated his actions.

Rebecca flew back to the kitchen to start pouring boiling water through the filter. "Hurry up!" she whispered, shifting from one foot to the other as the coffee began to drip. "Hurry, hurry!" she chanted, filling the filter to the brim before running again to the bathroom.

"We're starting to get somewhere," Jason said. "Turn off this water, please, Beck?"

Rebecca did, then stood at the ready as he hefted Agnes out of the stall and kept her upright while Rebecca began briskly toweling her dry.

"You're going to be okay, Agnes!" he said at top volume, holding her by the shoulders as Rebecca worked her arms

into the terry-cloth robe she'd found on the back of the door. "Let's get her into the living room. Beck, you take one side. I'll take the other. Your friend's going to do a lot of walking the next few hours."

They got Agnes into the living room and propped her against the arm of the sofa while Jason plucked at his sodden shirt-sleeves, saying, "I've got to get out of these clothes."

"Give them to me. I'll throw them in the dryer."

He stripped down, saying, "Think maybe you could find something I can wear till they're dry?"

"Sure."

She got a pair of Agnes's baggy slacks and one of her cardigans, gave them to him, then went to bring in the coffee and a mug.

"I could use a cup myself," he said, shaking his head in disbelief as he dressed quickly. "This is a beautiful woman. Why the hell would she want to die?"

"I don't know." Rebecca knelt down and chafed Agnes's hands, relieved to feel some response in the long cool fingers; even more relieved when she lifted Agnes's eyelids and Agnes tried to turn her head away. "Hey!" Rebecca exclaimed. "You're waking up. Come on, Aggie. Stay with us!"

Jason got two more mugs and poured the coffee. "We'll need at least another full pot, toots. It's going to be a long night."

"I'll make some more in a minute. Jason," she said tearfully, "thank you for getting here so fast, for helping."

"Are you kidding? With all the nonsense that's been going on at your place, you don't think I'd come on the run? Be real, woman! Anyway, don't go thanking me. We're not there yet." He drank some of the coffee, his eyes on Agnes. "Seriously, Beck," he said quietly. "Your friend's beautiful. She's got an important job, nice house, late-model Beamer in the drive. Why would she do this?"

"I can't give you an answer." All at once remembering

Teddy, she said, "I'll be right back," and went to the bedroom to gather up the pieces. Determined no one else would see this, she pushed the remains of the bear into the trash can outside the back door. Then she put the two envelopes from the bedside table in her handbag before joining Jason in the living room.

"I've got to call in," he told her, gulping the last of his coffee. "See if you can get her to swallow some of this." He handed her a half-filled mug. "Better get a towel. Most of it's going to spill."

He was right. She got Agnes to swallow only a few teaspoons. The rest ran down her chin. When Jason came back, he refilled the mug and took over, saying, "Rest for a couple of minutes. You might want to grab some of this yourself, and get another pot going." He slipped into place on the sofa beside Agnes, got his arm around her and starting coaxing her to drink.

By the time Rebecca had a second pot of coffee keeping warm on the stove, he had Agnes up on her feet and was ordering her to walk as he half carried her back and forth. Her eyes closed, her body slack, she appeared to be still unconscious.

"Get hold of her on the other side, Beck," he said, firming up his grip on Agnes's waist.

"Are you going to have problems because of this?" Rebecca asked him, getting Agnes's arm across her shoulders.

"Doubtful. Anything comes up, they'll call me here. *Hey, Agnes!*" he yelled. *"You're not walking! Let's get those gorgeous legs moving!"*

"Leave alone," Agnes slurred.

"Not a chance," Jason said, increasing the pace.

"Stop it!" Agnes protested distinctly.

"Nope."

"Maybe we should try to get her to drink some more

coffee," Rebecca suggested, her arms and upper body aching from the strain of keeping Agnes on her feet and moving.

"In a few minutes," he said, readjusting his hold to take most of Agnes's weight. "This is rough, I know. Soon as she starts helping a bit more, we'll go back to pouring coffee into her."

They fell silent for a time, parading Agnes back and forth the length of the living room. It seemed as if hours had passed when it dawned on Rebecca that Agnes seemed to weigh less, and she looked down to see Agnes's bare feet moving hesitantly one in front of the other.

"She's walking!" Rebecca said exultantly with the feeling that a miracle had happened.

"She sure is." He grinned over at her. "Coffee time, Agnes!"

They collapsed on the sofa with Agnes still anchored between them, and sat for a few moments. Rebecca's lungs labored as she tried to slow down her heart and her breathing. According to the clock on the mantel, it was nearly three-thirty. It felt as if she'd been here far longer than just two hours. Jason refilled the mugs, then took the empty carafe out to the kitchen. Rebecca turned to look at Agnes, who was sitting with her eyes half open, head drooping.

Rebecca took hold of her hands and held them tightly. "Agnes?"

Agnes's head jerked up, her eyes focusing for a second on Rebecca. "Sick," she whispered, and made an effort to free herself as her throat began to work. She shuddered helplessly, then liquid gushed from her mouth.

"Poor Agnes," Rebecca crooned, reaching for the towel. She dried Agnes's face, then blotted the front of the robe as Agnes moaned, tears leaking from the corners of her closed eyes.

"She throw up again?" Jason asked. "Good. That's good.

You're doing great, Agnes," he said, sitting again beside her. "Now we're going to drink a bunch more coffee. And if we're lucky, you'll vomit another two, three times."

She swatted feebly at his hand, and Rebecca reached to stop her.

"Hey, Beck, it's okay. Let her beat up on me. It'll get her adrenaline going. Right, Agnes? Come on. Give it your best shot."

It clearly took a mammoth effort, but Agnes raised her head, got her eyes slitted open, and asked thickly, ". . . the bloody hell're you?"

"I'm Jason, your new friend."

Drunkenly, Agnes turned to look at Rebecca, her eyes already starting to close. "Hate you," she muttered.

Knowing it was absurd under the circumstances, Rebecca was nevertheless wounded.

"None of that," Jason said, his hand on her chin turning Agnes's head toward him. "Here comes the coffee, Aggie. Over the teeth and cross the gums. Look out, tummy, here it comes!"

"God, Jason!" Rebecca smiled tearfully.

"Something we'll teach the kiddies, Beck," he said, tipping the mug to Agnes's mouth. "Down the hatch now. Good girl!"

"Hot!" Agnes protested.

"Sorry, Aggie, cold coffee isn't going to do it."

Rebecca marveled at the way he was handling the situation, impressed by his practicality and kindness, by his ability to maintain his sense of humor even under the most trying circumstances. Watching him minister to Agnes, she was overcome by certainty, and understood why her mother had so readily embraced him. He had no pretensions and no fear of revealing himself. He was someone who cared about others.

His pager and the dryer signal went off simultaneously.

"What's that?" they asked each other.

"My pager."

"The dryer."

"Okay," he said. "Keep pouring coffee into your friend. I'll get my clothes and phone in."

Agnes didn't want to drink any more. She turned her head away and pushed at Rebecca's hand. "Let me sleep," she said.

"You've got to stay awake."

"Sleep!" Agnes pushed the mug away.

Frustrated and weary, Rebecca cried, "Drink the god-damned coffee, Agnes! I'm not letting you go to sleep. If I see your eyes closed, I'll hit you." Grabbing hold of Agnes's hand to keep it out of the way, she held the mug to Agnes's mouth and yelled, *"Drink this!"*

Defiantly, Agnes shook her head. Rebecca pinched her arm, hard enough to bring a gloss of tears to Agnes's eyes. "You think I'm kidding? Drink this!"

Guilty at having to hurt her, Rebecca again held the mug forward. With the hangdog expression of a thoroughly chastised child, Agnes obediently drank.

"You going to be able to manage on your own for a while?" Jason asked, his dry clothes over his arm. "I've got to go on a call."

"I'll manage," Rebecca said, grimly determined.

"The thing is, I don't know how long I'll be," he said, pulling off his borrowed clothes.

"I'll manage," she repeated. "I think she's over the worst part, if giving me a hard time's any indication."

"Keep her moving. Don't let her close her eyes for more than a few seconds, and definitely don't let her lie down. I'll try to get back fast."

He went to the bathroom and came back fitting on his shoulder holster, then jammed his cuffs and bullets and IDs into various pockets. The pager went into his inside jacket pocket. He folded the garments he'd removed and placed them on the arm of one of the chairs. Then he crossed the room to stroke Rebecca's hair as he bent to look close-to into Agnes's eyes.

"Give it up, Aggie," he said gently. "Nobody wants you to die." Lifting her chin with the side of his hand, he kissed her on the forehead. "I'll be back soon's I can," he promised, and left.

"Coffee," Agnes said, bringing Rebecca's attention back to her. She took a good swallow. Her eyelids fluttered, but she forced them open, saying, "We'd better walk."

Rebecca stared at her for a second or two, then stood, grasped both of Agnes's hands and helped her up.

"Don't know if I'll forgive you," Agnes said as Rebecca got an arm around her and started her moving.

"Of course you will," Rebecca said.

"It's a complete mess."

"We'll take care of everything," Rebecca promised. "Just keep walking."

CHAPTER

Eighteen

The coffee gave Rebecca the shakes and made her slightly nauseated, but it revived Agnes. After almost three hours of walking and her consumption of at least a quart of the powerful brew, Agnes was fully awake and moving on her own. One arm wrapped around her chest, she paced back and forth with a cigarette, smoking furiously. Now that the danger had passed, Rebecca was overwhelmingly tired. She sagged into one of the armchairs and watched Agnes march up and down the room.

"Why couldn't you leave me be?" Agnes suddenly demanded, pausing to toss her cigarette into the fireplace. "Who asked you to play Nancy Drew?"

Rebecca reasoned it was only logical Agnes would be angry, but understanding didn't take any of the sting out of the words. "I'm sure," she said quietly, "if our positions were reversed, I'd be outraged at your wrecking my carefully planned suicide."

"Don't expect me to be grateful," Agnes said bitterly.

"I don't *expect* you to *be* anything, except alive."

"That doesn't strike you as just a bit selfish?" Agnes challenged.

"Yes, it is. It's a hundred-percent selfish. All caring is, because it makes the one who cares feel good."

"You *believe* that?" Agnes asked, bewildered.

"Yes, I do," Rebecca said stubbornly. "And there's nothing wrong with that kind of selfishness."

Her bewildered expression holding, Agnes sank down on the edge of the sofa, her arm still wrapped around herself.

"Why did you do it?" Rebecca asked, crossing to sit beside her on the sofa. "Please, tell me."

"Why? So you can again suggest I seek counseling?"

"Maybe you only need another viewpoint. Maybe you've blown whatever it is out of proportion."

"I doubt that."

"Tell me," Rebecca coaxed. "It can't make things any worse."

Agnes continued to sit staring at her feet. Then she dropped her head into her hands. "All these years," she said, her voice muffled, "my professional behavior has been above reproach. Whatever I did on my own time was done with discretion. I threw it all away, put everything at risk."

"How?"

Her voice dropping even lower, she said, "Thirty years ago, a teacher interfered with me. I made history repeat itself by becoming involved with one of the students."

"Oh, my God!" Rebecca said, jolted. "I see."

"What the hell do you see?" Agnes rounded on her.

"I understand." All at once Agnes's remarks about sleeping with the right men made horrible sense.

"You do, do you?"

"Stop attacking me, please," Rebecca said tiredly. "God, Agnes! I know damned well what the repercussions would be—personally and professionally. Give me a little credit.

Whether you like it or not, I'm here and I care. It's not my place to judge you. Not that I'm minimizing the seriousness of what you've told me. But now I understand."

Agnes grabbed for the cigarettes on the coffee table and lit one with trembling hands.

"Tell me about it," Rebecca invited, trying not to show how much this revelation shocked her.

"Please don't say it'll make me feel better," Agnes snapped. "Play Pollyanna with me, Rebecca, and I swear to God, I'll hit you."

"I'll bet at school you were the tough kid," Rebecca said. "Probably played it to the hilt, did everything you could to get yourself thrown out."

"You'd be wrong," Agnes said evenly. "I was a toady of the first order. I was obedient, courteous, and a top-grade grind. I told you, you don't know me."

"All right. I don't know you." Rebecca gave up and just waited, running a mental list of all the possible repercussions should it ever become known that Agnes had violated her position of trust. The implications were harrowing.

Agnes took a hard drag on the cigarette, then exhaled a thick plume of smoke. "What prompted you to come flying over here in the middle of the night?"

Rebecca sighed heavily. "It was a combination of things you'd said recently, your moods. And you said good-bye, Agnes. Not see you in the morning, but good-bye. I was awake for hours, putting it all together. Then when I phoned at a quarter after one and got your damned answering machine, I knew you'd really meant good-bye. So I came on the run. And seeing you that way"—she winced at the recollection—"I knew I needed help, so I called Jason. I didn't dare call an ambulance, given how the school board views even the slightest deviation from the curriculum."

"No," Agnes agreed solemnly, "you could hardly have done that. Why must you always be so bloody *good?* Have you any idea how maddening that can be to those of us who are considerably less morally upright?"

"I'm sorry," Rebecca said curtly. "I'll try harder in future to behave in a more acceptably reprehensible fashion."

"Damn it, Rebecca. It was so much easier my way."

"You believe you've committed a cardinal sin, but I don't believe it's worth dying for. You got involved with a student. That's definitely not good. But worse things have been known to happen. Men're forever doing it, college professors having affairs with freshmen."

"This isn't college," Agnes reminded her.

"Are we talking about a freshman?"

"No, we're talking about Murray Beckworth."

Of course, Rebecca thought, suddenly able to put any number of things together. It really was a mess. Agnes hadn't understated the case. "But Murray's at least eighteen. He's a grown man, Agnes. It's not as if you've corrupted the morals of a child."

"He's my *student*."

"He's also an adult. Is it still going on?"

"It's over," Agnes said dully.

"If it's over, why try to kill yourself?"

Agnes took another puff on her cigarette, then put it out and again buried her face in her hands.

"What?" Rebecca asked softly.

Agnes shook her head into her hands, her breathing going ragged.

Shaken, Rebecca kept silent. She'd never seen Agnes cry. It was unnerving to see her so undone.

"I can't do this," Agnes said. She blotted her face on the sleeve of her robe. "I wish to Christ you'd left me alone. It would have been best for all concerned."

"Maybe you should talk to him, Agnes, satisfy yourself once and for all that you didn't harm him."

"Oh, *please*! That's the last thing I could do."

"All right. Would you mind if I talked to him?"

Her reddened eyes widening, Agnes asked, "Whatever for?"

"So we can clarify matters. So you can be satisfied you haven't done him any harm, that you haven't destroyed your career."

Agnes looked away and busied herself pouring yet more coffee. Holding the mug with both hands, she stared into space. "It's so goddamned pathetic. Spinster schoolteacher smitten with handsome, virile young student."

"Don't talk that way. You're nobody's idea of a spinster schoolteacher. And Murray's no one's idea of a child."

"Look," Agnes said wearily, "do whatever you want. I don't care."

"I think it's important, Agnes. You and I both know how serious this is. You can't just leave things dangling. For your own peace of mind, one way or another, you've got to know Murray's position. If he can assure you no harm's been done, then you can quietly bury the whole thing. But as long as it remains an open issue, you'll just keep on wanting to punish yourself."

Agnes swallowed some of the coffee, then returned the mug to the table. "What have you done with the letters?"

"They're unopened, in my bag."

"I'd appreciate their return," she said coldly.

"I'll get them." Rebecca went to the bedroom for her handbag, wishing she could find some way to break through Agnes's resistance. God! Agnes must have felt truly desperate to have become involved with a student.

Agnes sat holding the envelopes for some time, looking at them front and back, before tearing them in half, then in quarters. "Anticlimactic, isn't it?" she said sardonically.

"No, just a big relief." Rebecca looked at the time on the VCR. "I'd better call the school, tell them we won't be in. I'll hang around here today."

"Keeping an eye on me."

"Correct."

"I'd actually be glad of the company," Agnes admitted.

Rebecca sat down and hugged her. "I care about you, and I don't want you to die," she said, on the verge of tears. "Why do you feel killing yourself is the only solution?"

"You may have noticed I have some difficulty with my emotions. I don't have your candor, or your courage."

"Maybe I'm candid, but I'm certainly not courageous," Rebecca said. "You don't have to die because a situation seems impossible. I know you think I sound like Pollyanna, but, God! Death doesn't solve anything. All it does is leave the people who love you with an immense hole in their lives and too many questions that'll never be answered. Do you *know* how glad I am that I got here in time? D'you have any idea of how guilty I'd have felt if I hadn't heard that goodbye? I'd have felt guilty for the rest of my life," she said mournfully, the tears finally overflowing. "I'd have thought about how I failed you, and I'd have been miserable that my dearest friend died because I wasn't paying close enough attention."

Cowed, Agnes looked away.

"Talk to me, please."

Agnes shook her head.

"Okay." Rebecca wiped her eyes with the back of her hand. "I'm going to call the school now, get that out of the way."

After explaining to Eileen, the head secretary, that Agnes was ill and that she planned to spend the day with her, Rebecca called Lou Gianelli. He was the one faculty member who would respond without asking too many questions. She also knew Agnes was fond of him.

For a pleasant change, she didn't connect with an answering machine, but with Lou himself.

"I'm glad I caught you before you left. I can't go into the details over the phone, but I'm with Agnes, and I'll be here all day. I've already notified the school. Lou, could you possibly come over here after classes today? I'm going to have to go home for a couple of hours and I don't want to leave her on her own."

"Sure," he said at once. "Is she all right?"

"We'll talk when you get here."

"I can be there by two-fifteen. I've only got one class after lunch."

Rebecca thanked him and hung up, thinking Jason obviously wasn't going to make it back from his call. She yawned, then rubbed her eyes. The nausea had passed, but her stomach was still unsettled from the coffee.

"Could you eat something?" she asked Agnes.

Agnes blinked, then laughed so hard tears came to her eyes. "I'm supposed to be dead, for God's sake! But yes. I'm desperately hungry."

"Good," Rebecca smiled, encouraged. "Let's make breakfast."

Agnes got up from the sofa, lifting a handful of her hair. "I must look a sight."

"Well, you have seen better days."

"I'm trying my best not to hate you."

"Go ahead and hate me, Agnes. I'd rather have you alive and hating me than dead and beyond all emotion." With that, Rebecca turned and headed for the kitchen.

"I know you'll have a fit, but I asked Lou to come over after his last class."

"Another baby-sitter?"

"If our positions were reversed," Rebecca said for the second time, "would you leave me to spend the night alone?"

"You've asked him to stay the night?"

"No, just a couple of hours. I want to go home, get cleaned up and change clothes. Then I'll come back."

"I resent your involving him," Agnes said, reaching for a cigarette. "I resent every last bloody thing you've said and done here."

"Will you *please* stop all this!" Rebecca said, exasperated. "Lou's one of the most decent people we know. And he thinks the world of you. I'm not going to leave you here alone, and that's that!"

"He thinks of me as just another teacher. Stop trying to inflate my ego! Why," she asked, shifting stiffly, "do I feel as if I've been the victim of a hit-and-run accident?" Standing she lifted the robe and looked at her backside. "It would appear you and your new paramour gave me a fair old bashing. I'm a mass of bruises."

"You'll have to blame me for that," Rebecca confessed. "I dragged you into the bathroom. Jason got here maybe half an hour later and took over."

Chagrined, Agnes sat with her fist held to her mouth. "Dreadful," she said, again averting her eyes.

"It's okay, Agnes. We were too busy trying to force you to vomit to spend any time looking at you. Don't even think about it."

"Easy for you to say. You weren't stark naked in the shower with a stranger; you're not the one who's vomited all over the house. Christ! It's so humiliating." For a second time, she began to cry.

"Look. All that matters is that you're here and that you've actually eaten a decent amount of food for the first time in ages."

"Why did you have to call Lou?" Agnes asked miserably.

"He's the only one I trust not to talk."

The doorbell rang. Both women automatically looked up.

"Maybe it's Jason," Rebecca said, rising and going to the door.

Jason stood there with a bag of food from McDonald's.

"How's it going? Sorry I couldn't get back sooner. We had a little joint kerfuffle with the Staties busting some dealers at the service center on I-Ninety-five. It was a whole lot of fun." He gave her a kiss, shucked his ratty jacket, and followed her into the kitchen.

"We've just finished breakfast," Rebecca said, sliding back into her chair.

"How're you doing, Agnes?" he asked, placing a hand on her shoulder.

"I've had better days," she replied coolly, shrugging off his hand.

"I'll bet you have," he said matter-of-factly. "I brought us a bunch of Egg McMuffins. I guess I'll have to eat them myself."

"If you'll excuse me," Agnes said, "I think I'll put some clothes on." Avoiding eye contact with either of them, she went off to her bedroom.

Jason sat down, asking, "How's it been?"

"She's very angry with me," Rebecca told him.

"That's to be expected." He unwrapped an Egg McMuffin, removed the lid from a container of coffee, and began to eat. "She'll get over it. You look wiped, toots."

"I am."

"You want to grab some zees, I'll keep Agnes company."

"That's okay. I'll hang in. Lou Gianelli, head of the math department, is coming over this afternoon to spell me for a couple of hours so I can go home and get cleaned up. Besides, you must be tired, too." It was amazing, she thought. It felt as if they'd known each other for years; they were perfectly attuned.

"I'm used to long hours," he said, finishing the sandwich. "Think she'll try again?"

"God! I hope not." She sat thinking as he looked into the McDonald's bag, then folded it closed and sipped his coffee. "I don't think so," she said at last. "I really appreciate all your help, Jason. I could never have managed on my own."

"Forget it," he said. "This Lou, is he okay?"

"He won't talk, if that's what you mean."

"Good. So, I guess tonight's a bust."

"It looks that way. I can't leave her on her own."

"I could pick up some Chinese or something, swing by here if you like."

"You don't have to do that."

"I know that, Rebecca, but I'm offering. I'd like to. What d'you think?"

"Let's leave it up to Agnes. Okay?"

"Sure, no prob." Leaning toward her and dropping his voice, he said, "I was really looking forward to nibbling your tiny pink toes, toots."

"A foot fetishist, are you?" Agnes said archly, coming back into the kitchen and making her way to the stove to pour herself more coffee.

"Definitely," Jason said. "So, what d'you think, Agnes? Should I pick up Chinese and drop back around six?"

Her eyes slightly narrowed, she looked over at him. "And I suppose you'd like to play Trivial Pursuit, too?"

"Hey! I'd love it," he said, deliberately ignoring her acrimonious tone. "I could bring my Silver Screen edition. I'm into movies in a big way, have been since I was a kid. Or how about the Baby Boomers one? We're all Boomers, right? There's always gin rummy, or three-handed poker. Or we could get Lou to make a foursome and do group games in the shower. He a fun guy, this Lou?"

"Christ!" Agnes couldn't suppress a smile. "Pollyanna and Mister Indefatigable. This is too bloody much!" Defeated, she came to sit at the table. "I give up. We'll celebrate my failed suicide attempt with Chinese food and party games. I actually happen to have the Silver Screen edition."

"Oh, neat!" Jason teased her. "This'll be swell, won't it, kids?"

"Just peachy," Agnes snapped.

"Seriously," Jason said, "how d'you feel, Agnes?"

"Why on earth do you care?" she asked him.

"Because you're Beck's friend, and she cares," he replied. "Besides," he added, getting his pipe from his inside pocket, "I like you."

"Then you're an idiot!"

"Wait!" he cried. "I've got it. Baby Jane to Blanche. Right?"

"What?" Rebecca looked first at him, then at Agnes.

"Right!" Agnes smiled at him approvingly.

She was going to be okay, Rebecca decided, watching Agnes respond positively to Jason. Her relief was such that she could have gone to sleep right there at the table. Now if only the son of a bitch who was trying to drive her crazy would quit and leave her alone, everything would be fine.

Pete felt lousy, like he had this loser acid rock band playing its biggest hot number inside his skull. Gave him the worst headache. Plus he couldn't keep track of stuff. People telling him do this, do that, and him going yeah, okay, sure. But he'd forget. Then last night his mother got into her latest pitch which was how she couldn't wait for him to go the hell off to some college and get out of her face. The same old jazz about what made him think he could treat her the way he did, and if he didn't clean up his room, she'd burn everything in it.

Number one, he could hardly wait to get to college himself. Only problem was, he positively could not remember if he'd mailed the applications. He could see himself filling them out, getting Xerox copies of his transcript and all that, but he couldn't remember mailing the envelopes. He couldn't find them anywhere, so he was just hanging. He'd know if he sent them when he started getting rejections, which he was bound to get because his grades were in the toilet. Man! All he wanted was to put in maybe twenty-four hours straight sack time.

It was all bullshit. Everything. Bullshit. He had maybe sixty bucks the old man had laid on him, enough to score some serious pills if he made a quick trip to the service center. One thing for sure, he wasn't into staying at school today.

The word was Leighton and Tyrell were no-shows. That got him kind of curious. So he decided to cut out after the second class, threw his books into the locker, and walked out. He didn't have the energy to ride the bike to the service center, so he headed home.

Wheeling into the driveway, he saw that the wagon was there, but the Olds was gone. Maybe it was his lucky day, and his mother had actually gone out for a change.

The house was stuffy, reeked of cigarette smoke. The curtains were drawn in the living room, but his mother wasn't home. Great! He chugged some orange juice right from the carton, then went to his room. Opened the door and felt like he'd been kicked in the gut. He couldn't believe it. All his stuff was gone. Only the furniture and his boom-box were left. Everything else was gone: his tapes, photographs, all the posters, his books and magazines. He ran to check the closet, then the dresser drawers. Half his clothes were gone, too. She'd cleaned him out. Even his fucking school yearbooks.

He tore outside to check the garbage cans. Empty. Ran back inside to look at his room again, as if maybe he'd been hallucinating or something. But it was the same as before. "What the fuck!?" he yelled, completely freaked. Then he thought she might've stowed the stuff somewhere in the house, so he went from room to room checking the drawers and closets, under the beds. Went through every possible place in the house where she could've hidden his things. Gone! The bitch had actually burned his stuff! How could she *do* that? She had no *right* to do that! Breaking into tears, he punched the wall with his fist, put his fucking hand right through the drywall. Good thing she wasn't there, he'd have put his fist through her face. He'd have killed her, beat her until she was fucking dead.

His chest hurting, he grabbed the key ring from the counter in the kitchen and went out to the car. Reversed out of the driveway, then floored the accelerator, knuckling the tears out of his eyes. Look what that bitch Leighton had done! Because of her, every last fucking thing he cared about went up in smoke. Because of her, the family turned to shit. Years now, things'd been falling apart, and it was all her goddamned fault. Why'd she have to mess with his father? Why the hell couldn't she find somebody else?

He cruised the Shore Road. No Jetta. He drove on past and parked the wagon in the driveway of this empty house with a for-sale sign out front. Then he walked back down the road, fished the keys out of his pocket and let himself into the bitch's house. He stood in the mudroom looking around, spotted a screwdriver on the shelf and had an idea.

Grabbing the screwdriver, he went to work on the screws holding the safety chain. He loosened them just enough so that it wouldn't be noticeable, but one good push against the door from outside would pop them right out of the wall. Satisfied, he put the screwdriver back on the shelf.

He found a couple of candles in one of the drawers, and some packs of matches. He jammed the candles and matches into his jacket pocket, then grabbed a diet Coke and a hunk of cheese from the refrigerator. There was an unopened box of wheat crackers in one of the cupboards. Carrying all the stuff in one arm, he lifted the trapdoor and climbed down into the cellar. He'd hole up and wait for the bitch to come home. Then he'd fix her once and for fucking all.

When he actually saw the crawl space in the light of the candle, it was bone-dry, with not a bug to be seen. In fact, it looked pretty decent. He scooted over into the far inside corner and settled in. There was just enough room for him to sit if he hunched a bit, so he leaned back against the foundation wall, popped the tab on the diet Coke and chowed down on some of the cheese and crackers.

While he was eating, he started crying again, thinking about what his mother had done. She'd fucking destroyed everything he owned. All his bootleg live-concert Dead tapes, his dubs, his original Zeppelin posters, everything. What he felt was way, way beyond hate. It was this whole other emotion that didn't have any name. And mixed in with that was this killer pain, this little-kid kind of hurting that made his throat feel like he'd swallowed a peach pit.

He cried until he was so wiped he couldn't keep his eyes open. Bunching up his jacket for a pillow, he put the matches within reach, then snuffed the candle.

CHAPTER

Nineteen

By the time she was on her way home at a quarter to three that afternoon, Rebecca felt as if she were moving through a sea of quick-drying cement. She was utterly drained, yet every time she thought about seeing Agnes laid out in that bedroom, her brain seemed to start sizzling and she was gripped by an anxious need to get back to Agnes as quickly as possible. It felt vitally important that she keep a personal, vigilant watch over her friend.

After pulling into the driveway, she took the key from the ignition, then rested her cheek on the steering wheel as she looked at the house. She didn't want to go inside, not even in daylight. It was ironic, but she'd have given a lot to have back her old, boring life. Anything was preferable to what she was going through now. Just a couple of weeks, and everything had been turned inside out. Her best friend had tried to kill herself, and someone was doing his damnedest to destroy her sanity. She didn't know if she had enough strength left to keep on fighting.

Resigned, she got out of the car and took a walk around the house. She was so done in she doubted she'd notice, but nothing appeared out of place. She completed the circuit and let herself in the back door.

Standing in the mudroom, she was again overcome by reluctance and had to force herself to hang up her coat before making an inspection of the interior of the house. Again, everything looked okay, and she returned to the kitchen.

Yawning, she listened to the messages on her machine. The first was the locksmith, asking her to call again for an appointment. He sounded disgusted, as if returning her original call had been a complete waste of his time.

The second was the electrician, saying something had come up and he'd have to reschedule from Wednesday to Thursday evening. Would she please let him know if that was no good for her.

The third, fourth, and fifth were hang-ups, each followed by thirty seconds of dial tone, then a recording of a robotic female voice saying, "Please hang up and try your call again."

The sixth was Ray, calling, he said, from St. Louis. "It's now ten to eight Monday morning. I'll try again later. Sorry I missed you."

The seventh was her mother, saying, "I've already made three trips to the dump this morning. Where did all this trash come from? Call me when you get home from school, sweetheart. 'Bye."

The eighth and ninth were more hang-ups, with more dial tones and the female robot again.

After resetting the machine, she checked all the doors and windows as well as the appliances, the TV and the stereo. There were no more hidden timers; the skylights were clear; the shutters and curtains remained drawn over the windows. Of course just because she couldn't see anything didn't mean someone hadn't been inside. She phoned the locksmith, who informed her that the soonest he could make an after-school appointment was Wednesday. She booked the date, then remembered and went out to get the mail. Bills from Southern New England Telephone, NorthEast Utilities, and Visa, a couple of magazines, but no check.

She called the electrician, got his machine, and left a message saying Thursday would be fine. Finally she dialed her mother's number, but there was no answer. After that, she went upstairs to take a long, hot shower.

Twice in the shower she found herself falling asleep. If she didn't rest for a little while, she'd never make it through the remainder of the day. Taking care to set the digital alarm to P.M., she climbed into bed in her underwear to sleep for an hour and a half.

In the crawl space, Pete lay with his head on his jacket, deeply asleep. He dreamed he was boinking the bitch, going at it like crazy. And the totally weird thing was, they were both hot for it, really into it, like they were in love or something. They were doing it, and he was looking at her face, freaked because she was so beautiful. She had these phenomenal turquoise-colored eyes, all this thick curly black hair, and an amazing body. She was letting him do absolutely anything he wanted, and loving it, begging him to do more.

Then, flash, with no warning, he was back at his house, standing in the burnt-out shell of his room. A feeling of desolation took over him, and he wanted to get out of there. But the door was gone. He was trapped in this reeking black box with no way out. He ran around the perimeter, pounding on the charred walls with his fists, screaming for somebody to come let him out.

He awakened with a start and was freaked, not knowing where he was. Then it came back to him, and he found the matches and lit one to look at his watch. Coming up to four o'clock. He got a candle going and sat thinking. He was so wiped he almost nodded off again. His head fell forward and he came to with a jolt.

He didn't want to go home. Not after what his fucking mother had done to his room. But if he didn't turn up, she'd probably report him missing to the police. And that'd be all he needed, having the cops looking for him. He was screwed; he'd have to go home.

He stowed the candles and what was left of the food in the corner, then worked his way over to the opening of the crawl space. Shit! What if the bitch was home? His legs cramped, his body stiff from sleeping on the concrete and dirt, he stood at the bottom of the ladder. He didn't want to go out the storm doors because then she'd know he'd been inside. If he left by the back door, she'd have no way of knowing.

At the top of the ladder, he listened. Not a sound. There was a good chance she wasn't home. His heartbeat picking up, he eased the trapdoor up an inch or so. Quiet. Now or never. He scooted up the ladder. His heart pounding, he stepped into the room, lowered the trapdoor, took a couple of steps, looked out through the back door. The Jetta was parked in the driveway. The chain was on the door. Shit!

His eyes went to the spiral staircase. Was she up there? Total quiet. He sneaked over to the stairs, began inching his way up until he could see into the room. His heart slammed. She was there, sacked out. He made it to the top of the staircase, took a couple of steps, stopped, holding his breath.

The dream came back to him, the two of them boinking, but he couldn't get the dream into sync with what was actually happening. He was right there in the bitch's bedroom. She was totally out. He could do anything. Except he couldn't. He could only stand there, blown away by how she looked like a kid, curled up asleep, her hands tucked under her cheek. A kid with all this black hair and these long eyelashes and a completely great face, like a fucking angel, or a painting or something.

He felt weird, like something out of a horror flick, some unbelievably hideous, lizard-skinned, grotesque mutation. And she was this innocent dreaming angel. None of it fit with the way he'd been feeling about her. His chest was hurting again, and he knew he had to get the hell out of there.

Down the stairs without making a sound and straight out the back door. A few seconds and he was running up the road to where he'd left the car.

As he drove home, he shook off the weird feeling and decided the only way to deal with his mother was not to say one fucking word to her. No matter what she said or did, not if she went to burn him up just like she'd burned all the stuff that'd ever meant anything to him, he wasn't saying one word. And while he was giving her the silent treatment, he was going to be figuring out a major, major pay-back.

"What happened, Agnes?" Lou asked.

"Rebecca didn't tell you?"

"No. She just asked if I'd mind keeping you company for a couple of hours."

"And you agreed," Agnes said. She was sitting on the sofa with her feet propped on the coffee table. Lou was seated comfortably in one of the armchairs. "A demonstration of admirable restraint, Louis." She gave him a tight smile.

"You're in a nice mood," he observed, unruffled, thinking what a wonderful-looking woman she was, in spite of her visible tiredness. He'd always been awed by her, by her ferocious intelligence, by her looks, and her glossy mane of fiery hair. Today, for the first time, he saw that her eyelashes were a rare russet color. Not that he'd ever doubted it, but the eyelashes proved her hair was natural, not dyed.

"I'm in a filthy mood," she said flatly, lighting a cigarette. "This is service above and beyond the call on your part."

"I don't know about service," he said, looking around. "I

like your house. I've been renting an apartment in Stamford since the split. It's getting on my nerves. The noise," he clarified. "Every time the people above me take a shower or flush the toilet, it sounds as if I'm in a diving bell."

"Good imagery," she said, openly studying him. He didn't seem bothered by not knowing why he was there. "Aren't you curious, Louis?"

He crossed his legs, then smoothed his mustache. "Sure," he answered, enjoying this singular opportunity to talk with her in her own home. She had good taste. He liked what she'd done with the house. "But I can live with it. The staff and students were busy speculating on why you and Rebecca were both out today. Apparently your intern lost control of the senior lit class. Crandall had to go in and take over."

"He must have loved that," Agnes said, eyebrows raised. "It has to be ten years since he taught a class."

"At least," Lou agreed. "He'll never make principal, but he keeps on trying. Me, I'd transfer to another school in the system. But not Jake. He wants Nortown High. He's ridiculous. Ever see him patroling the cafeteria?" He smiled. "The kids pelt him with peas, bump into him and leave Hit-Me signs Scotch-taped to his back. Anyway, things got so out of hand he finally had to dismiss the class. They were all in the cafeteria wetting themselves over Jake and the intern."

"I took twenty-six sleeping pills with a glass of Ballantine's," she said baldly, watching closely to see how he'd take this.

"God almighty, Agnes. Why?" He looked grieved.

"That should be obvious."

"I know. But why? What made you do a thing like that?"

"Oh, this and that."

"No, really. Why?"

"I don't think I can tell you."

"Sleeping pills you said?" He leaned forward, his eyes troubled. "Mind if I ask what kind?"

"That's an odd question." She looked bemused. "Triazolam, I think."

"Triazolam," he repeated. "How long have you been taking it?"

"About two and a half years."

"Surely you're aware of all the negative press Halcion's been getting."

"What do you mean?" she asked, thrown. "I haven't been taking Halcion."

"Triazolam's the generic name," he told her. "I know all about it because my mother was on the drug for ages, and after a while I started noticing she didn't remember things; she got restless as hell and complained that food didn't taste right. She was edgy, said her eyesight was going; she was tired but couldn't sleep without the pills.

"Finally I started getting really worried, so I took her to a new internist for a checkup. First thing he did was get her to list all the medications she was taking. When he saw she was on Halcion, he said he was ninety-percent sure that was what was causing her problems. He took her off it, and within six months she was way better."

While he'd been talking, Agnes had taken her feet off the coffee table and sat very straight. Now she said, "She suffered memory loss? And nervousness? But sometimes she was hyperactive? Did she ever tell you she felt confused, or depressed?"

Lou nodded. "She was terrified she had Alzheimer's. But it was the Halcion. Believe me, Agnes. I researched the hell out of that drug. I don't know why doctors still prescribe it, especially in view of the side effects that have come to light. There have even been cases of people becoming violent on the drug."

"Oh Christ!" she whispered, stunned. "Aside from becoming more and more depressed, I've been forgetting all sorts of things. In the past few months there have been days when I've been positively wired, fizzing with a kind of manic energy, but desperately tired at the same time. Seeing things, imagining things, uninterested in eating, weak, yet energized. I thought I'd contracted something terminal. And you're sitting here telling me it's all as a result of my being given a drug I wouldn't knowingly have taken. Louis!" she exclaimed. "I thought I was losing my faculties. Every day, for months now, it's taken all my willpower and strength to get to school and make it through the day. It reached the point where I decided I'd prefer to die than continue living this way."

"Didn't you go see your GP?"

"He told me to take multi bloody vitamin tablets and gave me a brochure on menopause! It was so *offensive*. Not that I mind being menopausal, if that's what I am. But vitamin pills and a brochure when I sit there on the verge of hysterics, telling him I'm losing my mind! Christ! And never a *word* about the so-called Triazolam he'd prescribed and kept refilling because I couldn't sleep."

"You're not crazy, Agnes," he said with conviction. "But it sounds like you need a new doctor."

"Clearly!" she agreed. "I might as well tell you the rest of it," she said, shocked beyond her anger, and anxious to confide in him because what he'd just told her made such a sudden and enormous difference to how she felt about herself. "I became involved with one of the students." She wanted to look away, but forced herself to keep her eyes on his. If he passed judgment on her, she didn't know what she'd do.

"Murray Beckworth."

"You *knew?*" she said, terrified to think it was common knowledge at school.

"I was afraid it might be," he admitted. "I was hoping I was wrong, but you were on your way to the English office one morning, maybe three or four months ago, and I happened to see Murray watching you. It registered. I hoped I was wrong. I mean, in twelve years working together, I've never known you to be . . . I don't know . . . rash, I guess. Anyway, as I said, I hoped I was wrong."

Worriedly, she asked, "Do you think anyone else guessed?"

"Highly doubtful. I probably wouldn't have picked up on it myself, except that I was, well, interested." He changed position in the chair, looking uncomfortable now.

"What do you mean?"

"It's just that I was watching you myself," he admitted, one finger nervously smoothing his mustache. "I suppose I recognized something in the way he was looking at you."

She reached to put out her cigarette, then sat bent over her crossed arms. "I tried to kill myself because I thought I was going mad, because I was so unutterably depressed, because I'd broken the rules, because I couldn't sleep and was walking around in a daze." She shook her head mournfully and bent more until her chin was resting on her knees. "If Rebecca hadn't come here last night, I'd have died. God, the things I said to her!"

"She won't hold it against you, Agnes. Rebecca's not like that."

"I was vicious, positively vicious." Tears streamed down her cheeks, and she shook her head again.

"What's the status with Murray?" he asked awkwardly.

"It's finished."

"That's good," he said, not sure what to say. He felt sorry for her, and strangely sorry for himself, too. It saddened him to learn he hadn't been wrong, that she'd put everything on the line by becoming involved with one of the kids. But at least it was over. That was something.

Covering her eyes with one hand, she said, "That story about your mother, it's the truth?"

"You can phone her if you like. She's become a real crusader, trying to organize a lobby to get the stuff taken off the market."

Agnes sat up and let her head fall back against the sofa, wiping her face with shaking hands. "Poor Rebecca. As if she hasn't got enough on her plate, with someone vandalizing her house, putting drugs in her tea. She rescues me and I heap verbal abuse on her. And on Jason, to boot."

"I know she won't hold it against you," he said, wishing he knew how to comfort her. It upset him badly to know she'd tried to kill herself. Agnes was a woman who'd always seemed to have a zest for life. It was awful to learn that she was anything but, and that he'd been blind to her unhappiness. "Who's Jason?" he asked.

"A policeman Rebecca's seeing," she answered dully. "I am so tired, so horribly tired."

"Maybe you should try to get some sleep." He had a flash image of himself putting her to bed, holding her hand until she fell asleep. His imagination was out of control.

"Not yet. The drug's still in my system. Besides," she said, slowly sitting upright again, "I'm afraid to go to sleep. Isn't that ironic? Now I'm afraid I won't wake up. What must you think of me?" She looked over at him somewhat fearfully.

"The same as I've always thought of you," he replied. Now was not the time to dance around the truth. She was being so honest, the least he could do was be equally open. "Right from that first day of the first semester, when we were both new to the school, I thought you were the most exotic woman I'd ever met. I couldn't figure out what you were doing at the school. I was convinced there was some kind of mistake." He gave her a smile. "But I was glad there wasn't. It gave me a charge just seeing you in the halls."

"You were married to what's-her-name."

"Maybe so, but I wasn't blind. Anyway, what's-her-name

and I have been history for close to two years. Which is neither here nor there, but I'm still not blind."

"Evidently not."

"Murray's leaving at the end of the semester, isn't he?"

"I'm so ashamed. I feel like a child molester."

"Don't," he said. "I know how serious it is, and how upset you are, but Murray's got a lot of maturity for his age. I don't think this would be harmful to him. You're being very hard on yourself, Agnes. I understand why, but if the whole thing's over and done with, maybe you should consider the matter closed and try not to think about it. To tell the truth, I have to admit there are a couple of senior girls who do awful things to my blood pressure."

"Yes, but you didn't take them to bed. Did you?"

"No," he said soberly. "I didn't. It doesn't mean I think any the less of you, Agnes."

She looked up at him.

"It doesn't," he insisted. "You had a bad patch, but it's over now."

"You're very generous," she said, stretching out again and returning her feet to the coffee table.

"Not really. I'm just trying to be fair. I mean, it bothers me. I'll admit that. But it bothers me because you've obviously been having a bad time, and I wish there was something I could've done to help. Listen. You want to get some air? I thought I'd go home, pick up a few things. Why don't you come along for the ride?"

She gazed at him for several seconds, touched by the generosity he was so quick to deny. Then she turned to lift the curtain and look out the window. "Yes, all right," she said. "Give me a minute to put on some shoes and let Rebecca know we're going out. I'd hate to have her arrive and find the house empty."

"Tell you what. I'll call her while you're getting your shoes. Okay?"

"Louis," she said, "I have to tell you I was furious this morning when Rebecca told me she'd asked you to come here. Now I want you to know I'm deeply grateful. What you've told me about those pills changes everything. I had *no* idea what I was taking. No idea at all."

"I'm just glad I happened to know. It scares the hell out of me to think you might have died because of them, and because of Murray. I like you, Agnes. For purely selfish reasons, I'm glad you're still alive. Please don't ever think about suicide again. Okay?"

He spoke with such feeling that she was thrown. And it occurred to her she'd made a mistake not inviting him to dinner when she'd wanted to.

"So, Lou," Jason was saying as he helped himself to more pork-fried rice, "you teach math, huh? My kid sister's the entire math department at her school up in Vermont."

"Computer sciences, too?" Lou asked interestedly.

"Definitely. Mimi's a whiz. She's got her whole life programmed into her NEC system."

"NEC," Lou said almost reverently. "Good products. I've got an IBM, so I'm compatible with the school's system. You have a PC, Jason?"

His mouth full, Jason shook his head, swallowed, then said, "I'm not into it. You're looking a whole lot better now, Aggie. Still up for the big event?"

"I am. Louis," she said, "how are you on movies?"

"I love movies. Are we going to watch something?"

"We're going to play Trivial Pursuit," Rebecca explained. "The Silver Screen edition."

"Great!" Lou carefully blotted his mouth, his eyes on

Agnes. "I'm crazy about games. My former wife hated them."

"What games?" Agnes asked.

"Backgammon, chess, dominoes, cards, anything."

"It's been years since I played chess," Agnes said wistfully. "We used to play backstage between shows. I rarely won. I was too impetuous, made hasty moves. We'll have to play, Louis."

"I'd love to play with you," he said earnestly.

Jason patted him on the back. "You've got good taste, Lou," he laughed. "Want to watch out for this guy, Agnes."

"This guy," Agnes said, deftly dipping her chopsticks into the cardboard container to pick up a shrimp, "told me something today that gives new meaning to my life. Louis, please tell them what you told me about the Triazolam."

"It's the medication Agnes has been taking to help her sleep," Lou explained. "More commonly known as Halcion." He described his mother's experience, then wound down saying, "When Agnes told me she'd"—he glanced over for approval and she nodded—"overdosed on it, we put two and two together and came up with a lot of answers."

"We certainly did," Agnes said angrily. "The long-term cumulative adverse effects had me believing I was losing my reason. Suffice it to say, I'm not going to be taking any more sleeping pills."

"We stopped by my place," Lou said, "and picked up some of the information I researched."

"Fascinating reading," Agnes put in. "All sorts of warnings about anterograde amnesia of varying severity, not to mention the danger of ingesting alcohol while on this medication. I wasn't told any of it."

"Doctors," Jason said disgustedly. "They're so damned cavalier about handing out prescriptions."

"Agnes, that's awful," Rebecca said. "That's why you overdosed?"

"That is primarily why," she confirmed. "And now I know I'm not going round the twist."

"I never thought you were," Rebecca told her.

"But *I* did, Rebecca," Agnes elaborated. "And I didn't want to live that way. Perhaps it's vain, or purely egoistic, but I've always taken great pride in my intelligence. The idea of having it drain away until I was left incompetent terrified me. I could cope with the rest of it—the banality of school politics, the petty rivalries between the departments, even my involvement with Murray. But I couldn't bear the thought of having my mind shrinking daily. And that's what I felt was happening. I went into a panic a month or so back because I couldn't remember the address of the house I grew up in. Nor could I recall the name of the actress with whom I was friends during the run of *Butternut*. I forgot our date for this weekend, you'll recall, my dear."

"Most of it comes back," Lou told her. "It did for my mother."

"It doesn't matter to me now, being unable to remember this or that. I'm not going to panic, because I finally know *why*. Everything had gone gray. I'm so grateful to you, Lou. I feel now as if there's color to the world again."

"I'm glad," he said simply. "We all want you alive."

"Yes, we do," Rebecca confirmed.

"It scared the hell out of me," Jason admitted, taking hold of Rebecca's hand. "I didn't even know you, but I sure didn't want you to die."

Choked, Agnes said, "Excuse me a moment," and left the room.

"Thank God you were here," Lou said in a whisper to Rebecca.

"She was great," Jason told him.

"No," Rebecca disagreed. "I was lucky, that's all."

"Never mind," Lou said. "It's just a good thing you were here."

Jason put an arm around her shoulders, saying, "You were heroic, Beck. I'm damned proud of you."

Unable to speak, she rested her head for a moment on his shoulder.

Jason won the game in half an hour. His knowledge was encyclopedic. They couldn't catch him up in any of the categories. He knew that the Harvard Lampoon Award for worst movie of 1978 went to *Looking for Mr. Goodbar;* that John Wayne's nickname of Duke was actually the name of Wayne's Airedale terrier; that Jack Lemmon won his first Oscar for *Mister Roberts;* and that Francis Ford Coppola directed *Finian's Rainbow.*

"It is not fun to play with you," Agnes stated. "Rebecca, take your friend home."

"Hey!" Jason protested. "I told you I was a movie buff. I've been into movies since I was eight years old. But I'll pretend not to know in the next game."

"Next time we'll play regular Pursuit. Perhaps your general knowledge is less extensive," Agnes said.

"My general knowledge is pretty well nonexistent," Jason laughed.

"I'm going to stay here with you," Rebecca told Agnes.

"Lou's agreed to sleep in the guest room. And you're worn out," Agnes said. "Jason, take her home and tuck her in."

"Okay, Chief." He saluted, emptied his pipe into the ashtray, then said, "Come on, toots. The chief here's given orders."

Rebecca said, "I really don't mind staying."

"You've been given your walking papers," Jason said, going for her coat.

Rebecca stood and went to embrace Agnes. "I love you," she said sleepily. "I'm so glad you're okay and that things are getting sorted out."

"Thank you for everything. You know I'm very fond of you," Agnes said inadequately, wishing she were able to be more forthright about her feelings. "I'll see you in the morning."

"Goodnight, Lou." Rebecca kissed his cheek, and waited for Jason to shake hands with Lou. Then Jason put his arms around Agnes and whispered, "You take good care of yourself. Okay?"

Overwrought, she said, "Okay."

"We're out of here," he said, directing Rebecca through the front door. "Uncle Jason's gonna put little Becky to bed."

In the car as she was fastening her seat belt, Rebecca said, "Isn't it amazing about those pills?"

"It's more like horrifying. You take any kind of pills, Beck?"

She yawned, then said, "Only Tylenol, sometimes."

"Birth control pills?"

"Had to stop," she answered, stifling another yawn. "They gave me mood swings." Hearing what she'd said, she looked over at him.

"Right!" he said. "Jesus H. Christ!"

"Tylenol's okay," she said somewhat doubtfully. "Isn't it?"

"I sure as hell hope so."

CHAPTER

Twenty

I traded off half a shift," Jason said. "So I don't have to clock on until eight tomorrow morning."

"Oh! Good." Rebecca held a hand over her mouth to conceal another yawn.

"So," he said, turning her by the shoulders and pointing her toward the bed, "I can tell you a bedtime story. I could even stay and play spoonies with you."

"What?"

He laughed. "Spoonies is strictly nonactive. We're both too wiped to get into any serious action, but I'd love to sleep in this nice big bed with you."

"Oh. Okay."

He folded back the blankets and she climbed in.

"I'll just grab a shower, if that's okay."

Her eyes closing, she mumbled, "That's okay."

By the time he came out of the bathroom, she was deeply asleep. For a minute or two he squatted by the bedside, happily watching her sleep, bowled over by how lovely she was and by the fact that they'd become a couple. She was everything he'd ever hoped to find: sweet-natured but gutsy, and smart as all get-out. He felt phenomenally lucky. It was amazing to think that whoever was harassing her was responsible for the two of them meeting. And now here they were, an item. He switched off the light, slid under the blankets and aligned his body to hers. She didn't move at all.

"You sure are a heavy sleeper," he whispered, kissing her cheek and breathing in the fragrance of her luxurious hair.

In a matter of minutes, he too was asleep.

Agnes looked at the clock on the bedside table. Ten-fifteen. She'd been trying to read for half an hour, unable to sleep and imagining that at any moment, Lou would knock at her door. Reaching for her robe, she slid out of bed to walk silently barefoot down the hall. Stopping in the guest room doorway, she held the robe closed with both hands. Lou was in bed, leaning on his elbow, reading. She liked seeing him there. A tall, well-built, dark-haired man with classic Latin good looks.

"Are you quite comfortable, Louis?" Her voice was huskier than usual from prolonged retching and too many cigarettes.

He looked up and smiled over at her. "Oh, sure. I'm fine."

"Do you feel awkward, being here with me?"

"To tell you the truth, I've been enjoying the quiet."

"Good." She could feel a draft winding itself around her ankles.

"Anything wrong, Agnes?" With her pale complexion and long red hair, in the black robe, he thought she made a highly dramatic composition, framed by the doorway. He felt a little shock of excitement at being alone with her in her house. For the past half hour or so, he'd been thinking about knocking on her door, asking if she was all right. He'd imagined her in bed with her hair hanging loose the way it was now, imagined himself touching her milky skin.

"I would like to sleep with you," she said. "I know it's rather inelegant of me, but perhaps we could view it as affirmative action." She gave what to her sounded like a fraudulent laugh, and felt a little ridiculous. She was too old for games.

"Inelegant? I'm not sure I know what you mean." He wondered if he was correctly interpreting what she seemed to be saying. He hoped he was. Since two-thirty that afternoon he'd been thinking about what it would be like to make love to her.

"A crude form of reaffirmation, perhaps." Why did she always have to use sex to prove her feelings, to make her points? Why was it the barometer with which she tested the emotional climate?

"Oh." He nodded several times. "That makes sense." He smiled, afraid of saying or doing the wrong thing.

She returned the smile, the tension easing slightly. "I'm afraid I'm not a very pretty sight at the moment."

"As far as I'm concerned, you are." He set aside his glasses and the book as she let her hands drop and the robe fell open. He looked over, feeling the reaction like a blow to his midriff. He could hardly believe this was happening. It was like having a fabulous dream, only to discover it wasn't a dream at all.

Still uncertain, she said, "You needn't feel you have to," and took a step into the room. She hated the idea that she was begging. What on earth must he think of her? "You've been very kind, most understanding, and your telling me about the Halcion has changed everything." She glanced over her shoulder at the darkened hallway. "I'd prefer not to sleep alone tonight."

He sat up, not taking his eyes from her. "You don't have to explain yourself to me, Agnes. Or to anyone. I mean, I understand." It was overwhelming. This was actually happening. She was talking about the two of them making love, but making it sound somehow one-sided, as if she didn't think he'd want her.

She took several more steps and let the robe slide off her shoulders. "Do you?" she said. "That's good." She'd arrived at the side of the bed. "You should have let me know you were watching. Murray would never have happened. I've been very lonely for a very long time. Isn't it dreadful how we'll never admit to that? It's like saying one has cancer. People prefer not to know. Have you been with anyone since the divorce?"

He shook his head and tentatively took hold of her hand. Her fingers were very cool. Automatically he began trying to warm her hand.

She smiled, moved by his instinctive kindness. "Think of this as a thank-you present for today if you like. No strings."

"I hope you know I'd never take advantage of the situation, of you." He continued stroking her hand.

"I know, but I've been sitting in my bedroom hoping you would. I like you for not doing it. Does that make sense?" She drew back the bedclothes and turned off the light. "I'd hate to have you see my bruises."

"It wouldn't matter. And yes, it makes sense. I was thinking about knocking on your door."

"But you didn't because you couldn't, could you?" She lifted one knee onto the bed.

He opened his arms to her as she sat across his lap. "I don't know," he said, bowled over. "I might have. I kept thinking about you being just down the hall. I definitely wanted to." She was even softer than he'd imagined. "You smell wonderful."

"I considered inviting you to dinner quite some time ago. *I* definitely wanted to."

"Why didn't you?"

"Probably for the same reason you didn't knock on my door. I was afraid."

"That's too bad. I'd have jumped at the chance to spend time with you away from the school."

"I've always found you very attractive, Louis." She rested her cheek against his as his hands slipped down her sides. Tears ran from her eyes. He touched her as if he thought she was no more substantial than a hologram.

"Why are you crying?" he asked with concern, his hand on her face.

"Am I behaving offensively?"

"Not at all. Why would you think that?"

"I frighten most people, you know. Men especially."

"I'm not frightened. Surprised, delighted, very excited, but not frightened."

"I'm glad you're not, because I am." She took his hand and placed it between her breasts so he could feel her heart drumming.

"Don't worry, Agnes. I'm a nice guy."

"I know that," she whispered. "The thing of it is, Louis, I'm not a nice woman."

"I know," he said with a soft laugh. "It's what I've always liked about you."

She directed his hand over her breast, then fit her mouth to his.

"Don't wait for the guy to call you tonight. Try him now," Jason said the next morning. "Most of the service people in town start early. You need to get these locks changed, Rebecca."

She found the locksmith's number and dialed.

A gruff voice on the other end said, "Yeah, Grady's."

"This is Rebecca Leighton. We have an appointment for Wednesday."

"Yeah, right."

"Would it be possible for you to come this afternoon instead? I'll be home by four."

"Lemme see. Hang on." He put down the receiver and she could hear him whistling between his teeth. "Four-thirty. That okay?"

"That'd be great."

"Comes under emergency service, cost you seventy-five for the call, parts and labor extra."

"That'll be fine."

"Cash," he added. "We don't take checks."

"Okay, I'll get cash. How much for two new locks?"

"Run you a minimum of ninety, depending on the cylinders."

"Fine. I'll have the cash."

"See!" Jason smiled, setting a cup of coffee in front of her. "You've got to know how the system works. Otherwise, you could waste half your life with these guys. What about the electrician?"

"He's coming Thursday evening." She lifted the cup and looked at him over the top of it. "This is strange."

"Strange good or strange bad?" He perched on the stool beside hers.

"Strange good. I'm not used to having someone around in the morning making coffee, fixing toast."

"I'm okay to have around," he said amiably. "Handy and good-natured, a generally great all-round fella."

She leaned on the counter and smiled at him. "What time are you off today?"

"Six."

"Want to come for dinner?"

"You're going to cook for me?"

"Uh-huh."

"Oh, boy! We're really humming right along here. Should I bring my jammies?"

"What?"

"You know, jammies. For the slumber party."

She laughed. "Doctor Denton's, with a trapdoor and padded feet?"

"You want 'em, I'll get 'em. Anything for you, toots." Also leaning on the counter now, he smiled widely. "Gorgeous," he said, winding a long strand of her hair around his finger. "Absolutely gorgeous. I could eat you up with a spoon. Your toast's getting cold."

She looked down at the plate, then back at him. "You really are good to have around. I could get used to it."

"I sure hope so." He removed his finger and watched the strand of hair bounce gently like a spring. "I like playing with you." He looked at his watch. "Time to go, Beck." He downed the last of his coffee and stood up. "Tonight," he declared, "we get down to some serious lovemaking." He bent to kiss her. "Tonight," he repeated. "Definitely."

"Definitely," she agreed, feeling the breath catch in her throat.

Agnes was already in the English office when Rebecca arrived.

"How are you?" Rebecca asked, deeply pleased to see her. "You look really well." Her heart was beating surprisingly fast.

"Makeup, my dear. Actually, I feel better than I have in a long while. I want to apologize for all the frightful things I said—"

"Forget it, please," Rebecca cut her off. "Were you able to sleep?"

"For a few hours. I expect it will take some time before I fall into any sort of normal rhythm. But now that I know I'm not going mad, I really don't mind."

"How did everything go with Lou?" Rebecca asked, sorting through the papers from her box.

"Oh, swimmingly."

Rebecca looked across the desk at her. *"Swimmingly?"*

"Literally, it means a great success."

Rebecca stared as Agnes lit a cigarette. "Well," she said finally, "you don't say! Swimmingly, huh?" She felt a flaring happiness for her friend.

"Before you go leaping to any conclusions, you might as well know it was all my doing. We'll talk at lunch, I promise."

"Damned right," Rebecca said. "It's wonderful to see you this morning, absolutely wonderful."

"I'm pleased to be here."

Rebecca opened the door to go, her heart still beating too fast.

"By the way," Agnes said. "I like him, your new gentleman friend."

"That's good. I do, too. And it just so happens I've always thought you and Lou would go well together." Rebecca smiled helplessly, pleased.

"You thought so, did you?"

"Yes, I thought so," Rebecca mimicked her. "See you later."

He couldn't have said why, but as he was pulling out of the Burger King drive-thru at noon that day, Jason hung a left toward Rebecca's house instead of the right he'd intended. He told himself he'd have a quick look-see, then head on to his original destination—a stakeout at a body shop they suspected was actually a chop shop, refinishing stolen cars or breaking them down into parts.

One quick look. He'd eat his Whopper on the way back to the stakeout, tell Truman he'd cover an extra hour to make up the time. But he really had to go look.

As he rounded the slight bend in the road, the first thing

he saw was a late-model Chevy station wagon parked maybe fifty yards up the road from the house. He couldn't be certain it was the same wagon he'd seen before, but he was pretty sure. And if it was, this guy was looking to get nailed.

He reversed back around the bend and parked the sedan out of sight, then got out and walked toward the house. No point trying to sneak around in broad daylight. That'd send half a dozen housewives to their phones and in no time flat, there'd be a patrol car on top of him.

Entering Rebecca's grounds via the neighbor's driveway, and keeping as close to the shrubberies as he could, he made his way around the rear of the house, alert to every movement and sound. Behind him, on the far side of the stockade fencing, cars whipped along the Post Road. No one seemed to be near the house.

Probably one of the neighbor's cars, he decided, about to move out from the minimal cover of the bushes when he heard a laugh. His hand instinctively reaching under his jacket for his gun, he froze, his eyes sweeping the property.

The laugh came again, a kind of drunken, unhappy sound. Where was the guy? Jason scanned the area. Remaining motionless, he strained to hear anything that would pinpoint the source of the laughter. An odd creaking sound, several cars speeding past on the Post Road. A twig falling to the ground caught his eye.

Looking up, he saw a kid sitting halfway up the copper beech, legs dangling, one arm looped around the trunk for support. Making laughing sounds, but crying like an orphan.

Gonna nail you this time, Jason thought, creeping cautiously back to the property line, his eyes on the tree, puzzled by the kid's strange emotional state. He was acting and sounding stoned. Jason went stealthily back along the front of the neighbor's house, across their driveway to the road. As he approached the station wagon, he memorized the plate, repeating it to himself as he strolled casually around the bend.

Once out of sight of the house, he bolted to the sedan, getting on the blower as he backed into the road. He had them running an DMV make on the plate while he repositioned the car in the driveway opposite Rebecca's.

While he waited, fully confident this was the day he'd put a wrap on the vandalism, he got on the blower again so someone could go relieve Truman.

"I'm sitting on a possible B and E," he explained. "No assistance required. Will advise. Ten-four."

"Ten-four," he said under his breath, stowing the handset. "Over and out. Roger, that's a ten-four. Come on, fella. Get down from the tree and into your daddy's big wagon. Uncle Jason's gonna follow you home and read you your rights."

The gig was old, Pete thought. Old and stupid and a hassle. He hated it, and had to wonder why the hell he'd ever started. Today he hated everything. He'd taken thirty bucks' worth of pills, just tossed them down with a diet Coke. Then he'd thrown his stuff in the locker and cut out of school. He couldn't handle being there, with Shell giving him these looks like he was the biggest loser of all time. And Cal and Tim not even saying hi, nobody talking to him.

Instead of going home and taking the scissors to his mother's wardrobe the way he wanted, he came back to Leighton's place. But now that he's here, he doesn't know why. The pills're kicking in and he gets this idea to sit in the tree. He's just sitting in the big mother tree when this totally down feeling comes over him. Then he laughs. Too weird. Next thing he knows, he's into a goddamned crying jag. His head's completely messed. He's thinking about his cleaned-out room, and about the way his dad's forever throwing money at him like it's medicine that'll make him healthy or something. He's thinking about seeing Leighton heading into the English office this morning and remembering how he dreamed he was boinking her, how he stood watching her sleep, thinking she looked like a goddamned angel painting. Now he's wondering why he's been hassling her. He can't remember how the whole thing started. He remembers being seriously pissed with her, but not the reason why.

He's laughing, then he's crying. He's fucked, and he thinks maybe he should head on down to the I-95 service center, see if he can score something to even him out so he can stop these bullshit swings back and forth. He's got to do something, 'cause his brain's destroyed. Maybe he'll buy enough to put himself away for good. Nobody'd give a shit, that's for sure. Except maybe Lee. He thinks about his sister and starts crying again.

Another ten minutes of waiting in the sedan, and Jason saw the kid come down the driveway, headed for the station wagon. Lurching drunkenly, and still crying, the kid was wiping his face with his sleeve. Jason moved to get out of the sedan, thinking to stop him from attempting to drive in that condition. But by the time he had the door open, the kid was in the wagon, revving the engine, then rabbiting toward the intersection.

"Oh, shit!" Jason muttered, throwing himself back behind the wheel as the kid rode the red light and skidded up the Post Road.

Glancing both ways, Jason floored the accelerator and followed, opening the window to put the flasher on the car roof. His finger on the siren, he hesitated. The condition the kid was in, the siren might freak him out. On the other hand, given his condition, he probably wouldn't even notice. All Jason wanted to do now was stop him before he injured himself or somebody else.

When the wagon turned a squealing right onto Nortown

Avenue, Jason got on the blower to alert the Staties. He'd make book the kid would get on I-95, probably heading for the service center. The turnpike was State Police territory, not local, and he wanted this one to go by the book.

"Proceeding southbound I-Ninety-five in pursuit of late-model Chev wagon, plate six-six-four Edward John Fox," he said into the radio, then hit the siren, watching the kid weaving at high speed from lane to lane, swinging way out to pass an old VW bug, then, doing at least eighty-five, cutting in front of a Mercedes that had to throw on its brakes and spin a hard left to avoid colliding.

"Holy shit!" Jason swore, vehicles pulling out of his way as he pursued the wagon. Glancing into his rearview, he saw the flashers of a Statie still a good way back, but really moving. Probably one of the Mustangs. Those suckers could really go.

Eyes front again, he saw the wagon whip into the center lane, then shoot back to the outside, whizzing past a cluster of half a dozen slower-moving cars. The radio squawked, and dispatch gave him the DMV readout on the plate. He acknowledged and switched off, puzzling over the name. Hastings. Hastings. Why the hell did that ring a bell? On the inside lane was a piggybacking tractor-trailer making good speed. Jason was maybe eight cars behind, his foot already lifting off the accelerator, as the wagon aimed for the inside lane to make the exit for the service center. The trucker, probably sensing what was coming, had started gearing down as the wagon shot in front of him. Too late.

Flinching as he rode the brake and eased over to the shoulder, Jason watched the truck plow into the passenger side of the wagon and take it seventy or eighty yards while the rear trailer slowly folded out into the center lane, causing the oncoming traffic to start swerving to the left. Three cars mashed together in the outside lane. Two more caught the rear trailer. The noise of metal grinding into metal, glass shattering, seemed to go on and on as Jason spoke quickly into the radio. "They're going to need the rescue squad, maybe half a dozen wreckers, minimum three ambulances, and a fire truck."

He jumped out of the sedan as the State cruiser screeched to a halt on the shoulder behind him. Grabbing some flares from the back seat, he got them going, then dropped them in the road as he sprinted through the steaming wrecks. The air reeked of gasoline, and he tried not to breathe it in as he headed toward the station wagon. He should've nailed the kid when he was up in the tree. He should never have let him get in the goddamned car. But he'd had no way of knowing the kid was so wasted. He just hoped to hell no one was dead.

Glancing into cars as he ran by, he saw white faces, some blood-spattered; a few stunned people shakily climbed out to stand dazed in the road as witnesses came rushing up on foot to help. The stink of the spilled gasoline from ruptured tanks was getting to him, making his head ache. He could hear sirens in the distance. Traffic on the northbound side was down to a crawl, people gawking. Hastings. What was the connection? Hastings, Hastings. The name kept rolling around inside his mouth like a sourball, then—flash!—he had it. Rebecca's ex: Ray Hastings. The kid had to be the son. Jesus H. Christ! There was the connection! The kid had been punishing Rebecca for being involved with his dad. That had to be it. He ran faster.

The trucker was getting down from the cab, his face frozen with shock.

"You okay?" Jason asked, his hand on the man's arm to help him to the ground.

"Yeah! Jesus! You see that? I couldn't help it. Kid cut right in front of me."

"I saw it," Jason said, hurrying forward to the station wagon.

The passenger side had taken the brunt of the impact. The car had been reshaped into a wide, shallow U, its midsection reduced to half its former size.

With the trucker loping along at his heels, Jason made for the driver's side, slowing as he saw the shattered, bloodied window.

"Oh, man!" the trucker said softly. "Guy's bought it, looks like. You don't wanna go opening that door."

Jason agreed and glanced back up the shoulder, looking for the rescue unit. Flashers still off in the distance. He pulled open the rear passenger door, dusted chunks of glass off the seat, then squeezed inside and looked at the kid draped over the wheel. Jason touched two fingers to the side of the boy's neck, relieved to feel a good strong pulse.

"How is he?" the trucker asked, stooping down to talk through the open door.

"Still alive," Jason answered. Fearful of moving the kid, he said, "Can you hear me?"

Incredibly, the kid responded. "Uhnm."

"Okay." Jason put a hand lightly on his shoulder. "People will be here in a minute to get you out. Okay?"

"Yeah. Stuck," he said, lifting his right hand and sending fragments of glass tinkling to the car floor. "Head hurt, man. Bad."

"What's your name?" Jason asked, keeping his hand on the kid's shoulder.

"Pete."

"Pete, I'm gonna be right here with you. Okay?"

To Jason's distress, the boy began to cry again. "Fucked up!" he sobbed. "Didn't mean to."

"I know," Jason said. "You just meant to scare her a little. Right? Mess her up to even the score, 'cause of your dad."

"Yeah. Am I gonna die?" he cried.

"You'll be okay, Pete. Hang on. I'm staying right here."

The boy's hand rose and Jason grasped it, feeling a sudden

pity for this kid. He could practically write the script, he was so sure he knew what Pete Hastings was going to tell him. "They'll have you out of here in another minute or two," Jason said, relieved to see the red rescue wagon pulling up alongside.

"Don't go!" the boy pleaded.

"I won't," Jason promised. "You're gonna be okay, Pete. Just hang in. Okay?"

CHAPTER

Twenty-One

At home that afternoon after her routine check indoors and out, Rebecca listened to her messages. She'd been so worn out the previous night she hadn't bothered.

Sitting at the island sorting through the mail—still no check—she heard her mother say, "There are some things here I thought you might want, sweetheart. Call me, please."

Then Ray came on. "It's ten past three. I'll try again in a couple of hours." He sounded irritated, and didn't bother with a good-bye. She must have been in the shower when he'd called.

The tone, followed by Ray again. "What is this, some kind of game? Why are you avoiding me? For chrissake! All I want is to *talk* to you." A pause, then he hung up.

The tone. "Sweetheart, this is your mother. Remember me, the woman who used to change your diapers? Call me tonight, please. Bye-bye."

The tone, then Ray, shrieking, "You bitch! I know

you're there. Who the hell d'you think you're playing with?" The receiver slammed down.

He must have come by the house while she and Jason were having dinner with Agnes and Lou.

Again the tone. "You don't waste any time, do you? Two cars in the driveway. New boyfriend spending the night? You'll be sorry you ever fucked with me . . ."

She fast forwarded. The phone had rung once the night before. Half asleep, she'd assumed that Jason must have answered, because the ringing stopped. But the machine had picked up after the first ring.

She felt thoroughly menaced. Ray had come by the house, spying on her. Convinced she was ducking him, he'd turned hostile. He probably was the one responsible for the vandalism, and had only pretended not to believe her. He'd miscalculated, and she'd ended the affair. Now he was out of control, threatening her. She'd have to save the tape for Jason to hear.

The next message was Jason, saying, "Hi, Beck. I wanted to let you know I'll be a little late, but I will be there. I've got good news and bad news. See you later, toots."

The tone, then the last message. "Ms. Leighton, it's Murray Beckworth. I got your message, and I'll see you at five-fifteen. 'Bye."

After inserting a new tape in the machine, she called her mother.

"I did try to call you, you know," Rebecca told her. "You were probably making another trip to the dump."

"Where have you been and what have you been doing since you left here Sunday? And how," she asked meaningfully, "is Jason?"

"Jason's great. I spent Sunday night and all day yesterday with Agnes." She explained about the suicide attempt, then wound down saying, ". . . which is why I haven't been able to phone you."

"Poor Agnes," Evelyn said. "Is she all right now?"

"She's going to be fine. It was a good thing Jason was around to help. I'd never have managed without him."

"It's a good thing *you* were around. And what about you, sweetheart? Any more incidents?"

"Not for a couple of days. I'm hoping maybe it's over." She wondered if nothing more had happened because Ray had been out of town. It seemed to fit. "Anyway, I've got a man coming soon to change the locks."

"Well, good. I wanted to tell you Mrs. Dunbar told me another unit is available. I thought you might want to take a look at it."

"Mother, on thirty-two thousand a year, I simply can't carry a mortgage."

"I'd help you out. And you could pay me back in time."

"I love you for offering. Let me think about it. Okay?"

"Rebecca, I don't like what's been going on. It worries me."

"That's precisely why I didn't want to tell you."

"But you did, and I'm worried. I want to know you're safe."

"Mother, I'm perfectly safe," Rebecca insisted with confidence she didn't feel. "The locks are being changed. The electrician's coming Thursday to put the outdoor spots on timers. The place is sealed up like a bank vault. Plus, Jason's around."

"Speaking of Jason." Evelyn's tone softened. "I'm expecting the two of you for lunch on Sunday."

"I see," Rebecca said, amused. "You've got my entire future arranged."

"Of course I haven't. What a thing to say, just because you're finally seeing someone I happen to like."

"Okay," Rebecca laughed. "I'll remind him when he gets here later. I've really got to go now."

"Let me tell Mrs. Dunbar you'll have a look at the apartment."

"I'll be happy to look at it, but I'm not promising anything."

"Good. That's all I ask. Give my best to Jason, and I'll see you both Sunday."

"I love you and good-bye."

"I love you, too. Be careful."

"I will."

The locksmith's bill came to a hundred and eighty-seven dollars and ninety-two cents. Rebecca counted out the cash, accepted the change, a receipt, and two sets of keys.

"By the way," he said as he was leaving, "that back-door chain was about ready to fall out of the wall. I tightened it up for you."

"Oh," she said, looking past him at the door. "Thanks very much."

Murray Beckworth pulled into the driveway as the locksmith was backing out.

"It's good of you to come, Murray," she said, inviting him in. "Would you like something to drink? Coffee, tea, a soda?"

"I'm fine, thanks," he said somewhat stiffly, obviously apprehensive.

They settled in the two wing chairs beside the fireplace. "This is a bit awkward," she began after a moment, "which is why I wanted to talk to you away from the school." She paused, not sure how to go about this, then said, "It's about Agnes."

Murray's brows drew together and his hands tightened their grip on the arms of the chair. "Oh?" he said with uncertainty.

"You're not in any trouble, Murray," she said, hoping to put him at his ease. He was so impossibly good-looking, she had to make a conscious effort not to stare at him. He had thick dark-brown hair, a naturally ruddy complexion, wide-set large gray eyes and enviably long lashes, a perfect patrician nose, a full mouth, and a squared, dimpled chin. He was tall, strongly built, and attractively dressed in gray flannel slacks, a light-blue shirt under a navy V-neck pullover, navy socks, and Ralph Lauren loafers. In spite of his relative youth, he exuded self-confidence without appearing either arrogant or vain. His eyes glowed with intelligence. Agnes had often said he was destined for success, and Rebecca had to agree.

"To be candid, I'm afraid Agnes is the one in trouble."

"Is she going to lose her job?" he asked fearfully.

"No, no," she assured him. "Nothing like that. It's just that she didn't feel able to talk to you herself, so I offered to." God, this was difficult! She took a breath and went on. "There are only two of us on staff who know about your . . . involvement with Agnes, and it won't go any farther." Color suffused his face, even turning the rims of his ears bright red. "I'm afraid she put both of you in a dangerous position, as I think perhaps you already realize." He nodded solemnly, keeping his eyes on hers in what she found an admirable display of courage. "She's deeply concerned that she's harmed you, even possibly taken advantage of you."

"She hasn't harmed me," he said at once, looking only a little less worried.

"I certainly hope not. But aside from the considerable difference in your ages, there's also her position at the school. You must appreciate that she's violated several moral and ethical, not to mention professional, rules."

"I kept telling her none of that mattered," he said guiltily, turning more toward Rebecca, both hands on one arm of the chair. "The way I see it, I took advantage of her. I'm the one who's really to blame. I mean . . ." He stopped, framing his words. "I was the one who started it. Not that I planned it or anything. Nothing like that. But right from my freshman year, I had this . . . feeling. I mean, it was the way she looked, you know, and the sound of her voice. I used to *dream* about her. I must sound like a real jerk."

"Not at all," Rebecca assured him, convinced his feelings for Agnes were quite genuine. "Sometimes we find ourselves in situations where the rules don't seem to fit. It happens to everyone."

"That's it!" he said eagerly, grateful for her understanding. "I kept telling myself it was just a crush, I'd get over it. But I didn't. Right up through last year I was actually going to bed at night and dreaming about her. Then this spring we rehearsed late one night, and I stayed after so she could give me her notes. I don't honestly know how it happened. I've gone over and over it, and I'm still not sure. We were sitting in the auditorium, and all of a sudden something changed between us. We never even discussed it. We just went back to her house. And that was the start.

"She said it could only be that one time, that it wasn't to happen again. It was an accident. It was dangerous. She'd be fired if anyone ever found out. But I wouldn't listen, and I didn't want it to stop. I covered by telling everyone she was tutoring me, helping with my application for Juilliard. The thing is, I really loved her. I know nobody would believe that, because I'm so much younger. But it's the truth. When she broke it off, I knew all the reasons why she had to. She'd been telling me why for months. But it didn't change my feelings. On my birthday last weekend, my folks had a little family party, and when it was time for me to blow out the candles, I wished I could still be with Agnes.

"She never *harmed* me, Ms. Leighton. I got scared that I was messing *her* up. She started changing; she'd be so depressed sometimes. I'd come over and she'd sit talking to her teddy bear as if I wasn't even there. Then she'd snap out of it, but it worried me. I thought it was my fault, because she kept saying it had to stop and I didn't want it to end. She'd tell me she was risking everything that mattered to her, but I didn't want to hear that, even though I knew it was true. If anybody did harm, Ms. Leighton, I'm the one who harmed her."

"Murray, I think you should know that she's been taking a medication that's had some very serious side effects," Rebecca said. "Her depression is mainly as a result of that, and only partly as a result of her concern for you."

"So what should I do?" he asked anxiously.

"It's most important that no one else learns about this."

"I know."

"It's also very important that the situation's resolved to both your satisfaction, so that neither of you feels there'll be any possibility of repercussions. The thing is, Murray, she was depressed and lonely. Otherwise, none of this would ever have happened."

"I understand."

"I believe you do. Perhaps you could phone her, tell her some of what you've just told me. We all need reassurance now and then, you know," she said with a smile, anxious to lighten the mood. "Even teachers."

"Tell me about it!" he smiled back. "Sometimes I get into these sessions with my mom and dad where I'm thinking, Hey, wait a minute! I'm the kid here, not the parent. How come I'm bolstering them up? No, I know what you mean," he said, sober again. "I'll call her tonight. I know we can't ever get back together, and that it shouldn't have happened in the first place. But I'll never be sorry it did. Maybe that's wrong of me. But I really loved her. I wasn't just a kid with a crush on his teacher. I admired her, and I learned so much from her. It probably sounds dramatic, or corny, but I'll always think of her as someone I love."

Her eyes filling, Rebecca said, "She cared for you too,

Murray. But what happened between the two of you was because she was frightened and lonely, and it made her vulnerable. And regardless of what you say, I think it's been stressful for you, too."

"It has been kind of rough," he admitted. "I feel a whole lot better, having this chance to talk about it. That's been the hardest part, not having anyone to talk to."

"I'm sure it must have been."

He stood up and offered his hand, saying, "I'm really glad we talked, Ms. Leighton. I appreciate it a lot, and I'll call her tonight, make sure she knows I'm okay and that I'm sorry about everything."

"Thank you, Murray. That would be very helpful." They shook hands and Rebecca saw him to the door. As he was leaving, he said, "I didn't know how much I wanted to talk about this. Thanks an awful lot. I really feel better now."

Agnes actually answered the phone on the second ring.

"I was all set to leave a message," Rebecca said. "Now, I'm totally thrown."

"I really can't have you flying over here every time I choose not to answer the telephone, so I've decided to answer when I'm home."

"Good. Listen, I've just talked with Murray, and you don't have to worry about him. He's just fine. He's planning to call you this evening. You know something, Agnes?"

"What?"

"He cares very much for you, and he was very concerned that he'd harmed you. He was quite shocked to find out you were afraid you'd had a negative effect on him."

"I see."

"I did tell you I was going to talk to him, to try to set the record straight," Rebecca said, unable to gauge Agnes's reaction.

"Yes, you did. Rather sooner than I anticipated, but there you are. Well," she sighed, "it looks as if you've pulled the fat out of the fire."

"Fortunately, it was never *in* the fire," Rebecca said. "Stop punishing yourself. Everything's going to be okay. You'll talk to Murray later, and that'll be the end of it."

"Thank you. You're far braver than I."

"That's bull! It's always easier being on the outside. You sound tired."

"I am, exceedingly. I might as well tell you Lou seems to have taken this baby-sitting business to heart. He's on his way over here even as we speak. I think he's more attracted to the house than he is to me."

"Oh, right! I'm sure that's what it is."

"You may laugh, but you haven't seen where he lives! I actually heard one of his neighbors cough. Tissue-paper walls, low ceilings. A horrid place."

"So rent him one of your rooms," Rebecca joked.

"Let's not go overboard, my darling. I don't know that I care to have someone underfoot. Speaking of which, is the sleuth hanging at your elbow?"

"No, the sleuth's not due for a little while yet. You are so rotten!"

"Rottenness is my stock in trade. Well, I'll see you tomorrow. And Rebecca? Two things. I didn't mean what I said just now about having someone underfoot. I'm really very fond of Lou. And thank you for speaking to Murray. For some reason, I just couldn't face it."

"No prob. 'Bye."

Jason put a bottle of wine on top of the dryer, then gave her a long hug.

"What's the matter?" she asked, feeling his tension.

"It's been a bitch of an afternoon," he said, keeping his arms around her waist. "It's good to see you, you know that?"

"It's good to see you, too. You look as if you could use a drink."

"In a minute," he said, letting his nose touch against hers. "You know that deal where the good angel sits on your one shoulder and the bad angel sits on the other?"

She shook her head. "No, but I can picture it."

"Okay. I had kind of an epic battle with those little guys this afternoon. I think I screwed up. Not officially. But unofficially, personally, I feel as if I did."

"Let me get you a drink while you tell me about it."

He released her, retrieved the wine and gave it to her, then took off his shabby tweed jacket. "Have you got any gin?" he asked. "A double martini would do the trick."

"I think I do, but no vermouth. Thank you for the wine."

"My pleasure. And forget the vermouth. We'll call it an extra-dry martini."

She fixed his gin, some vodka for herself, and they went to sit in the living room.

"The good news," he said after his first swallow, "is your vandal's been identified and the whole thing's over."

Her spirits soaring, she exclaimed, "That's great! It was Ray, wasn't it?"

He made a face. "Close, but no cigar."

"It wasn't? But I was so sure—"

"Peter Hastings," he said. "And here's where we get to the bad news and my screw-up. I saw the kid outside here today around noon. Instead of reading him his rights on the spot, I let him get in his car. The thing is, I had no idea how high he was until I saw him walking to the car. And then there was no time to stop him. He took off too fast.

I followed, radioed in for a make on the plate, then got on to the State boys when I saw he was headed for the turnpike. Shit!" He shook his head and took another swallow of gin.

"He had an accident?"

"Seven vehicles, one of them a tractor-trailer with a piggyback load. What a mess! Five people in Stamford Hospital, two listed as fair, three as critical. Pete's one of the three criticals. He's got a mild concussion, but his face is all broken up, fractured arm and shoulder, internal injuries."

"My God!"

"I should never have let him drive off. I thought I'd get a make on the car and a positive ID, then go to the house to make the charge in front of his parents, get them involved. You know the worst part, Beck? I sat there and held the kid's hand while the rescue guys were working to get him out of the wreck. And here's this kid, thinking he's going to die, telling me his life story, telling me how things got way out of hand. He never meant to do more than shake you up, because he found out about you and his father. His brain's a mess, but I felt sorry for him. He did tell me how the whole thing got started. Do you remember, one Friday night a few weeks back, three guys with a broken-down car?"

She thought back, then said, "I remember. God! One of them jumped right in front of me. I nearly hit him."

"That was Pete."

"It was?"

"Sure was. He recognized you and decided you were to blame for everything that was going wrong in his life. He was driving by one night and saw his dad's car parked in your driveway."

"Oh, no!"

"You got it. That's when he made up his mind to get you but good for wrecking his parents' marriage."

"But Ray moved out on his family months before I met him."

Jason shook his head. "Your ex-boyfriend never moved anywhere, Beck. The guy snowed you. But how was the kid supposed to know that? The parents were at each other's throats, had been for years, and he figured you were responsible."

"Ray *lied* to me," she said, sickened. "All those months, all that garbage about working out the divorce settlement, and he was lying. God! I probably should've known. I kept thinking it was taking too long. I feel like an idiot. Is the boy going to be all right?"

"Fifty-fifty. Anybody here's an idiot, I'm the one. I still can't believe I stood there and watched the kid sitting in the tree out back here, laughing and crying at the same time, and let him go ahead and get in that goddamned car."

"I was so convinced it was Ray," she said softly, thinking of those poisonous messages. "Well, now I understand why it happened."

"One thing," he said grimly, "at least there isn't going to be any more harassment."

"That bastard, Ray. It's all his fault. He was lying to everybody. God! Wait till you hear the messages he's been leaving! Then you'll know why I thought he had to be the one. I saved the tape as evidence."

"I feel for that kid, Beck. I know he put you through a lot, but I promised I'd go back to see him."

"Tonight?"

"Tomorrow, when I'm off. I wanted tonight with you." He put his arm around her shoulders.

"Are you hungry?" she asked, wondering why she couldn't let go of the idea that despite Pete's confession, Ray had played some part in all of it. According to Jason, that wasn't possible, but she had doubts. "I really want you to hear that tape. I'd like your opinion on how I should handle the calls."

"What I need first is a shower. Do you mind if I use your bathroom?"

She looked at her watch. "The casserole will be another thirty-five minutes. How would you feel about a bath?"

He smiled for the first time since arriving. "With you?"

"I thought I might join you."

"Fantastic! I'm starting to feel better."

"Come on," she said, taking him by the hand. "We can finish our drinks in the tub."

"Tell me the truth," he said, holding back. "D'you think I screwed up?"

"I think you did what you had to do."

"Okay," he said. "I'll buy that. I just wish to hell so many innocent people didn't have to get hurt because of my mistake."

"It's over." She gave his hand a tug. "Let's both try to relax now. I've always loved this house, you know, but lately all I've thought about is getting rid of it." She looked back from the doorway to admire the living room. "Maybe now I'll be able to start enjoying it again. Oh, I've got a spare set of keys, if you want them."

"Do you want me to have them?" he asked.

"I think so," she said with a slow smile.

CHAPTER

Twenty - Two

While Rebecca was making coffee after dinner, Jason took the tape to the living room and listened to it on the cassette player. The look on his face when he returned prompted her to say, "I know. What was I doing dating a lunatic?"

"The guy sounds like a real banana. That last message is a doozy."

"I only heard the beginning. That was enough for me."

"Well," he said, sliding onto one of the stools at the island, "now I know why you figured him for your vandal." He got out his pipe and tobacco pouch. "I'll tell you something. If I had a father like that, maybe I'd be doing drugs, too. Really does make me wonder."

"About me?" She reached into the cupboard for some mugs.

"You, no. Old Ray, for sure. I'm not crazy about the idea of him cruising the house, keeping tabs on you."

"I'm not too thrilled myself." She took the cream from

the refrigerator, then looked over at him. "I've been thinking about getting my phone number changed."

"Might not be a bad idea. In the meantime, he comes banging on the door, don't even *think* about letting him in. Call me or nine-one-one."

"Do you honestly imagine I'd open the door to him? Do I look crazy to you?"

"What you look to me, kiddo, is adorable. But given all the heavy action in your life lately, and given that I've developed this truly critical pash, I'd hate like hell to have anything happen to you."

"Pash?" Her eyes lit up with amusement. "Talk about old black-and-whites. You sound like Mickey Spillane."

"Yeah, well." He shrugged and started pushing tobacco into the pipe bowl.

She poured the coffee, experiencing a moment of awe. This dear, caring man had managed in a matter of only days to become the focal point of her life. He had such a depth of feeling for people that he could even care about a drugged-out teenager who'd exercised his imagination and anger at her expense. Again that sense of certainty seemed to cushion her. The tension of the past weeks had eased, and now she could look forward to deriving pleasure from each day. It was as if after months of being locked in a dark room, the light had been turned on. She found it somehow easier to breathe, knowing the torment was finally over.

"Let's go into the living room," she said, carrying the mugs. "You can put on some music while I get a fire going."

"Perfect." He went to the stereo and put on James Taylor's *JT* while she held a match to the newspapers crumpled under the grate. She smiled to herself. Even his taste in music pleased her.

"My mother's expecting the two of us for lunch on Sunday," she said.

"Did you think I'd forget?"

"No, but she made a point of reminding me, so I thought I'd mention it."

"Your mother's doing Italian on Sunday. You think I'd miss that? Next to you, toots, Evelyn's my favorite new woman. She's a knockout, your mother. You know that?"

"I think she's incredibly beautiful," Rebecca said quietly, "the best mother anyone could ever have."

"She sure is," he said. "So, what d'you think? Want to do the classic in-front-of-the-roaring-fire scene?"

"What?"

"You know. We go for black-and-white, lots of contrast. Start with a medium two-shot of the couple gazing meaningfully into each other's eyes, with the fire crackling away behind them. Then we move in for a close-up of the clinch. The camera holds as the couple slowly disappears down out of the frame, and the camera closes in on the darting flames. All that good movie imagery."

She sat for a moment, then got up, saying, "I'll be right back," and went through the guest room to the bathroom. James Taylor was singing "Handy Man" when she came back.

"That was fast," Jason observed.

"I was in kind of a hurry," she said, sitting on her knees in front of him. "I'm getting addicted to you, Jason."

He lifted a hand to stroke her hair. "I sure hope so. I'm working very hard at cultivating your addiction. You're my woman, toots."

"You've got such a way with words." She pulled off her T-shirt and leaned forward to kiss him, then stood up and removed her sweat pants. Brazen, she thought. He'd turned her upside down. She couldn't look at him without wanting to touch him.

"Time for dessert," he said, his hands closing over her hips and bringing her forward.

"Can you stay the night?"

"Got my jammies in the car."

"You won't need them," she said, sucking in her breath as his hand moved up the inside of her thigh.

"Peter Hastings?" Agnes's eyebrows lifted. "The one in my senior lit class? He's the son of Mister X?"

"I feel kind of sorry for him," Rebecca said, opening the thermos of coffee she'd brought. "He needed to blame someone, so he picked me."

"This young thug leaps in front of your car, and because you quite rightly refuse to stop and help him and his friends out, he decides to persecute you. He plays hell with your life, but you feel sorry for him. You really do take the cake, my dear. I'd *kill* the little bugger."

"He was badly injured. Jason's going back to see him this afternoon."

"Darby and Joan, the two of you. Next thing anyone knows, you'll be setting up housekeeping in a quaint little cottage."

"I've already got one," Rebecca reminded her. "My mother's pushing at me to sell it and move down to Greenwich. But now that the whole thing's finally over, and Ray will have other things to do beside spying on me and leaving vicious messages on the answering machine, I think I'll stay put. So, how are you? Manage to get any sleep?"

"Some. It doesn't matter. I'd rather sleep only three hours a night for the rest of my life than ever again take sleeping pills. Spying? Vicious messages?"

"All this outraged nonsense about how he wants to talk to me and why am I avoiding him when he's driven by the house and he knows I'm home. Forget it." Lowering her voice, she asked, "Did you talk to Murray?"

"I did," Agnes confirmed, folding her arms on the desk. "It was painful. There I was waiting for Louis to arrive, and talking to Murray. Has it occurred to you that you and I both have switched affiliations in a very short period of time?"

"It's occurred to me," Rebecca replied. "I've decided to be philosophical about it."

"Wonderfully convenient conscience you have, my darling."

"Don't give me any of that, Agnes. Things happen, that's all."

"Lovely. You're philosophical, and I feel like a slut."

Rebecca stared at her, saddened. Agnes was exquisite, with her pale, perfect complexion, large green eyes and generous mouth, her glossy hair held in a tortoiseshell clip at the back of her neck; her beauty was complemented by an open-necked, long-sleeved white silk shirt and a simple knee-length black skirt. Yet she felt anything but beautiful. "Why do you say things like that? No one else would ever think as badly of you as you do."

"Years of practice." Agnes sat back and reached for her cigarettes.

"It's time to stop. You're not a slut. Okay?"

"I'll try to remember that. It's unfortunate that our epiphanic moments are so short-lived. In between times, one tumbles pell-mell into the troughs."

Rebecca reached across the desk to take hold of Agnes's hand. "Lighten up, Aggie," she said. "The worst part's over."

"Could we have dinner tonight, just the two of us? If you could bear it, I'd like to bore you with a few, shall we say, domestic details."

"You never bore me, and I'd love it. I've got the electrician due at six-thirty. He called this morning to say he'd had a cancellation. I could meet you between seven-thirty and eight. But what about Lou?"

"He's off to a lecture in the city. And Jason?"

"He's working until midnight. Look, I know you're still feeling rocky. Just take it slowly. Okay?"

"I'll do my best."

"Good. I'll see you at lunch." Rebecca collected her things and went off to her first class.

The electrician accepted her check. His bill came to one hundred and sixty-eight dollars for an hour's work hooking up the timer in the breaker box and reconnecting the carriage lamp outside the back door.

"I wish that check would turn up," Rebecca told Agnes over dinner at a small Italian restaurant in town. "If I have to lay out any more money this week, I'll be overdrawn."

"I'd be happy to lend you whatever you need," Agnes said.

"Thank you, but I'll be fine once that check arrives. Do you *know* what these service people charge per hour? If I'd gone for technical training, I'd be a wealthy electrician now."

"If you'd waited another hour on Sunday, you'd be a wealthy woman now," Agnes said.

Rebecca froze, and glared at Agnes for a long moment. Then, hurt and very angry, she said, "Of all the awful things I've heard you say over the years, that has to be the most insensitive remark ever to come out of your mouth. Do you think that I'd have been happy to profit from your death? Don't even answer. I may just dump my antipasto in your lap."

"I'd rather you didn't." Chastened, Agnes took a sip of her Chianti. "I apologize. Have you ever lived with anyone?" she asked.

More than willing to change the subject, Rebecca said, "No, not actually."

"I look at Louis and wonder what he's doing in my house. Then he pops up at my elbow with a cup of tea, and I'm taken completely off guard by his thoughtfulness." She shook her head. "I've never lived with anyone, either. It's very odd.

Each night we set off to our separate rooms, and come daylight, I'm attached to him like a barnacle. This morning I sat on the side of the tub with my coffee and watched the man *shave*. I was captivated. He slapped on eau de toilette afterward and I breathed in this fairly edible fragrance, tart and crisp like autumn apples. There have been few things I've enjoyed more. Does it sound simpleminded?"

"It sounds nice," Rebecca said.

"Nice," Agnes repeated. "Nice is dreary."

"Stop it, Agnes. Nice is nice."

Agnes ate some roasted red peppers, then said, "We appear to be falling very quickly into a routine. We leave the house five minutes apart in order not to arrive at school at the same time. Before we parted this morning, he asked if I'd like him to stop by this evening when he returns from the city. He waited for my answer, smiling very sweetly, and I thought I'd have to be mad to say no. So I said I'd like that. And he said, 'And what about tomorrow night?' I replied that I'd like that, too. He gave me a splendid smile and said, 'Good. I'll marinate a leg of lamb.' "

"I'm jealous," Rebecca said. "He can cook."

"*I'm* frightened," Agnes confessed. "I'll become dependent on him, and then he'll shatter me like a sheet of glass."

"Not Lou," Rebecca disagreed.

"This whole business of trusting men is frightening. I like them. I like *him*. He claims he wants to be with me, but I can't help wondering why, and how long it'll take before he gets bored and I'm left in pieces."

"That scares me, too," Rebecca admitted.

"You're not serious!" Agnes was taken aback. "The two of you put me in mind of, I don't know, Fred and Ginger, or Rodgers and Hart. Some pair completely in sync."

Rebecca laughed. "Sorry, but I feel the same way you do. All of a sudden I'm in the thick of this affair and I have agonizing moments when I can't figure out how or why any of it's happening. Then I tell myself to stop agonizing and just enjoy it. That's what you have to do, too."

"I can't," Agnes said, pushing away the remains of her salad and reaching for a cigarette. "I trust Louis. He asks politely may he come back, and I say yes, please, but I'm convinced he's merely putting in time until someone younger and more attractive comes along."

"He's never going to find anyone more beautiful than you," Rebecca said. "Do you want to keep him?"

"Perhaps. What about you?"

Rebecca flushed. "I've been thinking about what it would be like to be pregnant."

"There's no risk of that, is there?"

"No. But it's easy enough to accomplish. Last night I dreamed I was hugely pregnant and they were wheeling me into this immense white delivery room. They put me naked on a stainless-steel table. I opened my legs, put my hands on my belly and started pushing. It didn't hurt at all. I was just embarrassed to be naked with all these people in masks and gowns watching. I pushed like a fiend, and there was this terrific down-rushing sensation. All at once my stomach went flat and I propped myself up on my elbows to look, and I'd given birth to Jason. He sat on the end of the table and said, 'That was great, Beck. Next time we'll make the baby.' "

"Bizarre," Agnes said, frowning.

"No. I've decided it was about trust, about how every time we fall in love, we get a chance to remake ourselves through the person we love. When I woke up this morning, I looked at Jason and knew I loved him. I just haven't told him yet."

Agnes was leaning on her hand, gazing at her. "Monday evening after you two left," she said, "I got Louis installed in the guest room, then went to my room. I sat in bed trying to read, very aware of him just down the hall. I had a very attractive, very nice man in my house, and until two nights before, I'd been going to bed with a bloody *toy*. My last rational act after taking the pills was to rip that damned bear to pieces.

"In any event, I went down the hall to put my hands on someone real. I was frightened, but I did it. Now I've started something, and I alternate between wanting it with all my heart and being terrified of having it."

"It beats hell out of being alone and lonely."

"That's the damnable thing of it," Agnes said. "I think so, too."

The waitress came with their entrées, and Agnes went on, "I feel like a transparent sack of unset gelatin. All this wobbly, dismal anxiety."

"Welcome to the human race," Rebecca said quietly.

"It's not in my nature to be confiding. I have the feeling everyone here is listening to what I'm saying, and privately snickering."

"Nobody's listening. And nobody would laugh, either."

Putting out her cigarette, Agnes said, "I find trying to be happy frustrating, enervating, and intimidating."

"All of the above," Rebecca agreed, winding angel-hair pasta around her fork. "But it's still way better than being dead."

"Why are you so endlessly optimistic?"

"I think that may be genetic," Rebecca joked. "Perhaps you've noticed my mother and I have optimism in common. Eat." She pointed her fork at Agnes's plate.

Agnes picked up her knife and fork, saying, "I'm more afraid of allowing myself to care than of anything else."

"Stop thinking so much about it," Rebecca advised.

Agnes cut into her chicken *parmigiana*. "I suppose I should tell you what's sent me into this panic."

"What?"

"Yesterday morning, while we were putting on our coats in the front hall, Louis got rather shaky. It took a few minutes before he could speak. I imagined he was going to say that our having slept together was a terrible mistake. Instead, finally, he confessed that he'd been in love with me for years."

"That's great!"

"It's a huge responsibility," Agnes said uncertainly.

"I think you're up to coping. The thing is, how do you feel about him?"

Hesitantly, Agnes said, "For close to a year I'd been feeling very alone, desperately lonely, and very afraid. I thought my mind was going, and it terrified me, but I couldn't bring myself to confide in anyone. Then one evening Murray and I somehow ended up being the only two people left in the auditorium. I'd been well aware for quite some time that he had a crush on me. But suddenly, foolishly, his affection seemed viable. Here was someone whose affection would bolster me. There was no need for me to be alone.

"The guilt was like slow asphyxiation. I'd taken this boy to bed, and it made everything ten thousand times worse. Well, we all know what the end result was. I simply couldn't live with myself. Then, with the best intentions, you invite Louis to play my attendant for a few hours, and the next thing anyone knows, I've invited myself into his bed. I had to wonder if I'd simply transferred my desperation from Murray to him. A distinct possibility," she said, looking off into space for a moment. "I truly like Louis. I have for years," she went on. "I enjoy having him around, but I can't help feeling I'm taking advantage of him."

"You felt that way about Murray, too," Rebecca pointed out. "Maybe your involvement with that French teacher established a negative precedent. I mean, Murray's one thing. But Lou's a grown man. Can't you just let things happen?"

Agnes finally took a bite of the chicken and chewed thoughtfully, then drank some more wine. "Imagine," she said at length. "He was still married, but he was secretly lusting after me."

"Don't reduce it to that," Rebecca said softly. "It's not just about sex."

Agnes put down her knife and fork. "Yes, I know," she said after a time. "But I have to put it into terms I can deal with."

"Why those terms?" Rebecca asked. "You're not just about sex, Aggie. There's far more to you than that."

"Sex has always been the equalizer," she said. "It's difficult to fool anyone when the both of you are naked. Once you've taken your clothes off, there's nowhere to hide."

"That's only true on one level," Rebecca argued.

"But it's a terribly important level."

"Come on, Agnes! It's only really important when everything else is working and you need to know, finally, if the compatibility's a hundred percent. Don't you realize you're lovable?"

Agnes was so thrown by the comment that she couldn't speak.

"My God!" Rebecca said. "Don't you *know* that? You *are*. There are so many people who love you. Even Murray, as inappropriate as that was, cared very deeply for you. *I* love you. Jason thinks you're sensational. And now you've discovered Lou does too. He's *told* you so."

"Yes, he has," Agnes conceded.

"See! And I'll bet it did your ego a world of good to hear that."

Agnes said, "It did, actually. That and making love with someone who didn't require instruction. I'm not making light of Murray, but I was almost old enough to be his bloody grandmother, and still I couldn't bring myself to end it because I was so afraid I'd never have anyone else, that no one else would ever want me. Pathetic, isn't it?"

"Not at all. It's just sad. You haven't responded yet to what I said about that French master."

"Perhaps it was damaging," Agnes allowed. "I've never

given it all that much thought. But when the situation arose
with Murray, it was unavoidable. I couldn't stop thinking that
I was inflicting the same sort of anguish upon him."

"But he's assured you that you didn't."

"He's young. Perhaps he's unaware."

"Listen, Agnes. He may be young, but Murray's definitely aware."

"You think so?" Agnes asked with much the same expression she'd worn when telling Rebecca about her sexual
initiation by the French teacher.

"Yes I think so! Please give yourself and Lou a chance.
You deserve to be happy. You really do. It's your right, as
much as any of us, to care and to be cared for."

"We'll see," Agnes said cautiously. "It isn't easy to aban-
don the reservations of a lifetime."

"Please try. Okay? *Try!*" Rebecca pointed with her fork
to Agnes's plate, saying, "How's your chicken?"

Agnes looked down at her food, then back at Rebecca.
"I'd say the chicken and I bear an astonishing resemblance to
one another. We're both on the stringy side and a bit tough.
But the sauce is zesty."

Rebecca laughed so loudly the other diners turned their
way, smiling automatically.

CHAPTER

Twenty - Three

Rebecca was delighted to be able to go home knowing the outside lights would be on and there was no need to be apprehensive about entering the house. There would be no more assaults on her sanity, and probably no further messages from Ray.

There were, in fact, no messages at all. The red light on the answering machine glowed steadily. The green call-number indicator was at zero. The house smelled pleasantly of last evening's wood fire and Jason's tobacco. She breathed deeply, contentedly, as she climbed the spiral staircase to the bedroom.

She'd just settled in bed, planning to get caught up on some of her reading, when the telephone rang.

"I didn't have one free minute to call before now," Jason said. "How's it going, love of my life?"

"I'm a happy little camper, all snuggled up in my bunk. No more harassment, no nasty messages. I can hardly believe it's actually over. How's Pete? Did you get a chance to see him?"

"That was the plan, but I phoned and they had him back in surgery this afternoon. He's going to be out of commission for a good long time. But he's off the critical list and out of intensive care."

"That's good."

"Yeah. I just wish I felt better about the whole thing."

"It's not as if you fed him the drugs, then told him to go drive the car."

"This is true. I thought about you while I was sitting in court all morning. Kept me from going squirrelly."

"It's kind of strange not having you here."

"You really are getting used to me." His voice brightened. "I knew you couldn't resist me."

"Don't be smug," she smiled. "I was getting used to vandalism as a daily diet, too."

"Nice. Go ahead and equate me with pillaging cossacks. See if I care."

"What time do you finish?" she asked, extending her hand to the pillows beside her.

"Midnight. I'm covering a half shift I laid off on Frank a while back. This'll square us. After tonight I'll be back to something resembling normal hours."

"What's normal?"

"Two weeks starting tomorrow, I'm on days. I'll be able to see you every single night, if you like. We can do all kinds of fun stuff. Go to movies, eat Greek, even buzz into the city and catch a show."

"I'd love it."

"Eat you up with a spoon," he growled. "Start on those tiny little tootsies and work my way up."

"That'd be nice, too. Midnight, huh?" She glanced over at the clock. It was coming up to ten. "If you're interested, you could come for breakfast in the morning."

"Aw, I was hoping you'd invite me to tiptoe in when I close up shop for the night."

"By midnight I'll be sound asleep."

"Fine. I'll creep in and we'll do spoonies."

With a laugh, she said, "When was the last time you slept at home?"

"Now I'm hurt."

"God, don't be hurt. I wouldn't want that on my conscience. You can creep in if you want. You've got the keys."

"Oh, boy! I get to watch you while you're sleeping."

"What are you, a necrophiliac?"

"I said watch, not molest. And I prefer my women alive, if you don't mind."

"That's good to know."

"Next time you open your eyes, there I'll be, toots."

Again she laughed. "Fine. I can't wait. Let me get some reading done now. Okay?"

"I love you, Beck."

"I know," she said, smiling, and put down the receiver.

Sensing Jason's presence, she drifted upward from the depths of sleep to a level nearer to consciousness. She came just close enough to the surface to want to be near him and made the effort to shift over to her left side. Her turning brought a searing pain down the outside of her right arm and she was instantly awake, sitting up, a cry of alarm escaping her throat.

Her left hand going automatically to her injured arm, she felt wetness and saw a shadowy figure jump away from the bed into the darkness. Not Jason. Someone else. Someone trying to harm her. She screamed, scrambling frantically backward off the bed, away from the figure that was already fleeing, hurtling in a noisy clatter down the spiral staircase. She kept on screaming, hearing him fall at the bottom of the stairs. Petrified, she tried to think what she could use to defend herself.

The screams ripped at her throat, roared inside her skull, colliding with the pounding in her eardrums. Her heart battered at her ribs. It wasn't over. She'd been wrong to relax. Someone was in the house, trying to kill her. Fleeing footsteps in the mudroom, the sound of the back door being thrown open. She forced herself to go to the window. A lengthy distorted shadow disappeared up the driveway.

"Ohgodohgodohgod," she whispered, trembling as she went to turn on the bedside light, her left hand still wrapped protectively over her upper arm. The pain was broad and deep, and she looked to see blood soaking the sleeve of her nightgown, dripping from her fingers. Sobbing, she saw more blood on the bedclothes, and something dark there. What was it? Grabbing up the phone, she dialed 911. She had to hold the receiver with both hands.

She was shaking so badly she couldn't seem to focus. Her head kept turning of its own volition toward the stairway. A voice came on the line, and she gave her address in a frenzied whisper. "He's trying to kill me!" she cried, almost swallowing the words. "Hurry!" She put down the phone, telling herself to go down and close the door. He might come back. But closing the door wouldn't stop him. Everything had been locked. He got into the house anyway. And what was that thing on the bed? She stepped closer, leaned in. Black fur. A small animal? Was it dead? It didn't move. So much blood—on the pillows, the sheets, dripping through her fingers.

She wiped her eyes and runny nose on her sleeve, afraid to know what that was on the bed. With her left hand she picked up a pencil from beside the telephone, reached out stiff-armed to poke at the thing. What? No depth or substance to it, just black fur. Fur? No, hair. Something else, too, catching a glint of light. A piece of mirror? The tip of the pencil wavered, then lowered, connecting. The lead made a faint metallic tink. A single-edged razor blade. And hair.

Hair? Dropping the pencil, her clumsy left hand lifted to her head, failed to find the familiar spiraling density; just wisps, empty space. Her mouth was open, emitting night sounds she'd heard in the underbrush as a child at summer camp and sometimes now at the far edges of her property. The clock's liquid green numbers pulsed. 12:07; 12:07; 12:07. Beat, beat, beat, beat; the numbers pulsing in syncopation with her heart; silently altering: 12:08; 12:08; 12:08.

The room, the furniture, the whole house was keeping time with the clock. 12:08; 12:08; 12:08. Her head was wobbling, bobbing; the blood pushed through, keeping cadence. The door was open; it was cold; she had to close the door before he came back. But she was paralyzed, eyes riveted to the luminous green-glowing numerals: 12:09; 12:09; 12:09. Her chest heaved up and down up and down; the pain in complete possession of her arm, from shoulder to elbow, throbbing along with the clock, with her chest, and with the raging pandemonium inside her skull; her entire being palsied with fear.

He wants to kill me, he'll come back and kill me, I can't live here anymore, got to get out of here. The thin whine of an insect, like a mosquito droning too near to her ear. A siren. They were coming. Police on their way.

Uniformed men came, bringing more noise, asking questions. One stayed, his lips moving, while the other went away through the house. Her eyes swiveled back to the clock: 12:10; 12:10; 12:10. Maybe she'd never be safe again. Every time she began to relax, there'd be another attack.

"Come with me, please, ma'am." The officer wanted her to go with him. She couldn't budge. The blood dripped, spilling on her toes. She could feel the carpet wet under her foot.

"An ambulance is on the way. D'you hear me, ma'am?"

Her head creaked up and down. In the distance was that sound that always made her think of the Anne Frank movie. *Wanh-aah, wanh-aah.* Like mechanical weeping.

"Broken window downstairs." 12:11; 12:11; 12:11. The other officer stood at the top of the spiral staircase, black-leather gloves on his hands. "She hurt bad?"

"Can't tell. Hell of a lot of blood. Ma'am?" The first officer had a blanket, wrapped it around her.

"Rebecca?" It was Jason. He was downstairs.

"Beck . . ." He paused halfway up the stairs, eyes sweeping the scene. She could feel him, and willed herself to move, to speak. She blinked, broke the numbing rhythm. The heaving of her chest accelerated. *"He tried to kill me!"* she cried, clutching her injured arm under the blanket. The two officers backed out of the way.

"Oh, Jesus!" He rushed over to take hold of her. "You're hurt."

"My arm," she sobbed. "I woke up, thought it was you."

"Ambulance is on the way, Jase," said one of the uniforms. "We just caught the call."

"What'd you find?" he asked, keeping hold of Rebecca.

"Broken window downstairs, stuff on the bed, that's about it."

"I'm so cold." Her teeth were chattering, her arm on fire.

The ambulance attendants came on the run with a stretcher.

"I don't need to go to the hospital," she told Jason.

"Let's go downstairs and they'll have a look. Okay, Beck?" He maneuvered her down the stairs to the kitchen, keeping hold of her hand while they sat her down and cut open her sleeve to look at the wound. The attendants conferred in murmuring tones, then chose to speak to Jason.

"Explain to Rebecca what you want to do!" he said

angrily. "Don't tell it to me, as if she's not here and can't understand!"

"Sorry," they apologized.

"He wanted to kill me, Jason," she whispered, watching fearfully as one attendant held her arm while the other began cleaning off the blood with a wonderfully cool solution. "It was a razor," she told everyone. "It's on the bed." She looked over to the doorway. "I thought it was a dead animal but it's my hair, he cut off my hair. I'm so scared."

"Don't be," Jason said soothingly. "I'm here now."

"It's one heck of a long gash, but not too bad," the paramedic told her. Very carefully he eased apart the edges of the wound. Fresh blood welled up the entire length of the slash. "It's clean, and not too deep."

"I'm cold," she said again, feeling as if she might fragment into hundreds of small frozen pieces.

"Have you had a tetanus shot recently?" the paramedic asked her.

Her lips oddly thick, terribly dry, she answered, "No."

He said, "Okay. Get yourself one the next couple of days, just to be on the safe side. This doesn't need stitches. We'll bandage it up. Keep it clean and dry."

"Okay." She watched them work, fascinated.

They swabbed the cut with another liquid. It evaporated quickly, making her shiver, feel even colder. Then an ointment. One man held her arm firmly, but with care. He seemed a kind person, even glanced up at her and smiled reassuringly. Then gauze went around and around, yards of it, encasing her arm from the shoulder to just past the elbow. A couple of pieces of tape, and they were packing up to go, telling her, "Don't forget that tetanus shot."

Jason thanked them. They left.

"You want us to file the report, Jase?" one of the uniforms asked. "Or you gonna handle it?"

"Go ahead and file," he told them. "I'm off duty. You caught the call. Find anything?"

"Zip. Intruder wore gloves. Naked eye you can see the blade's clean as a whistle, just blood and some hair. That's clean, it's a lock there won't be anything else. We'll write it up as assault, assailant unknown. Something you want us to do?"

"Walk the property, see if you spot anything."

"Okay, Jase. Goodnight, Ma'am. Sorry for your trouble."

After they'd gone, and while Jason was making her some tea, she said, "I changed the locks. I put the lights on a timer. I kept the windows and shutters closed. I did all the things I was supposed to do, but I woke up and he was trying to *kill* me." She heard the way she sounded and said hoarsely, "I'm sorry." Her throat was raw from screaming.

"For what?" Bemused, he curved his hand over her cheek.

"For acting like an eight-year-old." She hiccoughed and wiped her face. "No," she said. "I'm sorry I couldn't think properly or do anything. That's what I'm really sorry about."

"Hey! You were scared. It's okay. Nobody can know what she'll do in a situation like that."

"I want Ray arrested. I'll swear out a complaint, or whatever it is I have to do."

Leaving her side to go lift the kettle from the stove and pour water into the teapot, he asked, "Did you actually see him? Are you sure?"

"Who else would it be, for God's sake? You told me Pete's going to be out of commission for a good long time. Who else has a reason for attacking me with a razor blade?"

He came around the island and touched the side of her head.

"What?" she asked.

"It's just this one part here."

"What, my hair? Let me see." She got up, holding the

blanket closed with her left hand, and and went to look in the mirror in the downstairs bathroom. On the right side her hair had been lopped off just below her ear. There was dried blood on her face, in her ear, down her neck and shoulder. Stepping back, she could see it on her calves and caked between her toes. Her nightgown was still heavily damp with it, particularly on the right side.

"You need a bath," he said quietly from the doorway. "Rebecca, did you actually see him?"

"I was asleep. I turned over and felt this sudden awful pain in my arm. I started screaming, and he took off. The lights were out, so no, I didn't actually see him. But it couldn't have been anyone else."

"You didn't see him. You can't accuse the man without proof."

"There's a razor blade in my bed!" she cried. "That's proof. Look at me! *I'm* proof!"

Placing a calming hand on her shoulder, he said, "I'll get your tea. Then we'll put you in the tub, clean you up."

She stood looking with disgust at her blood-sticky toes, her arm stinging, her fear giving way to anger. "Why don't you believe me?"

"I believe someone was in here. I believe you got hurt. I don't believe this was attempted murder. I'm sorry, Rebecca. Somebody wants to kill you, he doesn't take off running when you wake up screaming. He's there with a razor in his hand, he cuts your throat. *But he doesn't run.* I'll tell you how I see this," he said, sounding all at once dishearteningly professional. "Whoever it was broke in intending, most likely, to cut off your hair, maybe rape you. You're asleep, and the intruder goes to work on your hair with a razor blade. Nice quiet tool, makes almost no noise. But you turn over. The razor's in mid-stroke, misses, and gets you in the arm. You wake up screaming and scare the shit out of him. So he takes off running. He practically breaks his neck falling down the stairs, he's in such a big hurry to get away. It's personal injury, and that's no small thing. But it is *not* attempted murder, and you *cannot* say for a certainty it was Ray Hastings."

"I see. So what'm I supposed to do, change the sheets, crawl back into bed, and wait for him to come try it again?"

"I know you're scared and angry and all the rest of it, but don't dump on me. Okay, Beck? I'm being straight with you. I'm telling you you've got no grounds to go swearing out a complaint against this man. There's absolutely nothing to prove he was here."

"You're telling me not to do anything?"

"No. I'm saying that it's unfortunate as hell, but you've got no cards to play. That is the sad reality of this situation. An incident report's the most you're going to get. A complaint's out of the question, even with those message tapes. Abusive telephone calls aren't enough. I could swing by the Hastings place, make police noises. The guy'll say he was home in bed with the wife, and that'll be the end of it."

"But there'll be a report of this?" she asked.

"Absolutely. Why?"

"Because I want it on the record, Jason! When they find my goddamned dead body, I want them to know I wasn't playing for attention here."

"Ah, shit. I'm not taking an adversarial position on this, Beck. You don't think I'm bothered? You don't think I'd nail old Ray's ass to the floor if I thought it'd stick? If he's the one who hurt you, you can be sure I'm going to get him for it. But I can't go doing stuff without probable cause. I'd end up out of a job, and you'd be no better off."

"Then why the hell do we have a police force?" she asked bitterly.

"Sometimes I wonder myself. But there are rules, laws, and we're sworn to abide by them."

"You're also sworn to serve and protect. What about that?"

"I am doing my very best for you, Rebecca. Christ! I've been patroling this place on my own time every chance I could get from day one. I've believed you from the get-go. I also happen to love you. For one godawful moment there, when I pulled in and saw the black-and-white, with the ambulance right on my tail, I was scared shitless you were dead. You're in shock. You know that? It's not possible to think clearly at a time like this."

She was so cold her toes were cramping and her jaws felt locked. "You're right," she said more quietly. "I'm taking it out on you."

"Look, I'll get your tea, then I'll help you get cleaned up. After that I'll take you to my place. Unless you'd rather go to your mother's or to Agnes's. Let's, please, take this one step at a time. Okay?"

"Okay," she relented. "But could I, could we, just stay here? We could sleep in the guest room. My mother's already worried. And Agnes is still pretty shaky. I don't want everybody upset."

He started filling the tub, then straightened, saying, "Don't want to spend a night in my swell garage, huh?"

She shook her head, watching the steam rise.

He went out, returned with the tea and handed it to her. "I'll find something to cover that window."

"There's some lumber in the shed," she told him.

"Right."

"The key's on the island."

"Right."

"Jason?"

He turned back.

"I love you, too. I didn't mean to dump on you. I'm just scared. The man really is trying to kill me."

"I know you're scared. And I'm not going to leave you on your own. I'll be two minutes," he promised, fishing the Mini-Maglite from his pocket.

After nailing a piece of wood across the window, Jason swept up the broken glass before returning to the bathroom, where, her tea finished, Rebecca lay soaking in the hot water, her injured arm propped on the side of the tub.

"How do you feel?" he asked.

"Better, warmer."

He took off his jacket, rolled up his sleeves, and got down on his knees beside the tub. "Get you cleaned up," he said, lathering a washcloth.

"Jason, I can't live here anymore. I'll never again feel safe in this house."

"I understand." With care, he scrubbed at the crusted blood between her toes.

"I'm going to let my mother lend me the money to buy a condo."

"You do have an alternative," he said, rinsing the cloth before lathering it up again.

"What? At the moment, I'm close to overdrawn on my checking account. I've been waiting for a check that was supposed to arrive days ago. That money would barely pay the legal fees for two closings, and I really don't want to dip into my savings. I don't have that much, and once it's gone, if there's an emergency, I'm in trouble."

"We could buy a place together, go fifty-fifty."

"We're talking a lot of money, Jason, even with what I could get for this place."

"We'd work something out, get it all in writing."

"God! I don't know."

"Think about it. One thing, though. If we do agree to go

into something together, we should get a decent-sized place."
He smiled over at her. "With room for a good-looking,
intelligent baby."

"God!" she said again. "Are you serious?"

"Nah. I'm only trying to cheer you up. Of course I'm
serious."

She leaned over the side of the tub to kiss him, then said,
"I have a horrible feeling this is never going to end. Every
time I relax and start thinking I'm safe, someone's going to
start coming at me again."

"Don't think that way. It'll end. Tomorrow you'll throw
a few things in a bag. You'll give your mother a call from
school, tell her you're coming to stay for a couple of days
while you get this house on the market and start looking at
those condos she's been touting. A couple of weeks after that
you'll be in a secure building, trying to decide where to put
the furniture, and the past few weeks will be fading fast."

"I'm not likely to forget any of this in a hurry, Jason."

"I'm not suggesting you will. I'm merely saying you'll
have other things to think about. Whether or not you decide
to take me up on my offer, you're going to be moving out of
here."

"There's no question of that."

"So, okay," he said, running more hot water into the tub.
"We'll take it hour by hour, day by day, and you'll get
through it." He smiled again at her.

She leaned over to give him another kiss, then said,
"Would you mind getting me a clean nightgown from upstairs?"

"No prob." He wrung out the washcloth, draped it over
the rack, and handed her a towel. "Won't be a minute." He
started to go, then turned back. "Pulling in here tonight,
seeing the uniforms, I was damned scared, too," he confessed.

"I'm not playing games with you, Rebecca. I believe some-one really is trying to hurt you. I intend to find out who, and I intend to make him one very sorry son of a bitch. Okay?"

She nodded and said, "Okay."

CHAPTER

Twenty-Four

G od!" Agnes exclaimed. "What on earth's happened? You look dreadful." She'd never seen Rebecca so haggard. Not only did she appear to be ill, she actually seemed physically smaller. Her eyes—that Agnes had always, rather whimsically, considered a Caribbean blue—had bruised-looking shadows under them, and there was a grim, yet oddly vulnerable, set to her mouth.

Rebecca put down her things and sat heavily in the chair by Agnes's desk. "It was a rough night," she said, touching the side of her hair to be sure none of the short ends had escaped from the ponytail she'd fashioned to conceal the uneven length. "I didn't get any sleep to speak of." Every time she'd closed her eyes, she'd relived the attack and fear had begun pounding inside her body like something trapped within the cage of her flesh.

"What happened?" Agnes repeated, feeling an interior frisson of alarm as she got up to pour them both some coffee.

Her left hand going protectively to the bandaged arm

beneath her sweater, Rebecca gave an abbreviated version of the previous night's events. "He's trying to kill me," she wound down. "But I didn't actually see his face, so there's not a hell of a lot anyone can do."

Agnes put a cup of coffee in front of her, saying, "I'll get the intern to take over your classes. You're in no condition to teach. You shouldn't even have come in today." She couldn't bear the thought of any harm coming to Rebecca. It came home to her forcefully how very much she cared for her, and how negligent she'd been in demonstrating her affection. Inwardly she cursed her perennial reticence, her apparently congenital inability to declare her feelings. Perhaps Rebecca was right, and she really did need to seek professional help in overcoming her fear of acknowledging her love for others.

"Please don't. I'd prefer to work. I need the distraction. I really don't want to sit around thinking about this."

Agnes gazed at her as if assessing Rebecca's ability to make this decision. After a moment she gave Rebecca's shoulder a gentle squeeze and returned behind her desk, saying, "I suppose you know best. You know, of course, that you're more than welcome to come stay with me." Bloody hell! *Why* couldn't she be more forthcoming?

"Thanks, but I'm going to my mother's. Aside from everything else, she could probably use help with the packing. And I've got to go look at some condos. I'm selling the house. I can't live there anymore. I feel as if I'm going to spend the rest of my life jumping at the slightest sound. Anyway, I have to go to my GP for a tetanus shot." She rubbed her hand lightly up and down her injured arm.

Agnes sat back, looking at her with a doubtful expression. "I am sorry, Rebecca. This has turned into a nightmare. I'd like very much to help." Her interior voice was saying, *Tell her how much you care!* but she couldn't get the words out.

"Thanks. I appreciate that, but there's nothing anyone

can do." Rebecca lifted the cup of coffee. It felt incredibly heavy. Her body was rebelling against the lack of sleep, as well as her continuing high level of fear. She gave Agnes a thin smile. "To think I used to complain of being bored." She shook her head.

"It doesn't make sense," Agnes said, toying with her pack of Dunhills.

"What doesn't?"

"Would this man be so overt?"

"There are a lot of crazy people out there." Rebecca pointed to the windows.

"But surely Jason—"

"Listen," Rebecca interrupted. "I meant what I told you last night, Aggie. I love this man. Okay? It feels as if I've been waiting all my life to meet him. We're probably going to be living together very soon, it's that serious. He's a cop; he carries a gun, and bullets, a beeper, cuffs, the whole show. He's the real McCoy, an honest-to-god cop. And he's explained to me in no uncertain terms exactly where I stand. Which is way the hell out on a sawed-through limb, because unless I happen to have a bunch of witnesses handy when I get attacked, there's no chance they're going to charge Ray with anything. Meanwhile, Jason thinks I'll be comforted when he says, 'It's okay now. I'm here.' Well, yes, I'm comforted. But there's no way I believe things are okay now. Because the minute he leaves, Ray will be back for another try. I'm on my own in this. Sooner or later, regardless of everyone's good intentions, I have to spend time alone. And that's when I'm at risk. Unless I want to go over to Chuck's Gun Shop and buy myself a little protection. Which I don't care to do."

"I'm sorry," Agnes said again. "I wish I could help. There must be something . . ." No matter how badly she wanted to, she couldn't make even the simplest declaration of caring. It was positively shameful.

"That's what I keep thinking. But there isn't, except for what I'm doing, which is getting out of that house. Ray knows my mother lives in Greenwich, but he doesn't know where, and she's not in the phone book. I'm sure I'll feel better once I get there. The thing is, I don't want her to know how serious this has become."

"She's going to know something's up simply from the look of you, my dear. I've honestly never seen you so . . ." She couldn't think of a word suitable to describe Rebecca's appearance.

"No, she won't," Rebecca declared. "Before I leave here today, I'll put on some makeup, and when I get there, I'll act perky as can be. Might as well put those years of acting classes to good use."

"Forgive me for changing the subject, but did your check arrive?"

"Not yet."

"I'll lend you however much you want. You really can't go about with no money."

Rebecca dredged up a smile of gratitude. "If it doesn't come today, I may take you up on that." She drank more of the coffee, then got to her feet. "I'm scared to death," she admitted. "But I refuse to play victim. I'm not going to wimp around waiting for Ray to come slit my throat. And next time, I don't intend to freeze, the way I did last night. I'm scared, but I'm furious. I understand now why people buy guns. No kidding. Anyway, my students beckon." She started to go, then stopped, asking, "How are you, Aggie? How's it going with Lou? Did you get any more sleep last night?"

"I'll survive," she said. "And I'm besotted with Louis, thank you for asking. At the moment, my darling, I'm much more concerned about you."

"I'll survive, too," Rebecca said with heat. "Count on it! See you at lunch." She turned to go.

"Rebecca!"

She stopped and turned back.

Agnes opened her mouth, but for a moment the words refused to come.

"Are you okay?" Rebecca asked.

"I care very much," Agnes got out.

"I know you do, Aggie." Rebecca was able to smile without having to force it. "I'll see you later."

Agnes slumped back in her chair, winded as if she'd just done a mile-long sprint.

Evelyn was immediately suspicious. "Of course you can stay, sweetheart. And I could certainly use the help. What aren't you telling me?"

"I can't go into it now," Rebecca hedged. "I've got a class in ten minutes. I just wanted to let you know I'll be coming. We'll talk when I get there."

"Is this about the vandalism?"

"Yes and no. I have to run now, Mother. I'll be there by four, and I'll fill you in then."

"You're sure you want me to call Mrs. Dunbar?"

"Positive."

"Well, that's good, at least. I'll call her now."

As she was on her way to the Jetta that afternoon, Lou caught up with her in the parking lot. "Agnes told me what happened," he said, his brow furrowed with concern. "Is there anything at all I can do?"

"I wish there were. Just keep your fingers crossed Jason gets it sorted out soon."

"Why don't they arrest the man if they know he's responsible?"

"That's what I'd like to know."

"Well, look, Rebecca. All you've got to do is call and we'll come running."

She kissed his cheek. "Thank you. I'll keep you posted."

"Take care," he said and waited, one finger smoothing his mustache, while she unlocked the car and installed herself in the driver's seat.

"Believe me, I will," she said fervently, turning the key in the ignition.

When she glanced into the rearview mirror before pulling out of the lot, he was still standing there. She waved. He waved back. She headed for the turnpike.

Jason sat beside the bed and listened to Pete talk. The kid went at it as if it was the first real opportunity he'd ever had to express himself, as if Jason's having been at the scene of the accident had created a singular bond between them. Maybe it had. Jason continued to feel an abstract responsibility for the kid, as well as a mounting sympathy. There could be no doubt that the family was dysfunctional as hell. Pete had struggled to cope as long as he was able, then he'd given up and taken to raiding his friends' medicine cabinets. He'd recited to Jason a list of prescription drugs he'd taken that should, by rights, have turned his brain to porridge. Yet, despite his tendency to wander off on tangents, he was remarkably lucid.

"I know you're a cop," Pete was saying, "but I don't care. You've been decent, man. No shit. Nobody else listens. You know? It's like they're so tuned in to their own stations they can't receive anybody else's signals."

"I know how that can be," Jason said.

"I mean, I can handle stuff if people will just let me alone to do it. But it's like they can't let you alone because they've already done the gig and they know how to do it better and faster, so they get on your case with a fucking vengeance because what they really want is to do it for you. You'll only fuck it up if they leave you to try. Can't do the laundry right. How come you won't clean your room? Like it's going to affect the world ecology if your room's not a hundred percent.''

Jason laughed.

Encouraged, Pete rushed on. "It's that whole Rodney Dangerfield thing, you know. I don't get no respect. The absolute positive truth. Anybody showed the least little bit of it, I'd pass out from shock. It's all power-tripping now, ragging on me instead of dealing with each other. Do this! Do that! You're twenty minutes late. You're grounded for six months. And they want me to respect them! What a joke! I'm supposed to respect these people who dump all their shit and grievances on me because I'm handy. Right? Dad tries to buy me. Forever laying money on me, like that'll convince me he's a good guy. Mom? She's turned into this major league psychopathic couch potato, just sits there in front of the tube with this thing, whatever it is, she's knitting. Chain-smoking, chugging coffee, doesn't even take her eyes off the set to give out orders. Take out the garbage! Rake the fucking yard! Clean your room! But cross her, say or do something wrong, and she'll come after you with a fucking screwdriver or a knitting needle. Oh, man.''

The kid was crying, tears soaking into the bandages covering most of his face. Jason held his hand. Pete clung.

"I don't know what happened, man," he said miserably. "I thought we had a regular family, just like the neighbors', like my friends' families. I can remember some decent times, barbecues in the back yard, tailgate picnics when we'd go to a football game. I remember that stuff. It was okay, good even. Then one morning I wake up and it's not there anymore. It's maybe four or five years later and it's just not there. I'm like the last one to notice, you know? Makes me out to be a real genius, I'm so clueless.

"She burned me out. She wanted to wipe me off the face of the fucking earth, but she couldn't, so she wiped out all my stuff. I just wanted her to feel what it was like. You know? To have all this stuff going down that really puts you face-down in the mud, but you can't do dick to stop it. You've got no power, you don't even know what the fuck it's all about. You know? There's all this weird shit going down every time you turn around, and you can't trust anyone because every time you do, they just fuck you over some more. They take everything that ever meant a thing to you and trash it, destroy it. You know?" he said pleadingly.

"I know," Jason said quietly, the controlled volume of his voice masking his sudden, almost sickening, surge of realization.

Listening to the boy talk, paying close attention to every word, it had all at once occurred to him he'd done what he'd been warning Rebecca not to do: *He'd assumed.*

When the kid had started talking in the wreck, Jason had held his hand, encouraging him to go on. But like some goddamned rookie fresh from the academy, he'd unwittingly made a dreadful and potentially dangerous assumption. *He'd taken for granted that Pete had been referring to Rebecca.* The enormity of his mistake had him sweating, but it was important—for the sake of all concerned—that he remain outwardly calm. He'd have to take great care not to compound his error by layering further assumptions over the initial one. It was vital to listen now without prejudice, because it was only a matter of a short time before Pete told him what he was waiting to hear.

The house was chaotic, with cardboard boxes everywhere, pale rectangles on the walls like ghosts of the pictures that had hung there.

Evelyn said, "I made up your bed. Why don't you put your things away, then come back down and talk with me in the kitchen?"

Rebecca went upstairs and along the hall to her old room. All that remained was the bed, a chest of drawers, the night table, and a lamp. The sight of the stripped room brought home to her as nothing else ever could the finality of her mother's move.

Her haven, this home, was gone. She'd never have it back. All the memories, the experiences the family had shared within these walls, were to be relegated forever to the past. The sound of voices calling from one room to another, the very feel of this place, would henceforth live only in her memory. No more corners to turn, no uneven edges of a carpet to trip her into reflection. Until this moment she hadn't understood what it would mean, not only to her, but especially to her mother, to leave this house.

She sat down on the side of the narrow bed trying not to cry. Every day was bringing another ending, more changes; her flexibility was undergoing a constant strenuous workout. This was the last time she'd be able in any historical sense to come home.

"This isn't easy," she said from the kitchen doorway, thinking how terrific her mother looked in narrow black slacks and a loose-fitting long sky-blue sweater. "I pushed you to sell this house, but I had no idea how hard it has to be for you."

Evelyn turned from the stove, folded her arms under her breasts, and said, "You'd better tell me what's going on, sweetheart."

Rebecca could feel her face begin giving her away. Her

lower lip and chin started to quiver; her vision grew blurry even though she was trying her damnedest to smile.

Evelyn said, "Come here," and Rebecca went obediently into her mother's arms—the safest place she knew—and sobbed noisily like a child while Evelyn cradled her head against her shoulder and held her consolingly. "Becky, sweetheart," she crooned, "what's the matter with my girl? Jason hasn't let you down, has he?"

"Nooo," Rebecca wailed.

"What then? This business with your house being vandalized? Talk to me."

The temptation was overpowering, but she knew she couldn't tell her mother about Ray's attack. There were a lot of reasons, but the primary one was her new understanding of the difficulties Evelyn was already experiencing. She didn't feel she had the right to encumber her mother with additional worries.

"I didn't know it would be so hard to leave here," she said, accepting a tissue Evelyn pulled from her pocket. "Just now, seeing my room, it hit me."

"Why do I have the feeling you're avoiding the issue?" Evelyn said cannily. "Nobody knows you better than I do, Rebecca. Nobody ever will. And you can't fool me. Why won't you tell me what's going on?" Her always expressive face was creased with concern.

"There's too much happening all at once," Rebecca told her. That was certainly the truth. "It's getting to me. That's all." She mopped her face with the tissue, offered her mother a watery smile, and sat down at the table. "A good night's sleep and I'll feel a whole lot better."

"All of a sudden, for no special reason, you've decided to sell your house. And you want to be rid of the place so badly you won't even spend another night there. Why?" Evelyn pulled out a chair and sat close by, placing one small delicate hand over Rebecca's.

"I've had enough. If it isn't something major every month, like the hot-water heater going on the fritz, it's somebody deciding to think up rotten stunts guaranteed to upset the hell out of me. I want to live in a nice, worry-free condo, pay the maintenance and let other people take care of the furnace and the lawn. I want twenty-four-hour security guards, surveillance cameras, and indoor parking. I want to stop getting up twenty minutes early in the winter to run out and start the car so it's warm by the time I'm ready to leave. I've got endless reasons."

"I see," Evelyn said with an inscrutable smile. "And does Jason fit anywhere in this?"

"None of it really has anything to do with him. I know you think it does."

"All right, sweetheart," Evelyn said, withdrawing her hand and getting up. "Whatever you say. You're a grown woman. I'm not going to push. Would you like a cup of tea?"

Rebecca said, "I'd love one. Thank you."

Evelyn went for the kettle. "By the way," she said, "Mrs. Dunbar says any time you like. She's got four—units, she calls them—to show you."

"Let's do it tomorrow evening. I'm too tired to look at anything tonight."

"Whatever you say," Evelyn repeated.

They were finishing dinner when Rebecca remembered the check. "I'm going to take a run up to the house," she told her mother. "I want to get the mail. Plus I forgot to turn down the thermostat, and the plants need to be watered." She looked at her watch. It was almost seven, and still light outside.

"Why not do it in the morning, on your way to school?" Evelyn suggested.

"If the check's there, I can swing by a bank machine and

deposit it. My account's very low. I had to pay out quite a lot this week."

"Surely it can wait until morning."

"It'll only take a couple of minutes in the house. I can be there and back in an hour," Rebecca said, her mind made up. Quickly she finished eating, then carried her plate to the sink. As long as it was still light, no one was going to attack her and risk being seen.

By the time she got to Nortown it was already growing dark. She parked the Jetta and went directly to the mailbox, then let herself in the back door. She'd get in and out fast. Why the hell hadn't she listened to her mother and waited until morning? She really didn't want to be in this house after dark. Leaving her coat on top of the dryer, she quickly sorted through the letters. The check had finally come. "About time," she said, getting her checkbook to write out a deposit slip. She'd swing by the bank machine up the road near the entrance to the turnpike.

Anxious to be on her way, she quickly turned the thermostat down to sixty, then hurried to fill the watering can and carried it to the living room.

It took her no more than five minutes. She was on the last of the plants when she heard a car pull in and stop at the top of the driveway. She stood listening. Expecting the bell at the back to sound, she was startled by a quiet knocking at the front door.

Cautiously she opened the top half of the Dutch door and peered around it to see an attractive blond woman in her mid-forties. "Yes?" Rebecca said, certain she was about to be asked for directions.

"Rebecca Leighton?" the woman asked with a tight little smile.

"Yes?"

"I, ahm, thought I'd take a chance on, uhm, dropping by in person instead of phoning. I'm Marla Hastings."

Why hadn't she listened to her mother? God Almighty! This was never going to end. Ray was trying to kill her. His son had harassed her, he'd vandalized the house, nearly driving her mad, and now Ray's wife had arrived for an impromptu visit.

When Rebecca failed to respond, Marla Hastings said, "It seemed more sensible to keep this away from the school."

The woman looked nervous. Rebecca thought she should probably slam the door in her face. But she couldn't. She'd been raised to be polite; she simply didn't have whatever it took to slam doors on people. Besides, not only did the poor woman have a first-class bastard for a husband, but her son was in bad shape in the hospital. They might as well clear things up once and for all. "Hang on a minute," she said while she got the door open. "Come in."

There was something familiar about her, Rebecca thought as Marla Hastings walked into the middle of the room. She'd probably seen her in passing on parents' night, or at the supermarket.

The two women stood studying each other. Ray's wife was about five-eight and painfully thin. She'd obviously taken pains to dress for this meeting, with a handsome tweed coat draped over her shoulders, and a tailored dark-brown dress belted tightly around a very narrow waist; gold door-knocker earrings, several long, gold chains around her neck, short brown leather gloves, good-looking expensive brown shoes with heels at least three inches high. Her shoulder-length hair was parted unflatteringly in the middle. Despite her makeup, she looked careworn, with deep hollows beneath her prominent cheekbones and many tiny wrinkles at the corners of eyes that were a gray so light they were almost colorless. She was a heavy smoker. Rebecca could smell the cigarette smoke that clung to her hair and clothes. There was even a faintly yellowish cast to the whites of her eyes. Once upon a time, she'd been very pretty.

Rebecca felt unkempt by comparison, in her sweater and skirt, and flat-heeled suede loafers, with strands of unruly hair escaping from her ponytail.

"I thought it was time we talked," Marla Hastings began in her raspy smoker's voice, clutching her oversized purse with both hands.

"I could use a drink," Rebecca said, hoping to forestall what was bound to be an uncomfortable dialogue. Ray's wife, for God's sake! It was too weird. "Would you like one?"

Marla gave her another tight little smile that didn't reach her eyes. Cold eyes, Rebecca thought.

"Bourbon, if you have it. Scotch, if you don't," she said.

"I have Scotch. How would you like it?"

"Neat, thank you."

"Sit down, please," Rebecca said. "I won't be a minute." She started toward the kitchen, trying to think what it was about the woman that seemed so familiar.

CHAPTER

Twenty - Five

Hi, Evelyn. This is Jason. How are you?"

"Just fine. And how are you, dear?"

"Peachy keen."

"Rebecca's not here, Jason. She's gone to Nortown to pick up her mail and water the plants."

"Oh. Okay." He took care to keep his tone casual. "Maybe I'll catch her there. How long ago did she leave?"

"About half an hour. She said she'd be coming right back. Would you like me to have her call you?"

"I'll try her at the house. But if I miss her, sure, you could ask her to call me. And I'll see you on Sunday. Right?"

"That's right."

"I can hardly wait."

They exchanged good-byes. He didn't want to waste any time phoning the house, and tore through the lobby of the hospital. She wasn't supposed to go back. He had a really bad feeling about her being there, didn't want her anywhere near the place, especially not now. He ran faster, wishing that he'd parked closer to the entrance, that he'd followed his own advice, that he'd warned Rebecca not to go back to her house under any circumstances unless he was with her.

Arriving at the sedan, he stabbed the key at the lock, missed, told himself to go easy, and aimed again. Got the door open and slid in behind the wheel. Mistakes were always made when a cop's emotions became involved in a case. Rule number one: Put your feelings on hold, because they'll interfere with your judgment.

Okay, so it wasn't really a "case," something that had been laid on his desk. He'd volunteered because he was interested in the woman from the top, because even covered with flakes of black paint and her hair soaked, she was gorgeous, and because she was spunky. Well, it had sure as hell turned into a case now, but he'd neglected a few basic rules. Pulling out of the lot, he cranked down the window, put on the roof flasher, and headed through the dark city streets toward the nearest on-ramp to I-95.

Construction had traffic backed up on the highway through Stamford for at least a mile. He swung onto the shoulder. Up ahead it was blocked by a couple of wise-asses. There were always jokers who'd clog the shoulder. Strictly illegal; too often it cost valuable minutes when ambulances or rescue trucks couldn't get to the scene of an accident.

He turned on the siren, watched the fools try desperately to get out of his way. *"Move it!"* he yelled, right on the bumper of an old Honda so rusted the lower body looked like lace. No room for the Honda to squeeze into the right lane. Finally a van held back to let the rattletrap in. Jason pushed the sedan ahead. He'd take the next exit, get on the Post Road. Jesus! He was getting himself all worked up, maybe for nothing. Operating on guesswork, a couple of hunches, and some phone calls. He'd get to the house, hustle Rebecca out of there, follow her back to Greenwich, make sure she was safely home with her mother.

Another moron on the shoulder. *"Get the hell out of there!"* He couldn't believe these people. Oblivious. This one was a teenage girl with the back window ledge of her Toyota full of stuffed animals, impairing her rearview vision. He came right up onto her bumper. Scared her. He could see her jump, realizing she had a cop on her tail. Automatically spun the wheel to the left. Damned lucky thing there was a gap or she'd have creamed someone.

A hundred or so yards and he was speeding down the off-ramp, slowing at the bottom for the red light. Nothing coming. He shot through the intersection, hung a hard left, cutting along the cross streets, zigzagging his way to the Post Road. He'd have a good, clear run once he got out of Stamford.

Rebecca got out the half-gallon bottles of vodka and Scotch. She took glasses from the cupboard, put them on the counter, then opened the freezer for ice. It was nagging at her, this idea that she knew the woman in the living room. Ray's wife. Brother! Wait till she told Agnes!

She could scarcely believe she'd put up with seven months of that bastard's last-minute cancellations, the complicated details of his supposed divorce, and the recent hectoring messages.

What *was* it about Marla Hastings? She tried to home in on it. Something subtle, some little thing. Why was it eluding her? She unscrewed the cap on the Ballantine's, her nose wrinkling at the smell of the Scotch. Lifting the bottle, her heart suddenly, painfully, constricted. *The smell.* That was it! *Perfume.* One that reminded her of insect repellent. She even knew the name: Poison. God! It hadn't been Ray . . .

She turned her head to see Ray's wife practically on top of her, her arm descending. The Scotch fell from Rebecca's hand. The bottle didn't break. The liquor splashed over the linoleum as she instinctively backed out of the way of the hammer that came crashing down on the edge of the island with a noise that made her jump, caused her heart to feel as if it were climbing into her throat.

She hadn't heard her coming because the woman had removed her shoes. She raised the hammer again now, her ravaged voice whispering, "You caught me off guard last night, waking up, screaming that way. This time I'm ready."

God! The whites of her eyes looked as if they were filled with blood; crazed, bulging eyes. God, God! "Look," Rebecca said, mouth dry, knees wobbly, hyper-aware of every detail as she edged around the island—the mechanics of the woman's lips and tongue shaping words; age-loosened flesh on her neck; tobacco stains on the index and forefingers of the hand closed around the rubber-covered end of the hammer; a glinting diamond solitaire on the left-hand ring finger.

"Your husband told me he was getting a divorce," Rebecca said, the pulse in her throat so rapid it affected the sound of her voice; she didn't recognize it as hers, way high in the upper register. "How was I to know he was lying? If you want to blame someone, blame him. I'm not responsible for your marital problems." Stupid inflammatory thing to say. Her hands braced on the rim of the counter, she tried to estimate the distance to the back door. Why was she trying to reason with her? This woman didn't care about blame. She wanted handfuls of hair, wanted blood and broken bones; she wanted death. *She actually means to kill me.* Inconceivable, but real. If she could get close enough, Marla would strike over and over until Rebecca was nothing but a skin sack full of pulverized bones.

"It doesn't matter now," Marla was saying in that hoarse, otherworldly whisper, like something from the sound track of a horror film. The voice of madness. This was what it sounded like on the other side of sanity. "Everything's destroyed because of you. But I'll have the satisfaction of putting an end to you. I don't care if they send me to prison. All these years it might as well have been prison, sitting in that house, waiting. The phone calls when they hang up because they hear a woman's voice. And that monster I was expected to love, just because he came out of me."

"I'm sorry you're having a hard time," Rebecca said. "But it has nothing to do with me." Why was she bothering when it was obvious the woman didn't hear her? But she couldn't stop. Making the words, getting them out, was the only rational part of what was happening. "I'm incidental," she rattled on helplessly, throwing up a barrage of sentences against a madwoman with a hammer. "I'm not even *seeing* Ray anymore. I'm involved with another man. This is a mistake." If she kept talking, maybe someone would come, something would end this. She tried to move without letting the woman see. Her chest was swelling with the need to scream; she could feel her ribs being pushed by the collecting volume, the density of her despair.

"You're young and beautiful, so you don't have to play by the rules. Rules are for the rest of us, the ones past forty who can't compete anymore. We have to sit home and take it, just take it, year after year, while *you,* all of you with your long eyelashes and your perfect bodies, you don't have to worry about what'll become of you because you never had a chance to learn to fend for yourself, you don't know how to do anything that'll pay your way. No." The woman stepped unheeding into the spreading puddle of Scotch, her lips barely moving as she whispered, unblinking eyes glowing like coals. "You're all the same. I could never get any of the others, but I can put a stop to you."

Rebecca inched around the island. Marla was closing the gap, going on and on with her monologue. Others, Rebecca thought. Ray had been cheating on his wife for a long time. She wasn't the first. Had the woman tried to kill the others? Oh, God! She was trapped inside this goddamned house with a complete maniac who couldn't be stopped by anything as inconsequential as logic. Why didn't someone come to help? Where was Jason? Where were the patrol cars? They'd been called off after Pete's accident. No one was going to come. She was going to die. This wasn't the way it was supposed to be. She wasn't supposed to die yet.

"My son"—Marla spat out the word "son" like something foul—"had a lot to say about you yesterday when he came back from the recovery room."

"I don't know your son." Rebecca held still for a moment, trying not to show how scared she was. She couldn't seem to take a breath. Her lungs were being squashed by the screams building up inside. She needed a weapon. Nothing within reach. She tried for another breath, got down some air, then made a break for the mudroom.

Marla anticipated, spun back and dropped into the doorway, the hammer swinging out in an arc. Rebecca twisted out of its path, clamped her hand around the woman's wrist on the downstroke. With astonishing strength—Rebecca could feel the stringy muscles under her hand—Marla wrenched her arm free, throwing Rebecca off balance. She lunged forward. Rebecca ducked out of range, keeping track of the hammer. Seeing her opening, she drove her fist into the woman's chest. The wound on her arm split open and began to bleed.

Marla hesitated, then swung again. Again Rebecca ducked away. If she could just get the hammer away from her, she'd have a better chance of defending herself. God almighty! How could this be happening? Fighting in her goddamned kitchen with a woman who would've looked right in place at a DAR meeting. If you didn't look too closely at her eyes.

"How long before dinner?" Agnes asked, charmed by the sight of Lou bending to check the lamb roasting in the oven.

"Another forty minutes probably."

"I was just thinking about poor Rebecca," she said as she straightened and removed the oven mitts. "She's been waiting ages for that check. Perhaps I'll nip over and collect her mail. If the check's come, I could let her know, possibly save her a trip in the morning."

"I don't know, Agnes," he said doubtfully. "With everything that's been going on over there, I'm not too wild about the idea."

"I'm not going inside, Louis. I'll simply fetch the mail and come directly back."

"Maybe I should come with you."

"You've got to keep an eye on all this food," she reminded him.

"You're probably starving," he said apologetically. "I should've put the roast in this morning and set the timer."

"Louis." She crossed the room to loop her arms around his waist. "Don't fret, my dear. It doesn't matter whether we eat at seven or nine. I'll collect Rebecca's mail and be right back." She ran her fingers through his thick black hair, kissed him on the chin, then on the mouth.

"I haven't really cooked since before the divorce," he explained. "My timing's a bit off."

She kissed him again, pleased by his sudden grin and his hands coming to rest on her hips. "Your timing's impeccable," she said. "I adore your timing. You like being here, don't you?"

"I love it. What about you?"

"I like having you here. I like *you*. I won't be more than half an hour."

"I still think I should come with you."

"I'll be fine, my dear."

"Be careful, Agnes."

She paused in the doorway. "You really do care for me, don't you, Louis?"

"Yes," he said seriously. "I do."

For a moment she studied his face, liking what she saw. "I care for you, too," she said, amazed at herself. "I'll see you in half an hour."

She slipped on her coat, picked up the keys and went out to the BMW. As she drove, she thought how pleased Rebecca would be to learn she'd been saved a bit of bother. It was quite a revelation to be able all at once to see that what Rebecca had told her was the truth: Caring was selfish. It did make the one who cared feel good. Declaring herself was remarkably restorative. This little errand was the least she could do in view of all Rebecca had done for her.

Jason tried to tell himself he was getting spooked for no good reason, but it didn't ease his sense of urgency or the intuitive jolt of comprehension he'd experienced waiting at the hospital. After talking to Pete, and to Pete's father—an odious prick, if ever he'd met one—he'd inquired about Mrs. Hastings. The Missus was supposed to be at home, having dutifully put in her hours at the boy's bedside during the day. But when he'd tried the Hastings' number, he'd reached an answering machine. And that was when all the tumblers clicked into place, when everything Pete had told him, and his own intuition, pegged Pete's mother as Rebecca's assailant. It added up: going after Beck's hair with a razor was something a woman would think of; as was running off when Beck got cut and woke up screaming instead of staying, using physical force to silence her. Plus the fact that Pete had been spilling his heart out about victimizing Rebecca to anyone who'd listen. Christ! He'd even had the stolen set of keys on him when they'd wheeled him into emergency. So Jason had called the house, ready with a reason for needing to speak to the Missus, but he'd connected with the answering machine. Which meant either the lady was screening her calls or she was on the prowl again.

Whatever happened to those nice, real-live people who used to have services to answer people's phones? Nobody had them anymore. The machines probably put all those services out of business. Why pay for people when you could have a machine, with cute, irritating outgoing messages?

Nine minutes since he'd left the hospital and he hadn't yet reached the Stamford city limits. Just coming up ahead. Two more traffic lights and he'd be over the line into Nortown. Then another couple of miles down the Post Road to Rebecca's house. Doing sixty-seven. He didn't dare put on any more speed, not approaching an intersection on the red. And never mind the flashers and the sirens. There were always clowns busy yattering on their cellular phones and trying to drive at the same time. A miracle there weren't more accidents, what with people conducting business from their cars. Portable FAX machines, cellular phones, handy-dandy micro-cassette dictating equipment. He wouldn't have minded one of those cellular suckers right then to call Rebecca, reassure himself she was okay.

There was the car radio, but if he radioed in and asked to be patched through, it might be begging for trouble. Unless it was legitimate police business, they tended to frown on taking time away from the board. Guys in dispatch didn't mind, but the big boys got hot about stuff like that.

He was over the town line. The road was almost free of traffic, and he put his foot down harder on the accelerator, reaching over as he did to kill the heater. He was already sweating like a beast.

Rebecca was getting dizzy. The smell of the spilled Scotch and this madwoman's Poison, as well as her efforts to evade the hammer, made her head spin. She was terrified of being hit and thereby incapacitated even for a few seconds. That would be all Marla needed to finish her off. One good whack in the head and Rebecca would be lucky to see another day.

Marla lashed out again, and instead of backing away, Rebecca threw herself forward, colliding with the woman and sending her flying into the wall. The shelf of decorative copper molds came loose from the impact and crashed on Marla's head. She was dazed. Rebecca grabbed for the hammer, at the same time sinking her teeth into the woman's wrist.

With a yelp, Marla dropped the hammer and yanked ferociously on Rebecca's ponytail. Rebecca stomped hard on the woman's stockinged foot, got a grip on the gold chains and tugged on them, intending to slam the woman back into the wall. The clasps gave way. Rebecca let the chains go, got a fistful of the dress and pulled her forward, ignoring Marla's effort to rip her hair out by the roots.

Breathing furiously through her nose, Rebecca stomped again on the woman's foot, then kicked at her shins as she tried to shake her head free. Overcome suddenly by rage, she dragged Marla sideways, while the woman tried with both hands to shove Rebecca away.

If she'd been grappling with a man, Rebecca would have kneed him in the groin. Doing that to a woman, she'd only hurt herself. So she jerked the woman's head down, brought up her knee, and connected with Marla's soft belly. Instead of doubling over, she reared back, her face going very dark. Her mouth dropping open, she gasped for air, then let out a chilling shriek and renewed her attack, aiming her fingernails at Rebecca's face.

Springing aside, Rebecca reached for the answering machine, got hold of it, lifted and swung all in one movement, connecting solidly with the side of the woman's head. A look of astonishment on her face, Marla bent forward, her hand rising to her face. Rebecca brought the machine down again, this time squarely on top of the woman's head. The impact caused the cassettes to fly out. The lid shot halfway across the room.

Marla didn't move, both hands now clutching her head. Keeping an eye on her, Rebecca sidled around the near end of the island. Panting, she put down the machine, snatched up the receiver and punched out 911. Before she could say a word, Marla shot forward, ripped the wire out of the wall, grabbed up the hammer and renewed her attack.

Her terror escalating at the sight of the woman knuckling blood out of her eyes with one hand while slashing out with the other, Rebecca ran to the living room, headed for the front door. She managed to get it unlocked but had to jump aside as Marla seemed to soar through the air at her.

Rebecca collided with the side of the wing chair, sending fresh pain shooting through her injured arm. She glanced at the fireplace tools. If she could get out from behind the chair, she'd be able to grab the poker. But Marla was blocking her way. She was cornered between the wing chair and the window. God! *I don't want to die!* She'd never intentionally hurt anyone, didn't deserve this. This lunatic was determined to kill her for things she hadn't done. *Godgodgod, don't let her kill me.* All avenues of escape cut off, she opened her mouth and started to scream.

CHAPTER

Twenty-Six

That was strange, Agnes thought. Rebecca's car was parked in its usual spot, and a second car had been left at the top of the driveway, its rear end sticking several feet out into the road. Rebecca was supposed to be with her mother in Greenwich. What was going on here? She pulled up beside the Jetta, removed the key from the ignition, and got out to hear Rebecca screaming.

At once fearful, she ran to the back door. Open. Through the mudroom to the kitchen. She saw the spilled Scotch, what looked like cassettes on the floor. Rebecca screamed again, a heart-stopping, purely primal sound. Agnes reached out, grabbed hold of the vodka bottle by its neck, moved to the living room. She took it all in instantly: the demented woman, hair matted with blood, waving a hammer about, Rebecca cringing in the corner behind the wing chair.

She didn't even stop to think about it, her arm flying out as she ran across the room. Putting everything into it, she caught the woman in the back of the head, the jolt of connecting sending a spike of pain right the way up her arm. The woman dropped like a stone. Agnes had to let the bottle fall; her fingers couldn't seem to hold on to it. They'd gone numb.

"Are you all right?" she asked Rebecca, unable to speak above a whisper.

Rebecca couldn't answer right away. She had to swallow several times as she came out from behind the wing chair. "Thank God you came!" she gasped, trembling violently inside Agnes's enclosing arm. "She was going to kill me."

"Christ!" Agnes exclaimed, trying to ignore the pain shooting up and down her arm. It felt as if she'd pulled a tendon.

"We've got to tie her up with something!" Rebecca exclaimed, breaking away. "You watch her while I find some rope. God! I don't have any rope." She ran to the kitchen. "Rope, rope." Spotting the ruined answering machine, she grabbed its wires, then ran back to the living room. "Agnes, help me get her hands. Then I'll call nine-one-one."

"Who is this?" Agnes asked, rolling Marla Hastings over onto her stomach.

"Ray's wife," Rebecca said breathlessly, working as quickly as she could, desperate to make sure this woman didn't come to and have another go at her. Looping the cords tightly around the woman's wrists, she said, "She's the one who attacked me last night. It wasn't him at all. It was her. She's completely insane, completely."

"Good God!" Agnes felt shock tremors rippling through her.

Rebecca chewed on her lower lip as she knotted the cords. "What're you doing here, anyway, Aggie?" she asked, swaying to her feet. Her stomach was turning over. "Call the police for me," she said, running for the downstairs bathroom. "I'm going to be sick."

Moving automatically, Agnes went to the kitchen, saw the telephone was broken, and started for the stairs as Jason came bursting through the rear door calling out to Rebecca. Turning back, Agnes met him as he tore into the kitchen.

"She's rather busy vomiting at the moment. I was just on my way to ring the police. I think you should see this." She indicated he should follow her to the living room.

He saw Marla Hastings trussed up on the floor, and shook his head. "Shit! Were you here, Aggie?"

"I arrived in time to help." She cradled her throbbing arm in her left hand.

Jason hugged her. "Good woman," he said gratefully. "Do me a favor and phone, will you, while I get her cuffed and read her her rights."

"Certainly," Agnes murmured, and went off to call.

Jason bent down to speak to the now conscious and struggling woman. "You are under arrest," he began, inspecting the knots in the telephone cord and deciding they'd hold for the time being. "You have the right to remain silent. You have the right to an attorney . . ."

He'd finished and had her seated in one of the wing chairs when the patrol car arrived. Agnes showed the two uniforms into the living room, then went to knock on the bathroom door.

"Are you all right, Rebecca?"

It was a few moments before she replied. "I'll be out in a minute."

"Jason's here," Agnes told her, then went back to the living room. She reached into her coat pocket for her cigarettes, got one lit and stood smoking, nursing her aching arm as she watched the officers deal with Marla Hastings.

Rebecca hung over the sink. The spasms had stopped. Her stomach was still quivery but had quit churning. She turned on the cold water and rinsed the basin, then drank from her cupped hands before soaking a washcloth and holding it to her face. The cold sent sparks shooting through her head. Her whole body hurt, her arm in particular. The blood had seeped through her sweater, which clung stickily to her skin. All the parts of her seemed to want to go in different directions simultaneously. But overriding everything else was her desire to get out of this house. She turned off the water, dried her face and hands, and gazed at her reflection in the mirror. She was a mess, but she was alive. If Agnes hadn't come, she'd have been dead by now. God! Agnes had come along to rescue her.

She saw it all again; the bottle crashing into Marla's head, the woman's blood-red eyes going wide with surprise for an instant before they rolled back into their sockets and she went down. Agnes had saved her. Rebecca closed her eyes for a few seconds.

She got to the living room as two uniformed officers led Marla out. One had her coat and purse, and the hammer in a plastic bag. The woman was whispering her grievances, reciting them like a religious chant.

"What'll they do with her car?" Rebecca asked, causing everyone to turn.

Jason at once came over to her, saying, "One of the officers will drive it back to the station. Are you okay, Beck?"

"I'm okay."

He put his arms around her, and again she closed her eyes. Then, unable to help herself, she started to laugh.

"What?" Jason asked, wondering if she was hysterical.

Rebecca pointed mutely at Agnes, who was leaning against the wall finishing her cigarette.

"What?" Agnes said.

"You should have seen her!" Rebecca laughed, her tender stomach protesting. "She was incredible. Like a Valkyrie."

Smiling but feeling dazed, Jason looked at Agnes, who was simply staring at Rebecca.

"She saved my goddamned life!" Rebecca howled. With no warning, her laughter turned to sobbing.

"I've hurt my arm, actually," Agnes said quietly, almost to herself, looking down at her arm.

"You still haven't told me what you're doing here," Rebecca said, wiping her eyes with the back of her hand. If one more thing happened, she'd go demented. She could almost feel herself letting go, spinning off into space.

All at once remembering, Agnes said, "Christ! I must call Louis." She started for the upstairs telephone, saying, "I stopped by to see if your check had come. I thought I'd do you a favor."

"You did!" Rebecca called after her. "She saved me, Jason. That woman was like some unstoppable robot. If Agnes hadn't come . . ." She shook her head and swallowed, a sour taste lingering in her mouth, her stomach clenching again with fear.

"It's my fault," Jason said quietly. "I was slow on the uptake, made a couple of serious mistakes."

"How is it your fault?" she asked, clinging to him.

"I assumed, Beck." He felt guilty, and silently offered up a prayer of thanks to the powers that be for sending Agnes along. "The cardinal rule, and I broke it. I automatically assumed Pete was referring to you. But he wasn't. He was way deep in this mental stewpot, talking about everyone at once. I didn't twig until a couple of hours ago. Then I hung at the hospital, waiting for his folks to show. When the father arrived alone, it made me antsy. So I checked their place and got the answering machine. Then I tried to call you at your mother's, and she told me you were here. I had a feeling Mrs. Hastings might just give it another try, and I wanted to warn you to stay the hell away from here."

"That doesn't make any of it your fault," she said, looking over at the door. The panic came back, squeezing her throat closed. "Jason, I've got to get out of here!" she said abruptly. "As soon as Agnes is off the phone, I'm leaving."

"Can I come, too?"

"Sure. You can try to explain it all to my mother while I climb into a hot bath."

"You mad at me, Beck?"

"No. I'm freaked out and exhausted. I want to go to bed for a week. But I'm not mad at you."

"Okay, good. I was worried. You know? I'll drive you back, visit with Evelyn."

"I'm okay to drive. I don't want to leave my car here. I *never* want to come back to this house!"

"You're not okay to drive, Beck," he said gently. "Let's worry about your car later."

Agnes came in shaking her head. "Poor Louis. His lamb roast is overdone, but as long as everyone's all right, he's not bothered. I think I'll run along now, if the two of you don't mind. Rebecca, take the day off tomorrow. Stay at home with your mother and relax. I mean it. Don't come in."

Too tired to argue, Rebecca said, "Okay."

"I'll call you tomorrow, see how you're doing." She kissed Jason good-bye, then put her arm around Rebecca and held her, saying, "I'm so glad I was here. If there's anything at all . . ."

"Agnes, *thank you,*" Rebecca whispered, hugging her. "I've never been so afraid."

Agnes rested her cheek against Rebecca's hair. Her tongue thick, she whispered, "I love you very much." Then, straightening with a shake of her head, she said, "We'll talk in the morning." Fishing in her coat pocket for the car keys, she went to the back door.

Rebecca stood staring at Agnes's retreating back.

"You okay?" Jason asked.

She turned to look at him and nodded slowly. "All I want is to leave," she said.

"Let's do it," he agreed, and went to switch off the lights.

As he was helping her into her coat, she asked, "Want to go look at some condos tomorrow evening?"

"You bet."

"Good," she said, grabbing her handbag and the check. "Let's get the hell out of here!" Without looking back, she ran from the house.

The hammer swung this way, that way, slicing the air like a scythe, while Ray's wife gave whispered vent to her lengthy list of complaints, real and imagined.

"You finished my world, kept him away . . . ignoring us as if we didn't exist, living his own life and leaving me to try to deal with his *son*. As if it was my fault, everything my fault, but all I ever did was try to keep up, make things the way he wanted. But it wasn't good enough . . . *I* was the one he wanted; he made such a big play, chasing after me even when he knew I was pinned to Bud. I could've married Bud, been happy, had someone to help me. But would Ray leave me alone? Never. I gave him everything. It wasn't enough."

Her outrage palpable, her eyes acquiring a red cast, her arm swung out, the deadly hammer directed at Rebecca's head. Bobbing and weaving like a prizefighter, the prize here being her life, Rebecca tracked the hammer's passage through space, fear coating her tongue. It was a taste in her mouth, a smell on her body. Fear, her new companion, a partner for life. It had taken up residence in her corpuscles, her cells. It sang in her ears, hummed in her head, circulated through her veins.

"Why do *I* have to be the one to deal with him?" Marla went on and on. "The things I find in his room—pills, prescriptions for people I've never heard of. A thief and a liar and some kind of addict, living off us like a fungus out of control. When they called to tell me about the accident, I hoped he was dead. I prayed for it. But he didn't die. You can't kill something like that so easily. No. No matter how much you want it, no matter how much better you know your life'll be with him gone, it doesn't work that way."

What, who, was she talking about? Rebecca wondered, feeling her heart starting to give way. It was wearing out, grinding down, done in from working so hard, sending blood flooding in waves through her arteries. Pumping overtime. Hearts could withstand only so much activity before they gave out, quit. If the hammer didn't crack her skull like an eggshell, her heart would beat a final time or two, then stop. *I want to wake up,* she thought. *I want this to end.*

It came to her that she had the power to stop the action. Like watching a movie on the VCR, she could press the "Pause" button, freeze the frame. She could even erase it, tape something else right over it. It was within her power to do that. All she had to do was concentrate, fix her attention on the possibilities, get herself functioning effectively. Put an end to this hateful event.

She pushed off the massive weight of the nightmare and opened her eyes. For a few seconds she had no idea where she was. Then she remembered and reached to turn on the bedside lamp. Shielding her eyes from the light, she looked at the alarm clock. Eleven forty-five. She'd only been asleep for an hour. One hour. It felt so much longer.

Her mother had turned down the thermostat for the night. Sitting up, Rebecca was glad of the cool air in the room. Her nightgown was damp. Perspiration saturated the hair at the back of her neck and at her temples. She got up and went to the door. The landing light was on. That meant her mother was still awake. She padded barefoot down the hall to the master bedroom.

Evelyn was sitting in bed, in white pajamas, a book

propped on her knees, her reading glasses balanced on the very tip of her nose. As Rebecca came into the room, Evelyn looked at her over the top of the frames.

"You were out like a light when I looked in on you fifteen minutes ago," she said, inserting a leather bookmark between the pages and closing the book. "Bad dreams?" she asked, putting the book and her glasses on the night table.

"Horrible," Rebecca said, sitting down on the side of the bed and looking at her mother. The lamp cast a faintly pink glow that was highly flattering to Evelyn's fine features. "You know," Rebecca said, "you shouldn't be alone. You don't have to be. Your life doesn't have to be over because Dad died."

"I like my life," Evelyn said. "There are worse things than being alone. You, of all people, must know that. Every time I think of what you went through . . ." She left the sentence dangling as she pulled Rebecca into her arms and cradled her to her breast. Rebecca could hear the steady, even rhythm of her mother's heart. "I shouldn't have let you go back to that house tonight."

"What happened isn't your fault," Rebecca said, comforted by her mother's hand stroking her hair, smoothing it away from her face.

"It isn't yours, either," Evelyn said strongly. "You try to make sense of people, but sometimes it's impossible. When I was a girl, we had a neighbor, Mrs. Parkinson. Something about that woman gave me the willies. I'd ride up with her in the elevator—we lived on the fourteenth floor, and it was an older building, so the elevator was slow as molasses—and the whole time I'd be afraid. She was always very pleasant, saying hello, asking after my parents. But her eyes bothered me. There was a certain light to them that always had me watching the floor indicator, quietly urging that elevator to move faster.

"Well, one afternoon I came home from school and there

were police cars outside, and an ambulance. The lobby was filled with people all buzzing away with a kind of furtive electric energy. I pressed the button for the elevator and waited, trying to figure out what was going on. I was very scared. I had the arbitrary idea something had happened to my parents or my sister. Finally an elevator arrived. The doors opened and there was Mrs. Parkinson with several policemen. She was in handcuffs.

"My mother told Bertha and me that Mrs. Parkinson had tried to kill her husband. She'd battered his head with an iron skillet. He'd been badly hurt, but he'd managed to get to the door and call for help before collapsing in the hallway. My mother heard him and phoned the police. Mrs. Parkinson was committed to an institution. The husband visited her every week for years. Then one evening when I was about seventeen, my mother told me Mrs. Parkinson had died. She'd killed herself. Not six months later, Mr. Parkinson remarried and moved away. I always hoped he was happy. He deserved to be."

"That's a sad story," Rebecca said sleepily.

"It was sad," Evelyn agreed. "My point is, there are a lot of people getting by who live right on the edge. It's awful you had to encounter one of them. I must say, the man never sounded quite right to me. I couldn't understand why you were being so naive, so willing to believe the things he told you. Without ever meeting him, I thought he was probably fooling around on his wife. Weren't you even a little suspicious, Rebecca? Did you really believe him?"

"Maybe I wanted to." Rebecca sat up and looked at her mother. "A few nights ago Agnes admitted she'd been feeling terribly lonely. I thought she was so brave to admit that, because I never could. It's just not something we want people to know. It makes us out to be defective or something. But I was lonely.

"When I first moved back from the city, I thought things

would be pretty much the way they had been. There'd be people to see on the spur of the moment, a movie or a play to go to if I was bored, new people to meet—new men. In the beginning some of my friends came out on the train to stay for the weekend. They were bowled over by how pretty it was, and how quiet after Manhattan. Salespeople were so polite, and prices were way lower. I was kind of smug, thinking I'd traded up for a much better lifestyle. But gradually I lost touch with most of my city friends, and everything centered on the school. There were no men around to speak of. A few dates here and there, but no one who interested me.

"By the time I met Ray, I was beginning to think I'd spend the rest of my life alone, and the idea scared me. What about the children I'd always thought I'd have? What about the family? I liked him well enough, but the important thing was how much he liked me. He called all the time, made a fuss over me. And it was so much better than sitting home watching *Jeopardy* every night. I mean, it got to the point where I was so hooked, I'd program the VCR to tape it if I had to be out. Ray came along and gave me something to look forward to, someone to cook for, someone to . . . to nurture, I guess. But I was never really in love with him, and I think I knew from the beginning we weren't going to have a future together. He already had kids; he certainly wasn't going to be the father of mine. But I had no way of knowing he was lying. I couldn't have known about any of it. But you know what?"

"What?" Evelyn asked.

"I feel terrible about Pete. Jason does, too. He's the real victim, not me. I'm going to go to the hospital to see him. I think he needs to know I forgive him."

"That's very decent of you," Evelyn said somewhat doubtfully.

"You think I'm nuts. Right?"

"No," Evelyn said. "Your eyes are normal. Bloodshot, but normal."

"Mother!" Rebecca laughed.

"It is decent of you," Evelyn said.

"It'll help me to see him, talk to him," Rebecca said, serious again. "It'll give me some perspective, maybe let me stop being so afraid."

"Maybe," Evelyn allowed.

"So," Rebecca said, "can I sleep in here with you tonight?"

Evelyn patted the space beside her, saying, "Just like when you were little. Come on."

Rebecca slid quickly under the blankets and cuddled up against her mother.

"I'm going to read for a while," Evelyn said.

"That's okay. I don't mind." Rebecca closed her eyes.

"Well," Evelyn said, "there's one good thing about all of this."

"And that is?"

"You found yourself a wonderful man. He could use a decent haircut. But he's wonderful. And he's crazy about you."

"I'm crazy about him, too."

"I'm very glad you're all right," Evelyn said quietly.

"Hmmn," Rebecca murmured, secure in her mother's warmth.

"So what do you think?" Jason asked, looking around.

"I think it's too expensive," Rebecca said, rereading the listing sheet Mrs. Dunbar had Xeroxed for her.

"Not if we go halvsies. And we don't have to pay the asking price, you know, Beck. We haggle, get them down, come in low the way your mother did."

"Even if we get them down a hundred thousand, it's still too much."

"How do you know that? You haven't asked me how much I've got in the bank. Are you assuming, toots?"

"Not unreasonably," she said, standing with one hand on her hip. "You wear clothes the Salvation Army would turn down. You live in an apartment that Dickens couldn't have dreamed up. The only halfway decent thing you own is your car, and it hasn't been washed since the day you got it."

"So now I find out what you really think of me." He scowled, thrusting his face close to hers. "You wait till the crunch, then lay it on me."

"Am I wrong?" she challenged.

"Totally." He rubbed his nose against hers. "I've got a trust fund, kiddo. What d'you think of them apples? My granny left me and Mimi a whole bunch of bucks. Mimi used part of hers to buy a house and put the rest into CDs to pay for college for the kids. I couldn't decide what I wanted to do with mine, so it's been sitting earning interest. My granny, I'll have you know, was a spunky little cookie just like you. When my granddad died, she decided to go into business. Five years before she died, she sold out. She left all the money to her seven grandchildren."

"What kind of business?"

"Food. She had a line of gourmet goodies—jams, toppings, sauces. Good stuff. It doesn't taste the same as it did when she owned the company. I think they use a lot of preservatives now. Kills the taste."

"Isn't that something?" she said. "Never know it to look at you that you're an honest-to-God heir."

"Well, I am. And I think we should buy this place. It's got plenty of room. The view's sensational. Plus it's only a floor away from your mother. In case we need a baby-sitter in a hurry."

"Don't rush me, please."

"What on, the condo or the babies?"

"Both. I need to think about this."

"The hell you do." He gave her a grin and took the listing from her hand. "Let's go get nice Mrs. Dunbar and put in our offer. This'll be fun."

"I don't know," she hesitated.

"Come on, Rebecca. We'll split it right down the middle. Halvsies on the taxes and maintenance, halvsies on the babies. And consider this! You'll have money left over once your place is sold, if we do it this way."

"That's true," she said, doing some quick mental arithmetic.

"Right. So if we get fed up with each other, we split back the cost of this place, we each take a kid and that's that."

"What's this 'we each take a kid' business? You're not going anywhere with my kid." She poked him in the chest.

"You're right," he said, slipping his hand around over the back of her neck. "Nobody's going anywhere. The happy family will stay put. By the way," he said, steering her to the door, "my dad's going to drop by for coffee on Sunday."

"What?"

"He's coming down to meet your mother."

"Does my mother know this?"

"Oh, sure," he said, pulling the door closed. "We talked about it last night while you were in the bath."

"And she *agreed?*"

"Yup." He poked the button for the elevator.

"She never mentioned it. Not a word."

"She doesn't tell you everything, you know." He ushered her into the elevator and draped an arm around her waist.

"Obviously. I can't believe it. How did you talk her into it?"

"I just said it was time she met a swell new guy, and that your dad wouldn't have wanted her to spend most of her evenings sitting home alone. She thought about it for a minute or two, then said I was right. He wouldn't have wanted that. She'd never thought of it quite that way."

"You're amazing," she said, dumbfounded.

"I am, a little."

"And so modest."

"Just your average guy."

"How much do you think we should offer?" she asked.

"I think we should let your mother do the negotiating. She's a whiz at it. Besides, she gets a charge out of wheeling and dealing."

"Okay," she said. "That's fine with me."

"So," he said as the elevator doors opened, "you want to get married or what?"

"What?"

"Hah!" he exclaimed. "Gotcha!"

"What?"

"It's okay. I heard you the first time."

"I'm swear I'm going to hit you," she laughed as Mrs. Dunbar came toward them. "Or what, for God's sake."

Jason turned off the engine, then shifted to look at her. "You okay, Beck?"

She nodded, looking at her mother's house. "Eighteen years I lived here," she said softly. "It'll be strange, not being able to come back."

He too looked at the house, saying, "I know. Couple of times I've jumped in the car and driven up to New Haven to cruise past our old place. It gave me a lump in my throat." He took hold of her hand.

"I don't think I'll ever be able to live in a house again. I'd be scared all the time."

"That's fine. I like apartments."

"Jason, what'll happen to that woman?" She looked at him anxiously. "Will there be a trial?"

"No way," he told her. "They'll plead insanity, and she'll spend the rest of her life in the funny farm."

"For sure?"

"Absolutely. She'll never set foot outside again."

"Good," she said fervently. "Because I don't think I'd be able to relax for a minute if I knew she was walking around free."

"Not a chance," he said, giving her hand a squeeze.

"I got very close to the edge, you know, Jason. I mean, I could feel myself falling over the line."

"Everything'll be okay now."

"It was incredibly tempting," she said. "Really. Once you cross over, you don't have to be responsible anymore. You can just be crazy, and everyone else has to do the worrying."

"Yeah, I know."

"My mother's waiting. We'd better go in."

"I love you to pieces, Beck."

She smiled and gave his cheek a gentle pinch. "Yeah," she said out of the side of her mouth. "I know. I love you, too, toots."

BESTSELLERS FROM TOR

☐ 51195-6 BREAKFAST AT WIMBLEDON $3.99
Jack Bickham Canada $4.99

☐ 52497-7 CRITICAL MASS $5.99
David Hagberg Canada $6.99

☐ 85202-9 ELVISSEY $12.95
Jack Womack Canada $16.95

☐ 51612-5 FALLEN IDOLS $4.99
Ralph Arnote Canada $5.99

☐ 51716-4 THE FOREVER KING $5.99
Molly Cochran & Warren Murphy Canada $6.99

☐ 50743-6 PEOPLE OF THE RIVER $5.99
Michael Gear & Kathleen O'Neal Gear Canada $6.99

☐ 51198-0 PREY $5.99
Ken Goddard Canada $6.99

☐ 50735-5 THE TRIKON DECEPTION $5.99
Ben Bova & Bill Pogue Canada $6.99

Buy them at your local bookstore or use this handy coupon:
Clip and mail this page with your order.

Publishers Book and Audio Mailing Service
P.O. Box 120159, Staten Island, NY 10312-0004

Please send me the book(s) I have checked above. I am enclosing $ _____
(Please add $1.25 for the first book, and $.25 for each additional book to cover postage and handling.
Send check or money order only—no CODs.)

Name _____
Address _____
City _____ State/Zip _____
Please allow six weeks for delivery. Prices subject to change without notice.

HIGH-TENSION
THRILLERS FROM TOR

☐ 52222-2 BLOOD OF THE LAMB $5.99
Thomas Monteleone Canada $6.99

☐ 52169-2 THE COUNT OF ELEVEN $4.99
Ramsey Cambell Canada $5.99

☐ 52497-7 CRITICAL MASS $5.99
David Hagberg Canada $6.99

☐ 51786-5 FIENDS $4.95
John Farris Canada $5.95

☐ 51957-4 HUNGER $4.99
William R. Dantz Canada $5.99

☐ 51173-5 NEMESIS MISSION $5.95
Dean Ing Canada $6.95

☐ 58254-3 O'FARRELL'S LAW $3.99
Brian Freemantle Canada $4.99

☐ 50939-0 PIKA DON $4.99
Al Dempsey Canada $5.99

☐ 52016-5 THE SWISS ACCOUNT $5.99
Paul Erdman Canada $6.99

Buy them at your local bookstore or use this handy coupon:
Clip and mail this page with your order.

Publishers Book and Audio Mailing Service
P.O. Box 120159, Staten Island, NY 10312-0004

Please send me the book(s) I have checked above. I am enclosing $ _____
(Please add $1.25 for the first book, and $.25 for each additional book to cover postage and handling.
Send check or money order only—no CODs.)

Name _____
Address _____
City _____ State/Zip _____
Please allow six weeks for delivery. Prices subject to change without notice.

THE BEST IN MYSTERY

- [ ] 51388-6 **THE ANONYMOUS CLIENT** $4.99
  J.P. Hailey Canada $5.99

- [ ] 51195-6 **BREAKFAST AT WIMBLEDON** $3.99
  Jack M. Bickham Canada $4.99

- [ ] 51682-6 **CATNAP** $4.99
  Carole Nelson Douglas Canada $5.99

- [ ] 51702-4 **IRENE AT LARGE** $4.99
  Carole Nelson Douglas Canada $5.99

- [ ] 51563-3 **MARIMBA** $4.99
  Richard Hoyt Canada $5.99

- [ ] 52031-9 **THE MUMMY CASE** $3.99
  Elizabeth Peters Canada $4.99

- [ ] 50642-1 **RIDE THE LIGHTNING** $3.99
  John Lutz Canada $4.99

- [ ] 50728-2 **ROUGH JUSTICE** $4.99
  Ken Gross Canada $5.99

- [ ] 51149-2 **SILENT WITNESS** $3.99
  Collin Wilcox Canada $4.99

Buy them at your local bookstore or use this handy coupon:
Clip and mail this page with your order.

Publishers Book and Audio Mailing Service
P.O. Box 120159, Staten Island, NY 10312-0004

Please send me the book(s) I have checked above. I am enclosing $ _____
(Please add $1.25 for the first book, and $.25 for each additional book to cover postage and handling.
Send check or money order only—no CODs.)

Name _____

Address _____

City _____ State/Zip _____

Please allow six weeks for delivery. Prices subject to change without notice.